BOOK TWO

WEAPON

WITCH
WARS

I0588731

HM HODGSON

Ebook ISBN: 978-0-6455598-6-6

Amazon paperback ISBN: 9798272209856

Developmental edit by Sarah Proulx Calfee, Three Little Words Editing https://threelittlewordsediting.com

Proofread by Jo Speirs, Nurturing Words

https://www.nurturingwords.com.au

Cover by Laura Hidalgo, Spellbinding Designs https://www. spellbindingdesign.com/

Special edition print internal character art by Reyna Rochin Art https:// reynarochinart.carrd.co/

CONTENTS

For all the
magic makers -
keep shining

GLOSSARY

Aetts of Cogadh: (*aht of kug-ah*) Three sets of eight runes made from the bones of ancient Mors Dicen witches. Together, the three aetts form a powerful Mors Dicen weapon capable of perfectly divining the future.

Bone Guide: Mors Dicen witches who sacrifice the chance of future reincarnation to bind their souls to one piece of bone forever so they can share their knowledge and skills with future generations.

Bone Wielder: Powerful Mors Dicen witches who can channel Bone Guides to wield their skills for themselves.

Cnamh truaill: (*Kuh-vaw tru-ill*) specialized lead-lined, leather scabbard for a bone-handled Mors Dicen knife, with a sliding panel where the bone meets the wearer's skin, whilst leaving their hands free.

Caorthannach: (*Kwih-rah-nukh*) Legendary monster,

sometimes referred to as the mother of demons who can spit poison fire

Crystallos: *(Krist-ello-z)* Coven of witches who draw their power from crystals and stones. Often use their magic for healing.

Darklings: Pitch-black, faceless humanlike monsters that appear from the dark, usually outside. Can not exist in the light.

Divinators: *(Divin-ay-torz)* Coven of witches who draw power from the energy of humans, often gathering in large cities to fortify their power.

Druids: Ancient, terrible, (believed extinct) race of beings connected to the elements. Descended from the Old Gods, they are rumored to have created the vampires.

Elixirs: *(E-licks-erz)* Coven of witches who draw their power from chemical reactions. Creators of magical potions ranging from food to medicine.

Hedge witches: Witches who prefer practicing their craft (in whatever form they find comfortable, except outlawed Mors Dicen magic) outside of an official coven.

Inis Misneach: *(In-ish Mish-Nagh)* Island off the west coast of Ireland, in the North Atlantic Ocean. Translates to Island of Courage.

Madgewick: Family estate and home of Matthias Medea,

Baron Madgewick. The grounds are protected by an ancient spell only allowing blood relatives to cross the boundary.

Magicae: (*Magic-eye*) Coven of witches who draw power from within themselves and use spellcraft to create magic.

Mors Dicen: (*Mor-z Die-Chen*) Disbanded and outlawed coven of witches who drew power from the earth and who talked to the dead through their bones. Traditionally preferred to live in sparsely populated regions. Practicing Mors Dicen magic is banned.

Shifters: Ancient, patriarchal, secretive race of humans who can shift into animal form. Through millennia of evolution, family groups tended toward staying with one animal type, now known as clans.

Special Investigators: Witches who carry out the orders of the Witch's Council. Traditionally, they came from all covens; however, since the Conflict of the Covens twenty years ago, they have only belonged to the Divinator and Elixir covens.

Vampires: Highly secretive, matriarchal, long-lived society of ancient beings who, legend has it, were created by the Druids. Able to taste lies from a human's blood.

But battle-scarred and
heart-weary, what form can
magic take if all the love has left?

Betrayal and lies made for cold, stiff company, even in a luxury private jet recliner. And while fatigue dragged at Vella's eyelids, she blinked hard until they didn't want to close.

No sleeping. Not until she was safely home with Sara.

Safety. What did that word mean anymore? For one brief moment, it had meant Matthias Medea. The memory of how she'd left him hours earlier, standing between the blood-soaked monoliths of Stonehenge, sent a chill through her. Did he hate her now? Would he ever trust her again?

In the recliner beside Vella, Ellaine Priestley sipped icy champagne like a witch with zero cares in the world.

And why should she? Vella had done her job, Ellaine had the bone runes, and Matthias had been left at Stonehenge cleaning up the mess.

Don't let on that you know the truth. Pretend, pretend, pretend.

Another yawn overtook Vella, and she blinked harder to stay awake. And not just because of Ellaine, but because every time Vella had dozed off in the last seven hours, the dream—nightmare—had hit again.

Her stomach clenched. Maybe if it had been a dream, she could have handled it. But this was a memory, part hers, part someone else's, and it was harrowing every single time.

Vella yawned again, and tried to blink, but this time her eyes stayed shut.

The house they'd moved into had a little couch, but Vella hadn't minded because they'd all squished in together, even her baby sister, and squishes meant tickles, and tickles were the best. Beside the couch, a fireplace had held a yule log, but by far the best part had been the painting on the wall.

Dadda's painting, which had come across the ocean with them. She'd been there when he'd painted it with all the bright, magical colors of their home.

The smell of paint and cleaners had made her nose tingle.

"Trust me, little V, this will all make sense in the end," Dadda had said as he'd gently scooped another dab of a deep green paint onto his brush.

That painting had carried the promise of everything wonderful—magic and love and family, no matter where they were in the world.

Until that day.

Because Dadda held his most precious skull, but his hands were calcifying ... it trickled up his arms and to his neck. Down his chest, up to his cheeks, it spread and spread and spread till his laughing brown eyes and his curly dark hair all turned to chalk.

The skull. He needed to let go of the skull.

"Dadda!" She ran for him.

"No! No, baby. Get back." Mamma grabbed Vella, pushing her away.

Mamma tried to save Dadda. She tried and tried, but the chalk got her too, and Vella couldn't look away. Couldn't do anything.

Mamma's and Dadda's friend, Steven, arrived. His voice was calm, and his face kind as he told her to run upstairs and look after her sister.

"Can you do that?" he asked.

Vella blinked, and when her eyes opened, she wasn't in her memory anymore, but in Steven's.

He hid behind a curtain, choppy breaths rasping in his ears. But footsteps were getting close—two sets. Heels and softer, walking shoes.

Click, click. Pad, pad. Click, click. Pad, pad.

"Well, Monty, our plan finally worked," a feminine voice said. "They're gone."

"Excellent idea, poisoning their precious bones," a male replied.

"And well done on the poison. That is quite a sight."

"I really am impressed with my skill," the male murmured. "And the children?"

"Our foreseers have predicted with ninety percent accuracy the eldest child of the Mors Dicen ruling family will hand the ancient bone runes to me. I know there are other Mors Dicen witches in hiding—and once I have the runes, I shall finally track down every last one of them."

"The younger child?"

"I think it's time to see if your experiment finally works."

"I'm delighted to hear that. I have been playing with some additional elements, so as well as removing her power, the potion will keep her sick, and if you stop giving it to her, she will die—probably within forty-eight hours."

"Is there an antidote?"

"None we have found so far."

"Now that is perfect. I can use the youngest as leverage if we need the oldest to come to heel." The female paused. "We'll remove everything useful, then burn this place down. No evidence."

Steven held his breath and eased out from behind the curtain.

Ellaine Priestley and Montgomery.

"Monty? We have a problem." Ellaine nodded at the curtain.

"Move back," Monty murmured as he took out a vial and threw it—the glass smashed. A thick green vapor filled the air.

Steven screamed.

Sʟᴀᴘ.

Pain flashed across Vella's face, jolting her awake. She grabbed at her cheek, recoiling into the plane seat.

For a split second, reality swung between the dream and the here and now, entwined by the acid surging in her stomach and Ellaine staring down at her, eyes narrowed and calculating, poised like a predator ready to strike.

Ellaine ... the witch who had pretended to be Vella and Sara's aunt for twenty years. But also, the motherfucking *murderer* who didn't know that Vella had uncovered the truth.

"There is no need to look at me like that." Ellaine sank into the plush beige seat opposite and arched one perfect ash-blonde brow.

"Apologies," Vella gritted out. "I was ... deeply asleep."

Don't vomit. Don't think of the dream. Focus on the now, only the here and now. She crossed her arms, so her hands were hidden and balled them tighter and tighter until her nails dug into her palms and the pain from *that* obliterated the memory of the dream.

"If you had slept properly when we boarded, Velvet, as I suggested, instead of napping off and on, I would not have been forced to use such a harsh method to wake you." Ellaine's lips pursed, but then she sighed and glanced out the window at the darkening sky. "I realize there was some … unpleasantness … at Stonehenge; however, we are about to land in our home city. Present yourself as befits a member of this coven before we disembark."

"Of course," she gritted out, and lurched for the private jet's bathroom.

The door opened as she reached it, and Derrick, the man she'd thought was her cousin, held it open as they passed. His blue eyes creased. "You okay, Velvet?"

No. No she was not okay. And she was *not* Velvet.

My name is Vespera!

Inside, fury and hate and the clawing need for vengeance bubbled like a cauldron filled with a hot, seething brew. But she shoved a lid on that cauldron and buried it under so much ice the furious bubbles could never show.

"Yes," she somehow lied. "Just tired."

As soon as the door shut, she dropped onto the closed toilet seat. This was so Goddess-damned *fucked*.

Focus, Vel. She knew the truth now, and she *could* do this. No more stealing arcana for the Ellaine. Just finding a cure for Sara's poison—then taking down the Witches Council from the inside.

2

Two hours after landing in New York, Vella broke into a fancy apartment in a Murray Hill condo complex. The emergency access stairwell door snicked shut at her back.

According to Ellaine's predictions, Vella had nine minutes and thirty seconds before her window of opportunity closed, and her ass got busted for breaking and entering, while the apartment owners were dining in one of New York's fanciest restaurants on the ground floor.

She mentally gnashed her teeth.

Instead of finding Sara's cure, or even just telling her sister the whole, horrible truth she'd learned in the UK, Vella was stealing even more arcana for Ellaine.

"Vella, are you in? Any problems?" Derrick's voice floated through her earpiece.

Any problems? Vella bit back a bitter laugh. Let's see ... In the space of less than two weeks, she'd discovered she and her sister were among the last Mors Dicen witches—a coven believed to perform human sacrifices, hated worldwide, and who Vella had been told had killed her parents, and been responsible for a rebellion against the Witches Council twenty years ago.

Next up ... the *monster* pretending to be their aunt was really poisoning Sara and using her 'illness' as leverage to force Vella to steal arcana for the Divs ever since she'd kidnapped them—Vella at five years old, Sara as an infant—oh yeah, after *murdering* their parents.

Then Vella had located an aett of eight ancient Mors Dicen bone runes, runes so powerful they could divine a cure for Sara, only Matthias Medea, Councilor of the Magicae coven, and the man she'd come to ... have feelings for, was determined to keep the bone runes from falling into the Divs' possession because of the danger they presented to all witchkind, but then Vella had taken the runes to the very Div he hated more than anyone. And so now he might never want to talk to her again.

And now, to top it all off, a headache nibbled away at the back of her skull.

No, she was not fine.

But instead of giving in to the urge to scream, she forced in a long, deep breath. Sara was all that mattered here, and now Vella had the bone runes back in New York, she would fucking find a cure for her.

Focus, Vel. You can do this.

"Vella? I know you just got home, but this citrine bracelet is being sold after the dinner tonight, so we either secure it now, for the good of witchkind, or miss our chance."

For the good of witchkind, Vella's ass. But she couldn't let on that she knew about Ellaine's real intentions—not yet anyway.

"I'm in," she gritted out, restraining the urge to add, *now leave me the hell alone to focus.* And why had Ellaine ordered Derrick to join the op? Was she already suspicious of Vella?

Vella had to be very, very careful.Which started right now with somehow pretending to steal this arcana while not revealing Brianna strapped beneath her shirt.

According to the floor plan she'd hurriedly downloaded onto her cell, arched doorways lead to bedrooms on her right and to the south-facing living areas directly ahead.

Zero signs of anyone being home.

"Are you sure you're okay?" Derrick sounded worried, damn it.

"I am. I just need to focus, so silence from here on out. Going off comms now."

"But—"

"Back in eight minutes." She ended the call, yanked the earpiece free and fumbled under her shirt to open the window on her Bone Guide, Brianna's sheath. "Brianna? Can you hear me?"

"About time." Brianna's voice cut into the room, as clear as if she were standing right beside Vella, instead of speaking from inside the bone-handled knife. "Where are we? Why haven't you talked to me in hours? Do you have the—"

"Short version now, long later. And we're back in New York, by the way." Vella followed her mental map into the main bedroom suite. The layout was close enough to what Vella's rushed research had confirmed: bed. Sitting area. Television. In-built dressing table filled with jewelry boxes, overflowing with crystals in all shapes and sizes ... and on the wall, an oil painting of a mountain landscape.

Bingo.

"I'm stealing another piece of arcana—"

"What?"

"Ouch." Vella winced. "No one else might be able to hear you, but when you screech like that, you blow my eardrums."

"If you don't want me to scream, then don't tell me things that make me furious. Why? Why would you help that ... that—"

"Motherfucker?"

"Exactly. You should be actively fighting her—you are a Mors Dicen witch. We are the warriors!"

Vella's stomach roiled, and she had to take a harsh breath to force back the nausea.

"Vella?" Brianna's sigh breezed through the room, gentle, but with enough weight to lift every leaf of frustration. "I know this is all new—"

"I don't know how I'm going to do it, okay? But I am going to fight, it will just be on my terms, and only after Sara is safe, which means pretending nothing's wrong until I can get a Div to use the runes and find a cure for the poison." She crossed the plush carpet to the painting. "And right now, avoid getting caught talking to you by Derrick."

"Why is Derrick a problem?"

"Ellaine sent him with me, which she's never done before." Vella pressed a cheek to the wall and checked out the painting from the left side. The frame sat flush on that side as well.

"Then you must be careful. If Ellaine suspects you of being a risk to her plans, your life—and Sara's—are in great danger."

"Believe me, I know." Vella took a careful look at the right side of the frame ... also flush. "But I need to be here—and while I'm pretending to carry out Ellaine's order, I can find information on Ellaine's plans to feed to Matthias."

"And where is Matthias?"

Matthias ... The look on his face when she'd left him back at Stonehenge—

midnight stars whirling in his silver eyes, those beautiful lips flat, his jaw tight—flashed through her mind.

She'd done the exact thing he'd been utterly against: handed the most powerful bone runes ever known, still inside the skull of an ancient Mors Dicen witch, to the enemy responsible for killing both Vella's and Matthias' families.

Did he even want her to try and talk to him? What if he hated her now?

The pain in her skull throbbed harder and she grabbed her cell and stared at the screen. The urge to call him—even to send him a message, to connect *somehow*—was so strong she'd thumbed it on before she'd thought twice.

And if she did message him, what would he say?

If they had been back at Madgewick, like before she'd learned all the awful truths, before she'd gone against his only request, no doubt he'd have said something sexy and low and called her Rapunzel. Somehow, she'd come to like his nickname for her. But she'd been so harsh before they'd parted at Stonehenge—when she'd basically told him to get his shit together, because he needed to deal with his trauma.

Trauma. What she'd discovered about her own parents, and Sara, had to be classed as that, right? But it wasn't as if she or Sara could go and ask for help, although for damned sure they both could do with talking to a therapist at the very least.

Maybe she could find a book to read instead?

"Vella?" Brianna's voice softened. "This has been a difficult time, I know that, but your Matthias—"

"Not sure he is my Matthias," she mumbled. With a sigh,

Vella turned the cell off. "And I haven't seen him since we left Stonehenge."

"You ... left him?"

"I had to! This is the only way to save Sara, and I tried to explain that to him, but I don't know if he understood."

"Then speak to him. You have devices where you can talk to each other, do you not?"

"I can't trust my calls aren't bugged."

"You have bugs that creep around and listen to your conversations?"

"Not that kind of bug. It means *she* could be monitoring my calls, so until we find another way to communicate, using my cell is a no-go. Plus ..." Vella swallowed the lump that lodged in her throat.

She hadn't even told Brianna yet what she'd done with the bone runes. Would Brianna hate Vella too when she found out?

"Plus what? What are you—Vespera! I hear footsteps!"

"But I'm not touching you! You said Bone Guides can only hear their Wielders, unless they're in physical contact."

"Vella? Where are you?" Derrick's soft call pricked the hairs on the back of her neck.

Shit. Shit, shit, shit.

Vella reached under her shirt and closed the window on Brianna's sheath so that her Bone Guide couldn't hear or talk to Vella, and spun around as Derrick entered the bedroom, carefully surveying the space.

"What are you doing here?" And how was she meant to *not* steal the citrine bracelet now? "You didn't need to come up—"

"Is someone else with you?" Derrick ducked his head into the ensuite. "I heard you talking."

"To myself." She kept her expression calm. The perfect, cool, collected Div.

"You're sure nothing else happened? You didn't see anyone?"

"No, no one else. It's a thing I do, kind of a way to remember my training."

"Oh. I didn't know that."

"You've never been on a job with me before," she muttered.

"True. And it's nerve-racking, to say the least. Is that where the navitas is?" He nodded at the painting.

"The what?"

"Navitas. It's an old term for the Crystallo coven's bracelet we're here for."

"And this jewelry is dangerous to witchkind?"

"Not particularly—it's Crystallo magic, after all—but arcana like the bracelet can be seen as symbols, and the last thing we need right now is anyone clinging to long-lost symbology. As Grandmother says, we need to help witchkind, and humankind, leap forward together into the future."

If only she could puke right now. Did Derrick really believe this shit that Ellaine sprouted?

"Right." She turned away to hide the disbelief she had zero doubt was screaming from her expression. "That's why you're up here? To see the safe?"

"No, I'm here because you kept disappearing."

"What?" Vella pivoted back around. "How were you—wait. You can use Div magic to watch me?"

"Just as a safety measure to make sure you're okay. It's not something most Divs can do, but if I'm near enough in proximity, I can bring my future visions close to near time for a short time."

Oh shit, Mors Dicen magic was invisible to Div's foresight. Of course she'd disappeared from Derrick's vision.

"So ..." She moistened her lips. "What did you see?"

"Nothing. One moment you were there and the next you just disappeared." He shoved a hand through his hair, messing its usual precise style. "Which is why I ran up all those stairs to make sure you're okay."

"Oh. Ah, thank you. But as you can see, just me." Vella forced a smile, then made a show of checking the time on her cell screen. "And as we've now got less than five minutes, I need to do my thing." She gestured at the painting.

"How can I help?"

"By not touching anything. The frame is pressure sensitive, and if I press anywhere bar a one-inch section, bottom right, a silent alarm will be triggered." Vella eased the painting forward, the frame silently gliding away from the wall on well-oiled hinges.

And there it was, a HEG-93, single-stacker, round-turbine personal safe, ready for the picking.

"You can break into that?"

"Also"—Vella held up a hand—"by not making a single sound until this is open."

Derrick made a miming gesture to keep his mouth closed.

She might not want to be a frigging thief, but stealing was one of her few skills, so she took out her equipment and went to work.

What tangle of fate had made her actually good at this? Yeah, she had the training, but before he'd disappeared, even her human mentor had remarked often enough that she had a gift for breaking and entering, and all-round thievery.

"You did that fast." Derrick let out a low whistle.

Shit. Vella froze, mid-action of reaching into the safe. She'd cracked the combination dial without even thinking about it.

Focus, Vella.

And there it was. A single-strand of citrine beaded bracelet that Ellaine claimed would be terrible for witchkind if its current owner sold it.

"Perfect. Let's get this secured." Derrick reached past her and snagged the navitas.

Vella's stomach knotted all over again, and the nagging headache at the base of her neck grew to take over her whole head.

She'd just helped the Divs steal another piece of arcana. So much for no more thievery. This better be the only part of her returning-the-runes-to-New York plan that went wrong.

Get your shit together ... Vella's words from beneath Stonehenge echoed over and over in Matt's mind, along with the fierce glow in her lioness eyes. He sighed, rolling in his bed for the hundredth time to his other side.

The lights on his bedroom clock mocked him, yet again. One a.m. He usually slept well at Madgewick, but tonight nothing he did calmed his mind.

*Get your shit togethe*r. Was she right? Was he letting his past get in the way of his ... all their futures?

He groaned and flipped sides again. Vella had left less than twenty-four hours earlier, but he couldn't stop thinking of her. Was she safe? How was she handling Ellaine? Had she told Sara everything?

Gods, what he wouldn't give to be there with her now. His chest clenched like an actual hand had grabbed his heart and squeezed hard.

But Vella was an ocean away.

He'd fucked up so badly there. It was *his* fault Vella had run straight to Ellaine with the runes to find a cure for Sara.

He'd lied through omission, fearing Vella's reaction if she learned about Sara's predicament; he'd been so stuck on controlling the situation.

Manipulating Vella.

Even after he got to know her as a person. After he'd fallen in love with her.

He grabbed his cell phone and tapped on Vella's contact profile. If he could just talk to her—but bloody hell, he couldn't. His cell phone might be fine, and he could call a spell to keep him hidden, but he was too far away to know it would work on her end, plus, without question, the Divs would have Vella's cell bugged by now.

But gods, he wanted to talk to her. Wanted to say sorry. Wanted to hear her voice. Pain and longing made his chest go tight, and he scrubbed a hand over that spot.

Ping.

He turned on his bedside lamp and grabbed his cell phone—oh shit. Black stars shimmered under his skin, following the line of his veins along his hand and arm.

Why were they doing that?

Control, breathe, focus.

He willed his Druid power to settle and opened the message on his cell phone, a secure group chat with his cousins Ronin and Shannah.

> Ronin: Matt, you up?

> Matt: Yeah. Why? Is Vella safe?

> Shannah: Vella got back to Arcane Antiquities fine, but maybe ten minutes later, Derrick turned up and she had to leave again.

> Matt: WTAF? Why didn't you tell me?

Ronin: We are. Now.

Shannah: Sara's fine. I'm watching the shop

Ronin: And I'm tailing Vella and Derrick. They went to a Murray Hill apartment tower on Lexington, now are back in Derrick's town car. Directionally, they're headed toward Div Tower

Matt: Stay on them. I'm calling Sylvie now for backup

Bloody hell, what was going on? Why would Ellaine and Derrick have pulled Vella in for a job so soon after returning? Was this to do with the Mors Dicen bone runes?

Or ... what if this was to do with the Magicae coven grimoire? Vella had said she'd find the one Ellaine had stolen from Matt. And yes, Matt needed that grimoire to finally decimate the Div coven and exact his vengeance, but shit, what if Vella put herself in danger locating it?

Power surged along Matt's veins. The stars grew brighter, and the buzzing grew stronger. *Control, breathe, calm.* He refocused on his cell phone—this was not the time for losing control of his power.

Sylvie answered on the first ring. "Matthias. To what do I owe the pleasure?"

"I need your help."

"Again? I already delivered last time, Matthias."

"This is important, believe me. Vella has returned to New York—"

"Why does that sound like you have not come back with her?"

"I can't leave just now." He turned his hand over. Bloody hell, definitely getting stronger. "Which is why I'm calling. I need someone to watch Vella, and Sara too. Shannah and Ronin are—"

"Leave it with me. Although this is a disappointment. I thought you were our Bone Wielder's Primus and would see to her safety."

"I have no idea what that is."

"In vampire society, the Primus is the mate who provides us succor: physical protection, emotional support, sexual satisfaction, to begin with."

"And in witch society, we do things differently," he forced himself to say in an even tone. Although, satisfy Vella? He bit back a groan. Yes, he would like that very much. "However, as you can see, I am trying to protect her—them—which is why I've called. I'll be back as soon as possible."

"And that is how long?"

"A day or so, max." That would be enough time to get control of his Druid power again. And in the meantime, he needed something for this bloody headache while he tried not to think about Vella, or what she'd said.

But no matter how much he tried, he couldn't get her lioness eyes out of his mind. Or the nagging suspicion she might've had a point about getting his shit together, because when they openly opposed the Divs and Elixirs, which finally looked possible if Vella could help him retrieve his missing grimoire, he needed to be at his absolute most capable.

As soon as Vella joined Derrick in the back of a luxury sedan, Derrick instructed the driver to return them to Div Tower, only to pause and glance at Vella.

"We can head to Arcane Antiquities first and drop you off with Sara?"

Damn it, she really did need to get back to Sara, but this opportunity with Derrick was too important to pass up.

"We should get the navitas straight back to the vault. The less time out in the open, the better, right?"

"Absolutely." Approval lit in Derrick's gaze.

"So, since we're going to drop these off at Div Tower, how about we find the skull and the bone runes and use them in a reading to find Sara's cure?"

"Tonight? We just got back."

"I know, but this is Sara." Surely, Derrick cared for Sara? They'd grown up living under the same roof most of Sara's life. Vella and Sara had believed Derrick was their cousin all that time. And she'd thought, he did too. Could he really be in on Sara's poisoning?

"Let's talk to Grandmother."

"No." She grabbed his arm. "I mean, not yet. Once you've had a go, just a small attempt, if it's worked, then I'll go to Aunt Ellaine"—Ellaine was *not* her aunt, but for Sara's sake, Vella choked back the urge to be sick all over Derrick—"for help."

"Vella ..." Derrick's sigh wavered. "I'm still not sure this is the right thing to do, but I get it; you want to help Sara."

"Derrick—" She swallowed the lump stuck in her throat. "This means more than I can even find the words to say."

"Okay, let's secure the navitas and I'll see what I can do."

"Thank you."

Was Derrick really a part of Ellaine's plan? Was he an incredible actor, or was he telling the truth when he said he cared for Sara and Vella? If only she knew for sure, because if she could trust him, he was the best person—bar E, and

Vella was never going there—to do the divination with the bone runes and find the cure.

Because there had to be a cure out there. Any other outcome was unthinkable.

BY THE TIME they arrived at Div Tower, it was close to nine p.m., and bright streetlights lit up the sidewalk from the curb to the main entry—no risk of Darklings here—and Vella had to restrain a shudder as the glass doors to the main foyer soundlessly slid open.

Div Tower had been where she'd lived from age five to twenty-five, but no way had she ever thought of it as home, and now, knowing the truth behind *why* she and Sara had been raised here?

"Vel? You coming?" Inside the lobby, Derrick's face creased with confusion.

"Uh-huh." *You can do this, Vel.* She gathered herself and took a deep breath. *It's just a building ... you're here for a reason ... just a build—*

"It's been a long day." Derrick rubbed her arm when she reached him. "And damn, you're cold too."

"I'm fine," she said through stiff lips. And yes, she was cold. But cold was good—cold meant she could bury her feelings behind that ice so damned deep she could pretend that she hadn't just entered the home of the most evil, vile being she'd ever known.

They took the lift down to subbasement one, where the entire level was split in half, one side housing the secure vaults, the other the archives, and a security desk overseeing the lobbies for each.

As always, glaring lights announced the security desk

open for business, but instead of Nathan at the desk, an unfamiliar man greeted them and held out a tablet.

"Mr. Priestley, Ms. Knight. Vault one, cage three, is prepped for your arrival. Please sign the subbasement one access log."

"Thanks"—Vella eyed his name tag—"Paul. Nice to meet you. Doesn't Nathan usually do the weekday night shift?"

"Oh, Vel, I forgot you haven't been here for a few days. You aren't across the changes yet." Derrick took the log and tapped something in. "I've signed for you too."

"I could've done that." She stared at the tablet where her name, the date and time were logged.

"Why? I'm here." He smiled like she was being humorous, when she felt the total opposite.

"Of course." She faked a smile and took the lead when he gestured for her to cross the vault lobby floor first, their footsteps echoing on the cold marble expanse, all white, of course, but for a gold inlay depicting the all-seeing eye insignia of the Div coven.

The perfect location to hoard away all the stolen arcana.

"So, what happened in the last few days?" Vella waited as the impenetrable vault door slid open, revealing a series of internal wire-caged rooms, all the contents visible.

All the contents that Vella had contributed to stealing. Her stomach knotted.

"Grandmother is ... concerned ... about non-Div coven employees in high security areas, so she instigated a rule that only Div coven employees can work in specific positions, and only special investigators in high security areas, like here at the vault."

"So Nathan just lost his job? He might be human, but his wife, Felicia, is a Div. She works in admin, level five, I think? She's pregnant with their first child."

"He'll be reassigned somewhere, don't worry."

"But why? I mean, what risk does a non-Div pose here?"

"Vella, you're not old enough to really remember what life was like during the rebellion, and gods, I was only a kid too, so even my memories are patchy, but just look at what happened to our parents."

An image of the memory she'd been shown at Madgewick, of her parents' true death, replayed through her mind, and she couldn't stop a shudder as revulsion speared through the ice barrier.

"Sorry," Derrick murmured. "I know it's awful."

She bit back a bitter laugh. He had no frigging idea. Derrick believed—at least, she hoped he wasn't aware of the truth—that her Div parents had been murdered by the Magicae and Mors Dicen working together in rebellion against the Witches Council twenty years ago.

"And that's concerning to Ell—Aunt Ellaine—why?" *Come on ice, do your thing ... Bury that emotion ... pretend, pretend, pretend.*

"Because ... tensions between certain segments in the community have Grandmother concerned that old lies and hatreds might be reigniting. These changes are to make sure that we're all safe, and that the important work we do here" —he gestured at the three vault doors leading off the lobby —"is not at risk."

Tensions? What tensions? What segments of which community?

Ping. Ping. Ping.

Derrick pulled out his cell phone and stared at the screen. "Shit. Grandmother needs me upstairs, now."

"But the reading for Sara—"

"Listen, you finish here, then head home, and I'll be in

touch about the reading tomorrow." He squeezed her arm and backed away. "I promise."

The lift doors opened as he reached them, as perfectly as if they'd been synchronized for his arrival—pft, who knew, they possibly had been—before silently closing, and he was gone.

Along with her chance of a reading with bone runes.

She'd been so close!

"Ms. Knight?" Paul, the security guard, stood behind his desk. "Are you completing the drop-off?"

"Yes, yes, of course." She plastered a serene Div expression on her face and spun back to the vault.

What the frig had been so important at this time of night for Derrick to be called upstairs? And which level had he been called to?

Damn it, the questions were starting already, and she hadn't been back a single day.

Inside cage three, five rows of floor-to-ceiling plinths each held varying-sized transparent glass cases, all of them secured by individual locks managed from the security desk. Small flashing lights indicated their status: green for open, red for closed.

And inside each case were all the arcane items Vella had stolen—perfectly visible reminders of her thievery. Of the deceptions. Of the lies and the murdering and the atrocities committed by Ellaine.

But unbeknownst to Ellaine, she had a fox in the henhouse. And Vella was going to be the sneakiest, most deadly damn fox any henhouse had ever known.

"Case twelve is unlocked." Paul's voice echoed through the speaker system.

Vella gave a thumbs up to the camera in the nearest corner and wound her way to the correct case, the only one with a lock currently flashing green. Withdrawing the navitas from the bag, she placed the strand of beads carefully inside the case and closed the door.

Click.

The light on the case blinked red.

Another arcana locked away.

"Ms. Knight?" Paul's voice echoed through the speakers again. "Do you need anything else?"

"No—actually, hold on." She retraced her steps to the security desk. Fox in the henhouse time. "An item was dropped off earlier this evening. A skull containing a set of bone runes. It went into vault two, cage one, case nine. I'd like to check the security on it."

"No need, Ms. Knight. That item was called to level thirty-one earlier this evening. It's with the Councilor."

Vella's lips went numb. Oh shit. Oh fuck. Oh shit.

"Ms. Knight? Are you unwell?"

"Yes, I mean no. Everything is okay." Now *that* was a lie.

Fine. She wasn't getting a look at the bone runes tonight. But she could still do some foxing around ...

"Actually, while I'm here, I need to look at something in the archives."

Paul stared, but didn't stop her as she walked past the security desk and into the archives, a cavernous space illuminated by glaring fluorescent lights that amounted to what was possibly the most sterile, unwelcoming library she'd ever seen.

At least with only one way in—from Paul's security desk —she didn't have to worry about watching her back.

And even if someone did view one of the many surveillance feeds from the multitude of cameras and questioned why she was in the grimoire section, Derrick had given her the perfect cover—she was going to learn how to divine the future.

But how to find the grimoire she needed?

Thankfully, the rigid nature of the Div's organization came to her help. She followed the floor-to-ceiling shelves, arranged alphabetically by topic … A, B, C, D … E, F, G—

Sweet frigging Goddess. So. Many. Grimoires. An entire bookcase is taking up one whole side of the room. Shit. No way these all belong to the Divs. So, whose were they? And how long could she take to look through them?

She faked a yawn and stretched—based on the position of the surveillance cameras, she'd hopefully be out of sight once she was within the stack.

The first grimoires were decorated with crescent moons and crystals; the next had the all-seeing eye within the triangle, then more with cauldrons, and there—a snake within a circle. Shit. One, two, three … so many.

Magicae grimoires! Her breath whooshed out. Matt's lost spell could be right here.

And she was almost at the end of the shelf, but not entirely. Although the next section had padlocked doors. But given what she'd seen, surely there—

Footsteps echoed from the far end of the room—the end opposite the security desk. Shit. Someone else was here. Had they been in here all along? But then why had Paul lied?

She scrambled back to the Div grimoire section, grabbed the first one she saw and—

"Velvet, there you are." Ellaine, dressed in perfectly pressed beige linen pants and a crisp white shirt, blonde bob styled, even at this time of night, strolled around the corner of the aisle like she was walking a catwalk. "Why are you with the grimoires?"

Shit. Shit, shit, shit.

"I dropped the navitas off and detoured here to look for some training guides."

"Oh?" One of Ellaine's perfect brows arched. "What training are you considering?"

"Well." Vella moistened her lips. "Given how bad my divination power is, I thought the grimoires might hold instructions to help me learn and improve."

"You thought poorly. As usual. Come, there are more pressing matters requiring attention than your ill judgment."

Crap. Ellaine was pissed, but was this just about Vella's checking out the grimoires? A shiver crawled up her spine as Ellaine strode off back past the security desk, and while Vella smiled at Paul, Ellaine kept silent as the elevator door slid open, and Paul didn't meet Vella's eyes at all.

Inside the lift, Vella surreptitiously checked the time on her cell. Eleven o'clock. Sara should be asleep.

"Am I keeping you from something?" Ellaine stared at Vella's cell.

"No. Just keeping an eye on the time for Sara—"

"Sara is at home and safe." Of course, Ellaine knew Sara's whereabouts, courtesy of their fucking surveillance.

Fury threatened to erupt, but Vella clenched her jaw so tight it hurt and forced her gaze down to her feet. *Focus, Vel. Reinforce the ice. Pretend, pretend, pretend.*

As the elevator doors opened to the ground floor lobby, Vella stepped back, deferring to Ellaine's lead to exit first— because the Goddess forbid anyone walk through a door before Ellaine—and spied Derrick talking with another security guard in the foyer.

Maybe tonight wasn't lost, after all? If the bone runes

were up on the reading floor already, she could talk Derrick into a reading now.

But before Vella could say anything, the elevator opposite them opened, and two medical staff emerged pushing a stretcher.

"What happened?" Vella peered closer. "Is that Tess?"

"There was an issue." Ellaine waved to the guard standing with Derrick. "Escort the medical team out through the rear entry."

An issue? A Div being stretchered out of the tower was an *issue*? Only someone without an ounce of compassion in their being would think like that.

"Vella?" Ellaine snapped. "Did you hear what I said? It's time for you to go."

"Wait. I thought I'd talk to Derrick—"

"I do not 'wait' for anyone, especially a witch unable to put her cell phone away for a proper conversation. Derrick, you come with me. Velvet, go home to your sister. I am sure you wish to see her, given it is her birthday tomorrow."

"Of course," Vella murmured. "Whatever you say." *You murderous fucking bitch.*

Shit. Shit, shit, *shit*. So much for getting a reading with the bone runes. But fine, she could be put off for a day, but no way was she giving up for longer than that.

Although that meant it was time to see Sara and tell her everything, except, it was already so late, Sara might already be asleep.

But which was worse—wake Sara up and tell her tonight, or ruin her birthday tomorrow?

Vella's stomach sang with an entirely new set of nerves.

This was going to be tough for Sara to hear, but at least they had each other, and one way or another, they'd get through this together.

4

Arcane Antiquities was a lie. Gone were the sense of welcoming walls, of safety, of security, and not even the familiar sage-infused air could ease the strangling tension that caught Vella and refused to let her go as she crossed the threshold.

Because this wasn't a home. This building, and the business she'd strived to build into a profitable venture, what she'd thought had been her identity, had always been a part of Ellaine Priestley's prison.

"Come upstairs," Sara called over her shoulder as she all but bounced through the shop that occupied the front of the ground floor to their shared office in the back, then up the steps to the first floor. "I can't believe you got called away so soon, but you're back now, and it's so good to catch up just the two of us, even at this time of night."

"Right." Vella refused to give in to the urge to shiver as she followed closely enough for her body to block Sara from the surveillance cameras that were no doubt catching every movement she and Sara made on the ground floor. Thankfully, once they were upstairs she didn't have to worry about any cameras. Although, if listening devices had been planted downstairs, would they pick up anything the sisters said up here?

"Come and sit down. Is it too late for a coffee? And tell me everything about the trip. I want to know all about Matthias' club in London."

"Never too late, you know me." Vella forced a smile even as she twisted her fingers together under the table.

As Sara bustled and bubbled around their galley kitchen, Vella couldn't help but stare at the picture of health and happiness and vitality her sister had become. Gone was the pallor that had clung to her skin the last time Vella had been home; instead, her cheeks were pink—actually *pink!*

Anguish and regret panged in Vella's chest. Sara had never looked better, but Vella's horrific news was life-shattering. How would that impact Sara? Maybe Vella should wait a few days before sharing all her news ... no. Vella had promised to stop keeping secrets from Sara, and she was sticking to her pledge.

Vella swallowed hard. "How are you feeling, Sar?"

Instead of groaning at Vella's anxiety over her health, Sara grinned. "Brilliant, actually. The new batch of meds from the Elixirs is great—apparently Nevena Montgomery has taken over my case, and I feel fantastic!"

Vella winced.

"I can't remember the last time I felt so well." Sara did a little happy dance, but inside Vella, knots twisted in her stomach. "You, though—you're looking kinda rough."

"Yeah, it's just jet lag." And the fact that she hadn't properly slept in twenty-four hours. Any time Vella had managed to drift off, she either woke up from night terrors of seeing her parents die or reliving that orgasm with Matt at the henge in Scotland. The emotional whiplash made her feel like she was losing her mind. Not to mention the frigging headache that hadn't let go all day.

But all she said was, "Hand me some ibuprofen, would you?"

Sara handed over a steaming cup and a couple of pills and whispered, "So, how was Matthias? I know you two banged."

Vella's heart twisted at his name, a sharp and almost physical pain. Was he angry at her? Did he maybe even hate her? Everything was so messed up—had she done the right thing bringing the bone runes back?

Surely, she had ... no, she *definitely* had. Saving Sara was everything, plus, Ellaine didn't know what information Vella had uncovered—so she would never suspect that Vella was now positioned to bring Ellaine down from the inside. This evening had been a setback, that was all.

And look at what Vella had discovered in the archives— that was going to be helpful.

"Why don't we get comfy, and I'll tell you about my adventure?" But could they talk safely here? "Actually, let's head upstairs to my room. I'm so tired I'll probably fall asleep the moment we're done."

Understanding lit in Sara's eyes, and her gaze tracked around the living area before settling back on Vella. Her smile turned wooden. "Of course."

Damn. Vella was already bringing the mood down. But what else could she do?

Following Sara into her bedroom, Vella placed her coffee on the bedside table and then slid the bone-handled knife, Brianna, from her sheath and placed her on the bed.

"Vel? Wanna tell me what's going on? And what is that holder for Brianna?"

"A *cnamh truaill*."

"What is a ... Kuh-vaw tru-ill?" Sara traced a finger over the sheath.

"Daughter?" Brianna's voice eased into the room. "Where are we now?"

"You're here with Sara and me, in our hom—in the house where we live, above our shop, Arcane Antiquities."

"Make contact with me, so that I can see this house through your eyes."

"In a moment, Brianna." Vella watched for any sign of hearing the Bone Guide on Sara's face ... nothing. "Sar, a *cnamh truaill* is what the Mors Dicen call lead-lined sheaths for their weapons. Lead is a natural barrier that stops Mors Dicen talking to the dead, and this sheath has a window in the side that slides open in one direction so Brianna and I can talk, or the other way so that when Brianna is strapped beneath my shirt, we can still be in contact without me having to physically hold her."

"Wow," Sara breathed. "And she's here now? Brianna? Can you hear me?"

"I'd have to actually be touching her for Brianna to hear you—"

"Vespera." Brianna's voice snapped through her mind. "Is there someone with you?"

"Wait. You can hear Sara?"

"Not enough to make out words. It is more like a fly buzzing in the background, but buzzing in a way that makes it sound like words."

"Brianna can hear me?" Excitement flooded Sar's expression. "Maybe I do have Mors Dicen magic."

"Hold on, Sar. Brianna, why would you kind of hear Sara? Could her Mors Dicen magic be coming in?"

"Perhaps. It is odd, though."

"Sorry, Sar. Brianna's not sure what's going on." But even

with Brianna's off comment, Vella's breath eased for the first time since she'd entered Arcane Antiquities that day. "Right. We're safe."

"What do you mean by 'safe'? As in, we're being spied on downstairs, but can't be heard up here?"

"Partly. But more than that, Divs can't see Mors Dicen magic in their visions. This conversation will be totally invisible to them. They can't spy on us when we're—I'm—using Mors Dicen magic."

"And what about you? Can you really not see anything when you use Bone Magic?"

"Not quite. When Brianna and I are talking, like now, there's no impact to my vision. But while I'm physical contact with her bone, my vision turns to charcoal—it's as if I'm seeing everything through a black and white filter—and that's when Brianna can see and hear everything I do, and she can also talk directly to you through me. But afterwards, when I'm not touching her anymore, that's when my vision goes dark, for the same length of time as I was touching Brianna."

"Like a balance—you get the use of Brianna's sight, but then you have to give up something for it."

"Exactly."

"Vespera." Brianna sighed. "Can we speak freely?"

"Yes, why?"

"Because we have not spoken in depth since you found my Tara. Where is she? Bring her out and hold me so that I might see her."

Vella winced. "Brianna, I need to talk to you, too. In fact, I've got a lot to tell both you and Sara. Why don't you sit down, Sar?"

Vella grabbed her coffee and took a long, fortifying sip.

Haltingly and staring into the murky brew, too raw to

watch any of Sara's reactions, Vella described everything she'd learned about the Mors Dicen and how Ellaine was fully responsible for their parents' death.

"Ellaine *murdered* our parents?" Sara whisper-shouted.

"There's more." Vella told her how the Divs and Elixirs had historically colluded, and in the past twenty years experimented with potions to control or destroy the magic of outside covens, including what had happened to Matthias and his family.

"Oh my fucking gods." Sara scrambled off the bed. "My name is Sienna? And you're Vespera? That murdering bitch changed our names *and* has been poisoning me this whole time to control you? Do you think that's why I can't hear Brianna? The elixir poison is stealing my magic?"

Shit. This was not going how Vella had expected—she'd thought there would be tears, a lot of consoling. "Maybe. Probably. But you can't tell anyone—not about our real names, not about the poison, not about any of it."

"Okay." Sara nodded to herself, took several deep breaths. "Okay. So what's the plan? When are we leaving?"

"What? We can't leave. We have to stay—I still have to find your cure. And you can't stop taking their potion—"

"Yes, I can. I'm going cold turkey."

"Sara, you can't. I'm pretty sure it would kill you. Don't you remember how sick you used to get when Ellaine kept your meds from you to punish me?"

"Fuck that. I want to join Matthias and his Magicae coven. They killed his parents and scarred him for life, for what—to terrify the remaining covens into submission?"

"Exactly that. They are horrendous, Sara. And it gets worse. Matt was only a teenager, but after the attack, Ellaine forced him to make a spell from his family grimoire, vowing that none of his coven would ever hurt Ellaine. So even he can't fully fight back until he finds that grimoire and undoes the spell."

"Well, what about those Mors Dicen witches you met? That's where we should go."

"We totally will, but first … Sara, come back. Listen. I do have a plan, actually. Please just trust me here. I gave Ellaine the skull and the first aett and—"

Brianna's screech would have split Vella's eardrums if her voice were physical. As it was, Vella still slapped her hands over her ears as the wail went on and on.

"You gave Tara to our greatest enemy?" Brianna's voice lowered.

"I had to! I have no foreseeing magic whatsoever, but Ellaine is the strongest Divinator alive, and Derrick is a close second. One of them must be able to use the most powerful arcana in living memory to find a cure for Sara. Ellaine said, even though the aetts are incomplete, she should still be able to get some leads."

"Do you know how bonkers you sound?" Sara snapped. "That monster is *actively* poisoning me. For all we know, she has the cure already. She is *still* controlling you. And you're letting her."

Vella's stomach heaved, but she sucked in a breath and forced back the urge to be ill.

"We get Tara now," Brianna hissed. "I must see her. It's been …" Her voice dissolved into loud sobs.

A lump stuck in Vella's throat, and her chest went tight as she tried to take another deep breath. Damn it. Sara was wrong. She had to be. Vella had absolutely made the right decision to hand over the bone runes.

"My plan will work," Vella gritted out. "We'll get Tara back as soon as I save Sara."

But panic made her heart race and turned her throat into a desert.

Brianna stopped weeping, and when she spoke again, determination filled her soft voice. "Vespera, Tara is my *bonded* mate. When we were young, we sacrificed our lives to become Bone Guides, powerful armament for Mors Dicen Bone Wielders to keep our people safe. For centuries, Tara and I fought together, until during a battle our Bone Wielder was slain, her armament scattered—and Tara vanished. I never knew where she had gone. Now Tara's back! I long to see my beautiful, perfect star. You must understand the ache in my heart since our separation."

"Brianna, I had no idea you'd been separated like that, but—"

"But nothing. Because you're wrong in your plan, Vespera. If Tara has been hidden with the Mors Dicen's most powerful armament, her purpose must be as a guard. Believe me when I tell you, no Divinator, no witch without a Mors Dicen connection, shall be allowed to scry using those runes."

"So that means a Divinator *can* use the runes?" Vella straightened as hope surged. "Derrick has already said he'll help me find the cure."

"Mors Dicen do not leave each other in the hands of the enemy!" Brianna shouted.

Sara stared wistfully at Brianna. "What's she saying?"

Vella hesitated.

"Vella! You promised you wouldn't keep things from me anymore."

"The skull that houses the runes, Tara, is Brianna's bonded mate ... and she wants me to rescue her immediately."

"Yes!" Sara rubbed her hands together. "We break into Div Tower, that would be the perfect revenge."

"No! We stay here in deep cover. We spy on Ellaine, gather information, and I find your cure."

"Vespera." Brianna's voice rang out. "You have betrayed me, my beloved, and the Mors Dicen coven. Until you make amends, I renounce you as my Bone Wielder."

A connection Vella hadn't been conscious of before dropped, leaving her more alone than ever.

First, Matt probably hated her. Now, Brianna had renounced her. And Sara's glare made out like Vella was the root of everything wrong with their world. Panic gripped Vella, terror clawing at the thought of losing Sara too.

"Of all people, Vel, I thought I could trust you to do the right thing!"

Trust? The word hung in the air—so painful it felt like a knife cutting Vella in two. What right did that word even have to exist after what the people Vella had *trusted* had said and done?

"You never should have handed over the skull, or the aetts, to that monster," Sara continued. "We have to get them back. Vel, even *if* Ellaine did tell you the truth about how to find the cure—which she won't—I would *never* have agreed to you putting my life above everyone else's. Don't you see what you've done?"

"Sar, listen, let's just take a deep breath. It's your birthday tomorrow, and we can spend the day together. I won't open the shop—"

"Vel, you're barking mad if you think I want to spend *my* day with you right now. I'm going to see Shannah. She said I can go up to Matthias' lake house any time, and frankly, I'd rather be there right now than talking to you."

"But your medicine."

"You mean poison, right? Never fear, I'll be back for that."

5

Against a velvety dark sky, Vella's curved, strong body rose above Matt. Standing stones circled them like silent sentinels as her scent filled his head, and her taste filled his mouth, and his cock filled the glorious liquid heat of her body.

"Vella!" His rasping voice echoed into the night.

Stars erupted in the dark sky behind her, spinning around and around, faster and faster, whisking Vella's cries away, along with the pressure in his cock, the feel of her body against his, her scent, her taste ... until nothing but those stars existed, and even they started to plunge, and a whirling black hole exploded in his chest, sucking everything in—even him.

Matt shot upright in bed, covered in a cold sweat, restless power writhing in his veins and a headache scratching at the base of his skull.

Dream. It had been the dream again. Just like every other time he'd fallen asleep since Vella had left.

Gods, so much for being back in New York in one or two days. The charcoal sky outside signaled dawn wasn't far away, which meant this was day six, his Druid magic running rampant and out of his control.

Six days of being forced to stay at Madgewick to keep the secret of his Druid lineage.

Six days since Vella had left him at Stonehenge and the most powerful arcana ever known had been delivered into the lair of the devil.

Power surged in his veins again, painful and heavy, and he bit back a groan. Gods, would this pressure never release? Although, fuck, maybe release was what he needed.

He kept the ensuite lights off; the moon's glow was more than enough for him to pick out the body wash and tap handles. And as hot water sluiced over his shoulders, memories from when he and Vella had been right here together streamed through him.

He palmed his cock, and it was her hands on him. Her lioness eyes glowing as her delectable mouth kissed down his chest. Her thrilling heat enveloping him. And gods it felt so fucking good because she was with him, and he wasn't alone.

"Matt," she whispered as she kissed her way back up his chest. "I need you."

She licked into his mouth, and he caught her tongue and sucked it in, then chased it back, surging between her lips, as his cock sank into her body and a groan tore through his chest. So. Bloody. Good. The pressure in his veins fused into a tight, hot ball at the base of his spine. Splinters of pleasure shot up his shaft, and instead of his hand, it was Vella he saw himself thrusting into, over and over and over until finally that pressure released and he came with a shout.

But when he finally opened his eyes, it was just him in the shower, the stars still shone under his skin, and the headache returned. As bloody good as it had felt, the release hadn't been enough.

MIDNIGHT ROLLED over on Vella's cell phone screen as she stared into the dark, fruitlessly willing herself into a peaceful sleep. That meant one more entire day had passed with Sara not talking to her, Brianna not communicating and Derrick not answering her calls. Twenty-four, Goddess-damned, more hours of Ellaine ordering her to stay away from Div Tower, of nothing in her mind but reruns of the nightmare that was her parents' and Steven's murder, and the awful frustration of being not one motherfucking step closer to finding Sara's cure.

She wanted to scream. But she couldn't because the freaking listening devices would probably pick that up, and then she'd have to explain why.

So she balled her fists again and tightened every muscle and forced the rage down ... down ... down ... beneath the ice. At least she was getting good at hiding the pain and bitterness and frustration. Pft. She was so damned cold on the inside it seemed to permeate her outer self too, and she huddled deeper under the thick blanket. But still, her chest panged with one emotion she couldn't control. Loneliness. She was so freaking alone.

She squeezed her eyes shut. Come on, mind, no night-mares tonight—a dream of Matt, now that would be welcome.

A coil of delicious heat tightened deep in her core. Vella shot upright. What was—

She and Matt were back at the ancient henge, the craggy

stones standing as sentinels keeping the rest of the world out and containing their magics within.

At least it was the Matt dream, not the other. And even knowing this wasn't real didn't matter because she'd relive the exquisiteness of being wrapped up in his strong arms, of the heat of his body sliding against her, his beautiful lips claiming hers, every night—any night—she could get it.

He kissed his way to her pussy, and as his tongue delved deep, more of that liquid fire pooled in her core, and she held him to her, let him feast, but before she could come, he stood and thrust into her and the fire turned into an inferno. With every thrust, that pleasure seared through her nerve endings, bringing her closer ... closer—

Stars shot across the sky, and where Matt's body had warmed her, cold seeped in. Colder and colder, it grew, freezing the henge stones one by one until they collapsed inward, and where Matt had been, nothing remained.

Waking with a jolt, Vella lay in the bed panting, hot and restless and achy on the inside, but still cold on the out.

Well, damn. Not even a hot Matt dream could warm her all the way.

Sleep seemed a million miles away, so she grabbed a robe and tiptoed out of her room, pausing outside Sara's closed door. If Vella opened it to see if Sara was sleeping okay, she'd probably wake her up too, which wouldn't help anyone, so she left it alone and padded downstairs to their kitchen.

Maybe a hot chocolate would help. But to sit here with the possibility of the listening devices picking up her movements? Ick, ick, ick. No, better to make it here and head back upstairs. She took out her favorite mug—

Hot tension flooded her core, and she jumped. Her mug fell. The handle broke. Frig! What was going on?

The tension grew and grew and grew. Her breath turned to pants and she gripped the edge of the counter. Oh fuck. Oh fuck, oh fu—

Sensation burst inside her and it took every inch of her control not to shout out as the full-on orgasm made every part of her tingle.

Only when the last of that incredible sensation dwindled, could she haul in a shaky breath and steady herself. Wow. Wow, wow, wow. She'd just spontaneously orgasmed. But why?

Well, there was only one explanation that made sense: Matt. But the last time sudden-onset orgasms had happened, they'd been sharing a hotel room in Scotland. He'd been in the ensuite, and she'd been in the bedroom. Did this mean Matt was nearby? Or could he trigger an orgasm in Vella from anywhere in the world? And was he alone, or with someone?

What she wouldn't give to be able to pick up her cell and text him or call him or simply roll over and ask him.

After clearing up her poor broken mug and getting out a different one to make her hot chocolate, she took her drink and the waning heat of that orgasm back to her bedroom, but by the time she huddled under the blankets the cold and loneliness enveloped her again.

She rolled over and stared into the night sky. Where was he? Was he okay? Did he hate her?

6

By midday, Matt slammed the tome shut he'd been staring at for way too long and shoved back from his desk. The low-grade headache hadn't fucked off, fatigue dragged at his entire body, and thoughts of Vella refused to vacate his mind ... no bloody question why he couldn't concentrate.

He paced past emptied bookshelves to the twin sofas, dodging piles of books that might as well have been jail bars, given he hadn't been able to leave Madgewick.

"Matty?" Mrs. B appeared at the doorway, concern on her face, carrying a tray with a cup of coffee and a green crystal pendant. "Any change?"

He held his hands out and scowled at the black stars shimmering beneath his skin, tracing the pathways of his veins.

"Ah, lad." Mrs. B sighed and picked up the crystal pendant. "And the headaches? Still as bad?"

"No," he lied through his teeth. Mrs. B didn't need to worry any more than she had the last week. "And thank you for the coffee, but—"

"Matthias Achelous Medea, if you think you can fool me after all these years, you are utterly mistaken." She bustled over to him, picking her way between books and furniture. "What? You think you can figure out what's going on with your Druid magic when you can hardly stop yourself from wincing? Sit and let me do another session."

"Mrs. B—" The look on her face took him straight back to his teenage years, and he knew better than to argue.

"Good lad. Now hold still while I hold my citrine over your head."

"One week, Mrs. B," he murmured as she did her thing. Thankfully, the pain reduced from the front of mind to a background ache. "My Druid keeps showing, no matter what I do."

"And the headaches. Although my crystal is resonating with a reduction in your pain. Is that better?"

"Aye. And thanks."

"Excellent." She tucked her citrine away. "And you've found nothing in any of the books here to explain what's going on?" She made a tsking sound. "Well, Ronin arrived not long ago—he's downstairs having a cup of tea with Burrows and Amelia as I asked him to let me have some time with you. He's worried, the poor dear. As are we all. I'll send him up now. Maybe he's found something."

Once more alone, Matt turned to the view of Madgewick's gently rolling hills.

Maybe Ronin *had* found something ... Gods but Matt hoped so, not that he held out much hope. Amelia had been searching for any hedge witch knowledge. Ronin had been on the internet for days before desperation had sent him to the vamps' London enclave for help.

Because if Matt's allies in the war against the Divinators ever discovered his secret, they might reject his participation entirely. Not to mention the Elixirs—what wouldn't they do to get their greedy, magic-stealing paws on him?

Matt's mom had hoped he'd only be a Magicae for his sake. But she'd died long before his Druidic power had blossomed, so he'd had to teach himself as a grief-stricken teen through trial and error.

And now his power surged once more, along with his desperation for knowledge to get himself under bloody control. He'd never been so frustrated—there had never been *any* information about being a Druid. Not even here at his parents' home, even though his mom had been one. Where in the hell had she come from anyway? Gods, he wished he'd thought to ask her as a child.

The Divs had a lot to answer for, including exterminating Druids over a thousand years ago and destroying all grimoires or documents describing their use of dark energy. They'd been thorough, too. For the last ten years, Matt had sought out and scoured every grimoire he could find, some going back hundreds of years, without any success.

His cell phone pinged, and he scrambled back to the desk, hope and fear clashing that it would be Vella. Ruby Chevalier's name flashed across the screen.

His heart sank—even though he knew it was for the best that it wasn't Vella—but still, he hovered a finger over decline. Except, damn it, it could be important, and they were so close to taking their fight openly to the Divs. He shoved a hand through his hair and sank into the chair. Hit accept on the video chat.

Ruby's face filled the screen, stylish as ever with her asymmetric haircut and Hermes scarf draped casually around her neck.

"This channel is secure against hacking, however,

subject to divination, so we must speak quickly," the Crystallo Councilor said in her light French accent.

"Okay, give me a moment."

Matt's cell phone was also fine, but to be sure, he heated the air over a candle to light it using his dark energy and called his spell for protection against scrying—the bloody entire candle froze.

Fuck.

"Done," he bit out.

"Medea, we have a big problem. My sources in New York have informed me that Councilor Priestley threw a lavish party, with only elite Divs and Elixirs present, at Div Tower to celebrate the acquisition of an ancient and powerful set of Mors Dicen runes—the Aetts of Cogadh. Apparently, they give her the power to divine at any distance, through any magical protections, and with one hundred percent accuracy."

"Ellaine's exaggerating there," Matt said, working hard to keep his tone even. "I know for a fact the runes were divided into three sets, and she only has one and no clue where the other two are. And since they're Mors Dicen, she may not even be able to use them herself."

"I suppose she'll make this MD arcana legal, *la vache*. Frankly, I can't be certain this conversation is safe. And it gets worse. Councilor Priestley has announced her intent to build Divinator towers in Paris—*putain de merde*—Dublin, Belfast, Cardiff and Edinburgh. She already has an entire skyscraper secured in London at Canary Wharf thanks to Nevena Montgomery. I believe we need to work together to address the threat, and I am calling a meeting of the Coven Union."

Shit. Shit, shit, *shit*. "At Cristal-Science Laboratories? When?"

"In three days. On the twenty-ninth. At nine o'clock. I am extending two more invitations."

Matt tunneled his fingers through his hair. Go out into the world right now? Fuck. Fuck, fuck, *fuck*. But he had to, which meant somehow keeping himself zipped up tight, no matter how painful.

"I'll be there," he gritted out. But bloody hell, he had to get his shit together because that was one meeting he couldn't miss. "Any news on the other matter?"

"Indeed, yes. We might have a crystal that could help sort out your friend's elixir situation. We can talk about it at the laboratories. *À bientôt.*"

Now that was good news. Vella would be so relieved— shit. *Vella.*

Bloody hell but he missed her.

His Druid magic flared; black diamonds pulsed through his veins. Were they whirling in his eyes too? Matt banged his head on the massive, centuries-old oak desk that Vella had salivated over not so long ago.

Knock, knock, knock.

Ronin, followed by Amelia, stopped just inside the study and traded glances.

"Told you." Amelia rolled her eyes. "He's gone through every shelf. You should see the library." She shook her head, but then peered closer at Matt. Froze.

"Mate," Ronin breathed as he walked over and hugged Matt. "It's damned good to see you again, but freaking hell, your snake tats are moving! Did that start when—"

"You, too. And thanks for coming." He returned the embrace hard. "And yes, ever since Vella left." Another example of his out-of-control power. "Did you get to the vamps?"

"Nope, the fuckers wouldn't even talk to me. I went

straight there after I landed, but whoever's left in London is locked up tight in their mansion in Highgate. I jumped the fence, but their security escorted me out before I could get inside the walls. Said I was alive *only* because of my connection to the Mors Dicen Bone Wielder."

"Bloody hell." There went his last, last shot at getting *any* information on Druids. "I just got off the phone with Ruby—the lab came through. She might have something for Sara." Ronin beamed, but Matt shook his head. "Don't get too excited. There's more."

Matt updated Ronin on everything, including the Coven Union meeting.

"*Hell.* But, Matt, you cannot go in public like this!"

"I don't have a choice. What's the news from New York?"

"Not great. Reports are that the special investigators are on a massive recruitment drive. Specifically looking for anyone with anti-witch sentiment."

"That hasn't come before the Witches Council for approval. Ellaine is hiding the increase."

"Which begs the question, why now?"

"Good freaking question." A whole different level of unease snaked through him. "What about Vella—and Sara?"

"Good and bad. Healthwise, Sara is doing really well— Shannah has never seen her so strong. And when she gave Sara the invite for the New Year's Eve party at Nocturnal, she RSVP'd for herself and Vella but ..."

Ronin's words disappeared as Vella's face punched into his mind.

Power surged through his veins, crackling, fiery, uncontrollable. Strong enough he couldn't risk even a minimal air shift to offset his power. *Oh fuck.* He bolted from the chair and ran for the door.

"Matt?" Ronin called. "What are you—"

"Hey, Matty!" Amelia's voice trailed after Ronin's. But he couldn't stop.

Breathe, calm, focus. He made it to the ground floor. Kicked his shoes off as he ran.

Breathe, calm, focus. He lunged for the nearest doorway.

Breathe, calm, focus—

He leaped over the short flight of stone steps and plunged his feet into the icy dirt and snow. Power released. The ground shook. And finally, finally, he could breathe easy again.

"You've got to be shitting me," Ronin said from behind him. "We cannot go to Montignac like this. You look like a bloody Christmas tree, and the star blinking on your head is flashing 'Druid' over and over again."

Breathe, calm, focus. Breathe, calm, focus. Matt closed his eyes and concentrated hard, yanking back his seeking magic, dampening down his Druid. Stuffing it, himself, into a box.

What a fucking awful sensation.

No way could he repress the shiver that ripped up his spine, but at least the damned magic seemed to stay contained.

"Matt, have you noticed you lost control when I mentioned Vella? Are you *sure* you completed your bond with her?"

"No clue. I know next to nothing about bonding, except it's a dark energy thing. My mom, a Druid, bonded with my dad—but did he even reciprocate as a Magicae?"

"Vella *would* reciprocate as a Mors Dicen but—look, this could be really bad. Tell me about your bonding experience with her."

"Like I said, after the fight at Stonehenge, I sensed Vella

leaving. I could literally feel her walking past the heel stone. And before that, we, ah, had this rather intense sexual encounter at these standing stones in Scotland."

"Fuck." Ronin shook his head. "That's one of *the* most ancient, most powerful bonding sites, you great numpty. And the way you two—" He stalked back into the house. "I need a drink for this conversation."

Back in the study, and tumblers filled with at least three fingers of whiskey for each of them, Ronin gestured at Amelia as he sat across from Matt. "You know about bonds, right?"

"Magical bonds? Sure." Amelia's expression turned wary. "But they're damned rare."

"They are in the shifter world, too. When we find our soulmates, we bond through a bite, leaving a mark that physically cements the emotional bond. I suspect it's similar for the vamps. No idea what Druids or Mors Dicen do, but even *with* a mark, sometimes a pair is only half bonded. I'm ninety percent sure that's what happened to you, and that means your Druid powers are erratic because they're searching for Vella, looking to cement the bond that you guys started, but never completed."

"But *why* do you think we didn't cement or complete or whatever?"

"Are you serious? Is Vella Knight at Madgwick fighting by your side right now, or did she flee back to her evil aunt? *Besides* the baggage of your combined pasts, the two of you have a mountain of therapy to unpack. You two have issues, and the bond knows it. Of *course* it didn't fucking complete."

"And, Matt, being half bonded is bad. Real bad." Amelia downed her whiskey in one gulp. "I needed that."

"Why?" With his stomach already filling with lead-lined dread, Matt couldn't bring himself to even touch his drink.

"The worst outcome is if it's neither completed nor severed entirely, the couple can ... lose their magic entirely."

"Amelia is right, Matt," Ronin added. "With shifters, sometimes we revert to our animal selves permanently. Not sure what happens with other dark energy users, but it can't be good."

Breathe, calm, focus. Matt took his guilt over Vella, his frustration over his ignorance about his heritage, his fear about the future and shoved it down, deep, deep down. What mattered right now was problem-solving. "How long do we have before the worst outcome? What do you think I should do?"

Ronin and Amelia traded glances before Ronin leaned forward. "You and Vella need to get back together as soon as possible. You'll deteriorate faster if you remain apart. I'm pretty sure being in the same location will slow ... whatever is happening now. And if you're being affected like this, you can be damned well sure it's happening to Vella, too."

7

Nine days after returning the bone runes to Ellaine, Vella woke to a frozen grayscale landscape that made zero sense: cast-iron lampposts dispersing misty glows into the night, most of them still wrapped in festive season decorations. Snow-covered ground. Glowing city windows peeking through tiny gaps in the treeline. This was not her bedroom.

But it was frigging freezing, and as if her body recognized the cold the moment the thought hit, her teeth and entire body started shaking. The back of her neck and palms itched like crazy, as though she'd been using her Mors Dicen magic overtime, and she reached for Brianna before she could think otherwise.

"Brianna?" she whispered. "Brianna!"

Silence. Brianna might as well have been back in her lead-lined box.

Why the frig was she outside? The last thing Vella remembered was running, searching for something ... Matt. She'd been looking everywhere for Matt. Or had that been a dream?

And, oh shit, she had on her sleeping tee, but nothing else. At all. With effort, Vella sat up, a groan escaping past her chattering teeth. Her head ached like a bitch, and besides being colder than she'd ever been before, every muscle dragged like a limp rag. But at least she could make out the outline of familiar buildings and trees ... This was West Village Park? What the actual fuck?

She'd been asleep in her bed, and now she was at the park? Vella clutched the knife tighter. "Brianna? Damn it, *Brianna!*"

Nothing.

Damn it all, how long was Brianna going to shut her out?

Swish ...

"He—hello? Is someone there?"

Shhhhh ... crick ... swish ... Cr, cr, cr ... snap, snap, snap.

In the faint illumination of the lamplights, lurching toward her on the dry grass, were ... rats? Except, they were just bones, though some had bits of flesh clinging onto them, with massive front incisors clicking and clacking.

Motherfucker, was this how she died?

Footsteps thudded behind her, coming fast. Vella whirled, a gasp sticking in her throat as the silhouette of a large man filled her view. She instinctively gripped Brianna in a forward hold and forced her aching, frozen-ass body into an attacking stance—

Fatigue crashed over her in a tidal wave, and everything went dark.

"BONE WIELDER, Bone Wielder—are you awake?" A vaguely familiar voice permeated the warm, oh, so blessedly warm, darkness.

Vella snuggled into the sensation of being wrapped up tight, the soothing rumble of a motor running lulling her back into the cozy depths of sleep.

"Bone Wielder?" The voice pressed against her consciousness again.

As if her eyelids were deadweights, she cracked one open, then the other.

Well, hell. Now she was sitting in the back of a car a fancy car. The just-rising sun shone through the windscreen onto a dark-haired man driving up front. And at her back—

WTF? She was *sitting* on someone. Vella scrambled off the lap she was squishing, but her muscles responded sluggishly, and the move was more a flop and roll onto the heated vacant seat. Who were these dudes, and why was she in a car with them, and where was—

"Brianna!" Adrenaline surged, and she fumbled for the bone knife's sheath.

"Do not worry, Bone Wielder," the golden-haired dude who had been her seat murmured. Vella twisted and met an oddly familiar, lazy, caramel gaze. Then he grinned, and despite a set of scary-looking fangs, he gave off a weirdly boyish vibe. "I put Brianna in my coat pocket, which you're currently wearing," he said. "You should feel her there."

"Right, like I'm meant to just believe a stranger." Although, he *was* familiar ... and the jacket was welcome— for both coverage and warmth. But she kept an eye on him as she fumbled for the pocket. Relief sang through her as her searching fingers touched Brianna's knife, even if she still had no response from her so-called Bone Guide.

"Distrustful little witch, aren't you? This is good, but unneeded with us as we've met before. I'm Alex, and driving us is my brother Tannis. We are your protectors."

Vamps. These were the vamps she'd met at Matthias'

club, and again at his lake house. As if just thinking Matthias' name was a trigger, his midnight eyes flashed through her mind. An entirely new warmth stole into her belly, but she squashed it flat. No word—not a call or an email or a text—let alone actually seeing him, in the last nine days.

"Are we going to see Matthias?" Because if so, she had some words to say to the deliciously hot, deliciously talented—in more ways than one—spellcaster.

That traitorous warmth licked back through her so strongly and fast she had to clench her thighs this time.

"The Magicae coven leader?" Alex chuckled. "No, we do not take you to see him. He cannot protect you well enough."

"Then where—" Tannis pulled the car to a stop, and when Vella looked over Alex's shoulder, she relaxed back into the seat. "Well, at least I'm home."

"Actually, our home," Tannis said.

"While we can call it that, anyway," Alex muttered. "The human government of this country is about to enact a law restricting vampires and shifters from owning property."

"Why would anyone do that?"

"Because she wants more and more power, and vampires will never take her orders."

She? Who would— Vella snapped her mouth shut. Ellaine.

The front door to the gorgeous, pristine-condition brownstone neighboring her shop opened, and Sara was there, standing just inside the doorway, beside a small female vampire with snapping black eyes.

"Sylvie," Vella murmured. Of course, Sylvie was here. Alex and Tannis were her brothers—not that you'd guess it going by their size difference. Vella glared at Alex since he was closest. Though it was at least a hundred years old, the *entire* building remained a single-family home, and to this day, Vella had never met the owners. "Wait. You didn't ... eat the previous owners, did you?"

"You witches, always so funny," Tannis said without cracking a smile.

"Ha, ha." Vella eyed the vamp brothers. Yeah, they might seem all boyish and fun, but their teeth were sharp, and she knew just how fast—and strong—they were.

"Come, I shall carry you in." Alex reached out.

"Ew, no way. I am perfectly capable of walking into *my* house."

"I think not." Alex shrugged. "You are like a newborn foal with your limbs all floppy, and it is just as well as we need to keep your journeying hidden."

"Hey, stop grabbing me—" But damn it, Alex had one thing right. Given she didn't have the strength to stop him picking her up at the best of times, she had zero hope now. But that didn't mean she had to like it. And seriously—they were trying to hide her? Pft. They probably made an even bigger spectacle with Tannis running around to stand close on one side and Alex pulling the jacket collar high to cover her face.

But at least vamp strength meant she was inside the brownstone townhouse in moments.

"Vel! Thank the gods!" Sara rushed to her.

Vella tried to respond, but her grasp on consciousness went sliding away again.

"Sylvie? What's wrong with her?" Sara's anxious voice chased Vella into the darkness.

"That's magic fatigue if I've ever seen it," were the last words she heard.

. . .

VELLA'S NIGHTMARE shoved her out of sleep as forcefully as if she'd been thrust into an icy lake—her parents again, calcifying.

Seriously, give her the horny ones at the standing stones with Matt any day.

"Vel? You okay?" Sara was under the same quilt, her knees drawn up and her iPad out, sketching something.

"Sara!" Vella hugged her tight, pressing the iPad awkwardly between them, but given this was the first time Sara had stayed in the same room as Vella in the last eight days, let alone shown any affection, Vella held on tight.

"Okay, squishing me." Sara prodded her under the arm, and Vella reluctantly eased back to the padded headboard of the four-poster timber bed—

"Whose bed is this? Where are we?"

"We're at Sylvie's house. Literally next door to us." Her voice wobbled. "You scared me, Vel. How are you feeling? And how did you end up at the park? In your jammies?"

"I'm feeling okay. A headache, but what do you mean by Sylvie's house? And ... the park?" Vella couldn't restrain a shudder at the memory of undead fucking rats lumbering toward her like zombies. Had that been *real*? "I honestly don't know. Please explain what's going on. I'm so confused."

"You remember Sylvie, right? She told us about being Mors Dicen?"

Another shudder scrambled up her spine. Like Vella could ever forget the vamp who'd tasted her blood and smelled her lies. Who'd been the first to proclaim Vella and Sara Mors Dicen witches.

"Well," Sara continued, "we've stayed in touch. Apparently, her family owns the brownstone next door to the shop. They're here to"—Sara made air quotes with her fingers—"protect us."

"What do you mean?"

"To be honest, it's way more like stalking. Anyway, last night, I went to the bathroom, walked past your bedroom and the bed was empty! But your keys, wallet, cell phone were all on your desk, so I panicked. I called Sylvie, and she sent her brothers over to smell your room, and off they went to hunt you down. Don't worry, they came through my window so they wouldn't be caught on Ellaine's surveillance cameras. Alex found you in the park near one of your fave running spots. Did you ... sleepwalk?"

"Maybe? How does Alex know where I like to run?"

"I wasn't joking about vamp protection methods. He has your schedule down."

Tap, tap.

Vella shifted to look around Sara as Alex strolled in. Most vamps had an ultra-cool energy, but this one had more of a golden retriever vibe. He held out a pastry bag and coffee from Crystal Brew. "I brought your favorite bagel— cream cheese—and a double-shot coffee, no cream. And for you, Sar, caramel latte and choc croissant."

"Thanks, Alex." Sara took the proffered gifts, and Alex flopped onto the bed, wagging his nonexistent tail. "We're not quite finished with sister time, though."

"Sibling time is vital." Alex popped back to his feet and bounded out the door. "Come down when you're ready!"

"He knows my coffee and pastry order?" Vella frowned. "And where I get it from?"

"I'm just grateful they're on our side, man. But, Vel, seri- ously, we need to talk. You must've noticed I've been avoiding you—"

"Yeah, that's been apparent."

"It's because I was—am—furious with you. But ... you terrified me last night. I guess I kinda got a taste of what you go through all the time with me being sick and all. So I think I understand *why* you did what you did with Tara—"

"Sara, I know you hate this. I do too, I promise you that. As soon as I—"

"Just stop. I don't want to fight about it. What I'm deeply concerned about is *you*—your physical and mental health. Since you got back from England, you barely sleep, and when you do, apparently you sleepwalk into the cold winter night, and you've got constant headaches—don't think I haven't noticed all the ibuprofen you've been popping."

"I'm not that bad." She took a sip of coffee—thank the Goddess, it was exactly as she liked it—to hide from Sara's truth.

"You look awful—pale with dark circles under your eyes. And Sylvie says that the reason you passed out unconscious is because you've somehow completely exhausted your entire store of magic. How did you manage that? You're not even using Brianna these days. What's going on with you? Please, be honest, talk to me."

Vella's heart cracked, and she squeezed her eyes tight to stop the tears that sprang up from falling. She *longed* to confide in her sister, to admit how awful these past days had been. Ever since she'd dropped off Tara and the runes at Div Tower, she'd heard exactly zero from Ellaine and Derrick— had even been refused entry to Div Tower, told they were both 'busy' and ordered to just concentrate on Arcane Antiquities and Ellaine would get in touch when it was convenient for her. The whole point of handing Tara over was to find a cure.

And she was lonely. So damned lonely. The holidays had passed with Sara's absence like a gaping wound in her heart; she missed Sara's soft laughter, her raunchy jokes, her companionship. Sara's yule present still sat wrapped and unopened in Vella's bedroom. And Brianna hadn't been making an idle threat with the whole renouncing Vella stance; pft, Brianna might as well be a regular non-magical dagger at this point. Vella hadn't realized how deeply she'd come to depend on her Bone Guide's friendship. And then there was Matt.

Now that was a hurt far deeper than she'd been prepared for. She carried this visceral longing to see him, to touch him, to be held by him.

But he'd betrayed her with his lies, and then she'd betrayed him right back, and everything was so fucked, and even though she knew contact between them was a no-go, all she wanted was to hear him call her Rapunzel again.

Vella stared at Sara—the only person on this planet who loved her, who she could call family. If Vella confessed *any* of her fears or doubts, she'd break. Cease being able to function. And who would save Sara then?

"I'm fine," Vella finally squeezed past the lump in her throat. "Just stressed. I'm struggling to get a lead on your cure. In fact, I'm going to Div Tower today. I'll break protocol if I have to."

Sara rolled her eyes dramatically. "Why do you keep saying the same freaking thing? It's like no matter what new input I use, your response is always 'must get Sara's cure no matter the cost.'"

"I am *fully* aware of the cost." Vella rubbed at her chest, pressing down against the void that was Matthias Medea. "And you're right, I am determined to make you safe. And after that, we can work on fixing everything else. Come on, Sar, *please*. Let's just go home. We can make hot chocolate and get your favorite s'mores, and I'll tell you about Madgewick and Mr. and Mrs. B—you are going to love them, and it, so damned much. And I *promise*, we will get there—"

"I don't want that murderer to use the runes to find my cure. I don't want *her* to touch the runes, full stop. I'm not doing this anymore. I'm moving out. Sylvie said I can stay here."

"Ellaine won't—"

"I don't care what that evil motherfucker wants!" Sara snatched up her iPad. "I'm done. There are options outside of *obeying*, Vella. For starters, days ago, I gave Shannah a sample of the Elixir's potion—Matt is working on some kind of plan to replicate it. If they succeed, I can go anywhere."

What the fuck? No. No, no, no. Sara couldn't just *leave*! "And if it doesn't work?" Vella's voice rose, and she couldn't stop her words or her volume if she tried. "What if you get sick? What if you—" The words stuck in her throat.

"Then I get sick." Sara's chin shot into the air. "Maybe I'll even die, but I'll do it on my terms. Not yours and not Ellaine's."

Vella recoiled at the absolute certainty in Sara's expression, and for a moment, the room spun, and she had to force herself to breathe.

"Seriously?" Sara scowled over Vella's shoulder and reached past her, grabbed Vella's cell and held it out. "Didn't you hear it ringing?"

Vella stared at her cell phone for a second, but before she could take it, Sara hurled it so hard that it bounced on the bed.

Vella caught it on the second bounce. Aunt Ellaine's name flashed on the screen.

Vella's stomach clenched.

"Where are you?" Ellaine's tone was as cold and sharp as her words. "You haven't been down in your shop all day, and we saw Sara exit at four thirty this morning. And she hasn't reentered. What is happening?"

Vella's brain whirred like an undead rat on a running wheel, trying to come up with an answer. Behind her, the bedroom door closed with a quiet snick.

"We ... ah ... had a fight. She's fine, though. Just blowing off some steam. I'm about to open now. Aunt Ellaine, about the cure—?"

"Sara is well, is she not? Are you asking me to waste valuable foreseer time and energy when we are dealing with a crisis? If you were just a little bit more talented, you could help, but you cannot. Stop being so selfish."

The call ended.

Vella gaped at her phone, numb, unable to fully comprehend what the frig just happened. The entire reason she'd brought the runes to Ellaine was for Sara, and now Ellaine refused to cooperate.

"Knock, knock." Sylvie's voice lilted into the room moments before she entered. "Alex grabbed a few things for you." She placed a small bundle of clothes onto the chair, resting Brianna on top in her sheath. "By the way, my dear, you stink of denial. When you're ready for some advice—"

Damn it, why did vamps get to be able to smell a lie? Vella opened her mouth to object, but Sylvie held up a finger. "*When* you are ready, come find me."

8

"Welcome to Cristal-Science Laboratories." Steadying herself on a crystal-tipped cane, Ruby Chevalier, Councilor for the Crystallo coven, waved an elegant hand for Matt and Ronin to follow. "You may notice a slight ... hum, as you enter."

They passed through double steel doors and down a series of steps into an underground facility. Energy flashed across Matt's skin, like when he passed over the boundary spell at Madgewick, raising the hairs on the back of his neck and arms.

Bloody hell, his Druid power. He raised an urgent eyebrow at Ronin.

Ronin's gaze traveled over him fast, and he shook his head once.

Relief made Matt's chest tingle, but forcing a calm smile, he followed Ruby as the stairwell opened out to an immense, crystal cavern. Above them, millions of crystals transformed the soaring ceiling into a nighttime wonderland, while from the floor, room-sized, hollowed-out quartz points grew into a complicated matrix of labs, bustling with equipment and technicians.

"This is spectacular." Ronin spun around. "It's like we're inside an ancient geode."

"*Très bien*, Ronin. Our geochronologists aged these caverns at over two million years old."

"And the doors?" Matt nodded to where they'd entered. "Reinforced steel?"

"And crystal-lined, with mineral wool interiors."

"That was the hum?"

"Correct. A petite ... idea we came up with after the coup."

"I think we've all been rather busy with our own ... processes, in the last two decades, haven't we? And apologies for the delay," he murmured. "Traffic was bad," he lied.

No way in hell could he tell Ruby the real reason had been to make sure his Druid power wouldn't explode while he was on board the plane. They needed to work as allies, but given the historical hatred witchkind had for Druids, he couldn't risk anything alienating her.

And if today's meeting went to plan, Matt would get the Coven Union's agreement to end their covert operations, and take their fight against Ellaine into the open, and finally, they could take their vengeance and free their covens from Ellaine's control.

"You are worth the wait, Matthias." Ruby's accent grew stronger as she turned to the salt-and-pepper-haired witch at her side. "Emil, please prepare the item we have been working on for Matthias. Now, come, we have important matters to discuss."

Ruby led them through to another small crystal-lined cavern, though this one only held a single, long timber trestle table, something that would have fit inside

Madgewick centuries earlier, filled the space, and sitting at it were a hedge witch, a vampire and a shifter.

Carys Llewellyn, Lucretia, and Broderick Mac Daniels.

Ronin stiffened.

Matt cursed under his breath. When had Broderick joined the Union? Matt shot a fast glance at Ronin, whose eyes glowed neon green.

"Ronin," Matt warned under his breath.

Bloody hell but he wished he could kick his own ass. He should've considered the possibility Ruby would widen their union, and of course, as the current head of the shifter clans, she'd reach out to Broderick.

And how was Ruby to know Ronin hated Broderick, and the feeling was mutual?

"It's okay," Ronin clearly lied through his gritted teeth.

Across the table, Broderick's eyes also turned a neon green, though whatever the shifter leader thought of sitting with his estranged son, he kept it hidden within his bulky jaw.

Which was just as fucking well.

"Well, it appears our Union has grown," Matt murmured. "Carys, it's an honor to have you representing the hedge witches at this table. I'm sorry Kathleen couldn't be here."

"The feeling's mutual, Matthias." Carys's smile was fleeting. "And Mom would've been thrilled to see this meeting finally happening."

"Matthias," Lucretia purred. "How lovely to see you again."

"Lucretia. I thought you were going to the countryside?"

"Oh, I did, however, given recent ... events ... it appeared time to reacquaint myself with those in our community who share similar goals." She smiled vaguely and waved a hand through the air. "And now I find myself in a different, though equally delightful, countryside. And hello, youngling," she said to Ronin, her deep red lips turning up in a slow appreciative smile. "Another new friend. How utterly delightful."

"My lady." Ronin nodded once as he took a seat.

"Ooh, I do like you." Lucretia's laugh was a gentle tinkle, but across from her, Broderick scowled even harder.

"Enough of this fuckery. What's he doing here?" Broderick said in a thick, Scottish accent, tilting his head at Ronin.

"Broderick—" Matt forced every note of disdain from his voice. "What a ... nice surprise to see you."

"Can't say the same, *Nephew*." He kept his gaze on Matt. "So?"

"Broderick," Ruby said with authority. "Once Lucretia joined our mission, I felt it only right to include the shifter community at the table, too." Ruby wobbled as she eased onto the seat, and as Matt helped steady her, he had to hide his surprise at the frailty she hid beneath her voluminous coat. She flashed him a warning smile, her eyes indicating she knew what he'd felt. Shit. Was Ruby unwell, or was this age-related? "However," she said with the same forcefulness, "in my home, I expect courtesy toward all guests *I* invite."

Broderick grunted, which, given his dislike of Matthias and Ronin, was more than Matt had expected.

"I invited you all here to discuss the imminent construction of Divinator Towers in cities near where we all live."

"And what does that have to do with us?" Broderick locked his arms over his chest. "Your magic spat got decided two decades ago."

"Broderick—" Ronin leaned forward.

"I am your father," Broderick spat. "You can call me Sir

or Laird. What kind of meeting is this that a non-representative can speak?"

"Don't punish the Union because you're pissed at me."

"You speak to me like that in front of others?" Broderick leaped to his feet far faster than Matt had realized his uncle could move, and beneath Broderick's shirt, his muscles writhed like he was about to shift. "If he stays," Broderick gritted out. "I go."

Matt instinctively moved in front of Ronin. "Bull—"

"Matt." Ronin gripped his arm. "This union functioning cohesively matters more than my presence. I'll be outside when you're done." As he left the table, he ducked his head and whispered, "Remember your stars."

Bloody hell, Matt's power was *surging*. That couldn't happen. Not here. Not now. *Breathe, calm, focus.*

"Broderick." Ruby stood, and while she used her cane to steady herself, there was no weakness in her voice.

Shit. Ruby had done the right thing bringing their whole community together—even if he didn't like the being that represented one of them—because to overcome Ellaine, they had to work together, and if Ruby felt they needed the shifters, Matt would heed her opinion.

"Ruby, please be seated," Matt soothed. "I appreciate your intervention on behalf of my cousin; however, Ronin is right in that we are here to discuss the Towers." And hopefully, dispense with the covert nature of their fight. "Please continue."

Ruby's displeasure remained open, but she finally nodded and resumed her seat. "Thank you, Matthias. As I was saying, the Divinator Towers will bring great numbers of their coven witches into our cities, and once there, they will feed off the energy of humans within these cities to power their foresight. Any hope we have of running our lives as *we* wish, without Divinator intervention, will be ended."

"There is more," Matt murmured. "My team has confirmed the special investigators are increasing their numbers too, giving Ellaine the physical means to enforce any order."

"Do we know if Nevena Montgomery, the Councilor-elect for the Elixir coven, will continue her coven's support of Ellaine's plans?" Carys asked.

Ruby ran a hand over the crystal tip of her cane. "Nevena had never openly disagreed with Charles in the past, but she was also only at Witches Council meetings as Charles' Second, and he never let any of his Seconds say much. Matthias, did you ever surveil her?"

"Yes, but our recon never found concrete evidence, one way or the other, of her personal view when it came to supporting Ellaine's orders. I'd place her as an unconfirmed threat at the moment." But that had to change. Matt made a mental note to get the Magicae coven to conduct a deep dive into Nevena's history.

"The vampires can observe her London residence given it is not far from one of our city sanctums. As the raven flies," Lucretia added with a small smile.

Matt met Lucretia's gaze and gave a subtle nod. Vamps weren't known to read minds, which meant Lucretia already thought along the same lines as Matt. Good to know.

"And you and I will no doubt get to see firsthand how she responds to Ellaine's proposals at our first Council meeting in mid-January." Ruby nodded at Matt. "However, the SI and Towers are still my immediate concern."

"What do you want from us?" Broderick's tone was calmer now, at least.

"We need to establish relationships with our human

government counterparts to counter these proposals and use every magic or power within our communal grasp to halt these expansions."

"The Magicae support resistance of the Div plans. Fully and *openly*." Matt held his breath. 'Openly' was the key to the Coven Union taking the final step in pushing back; they had to be willing to—

"No bloody way," Broderick growled.

"Why not?" Carys leaned forward. "I say we prepare for war."

"The vampires stand ready to take any action needed," Lucretia said.

"You are all mad!" Broderick leaned back in his seat, but his gaze locked on Matt. "Look at what you cost our community last time, Medea."

"Broderick." Ruby thumped her cane on the ground, and a bolt of energy shot around the room, booming from crystal to crystal. "The Coven Union will not survive if we rehash the past. Matthias is not responsible for the actions of others. And you will not use his victimhood to hurt him under my roof. Now, what do you say?"

"I say no. This shifter community will not participate in any scheme. We are alive and safe in our compounds, and that is all we need." He held up a meaty hand. "We wish to be left alone, nothing more, nothing less. That means I won't go blathering to anyone else about what has been said here, but no shifter who is a"—Broderick's gaze flicked to Matt—"clan member will support what could lead to an all-out war and risk all our lives."

"Well, Broderick, you have had your say. I should also like to say my piece." Ruby stood, and diminutive she might've been against the backdrop of the cavern and the beings surrounding her, but she still captured their attention. "When we started the Coven Union seven years ago, we agreed that we would only proceed with a course of action if all who wished to participate at the table were in agreement. Now, it appears Broderick is wishing for the shifter clans to depart this table?" She held Broderick's gaze, and when he nodded, she did too. "Fine, then you may leave, and we thank you for keeping this meeting to yourself."

Bloody hell. Could Broderick be trusted to not say anything?

As soon as Broderick had cleared the cavern, Ruby spoke again. "Well, now that Broderick has left us, I need to inform you, I also do not think we can proceed in an open resistance."

Fuck. Fuck, fuck, *fuck*.

AFTER ANOTHER HOUR, the Coven Union's remaining members agreed on a *covert* approach to monitoring and resisting the Div Tower builds, and Matt met Ronin back in the main cavern, inside one of the room-sized hollowed-out crystals.

"That asshole," Ronin hissed as soon as the crystal door closed behind Matt. "Can't believe he's here."

"He's not anymore." Matt filled in the gaps quickly about the rest of the meeting.

"So we're hacking any records about the Tower builds?"

"The others will focus on the build plans in each city. We're to identify who they're working with in the respective governments."

"I can do that." Ronin scrubbed a hand over his face. "But why only covertly? We're so close to being able to fight back! If we get the grimoires—"

The door to the crystal room opened, and Ruby joined

them, her cane in one hand and a hessian-colored bag carefully held in the other.

"Ronin, my apologies." Ruby sighed and settled into the nearest chair. "I did not understand the depth of the schism in your relationship with Broderick. If I had, I would have done you the courtesy of advising you beforehand of his joining us."

"Thank you, but it's not your place to apologize. Broderick is an ass. How and why the clans agreed on him being their representative is beyond me."

"Might is right," Ruby murmured. "Isn't that the shifter motto?"

"Fucking idiotic motto." Ronin grimaced. "Sorry, Councilor—"

"Ruby, please, Ronin. We must adhere to Witches Council protocol in certain places and around certain people, but among us, we know that titles are useless. Let us have that honesty between us here, in this place, at least."

"Of course, Ruby."

"Thank you, Ruby." Matt shook his head. "And if anyone is at fault here, it's me. I should've realized who you were bringing in, but I've been focused on other matters recently. The reason Broderick is such an ... ass ... is Ronin's business, so I won't—"

"Stop." Ronin sighed and sat beside Ruby. "Ruby, you deserve to know the truth. In fact, you should know who you're dealing with when it comes to Broderick. He and I haven't talked in years—ever since my younger sister, Shannah, left the compound in the Highlands to live with Matt and me, and refused to go back. Broderick blamed me, but the truth is, while I helped Shannah get out, she left because under the clan rules, she had to be the perfect chief's daughter—never saying or doing anything he didn't want."

"Shifter clans have always traditionally been reclusive."

"It's become so much worse than that." Ronin's eyes flashed green but settled just as fast as he regained control. "Broderick took all the shifters from his region to a compound and won't let anyone else in. He has absolute control, and if you don't agree, you're punished. He's awful, and I'll help anyone escape that hellhole who wants to."

"Ronin's right, Ruby. Broderick's not a decent man. And for that, I'm sorry I didn't tell you sooner. I still can't believe he got elected to rep all the shifter clans. And for what it's worth, I'm not surprised he didn't want to get involved in a fight outside his own compound."

"Matthias, I will be honest. Even if Broderick had said yes to your request, I would have said no. We cannot make an open move until we understand exactly what Ellaine is after. She has succeeded for twenty years—so why now this sudden Div Tower expansion? Once we have that answer, then we fight. And in the meantime, as we agreed in the meeting, we prepare as best we can: our people, our magic and our weapons."

"I agree that understanding why is crucial." Frustration hit hard, and he took a deep breath. Please, please don't let his stars be shining. "However—"

"*However*, you tire of waiting, no?" Ruby's smile was a sad, sad thing. "I, too, am weary of having her control our lives. But, Matthias, we must act strategically. When the coup happened, those in charge were caught off guard and reacted in haste. They—we—threw everything we had at Ellaine and Monty. And lost. So many were lost."

Matt's chest tightened at the depth of sadness in Ruby's eyes. She'd lost her family in the coup—of course her pain ran deep.

"I understand, Ruby." He reached out and gripped her

frail shoulders. Her pain was one he knew from the other perspective all too well.

"Yes, sadly, we have this sentiment in common. Which is why, this time, we must move strategically." Her expression shifted until determination lit in her eyes—another feeling he understood. "Not looking far enough ahead is what cost us last time, and I am determined to free our communities from her tyranny just as much as you. Now, I have something else for you." She lifted the pouch. "You asked for my help with an elixir potion. Sadly, our scientists could not find a permanent solution; however, they did make this." She withdrew a deep, blue crystal pendant on a silver chain. "This tanzanite navitas will nullify any toxins in the wearer's blood, provided they wear it continuously."

At Matt's side, Ronin tensed. Bloody hell. They had a cure for Sara—even if temporary. Which meant Vella could be free to focus on the fight and finding his stolen grimoire.

"Thank you," Matt said past the anticipation thickening his throat. "Thank you, Ruby."

Vengeance was one step closer.

9

Well before sunrise on December 31st, Vella knocked for the third time on the front door of a well-maintained, two-story Colonial in the heart of Little Neck, a good hour's drive from Arcane Antiquities.

Surely the vamp's intel that Derrick had been staying here was wrong—this house, the suburb, the pretty tree-lined street, were all about as far away from Div Tower living as Vella could imagine.

Finally, the door opened, and Vella froze. Derrick's eyes were bloodshot, his face gray, and his hair sticking out.

"You look awful," she blurted. Mind you, given her lack of sleep and the headache she'd had for the past eleven days, she probably didn't look any better.

"Vella?" He glanced over her shoulder up and down the tree-lined street. "What—how did you find me?"

"I have my ways." And thank frig she did—not that she'd actually believed the vamps' intel until this moment.

"What are you doing here?" Suspicion filled Derrick's eyes—the first time he'd ever directed that kind of look at her, and she wanted to blurt out everything. Wanted so badly to trust the person who she'd believed was her cousin for most of her life—for the sake of the boy she'd grown up with, who'd been punished, albeit it with different consequences, alongside Vella when they'd both gotten into trouble as teenagers, who'd comforted her when it looked like they were going to lose Sara. Who she thought had been family *and* friend.

But no, she couldn't trust him. Too many lives depended on Vella not messing up any more than she already had.

She reached deep into her center and found her icy core, the one she relied on to get her through this hellscape.

"Well, since you haven't replied to a single one of my texts or DMs or phone calls since I last saw you at Div Tower, I think you know."

"Shit." He ran a hand through his messy hair and glanced back inside. "Give me a second."

Muffled voices echoed through the door—Derrick's and a woman's—followed by silence. Moments later, Derrick was back.

"Come in." He glanced up and down the street again before closing the door fast behind Vella and leading her down a short corridor, past multiple doors shut tight, to the kitchen.

"Coffee?" Derrick dropped into a stool at the counter, opposite two steaming mugs, poured and ready to go.

"Sure." She took the mug he held out, but the sudden butterflies in her belly made taking a sip impossible. "I'd like you to take me to Div Tower this morning," she blurted. "And I want you to divine with the Mors Dicen runes I risked my life to find, and ask whether there is a cure for Sara, if at all, and if it's yes, what is it."

Derrick groaned and took a long sip of his coffee. "Vel, I

can't. I'm so sorry. And it's under Grandmother's orders that I haven't been in touch with you. We've been"—his eyes flicked toward his bedroom—"having some difficulty and Grandmother is, ah, disappointed."

Vella's heart picked up pace, but she managed to keep her expression calm as she asked, "What's going on?"

He lowered his voice. "The truth is, she's livid. I've never seen her so angry. And—" He gulped, his Adam's apple bobbing. "And, Vella, we *have* been trying to use the runes, but divinators are either dying or going, like, properly mad."

"What? Hold on—is that what happened with Tess?"

"Tess was the first to try. She ..." Derrick's face paled. "She's still in a coma. We used mid-level Divs at first to see how far they could go, and they just dropped fucking dead the instant their fingers touched one. Lydia and George, two of our most advanced foreseers, are now completely mental: one is repeating the words 'they're waiting' over and over again, and the other is screaming in terror—something about a zombie apocalypse."

"Zom—" Huh. Maybe Derrick wasn't well after all. Because none of this made sense. "Listen, maybe you need some rest—"

"No, you don't understand. With Nevena's help, we've figured out that the skull is some kind of protector, keeping non-Mors Dicen witches from accessing the runes. We tried to separate the runes and skull, but there's a limit to how far they can be taken apart. We've tried *everything* to negate the closeness spell, and later to demolish the skull—magic, incineration, a sledgehammer, even a pneumatic drill—nothing works."

Fuck. Off. They were trying to destroy Tara? Brianna's Tara? Once again, Brianna's shout echoed through her mind, *Mors Dicen do not leave each other in the hands of the enemy!*

But whether or not Vella had made a mistake handing Tara and the aett of bone runes to the Divs, if Vella didn't at least get a reading, then it was *all* for nothing. Her separation from Matt, Sara, Brianna, these terrible weeks alone, questioning and doubting every single thing she'd done, all for fucking nothing.

"Vel? Hey, Vel? You okay?"

Vella called up her ice barrier until it was such a tight shell around her that not one frigging ounce of emotion could get through.

"I'm fine. I just had an idea. Call Ellaine for me."

"Are you *sure* you want to do this?"

"Yes."

Ellaine's ice-gray hair and makeup were as chic as always. One brow arched. "Velvet Knight." Her glacial tone would've frozen a younger Vella in fear, had her scurrying back to do whatever bidding she'd been ordered. But this Vella? No fucking more. Never again would she let this monster get away with hurting people Vella loved. "You have succeeded in contacting me using a rather deceitful method, knowing I do not wish nor have time to speak with you."

"Well." Vella moistened her lips. *Careful, Vel. Tread, very, very carefully.* "I know you're busy at the moment, and I know your coven resources are, ah, strained. Derrick gave me some background info on the runes"—Derrick flinched —"and I've just had an idea about how I could help search for a cure. What if *I* were present in the room during a divination?"

"Interesting." Ellaine stroked a hand down the sleek curve of her bob, and whatever thoughts brewed inside that cold, calculating brain of hers, none were evident on the brutal perfection of her face. "That might work well after all. Meet me at Divinator Tower at seven-thirty sharp. Bring Derrick."

Ellaine ended the call, and a shiver crawled up Vella's spine. Please, please let this be the right thing to do. It was about time the good guys got a win on the board against Ellaine motherfucking Priestley.

DERRICK AND VELLA arrived at the thirtieth floor lobby of Div Tower, where the primary divination rooms were located, exactly at half past seven.

A receptionist stood up from a high-tech workstation and greeted them as Derrick approached.

"Loads of cameras," Vella murmured. They gave her the same ick feeling as she got at Arcane Antiquities.

"They're for our safety." Derrick's voice was softer than usual. "We deal with dangerous and powerful arcana up here, so Grandmother takes security seriously. And you don't have to worry, all the reading rooms have surveillance cameras." Derrick nodded back at the reception desk. "The feeds are monitored there so we can keep an eye on everyone in case of a problem mid-reading." Withdrawing a swipe card from his pocket, he buzzed them through double security doors.

Vella glanced over her shoulder before the doors closed and sure enough, the desk held several screens, each displaying the inside of a reading room.

"Where is everyone?" Vella pitched her voice low as they passed a wall cabinet containing divination equipment. A medieval dip pen, sets of tarot cards, pendulums, crystal balls, scrying boards ... some old, some new.

"Working." Ellaine appeared from an office doorway in a

cream silk blouse with matching woolen pants. Perfect. Expensive. Monochrome down to her leather heels. "As we will be when you discontinue talking."

If Vella never saw another piece of beige clothing in her life, she'd die a happy witch.

"Sorry, Grandmother." Derrick gestured for Vella to precede him after Ellaine, his expression calm, but his face pale. "Now, Vella, have you been in this reading room before?"

"Of course she hasn't." Ellaine pursed her lips. "This floor is for senior and specialist practicing Divinator witches only. And pending the success of today's reading will decide if she ever returns. Shall we sit?"

At the center of the room, a small circular table has three comfortable-looking chairs arranged at perfect intervals. Soundproof walls, looking something out of a luxury interrogation room, surround them and three triangles hung from the ceiling.

"Derrick." Ellaine gestured to one of the chairs. "Since you were so ... cooperative in helping Velvet contact me, I think perhaps *you* should be the Divinator to try and use the bone runes this time."

Shit.

His face went stark white, down to his lips.

"Yes, Grandmother," he said, and to his credit, his voice stayed even. "Standard protection protocols." With the faintest of tremors shaking his fingers, he touched three triangles, one at a time, and a sweet, resonating hum filled the room. "Vella, sit to my right under the east triangle. Grandmother, if you would sit beneath the west, and I'll be beneath the north triangle."

"I'd like to ask a question." Vella kept her expression

calm, but damn it, she had to try something to keep Tara from harming Derrick.

Derrick glanced at Ellaine, who nodded once. "Okay," he said. "When it's time, I'll call you into the divination. Keep the question simple. And make sure to stay absolutely focused; you can't let any other thought enter your mind."

"I will also make a query." Ellaine smiled at Derrick. "However, I will go last and be the anchor, in case the divination becomes unsteady. That way, I can withdraw you from the vision if you need assistance."

Vella blurted, "Can you keep Derrick"—*Alive? Sane?*— "safe?"

"I am confident in my and Derrick's power to succeed today." Ellaine's expression didn't waver. "Lydia had George as her anchor, but they were too weak and therefore unable to extricate themselves from the vision before it consumed their minds. Strength is what Divinators honor."

"Of course, Aunt Ellaine," Vella gritted the last two words out. Calling Ellaine aunt was becoming harder and harder to stomach. But she could do this—she just needed to keep the ruse up until they had a cure for Sara.

"Excellent. Now, one more point. Velvet, given your inexperience with readings, I have crafted your question for you."

"I'm going to ask to find a cure for Sara—"

"And my question will help us achieve that. I promise. Once we have the complete set of runes, our ... opportunity to find the cure will be at its strongest. Therefore, your question will be: how may I find the second and third aetts."

You can go fuck yourself. But Vella gritted her jaw and nodded. Obedient. Meek.

"Derrick, you may commence," Ellaine said.

He nodded and pressed a button, and the middle of the

table split open, a box from beneath rising. As it reached table height, all sides of the box sprang open.

An itch clawed into Vella's neck, shifted to prickle in her palms. Sweet Goddess, the runes—piled beside the skull—rose on some sort of pedestal to fill the table. Thankfully, Tara appeared to have zero damage.

"Vella?" Tara's voice whispered into the room. "Thank the Goddess, that *is* you. Are we safe? I've been fighting Divinators."

"Hello, Witchling," an unfamiliar voice called out.

"Good tides, Mors Dicen," another said.

"Welcome to the family," yet another murmured.

One after the other, eight voices called out a greeting.

Eyes straight ahead, Vel. Do not cry. Do not clench your fists. Do not scratch your neck—or your palms. Take a breath, and another, and—

"Vella?" Tara's voice grew louder. "Can you not hear us? We are here, your coven."

Derrick hit the three triangles again, and one by one their chimes filled the chamber, and then he turned the skull on its side, tipping eight small, irregular-shaped bones, each etched with a runic symbol, onto the table. He carefully picked each up.

No. No, no, no. This was wrong. These witches were *her* coven.

"I sense a Divinator," Tara hissed. "He touched my runes. I must kill him."

"Stop!" Vella shouted.

"You wish me to allow our mortal enemy to handle the sacred spirits of Mors Dicen who dedicated their afterlife as guides? Unpunished?"

"Velvet!" Ellaine snapped.

Vella yanked her hands back. Oh shit. Shit, shit, *shit*.

She'd almost grabbed the runes and Tara! How did she make this look okay? "Sorry. Just—thought I was to help—"

"Never touch the bones."

Ellaine's icy gaze, sharp enough to cut Vella in two right there, took her right back to her childhood, starving while Sara wept from pain—food and meds withheld for being bad girls.

"And where is my Brianna?" Tara demanded. "Why did you part us?"

Tears burned in Vella's eyes, but *no*, she was not letting Ellaine make her cry. No. No, no, *no*. She tucked her balled-up fists under the table to stop herself from wrenching *her coven* from Derrick and getting the fuck out of there.

"Vella, ask your question," Derrick said, the Mors Dicen bones clacking lightly in his shaking hands.

Focus, Vel. You can do this. "Where are the second and third aetts of the bone runes?" She took a fast breath. "And what is Sara's cure, and where can I find it?"

Derrick's eyes went wide, and he froze for a second before turning to Ellaine. "Grandmother?"

"How do we remove the magic from Mors Dicen monsters once and for all, and ensure they never pose a risk to Divinator dominance again?"

The question struck Vella like a punch to the gut, driving the air from her lungs.

Derrick dropped the bones, and they scattered on the table, forming a rough circular shape.

The chimes rang.

"A vision forms," Derrick whispered. Sweat beaded on his forehead, and he leaned closer to the runes. "But it's hard—so many pieces—like a jigsaw puzzle." He pressed his hands against his head, as if to keep it from flying apart. "More pieces," he moaned. "More. They're coming at me from all directions—Grandmother, it's like a storm, I can't focus, please help me withdraw, it's too much, I can't—"

"Derrick," Ellaine snapped. "Don't be weak! Pull yourself together and divine the future we seek."

He inhaled a long, shaking breath, and another, until he was close to panting. "I see a ... a woman—sixties, maybe—dark haired, in an apartment. Modern. Luxe. Behind her is a window to a balcony ... New York skyline. She's staring at a shelf filled with statues and plates. And ... a small yellow plate, shaped like a leaf, but with an image painted on the inside. Wait—the scene's changing ... I see a green hill somewhere."

"What else?" Ellaine leaned closer, her gaze locked on Derrick.

"Beneath is something deep, dark, so, so old, ancient and powerful ... from this source springs all life, all death." His teeth gnashed. "I can't—Grandmother, help, so many pieces —help."

He blinked. Again. Again. Suddenly, Derrick's eyes turned solid white. "So deep, so dark, so powerful. So deep, so dark. So deep, so dark." A tremble started in his hands, and within moments, shook his entire body.

"Damn it." Ellaine inhaled fast through her nose, and a crease appeared between her brows. "Derrick!"

"So deep, so dark, so deep, so dark."

"Well." Ellaine sighed as if she'd been let down. "This is disappointing." She pulled out her phone and started tapping, then made a tsking sound and strode to the door, throwing it open.

Vella gazed into the depths of Tara's eye sockets and whispered, "Please, stop."

Derrick was about to be killed because of Vella. Damn it,

she was a Mors Dicen witch; these were Mors Dicen bones, surely, she could do something to intervene.

Of course! But she had to act fast.

She risked a look at Ellaine. Still in the doorway, looking at her cell.

Heart pounding, Vella snaked out a hand and touched Tara. The charcoal film fell over her vision, and she recalled the one lesson Brianna had given her about traveling via dark energy: concentrate on the darkness and wait for the itch to collect in the center of her hands and the base of her neck to grow and grow and grow until—

A spiderweb of sparkling obsidian stars—the dark energy interlinking everything, and the source of Vella's magic—connected Vella to all that she could see, except for Tara. But trapped within Tara's skull, the dark energy also coated a struggling pale light, guttering, flickering. Derrick.

And his light was dying.

Following the spiderweb, Vella reached out, grasped him oh so gently and pulled. But while that light looked so fragile, tugging it free from the runes was like hauling a deadweight through quicksand. She strained with everything she had.

"I'm free!" Derrick shouted. His eyes went wide. He gasped. "The book holds the key."

And he passed out, falling to the carpeted floor with a graceless thump.

Vella physically let go of Tara, and everything went dark. Frig, how long had it been? Gasping for air, her lungs as desperate for oxygen as if she'd just finished running a sprint race, she forced herself to sit still because Ellaine couldn't discover what had just happened. So even though it felt like *she* was asphyxiating, she pretended to breathe normally while surreptitiously dragging in deep lungfuls of air, and counting the seconds in her mind.

One, two, three ... nineteen, twenty, twenty-one ... her vision started to return, and she dropped to her knees beside Derrick. His eyes remained closed, his cheeks ashen, and his breathing shallow and rapid. Because of Vella's pushing to find Sara's cure, Derrick was right now unconscious, maybe even dying.

Bile slicked through her stomach.

Thankfully, Ellaine was still busy fiddling with her phone, and when she did look up, Vella had caught her breath.

"How interesting." Ellaine strolled back to the table and leaned closer to the runes, considering them while tapping a single nude painted fingernail over her lips, never looking once at Vella. "Velvet, be a dear and clean up this mess."

"But Derrick?"

Two medics bustled into the room with a gurney.

"I have removed Derrick successfully from the vision. He'll be fine." Ellaine's eyes flicked in his direction briefly. "Most likely."

On trembling legs, Vella rose and got out of the way so the medics could see to Derrick, and then she collected the small, irregular bones. They were warm and comfy in her palms, just like when she held Brianna. *I'm sorry; I'm so sorry.* Vella blinked furiously. No way would she cry in front of Ellaine.

"Vella." Tara's voice was harder than she'd ever heard it. "I do not understand why you have allied yourself with these Divinators, nor why you refuse to address me freely. However, a word of warning: the bone runes, the completed Aetts of Cogadh, were hidden for a reason."

The Aetts of what? Frustration seethed through her.

There had to be a way to communicate with Tara. How ... how ...

"Aunt Ellaine." Vella choked back the urge to vomit at those words alone. "Thank you for the chance to be present when you did the reading. You know how much I love Sara, how worried I am about her health, and how she desperately needs a cure. I'd do anything for my sister."

I'm sorry I can't get you out now—but I will. I promise, I will get you out. If only Tara could hear Vella's thoughts.

Vella set the runes back on the pedestal alongside Tara, her heart sinking as her true coven, these ancient Bone Guides, descended once more into the possession of the Divinators.

"I believe I understand you, Vespera." Tara's parting words echoed into the room. "But Mors Dicen do not fear death. And you doing *anything* for your sister does have a price."

Something inside Vella shattered.

Ellaine walked right past the medic placing a facemask over Derrick's mouth, the other raising the gurney with a clunk. She paused in the doorway, giving Vella side-eye.

"Your gratitude does not negate that little rebellion over your question, Velvet. You may go."

No! If Vella left now, it might mean days or weeks or months before she got the one single answer she came here for. She dug deep, reaching for the numbness, wrapping herself in Divinator coldness.

"Aunt Ellaine, I apologize. I do get a bit emotional when it comes to Sara. May I please come with you to have Derrick's vision verified?"

A chillingly genuine smile curved Aunt Ellaine's lips. "Oh, Velvet, my dear. There are consequences for disobedience, as you well know. The existence of Sara's cure will remain a mystery to you for a while longer. Now toddle along to your little shop, Arcane Antiques."

"Antiquities," Vella hissed, glaring at Ellaine's back as she made her way to the elevators.

"Excuse us," the medic pushing Derrick murmured.

"Sorry, of course." Vella scrambled out of the doorway. "Is he going to be okay?"

The nearest medic replied, "Miss Knight, you do not have the authorization to—"

"Please?"

The medic's face softened. "He's stable for now."

They pushed Derrick down the hall, without a single squeak from the gurney wheels, as if even the medics knew not to make any errant sounds.

Shit. Shit, shit, *shit*. Vella had betrayed the Mors Dicen and blown up every single relationship in her life to find a cure and *still* had no answer. And Sara was right, as ever; Ellaine had come up with an excuse to push back the goalposts.

But Vella had just used Mors Dicen magic to save Derrick—maybe she could use it again to save Sara. Because the only monster here was Ellaine, and no way under the Goddess's moon would Vella let her win.

She just needed a bone. Where ... Her heart picked up. There might be one option nearby.

10

Vella staggered—her legs still unsteady after what had happened with Derrick—as she hurried down the beige on beige, seriously boring corridor of the thirtieth floor.

The art of a good thief: act fast. Vella didn't slow down as she reached the cabinet with the divination tools. Snatching the medieval dipping pen out of its cradle, she slid it into her purse in the one swift move.

Now she just needed to find a space ... but where ... where—a janitor's closet, and ... yes! Unlocked! Vella slipped into the blessed darkness, her nose tingling with the strong smell of cleaning chemicals.

Sitting cross-legged on the cement floor, she took out the dipping pen— Yes! A bone nib. Animal without doubt, but it was all she had. She pinched the nib between her fingers and focused on the dark like she had in the reading room. The tiniest of prickles gathered, then nothing. Damn it.

Come on. Vella clenched her fists, took a deep breath, shook out her hands. Tried to relax. Once more she focused on the dark. Her palms began to tingle and the base of her neck too, and then ... it all faded away.

Shit! Shit, shit, *shit*.

What the frig was wrong with her magic?

But Vella didn't have time to sit here figuring out why. Ellaine was probably getting answers about Sara's cure right now, and she was missing it.

Come on, Vel. Focus! She imagined the dark energy flowing and—

ELLAINE STOOD in her huge thirty-first-floor office. Shimmering cobwebs of midnight stars filled the room, and across from her, a silhouetted figure sat at Ellaine's desk, tapping on a computer keyboard. Satisfaction oozes from Ellaine.

Vella's gut clenched. Anything that could make Ellaine that happy had to be bad for someone—if not everyone—else.

"Yes, I can confirm," the shadowy figure said. "It appears Derrick's reading has given us a lead on an ancient ... source of ... some kind of power? *And* there's something else, hmm." The figure tapped a button, and Derrick's recorded voice replayed his words from the reading before the figure nodded. "Yes, I believe if Sara Knight were to be taken to that ... place, it could ... heal her *entirely*."

"Finally! The source of their power *does* exist. I knew it." Ellaine's eyes lit up. "Where is it located?"

"We don't have enough information to confirm the location yet."

Ellaine's face transformed back to an expression that Vella instantly recognized, and it turned her bowels to water.

"Darling," Ellaine said, looking off into the distance, "I require your assistance. This technician has been exposed to rather ... sensitive information. I need you to—"

The shadowy figure flinched. "Councilor Priestley, no, please, no, I swear I won't say anything to anyone—"

A wave of fatigue crashed into Vella, and her consciousness washed away.

BLASTING bright light shocked Vella back to wakefulness. What the fuck? Why did her body feel like one massive muscle cramping? She shielded her eyes against the too-bright light, and a figure moved into view.

Nevena Montgomery. Her graceful blonde tresses were artfully swept over one shoulder, and her matching seersucker pastel blouse, blazer, and knee-length skirt perfectly matched her eyes. She smiled, and Vella could've sworn she had extra teeth.

"Velvet?" Nevena said with a plummy British accent that reminded Vella of *Pride and Prejudice.*

"Nevena." Vella peeled her cheek from where her face pressed against a row of plastic detergent bottles.

"What are you doing in there, you sad girl? Your aunt noticed you never did arrive home, and then we found footage of you entering ... the janitor's closet? How odd." Her smile remained for the entire speech, and, strangely, her teeth seemed whiter—and were there more now?—than before.

Yes, how fucking odd indeed.

"Ah, I was tired." Adrenaline kicked in as the scene Vella had ... imagined? Dreamed? She hadn't traveled the dark energy to see it, so did that mean it wasn't real?

Whatever the frig that vision of Ellaine had been before Vella had passed out—replayed through her mind.

She shuffled on the hard, cold floor and rose to her knees. The medieval dip pen rolled off her lap, but she shifted and hid it with her leg.

Had Nevena seen?

"You must have been close to exhaustion, you poor lamb. Anyway, I'm taking Charles' spot as Elixir Councilor. That makes me Councilor-elect—technically. Best to keep within the bounds of protocol. Anyway, terribly pleased to make your acquaintance." Nevena reached out to help Vella stand —and Vella gaped. Was she going mad, or did that hand have six perfectly manicured fingers tipped with blush polish? "It's not contagious, just a little family heritage, shall we say?" All six fingers wiggled.

Oh shit, she was staring! Vella forced her gaze to Nevena's face and took the proffered hand, discovering she did need help to stand.

"Ellaine will be *so* relieved to know you're well." Nevena's smile didn't move. Was her face frozen in that position? And yikes, so many teeth! "I have a massive favor to ask. I'm new in town, and you know the Magicae Councilor? Matthias Medea? He's divine, isn't he?"

Matthias? Vella froze. What did Nevena want with—

"Anyway, he sent me a personal invite to Nocturnal's New Year's Eve party, and I know you must have been invited too. Shall we go together? Terrific! I'll meet you outside Nocturnal tonight at nine."

"Uh, I'm not sure—"

"Oh, you must!" Nevena checked an honest-to-the-Goddess wristwatch on her slim wrist, the thing glittering with gold and diamonds. "Oh dear, it is rather late already— that's only three hours from now! Goodness, you were in that closet for a while, weren't you? You had better hurry! By the way, a car is waiting outside to take you home. Ellaine is quite insistent that you exit the tower now. Toodles!"

Nevena left with a cheery six-fingered wave, and Vella shuffled out of the janitor's closet, only to startle as two SI agents seemed to pop into existence, flanking her.

But why the escort? What must Ellaine think just happened?

What *had* just happened?

If Ellaine had any clue about what Vella had just done— if what Vella had seen was even real—no way Ellaine would let her leave the building.

As soon as they reached the sidewalk outside the tower, a dark sedan approached and stopped, and Tannis exited the driver's side to open the car door for her. His chauffeur's hat hid his face at first, but then he winked as Vella staggered into the vehicle, almost hitting Alex where he sat in the back seat.

"Vella," Alex said with a smile in his voice. "You are perfection as always."

Pft. She *felt* entirely otherwise. "What the fuck is happening right now?" she croaked. "This is a Div vehicle. What happened to the driver?"

"Probably best not to ask." Tannis pulled away, licking his lips in a satisfied manner.

And chalking up yet another bizarre moment in her day, Vella found Tannis and Alex's presences reassuring enough that she didn't fight the urge to fall asleep.

VELLA AWOKE CRADLED in strong arms. "Matt," she murmured, and buried into his solid chest. A fresh green, spicy scent filled her nose. "Shit. Not Matt."

"Indeed, no, thankfully," Alex's voice rumbled beneath her ear. "No, no. Do not struggle. We are almost at the house."

"You could've just woken me up." And seriously, what was with all this falling asleep? She couldn't hold back a groan ... good Goddess, she needed to figure out what was going on.

"Why?" Alex paused as Tannis unlocked the front door to their brownstone. "Happily, I am more than strong enough and willing enough to carry you, Bone Wielder."

"How about because you don't carry someone without their permission." She scowled at him.

"Fine, fine." He grinned as she found her feet. "You know, I was impressed with your fighting form the other night in the park, right before you fainted. I have a studio where we teach self-defense classes. I think I could help further your training."

"I'm good in the fighting department. Now, why are we in your house and not mine?"

"We have news." With a flourish, Tannis opened a door down the hallway.

What now? Warily, Vella eased around the doorway ... to the living room of her dreams. Jewel tones of jade and ruby, sofas and artworks and gilt mirrors and green plants and the most gorgeous fireplace with an art deco surround, and three adorable cats lazing around.

And sitting on the sofas were Sara, Sylvie and Shannah.

"Vel!" Sara jumped to her feet. "Where have you been? You never opened up the shop. And what's wrong? You look awful."

"Nothing." Vella sank to the sofa seat Sara had vacated.

"Liar, liar, pants on fire," Sylvie purred.

Motherfucker.

Vella twisted the bare minimum required to check out her reflection in the nearest mirror. "You're right. I do look like shit." And damn it, her headache had returned too.

She collapsed back into the cushions, and the sweetest, fluffiest white cat popped onto her lap and started purring.

"Hello, gorgeous," she whispered as her heart melted. Who needed painkillers when you had this darling to cuddle?

"You'll stay for dinner," Sylvie announced. "Boys, can you throw something together, please?"

"Sure thing." Tannis made a kissing sound, and he and Alex vanished deeper into the house.

"Looks like she likes you." Sara scratched the cat behind its ear and then flopped onto the seat beside Vella. "And, Vel, I have the best news. Matt and Ronin just got back from France today and ..."

MATT'S SWIRLING STAR EYES, his snake tats, his smell ... a deep longing descended on Vella, and the base of her neck and the center of her palms prickled. Her magic erupted, plunging her into the world of dark webs and black diamonds, and there he was, Matthias Medea, and she wanted ... no, craved—

"VELLA? VELLA!" Sara's shouting forced Vella to blink her eyes open. Oh, shit, her fucking head *hurt*. Why wouldn't it fucking stop?

"Sar? Why are you shaking me?"

"What's going on with you?" Sara's cheeks were ghostly pale, and her eyes wide.

"I ... don't know. It's like my magic has gone loco. It

either doesn't work at all or it just blasts out completely. Sara mentioned Matt, and suddenly I saw him. I think he's at Nocturnal?"

"Yeah." Shannah let a long, low whistle, looking very impressed. "He's getting everything ready for the big New Year's Eve thing tonight."

"Hang on." Sylvie's eyebrows couldn't have risen any higher. "You have Mors Dicen sight? With no ritual? How much training have you had thus far with your Bone Guide?"

Vella frowned, concentrating on petting her new kitten. Did she have a name? "Um ... once?"

"Hmm. And we've reviewed all the footage from last night—we're piggybacking on Ellaine's cameras—and we never saw you exit the front or back doors of Arcane Antiquities, sleepwalking or otherwise." Sylvie let out a low whistle of her own. "That means as well as sight, you might be a journeyer. Well, no wonder you look half dead."

"What's this sight and ... journeying?" Sara's tone remained steady, but her smile seemed ... forced.

"Sight is basically sending your soul out through the dark energy; in the past, Mors Dicen witches used it to communicate over long distances. That was particularly useful in the days before phones. It remains a very handy way of spying on others' conversations and actions undetected."

"Hold on." Vella took a deep breath. "That means what I saw earlier—" The words stuck in her throat. That meant the conversation she had seen in Ellaine's office had really happened. Ellaine had uncovered some kind of wellspring of Mors Dicen power ... a power that could cure Sara. And destroy all the Mors Dicen, permanently—all she needed were the last two aetts of bone runes to find it. Oh fuck. Fuck, fuck, *fuck*.

What had Vella done?

"So Vella is basically a spy?" Sara crowed. "Now *that* is a skill."

"If that's how you choose to expend your life force." Sylvie shrugged. "And journeying is a rare ability ... no Mors Dicen witch has been able to do so in several centuries, and it isn't encouraged. It sends a witch's corporeal form from one location to another—from any distance—through the dark energy, but it too requires sacrifice. Both sight and journeying quite literally burn away the witch's life force."

What? Brianna had never said anything about—

"Vel, what does Brianna say about all this?" Sara leaped off the sofa. "Can we speak to her now?"

Sharp guilt twisted Vella's gut, and the thought of confessing her betrayal to everyone made her want to vomit. "She's in my room, next door."

"You don't have her with you?" Sylvie demanded, eyes narrowing.

"Vel," Sara said quickly, "I have some good news that might cheer you up." She withdrew a brilliant, deep blue pendant from beneath her oversized, long-sleeved tee. "This is a tanzanite crystal, from Matt. Apparently, there's this super-fancy Crystallo lab in ... um ..."

"Montignac, France," Shannah finished for her.

"Yes, and this crystal nullifies the effects of the poison Ellaine has been giving me. It means I'm free! It's not perfect. I ..." Sara swallowed hard. "They think the crystal will last two to three months before I'll need another one, and I have to wear it all day, every day, for it to clear the toxins from my system. But even so, that's weeks and weeks —and they can work on the next one while I use this one."

Everything in Vella shifted. "They—you—have a cure?"

"Not a cure." Shannah sighed. "But apparently the crystal will negate the effect of the poison safely, for a limited time."

So Vella could have kept Tara and the runes like Matt had wanted? She and Sara could be safely installed at Madgewick, fully free from Ellaine's clutches. She and Matt could be together, *right now*—sharp pain lanced through her heart.

If Vella had been patient, less stubborn, she'd have been able to work with Brianna, with Tara and the runes themselves to find a permanent cure for Sara.

Oh, frigging Goddess, Ellaine's question. And she'd gotten an answer that had made her *smile*. And Vella had orchestrated this divination herself—just like she'd stopped Tara from protecting her people.

Pins and needles tingled in Vella's fingers. Her lips went numb. The world narrowed, and she couldn't breathe; she couldn't fucking breathe.

Ellaine Priestley knew about the source of Mors Dicen magic, and it was all Vella's fucking fault.

"Vella, you smell of guilt." Sylvie raised an eyebrow. "What happened at Div Tower?"

Vella squeezed her eyes shut tight, unable to cope with the combined weight of everyone's gaze. But she'd fucked up, oh how she'd fucked up, and now she had to fix it.

"I'll tell you everything, but first, can you or maybe Alex fetch Brianna? She needs to hear this too."

"On it!" Alex shouted with abso-fucking-lutely too much cheer from another room.

11

They all moved to a gorgeous designer kitchen equipped with the finest cooking implements Vella had seen outside of television. On a long table, Tannis had laid out a feast while Alex bragged about an exclusive cooking course Tannis had completed in France.

"He's become rather a celebrity chef on the posh NYC restaurant circuit," Sylvie said.

"Only the best of the best can entice him to guest-chef for an evening." She inhaled deeply through her nose, clearly enjoying the smells.

"So, vamps eat food other than blood?" Vella placed an unsheathed Brianna beside her on the table.

Nothing but stony silence from her ex-Bone Guide.

"If we choose, of course. But personally, I only eat the good stuff." Tannis filled her empty plate with nigiri, maki rolls and chirashi. "Now, eat. It'll help with the magic fatigue."

Vella took a bite and had a mouthgasm. "Holy shit," she mumbled when she could speak again. "That's delicious."

"I know," Tannis replied as he sat up on the kitchen island next to Alex, examining his fingernails.

Vella shoveled several more bites into her, and when she felt better enough, physically, at least, she took a deep breath. Time to tackle another relationship she was missing.

"Brianna?" Silence. "We're going to get Tara back."

"When?" Brianna instantly demanded, and Vella's knees went weak with relief.

"Well, it's become complicated. Some things have happened, and you should be here for the explanation. And I'm so sorry for everything." Vella touched the bone handle, and the familiar charcoal film snapped over her eyes, turning everything black and white.

She'd missed the comfort of communicating with Brianna in this way so damned much. Had it really only been two weeks since Brianna had abandoned her? It felt like they'd been apart for so much longer.

"Hi, Brianna." Sara waved, and her smile had a tinge of shyness, totally out of character.

Brianna replied through Vella's mouth, her voice lower, resonant, and with a light accent. "Hello, my daughter. Greetings, protectors, your queen would be very pleased. Thank you, shifter. The Mors Dicen need all the help we can get in these evil days."

Doing her best to stay calm, Vella recounted everything that had happened at Div Tower that morning. It felt like years ago.

"Oh, Vespera." Brianna's voice vibrated with grief and rage. "You have given the Divinators our greatest secret—that our dark energy has a source. If they locate it, the Mors Dicen *will* never be a threat because we would lose our magic forever."

"There's more." Sylvie held up a hand. "This could

potentially give Ellaine the ability to finish exterminating all dark energy creatures, too: vamps, shifters"—she glanced at Vella—"any remaining Druids."

A dagger twisted in Vella's guts. "I never meant to hurt the Mors Dicen coven or anybody else."

"You love your sister." Brianna's voice gentled. "But you have no personal attachment to the Mors Dicen, no reason to feel loyalty, so you never even considered them, *us*, in your plans to save Sara."

"It's not that I don't care about the Mors Dicen, and of course I want them to be okay."

"Your word needs to be 'us,' Vespera. *You* are a Mors Dicen. Goddess, the power you have, all raw and untrained. You're a Bone Walker as well? I've only ever met a handful before, in all my centuries."

"Brianna?" Sara's voice was hesitant. "What are you talking about?"

"Mors Dicen abilities." Brianna sniffed. "We really must work on your coven knowledge, daughters. All Mors Dicen witches have bone magic in their blood, allowing them to talk to the dead through their bones. They are Bone Talkers. Then there are some with Bone Sight, where they send their consciousness to another place through the dark energy and see, hear, smell and feel the world. Rare Mors Dicen witches are Bone Wielders like Vella, who when touching a Bone Guide's weapon can tap into their fighting capability. And then there are Bone Walkers—Mors Dicen who can journey in their physical bodies along the dark energy. However, there are terrible dangers when journeying. If a witch is not properly trained, they can lose their physical body in the dark energy and never find their way out. I know of at least two witches who that fate befell."

"And Vella is a Bone Wielder and Walker?" Sara looked

queasy. "Are there any other abilities we need to know about?"

"As a child, I heard tales of a legendary Mors Dicen witch named Morrigan who was rumored to be a Bone Caller. But I have never heard of another, and do not know if that was mere myth."

Thank frig that was a legend only. Vella already had more bone abilities than one witch needed.

Brianna sucked in a swift breath. "This has been an awakening for me. Vespera and I have much work to do in her training. But, oh, Vespera, as such a powerful Bone Wielder, and a Bone Walker, in times of war, it is your duty to take up your armament and serve your people, protect them. You can no longer think only of yourself, of Sara."

Duty. Service. Frustration sparked bright and hot in Vella's heart. Did it never fucking end? But she shoved down the anger. She *did* want to fight Ellaine, and besides, this had happened because of Vella's choices. She'd been the one to fuck up big time, so she'd be the one to fix it.

"I am sorry, too, for abandoning you, Vella. My love for Tara … it caused me to betray my duty as your Bone Guide. I confess, I'd burn the world down to save her. We may be rather alike in our passions, and I hold no resentment. I hope, rather, we can be better allies, closer friends."

A hard lump formed in Vella's throat, and she could only manage a curt nod.

"What about that dark energy source?" Sara asked. "Could the Divs … use it for their own purposes?"

"I suspect so, with enthusiasm." Sylvie's expression turned grim.

"We must not lose hope," Brianna said to everyone. "If I understand the vision and Tara's warnings, I believe that as long as we can protect the rest of the Aetts of Cogadh—"

"What?" Sara held up a hand. "Um, sorry, Brianna. But what are the Aetts of ... Kug-ah, did you say?"

"The Aetts of Cogadh is the name of our oldest, most powerful, most sacred, Mors Dicen weapon. Each bone belongs to an ancient, powerful Mors Dicen Bone Guide, and while on their own, one aett of eight bone runes has considerable power, if a witch can wield all three aetts together, they will tap into the knowledge of all our forbearers—and knowledge is a weapon, my daughter. Knowledge, and the ability to act upon it."

"And Ellaine wants them," Sara whispered.

"There is more," Brianna called out. "Once a witch successfully reads the future using the Aetts of Cogadh, future readings with them become easier."

"So, Derrick can use the bone runes any time he wants?" Shannah's eyes narrowed.

"He will require a Mors Dicen witch by his side, at first. But if he is a strong Divinator it will not take him long to assimilate to the bone runes, and they to him. Then no Mors Dicen will be needed at all."

Vella swallowed hard. Fuck, fuck, fuck. Ellaine could never get the rest of the aetts.

"Which is why we must remove Tara and the bone runes from Divinator possession, then the power source should be safe from discovery. And that ... *Caorthannach*"—all three vamps burst out in delighted laughter—"can divinate no further using our runes."

So that was it—they had to retrieve Tara and make sure Ellaine never got the rest of the Aetts of Cogadh.

Vella let go of Brianna's bone handle, and as expected, the room went dark, but she let the flow of everyone's conversation guide her as to who was where.

"What's a Kwih-rah-nukh?" Sara said from beside Vella.

"She's a legendary monster," Sylvie replied from across the table. "The mother of demons who can spit poisonous fire."

"Hold on. What about the cure, though?" Vella couldn't stop herself from asking. "They said if Sara goes there, she'll be entirely healed."

"No, Vel, I won't fucking do it." Sara's voice went high. "I am not risking leading fucking Ellaine straight to the secret Mors Dicen power source to save myself. No. What I want is to *fight*! Stop them from harming any more covens, more families."

Sara fight? No frigging way. But the strain in Sara's voice was easy to make out, so she kept that thought to herself—for now. "We need to extract Tara and the bone runes first," she said instead. "But we'll need time to plan it properly. Div Tower security is no joke. Although, while I was in the archives I swear Ellaine appeared from the end of the room where there's nothing but a wall—which makes me think there might be a hidden elevator or entry there."

"Hell yes! The heist of the century!" Sara let out a whoop. "I can hack their systems."

"We can help," Sylvie added. "Tannis, Alex and I have skills other than cooking and procuring coffee."

"And I'm in," Shannah added. "I wonder whether you could get the Magicae grimoires, too?"

"We can definitely try, but—"

"Woohoo!" Sara's yelp was right at Vella's ear.

"—We need to keep *Caorthannach* complacent until then." Vella held her breath. No question Sara wasn't going to like what that meant.

"Ah, damn it. That means playing good girls again, doesn't it?" Sara made a vomiting sound just as Vella's sight returned.

"Afraid so. And I need to get ready for Nocturnal. I have to meet Nevena Montgomery there for the New Year's Eve party." *Where Matthias will be.*

The urge to celebrate like Sara had crashed through her, but she restrained the impulse. Right now, she needed to keep her emotions locked down behind that icy barrier so she could figure out how the hell to undo the damage she'd caused.

"I can't wait." Sara did the happy dance that Vella craved to indulge in. "I'm going to a party. An actual real-humans-and-real-witches party."

"Uh, no. No, you're not going."

"Uh, yes, I am. I RSVPed."

"And you're taking me with you," Brianna added.

"What?" Vella scowled at the knife, even though Brianna couldn't see her. "No way. It's too risky."

"Vella, take me in your hand. Good. Now, Sara?" Brianna said in a sweet voice that she'd never used with Vella. "If Vella doesn't take me, you do it."

"Sure thing, B!"

"What the frig, Brianna?" Vella dumped Brianna back on the counter. She'd only held Brianna for a few moments this time, so her vision returned just in time to see Sylvie stand.

"Actually," Sylvie said. "We're *all* going. Um, Vella, about your wardrobe ..."

"Don't worry, Syl." Sara smirked and preened for a moment. "I've already solved that ... issue."

"Hey! I've got good fashion sense."

"I ordered some dresses online last week. Here, take a peek." Sara passed Sylvie her cell phone. "This one is gorgeous. It's backless but has this center column that covers Vella's spine for maximum dagger concealment and a short, layered skirt to reveal her runner's legs for maximum Matthias Medea ogling."

Vella flushed at the teasing comment, but also, Sara hadn't teased her in two weeks, and sisterly ribbing had never felt so good.

"Also," Sylvie said. "I have a Crystallo bracelet you can borrow, Vella. It gives the wearer a boost of energy and should get you through the evening."

"As in I won't fall asleep every time I use my magic?"

"Yes."

"That, I will definitely take. I am absolutely over this whole fall-asleep-and-wake-up-who-the-fuck-knows-where thing."

But what if a fight broke out, and Sara got hurt? And even if Vella did have a dress to hide Brianna, what if something happened, and Vella got caught with a bone knife? What would happen to Brianna? Her stomach knotted. So many things could go wrong.

"All right, enough chitchat." Shannah clapped her hands smartly. "Let's get ready, party people! The night's not getting any younger. And we have people waiting for us."

People ... as in Matthias. The knots in her belly tightened further—this time in a mix of anticipation and heat and dread.

Please, Goddess, just for one night, could nothing go wrong?

12

Vella held Sara's hand as they strolled toward the VIP entrance, bypassing a massive queue of ultra-chic New Yorkers. Matthias Medea clearly still took looking after his people—from coven to staff to customers—seriously, judging by the way Nocturnal New York lit up the street. Floodlights at each corner, more illuminating the sidewalk, yet others directed up the red brick walls, all to the point that not a single shadow could be found from the road, keeping everyone safe from Darklings.

Shannah had left them to enter through the staff back door, and Sylvie, Tannis and Alex, the three as glamorous and beautiful as celebrities, had already sailed past humans and witches alike, vanishing through a secret VIP entrance with the entire queue murmuring *who are they?*

And whether it was anticipation about seeing Matthias any moment now, or the bracelet from Sylvie, or having Brianna and Sara talking to her again—not to mention seeing Sara frigging happy and healthy—the bone-deep weariness and headache that had followed her around for the last two weeks were gone, and instead a sense of hopefulness, and enough energy that she could've bounced through the extravagant oversized doors to Nocturnal, filled her.

"Hi!" Nevena Montgomery said right in Vella's ear, making her jump fifty feet in the air. "You're seven and a half minutes late but never mind."

Nevena wore a chic little black dress with cap sleeves, and her wavy blonde tresses cascaded around her face. Her smile was as creepy as ever as she turned to Sara. "You must be Sara! You are *so* adorable. And I'm ever so pleased my potions have you glowing with health." Nevena tapped Sara's nose. "Boop! Don't overdo it, though, girl! I'd hate to see you relapse!"

Sara looked at Vella, her widened eyes saying *what the actual fuck?*

Vella replied with her own *I know, right?* eye roll.

"Nevena?" Derrick's voice cut above the sound of the increasingly loud queue. "Vel, Sara, there you are."

Vella turned as Derrick ducked under the red velvet rope, looking tired but otherwise okay.

"Derrick." Vella threw herself at him, hugging him tight.

"*You* saved me," he whispered in her ear. "How?"

"Stinking Divs," a witch near the front of the queue muttered.

"Arrogant pricks," her companion hissed.

Nevena's smile grew even wider, her teeth triplicating before she addressed one of the bouncers. "Darling, get these two rascals' names and details, would you? Oh, and *do* eject them from the premises while you're at it. You need not be overly gentle."

Nevena snapped her fingers at Vella, Sara and Derrick. "Come along."

The second bouncer hurriedly unclasped the velvet

rope, and the muttering and murmuring followed them until the club doors closed at their backs.

"What the fuck?" Sara's eyes went wide.

"That's unfortunately pretty common, Sara." Derrick patted her hand. "People from certain levels of society will-fully misunderstand Divinators, our mission to keep the peace. I know you're not used to the sentiment, but this is what happens when you mix at Council-level events, or appear on behalf of the Council, which you are tonight."

Pft. The crowd's reaction wasn't because they were mixing in Councilor business—it was to the Council's ever-increasing control they exercised over witches, non-witches —and all led by Ellaine Priestley. Either Derrick was attempting to gaslight Sara and Vella, or he actually believed what he'd said.

"That's not what Sara meant," Vella murmured low to Derrick as they handed their coats to the attendant. "Nevena was a bit ... harsh."

Derrick accepted all their coat tickets and glanced nervously at a still-smiling Nevena as she gave specific instructions to the coat room team about handling her jacket. Were her lips even moving? "She's, um, very passionate about the mission."

"Yeah, I noticed." Vella bit back a grimace. "By the way, can Sara and I have our tickets, please? We may need to leave early, and I don't want to bother you."

"No need." Derrick shoved them into his pocket. "Just let me know when you're ready and I'll be there."

Sara shot Vella a pointed look. Yep, yet another example of Ellaine reaching out to control their lives. Vella suppressed the urge to yank the damn tickets out from Derrick's pocket.

"To be honest, I'd like an early night too," Derrick

continued. "I'm not feeling awesome after ... everything." His gaze drifted to Nevena whose smile now resembled the gaping jaw of a great white shark. "We should leave together."

Vella's internal guard went up. What the hell was going on? She had zero doubt Nevena had set up tonight's outing, and now Derrick was acting extra-odd. Was this to do with Vella's eight-hour snooze in the janitor's closet after she'd *helped* with the Mors Dicen bone runes?

Was Nevena's purpose to spy on Vella? Report on her behavior around Matthias? Could Ellaine be suspicious about Vella's knowledge of being a Mors Dicen witch?

"We're going to have to be very fucking careful around that ... *thing*," Sara whispered as Nevena, followed by Derrick, strode through the center of the internal doors as if she owned the place.

"Yes." Frigging Goddess, *yes*.

VELLA AND SARA entered the club proper, and a sharp pain gouged deep into Vella's palms and the base of her neck. Power surged within her, rising, raring to break free, and black stars started to shimmer everywhere.

Where was Matthias? She needed to see him. Now. Right fucking now.

"Easy, Vespera," Brianna murmured in her mind. "Your magic is going wild ... just try and calm down."

"What do you mean?" Vella gritted out under her breath. "You can feel it too?"

"I can hear multiple voices and the music of your time—and as we are not in physical contact right now, that should not be happening."

Oh shit. Her magic really was going loco.

"This is so fucking cool!" Sara shouted, looking around with wide eyes and dancing to the music Brianna had just mentioned.

Vella tried to yank back her magic, but it slipped through, seeking Matthias. He *had* to be there, existing just out of reach, hidden somewhere on the three floors of Gothic-meets-baroque inspired furnishings—all velvet and leather and chains and obsidian chandeliers.

Vella shoved through the sea of humans packing the dance floor on the ground level, standing three deep along the bar. Above, the first floor was obscured by the smoky-blue glass salons, and even more people crowded the rail on the second floor. None were Matthias.

Where. Was. He?

Her magic tugged upward, and she had no choice but to follow suit—apparently, she wasn't the only one because as she glanced to the grand staircase in the center of the room, it seemed like so did the rest of the club.

Matthias.

He stood at the very top, his long, blue-black hair, shaved at the sides, gleaming under the club lights. He'd pulled it halfway up into a tight bun, revealing the tattooed snakes with red eyes, the sign of the Magicae coven, that wound up each side of his long neck, their fangs poised, ready to strike.

Even the club lights caressed him like a lovers touch, highlighting his silver eyes, his high cheekbones and long, straight nose, and the ruby studs lining his right ear.

Vella's heart punched hard in her chest, accompanied by a beat of warmth so delicious, she hadn't realized she'd been frozen.

He was a walking, living wet dream.

"*Damn*, your orc is *hot*," Sara chortled.

Her magic finally, *finally* settled, and a pressure deep inside Vella released. She could breathe easy again, for the first time in what felt like forever, as if being in Matthais' presence was exactly where she was meant to be.

What if she ran to him and wrapped her legs around him and never let go?

Vella's eyes met Matthias', and even from across the dance floor, the flash of midnight stars glittering in his brilliant silver eyes made her entire body clench, and damn if an invisible bolt of electricity didn't zap through the club and connect them, tethering from low in her belly, vital and strong and hot and so frigging real she swayed toward him.

Mine.

His face tightened, and as if he felt that same tether, he began to descend the stairs, his gaze still locked on hers—

Nevena Montgomery marched up the steps and stopped, blocking him, extending her six-fingered hand.

What the frig was the Elixir witch doing? Vella's magic gouged deep into her palms and neck again.

Matthias sidestepped Nevena.

And from the base of the stairs, Sylvie, Tannis and Alex, followed slavishly by a crowd of humans and witches, swept past Nevena, dragging her away like a riptide, leaving behind a panicked-looking Derrick, who scurried after them all.

Sara pushed Vella between the shoulder blades toward Matt. "*Go*, you know you want to."

Vella almost gave in to the urge to run to him, but damn it all, she couldn't. Ellaine had been clear when they left Stonehenge that Vella wasn't to see Matthias socially. And making a spectacle in front of hundreds of witnesses—especially with Nevena there—was the last thing either of them needed. And Mattias seemed to get it because while his gaze remained locked on her, his stilled too, and his mouth pulled tight. He tapped something in his ear, and his lips moved as if he were talking, right before he looked over her shoulder—

"Ladies," a voice said right behind them.

Vella and Sara turned together.

"Ronin!" Sara's delight was real, and that alone made Vella smile. "You *are* here. I haven't seen you since—"

"Sar." Vella caught her sister's hand and murmured, "Not here."

"Damn, Vel, how are you always so cool?" Sara shook her head and rolled her eyes at Ronin. "Well, you know what I mean. And how awesome is this place?" Sara spun around, the black sequins on her strapless dress glinting under the club lights. "I've always wanted to come here."

Ronin looked at Sara like she was both something from his wildest dreams and his nightmares. Not that Sara noticed—she was too busy ogling everything and everyone around them, but Vella did, and she couldn't help but respond to the possibility of the latter, because Vella had zero doubt Ronin Daniels was far more dangerous than he let on. So when he turned to Vella and shook his head like he couldn't find words, Vella bared her teeth and made sure he saw she was dangerous too, and her little sister was not to be fucked with.

For some reason, that made him smile, but the grin disappeared fast when Sara turned back to them.

"Where are we partying?" Sara did a shimmy. "I want to get this night going."

"Upstairs, VIP floor. I'll take you there in the back-of-house lift, given it's rather ... crowded out here." His gaze shifted over her shoulder, and he nodded at someone, but before Vella could turn around, he gestured for Vella and

Sara to follow, and when Vella did glance back, Matthias had disappeared.

Damn it. She ground her teeth and forced her legs to follow Ronin through to an employee lift, and up to the second floor, when all she wanted was to run in the opposite direction.

"Vella, can you head to Matt's office? Down that corridor and take the third door on the right. Sara, I'll get you settled."

Anticipation clawed hot and deep in her belly, but she checked the impulse to run in that direction. What if something happened to Sara—

"Just go," Sara groaned. "If I have to see you making moon eyes at your orc one more time, I'm gonna hurl."

"Please, no vomiting in the club," Ronin murmured at their backs. "Now, Sara, this way, and, Vella, if you would ..." He gestured again toward the corridor.

"Hey." Vella leaned back out of Sara's eyeline. "Look after her."

"Heard that," Sara called back. "And I don't need looking after by anyone."

Ronin's expression stated what he thought of that comment, which eased Vella's nerves enough that she did the thing she wanted more than anything else and followed his directions.

The door to Matt's office shut with a quiet snick behind her, and the music quietened. She'd been here once before, but that night her interest in Matt had been fueled by anger. Now, intrigue filled her. This was where he worked. The room had an organized chaos vibe with a couch long enough for Matt to sleep there fully stretched out, a solid timber desk with stacks of papers and all the things that must be needed to run a nightclub, three fancy office chairs, and at the end, a blue glass wall that admitted muted shades of the strobing lights that lit up the rest of the club.

"Where are you now, Vespera?" Brianna let out a long breath. "I can hear myself think again."

"In Matthias' office. Alone."

"Show me."

"Later. I want to see Matthias when he gets here. In fact, I'm closing your window now. I'll talk to you later."

"Ooh, after some privacy for you and your Druid?"

"Did you just snicker at me?"

"Well, one of us has to laugh. And fine, but do not leave me closed for long, though!"

With a sigh, Vella wandered to the glass wall. Laughter? Didn't that require happiness? That was one emotion she couldn't even imagine feeling.

The club spread out before her in a series of decadent scenes. All the salons had their lights on, revealing their occupants mid-act, the VIP lounge's fancy booths seemed filled to the brim, and below, the dance floor heaved, bodies flashing under the strobing lights.

Snick.

"About fucking time," a delicious voice, tinged with a hint of a British accent and smoother than her favorite Fireball Cinnamon Whisky, said from the doorway.

A beat of warmth shot to her core—the first real heat she'd felt since returning to New York—and she spun around.

Somehow, Vella and Matthias were now standing inches apart. She inhaled his spice and sandalwood scent, taking it all the way into her lungs. If only she could trap it there and hold onto the scent and the warmth that it filled her with forever.

His snake tats, revealed by his unbuttoned shirt collar

and rolled-up sleeves, were actually *moving*, their sinuous scaled bodies curling, twisting, their tongues flicking, ruby eyes flashing. How good would it be to lean in and trace those tattoos with her tongue?

Frigging hell, talk about breathtaking.

Matthias' deep voice growled, "Rapunzel," and Vella nearly orgasmed on the spot.

13

Vella was here. Actually here, in his club. Alive, and safe, and *here*. And as the most delicious fucking scent filled the air—part butterscotch, part desire and all Vella—heat hit hot and hard low in his gut, and at the same time, his fight-or-flight instinct engaged.

Bend Vella over his desk right now and fill her and pound her hard until she was crying out with pleasure and he was emptying himself into her, and the world could end, but he'd be inside her so who fucking cared? Or throw her over his shoulder and flee Nocturnal, the city—hell, any-fucking-where a threat existed to Vella—and get far away, so bloody far they could be safe and together and nothing and no one else would matter.

Somehow, Matt suppressed the urge to pursue either path, and instead, brushed her hair back from where it shielded her face.

When he'd first seen her across the club, he'd registered something ... unusual about her, and now, he sensed it again.

Was she tired? Scared? Angry? All the above?

Her lioness eyes ensnared him, holding him still more powerfully than any binding spell he could ever have called.

He never wanted to leave.

Mine. Mine. Mine. The words grew in strength with every heartbeat. And for the first time in eleven days, the gnawing hole that had ripped open in his chest knitted back together, and the ever-present, writhing, searing surge of power in his veins retracted deep within him to curl up, satiated. Content. Even the fucking headache eased.

Gods, to feel so powerfully—and it was all Vella.

Were they cementing the bond right now?

"Matt." Her breath whispered over him, and his body reacted as if she'd caressed him.

It took everything in him to stay still instead of lunging forward and devouring her.

"We need to talk," he managed to say. Would she want his kiss? Did she want the bond? Did she feel any of this too? Fuck, so much to figure out. He pulled his hand back and ran it over his hair instead of down her body like he craved.

"Talk." Her eyes dipped away from his, and she stepped back, her arms wrapping around her torso.

"Are you cold?" He took out his cell and brought up the Nocturnal controls.

"I was." She laughed; a short, humorless sound even as she spun away from him and stared at the club.

"Vel?" He eased around her. "If you're worried about being seen, unlike the salons, it doesn't matter what the lights do in here; the only way someone can see us through that glass is if I change a setting."

"It's not that," she whispered.

"Then what?" Ice trickled up his spine.

"I thought you'd be angry at me after what I said—what I did—back at Stonehenge, but I guess I wasn't ready to see that with my own eyes."

"I'm angry?" What was his Rapunzel talking about now?

"Matt, so much has happened since then, but one thing I can't stop thinking about is how I told you to get your shit together. That—"

"You think I'm angry at you?"

"—wasn't fair on you. You've dealt with an atrocious situation for years, and I've just had my eyes opened, and yeah—"

"Wait, Vella—"

"—I think you take on way too much guilt and responsibility, but I get it, you love—"

"Vella!"

"What?"

You. I love you.

Bloody hell, how in the worlds had this happened? But the feeling was secure within him, to the point he could've said the words and not flinched. Except, was Vella ready for his declaration? Would she even want it?

And what if she didn't feel that way about Matt? Would that impact the bond? Could a magical bond happen without the emotional connection to back it up?

Fuck. Fuck, fuck, fuck.

"I'm not angry—not at you, anyway," he answered with another truth. "Your words gave me something to consider, about feelings I haven't confronted. Is that what you're worried about? Vella, I get you and I are still learning about each other, but this is my promise, I will never mind if you call me on my bullshit." He leaned on the edge of the nearest desk.

"Do you still feel like that? Guilty, in an unhealthy way, I mean." Memories of the last time they'd been on a desk flowed through him. What he wouldn't give to re-do that night, only this time bury himself inside her.

Pants suddenly way too tight, he got up and walked over to the one-way window. "Is that what you call it? Unhealthy?"

"Yes, absolutely. Unhealthy for *you*. I've been reading a lot at night, trying to work out how to help Sara and myself, given we can't exactly talk to anyone about everything that's happened. Thank the goddess Ellaine hasn't banned all books—"

"Yet."

"Don't joke. What she's doing is beyond fucked. But agreed, not yet. Anyway, the point is, that disgrace of a set of lungs, eyes and ears—who I won't even call a witch because witches don't deserve to be lumped in the same category with her, ever—is still winning if your guilt over what you went through, everything she did to you, still impacts you."

"She's not winning," he whispered.

"Then why were you still letting her actions determine how you see yourself?"

Because he'd been terrified of losing anyone else. But no more.

"Come here." He held out a hand, and when she took it, he turned back to the view of the club he'd built. "See all this? This is part of my fight back."

"When did you start?"

"Back in the UK, after the acid attack on me and the witching world stopped fighting back ... all I wanted to do was run away. And that's pretty much what I did. As soon as I was old enough, I left Madgewick—Burrows and Mrs. B were so damned good to me, but I couldn't stand myself there, couldn't stand to be where people looked at me, and I knew that they knew what had happened." He dragged in a breath.

"If this is too hard—"

"No. No, I want you know it all." To know me. "I ran away to London, and for years just fucked up my life. And then Amelia came up. She was more a sister than friend already, and she pretty much woke me out of a standing hangover and hauled my ass back to Glastonbury. Her mother had just died, and she was ... raging. At the Divs. At the Council. At me for abandoning her and them. And she was right. I had abandoned them—no. You don't need to try and pretend otherwise. While I'd been drowning out the rest of the world, the rest of the world had been drowning. I guess that's when I knew, or hell, maybe Amelia's rage was contagious, but either way, I couldn't go back to fucking and drinking. And I realized fast that if I wanted to help our people, I needed two things: my grimoires back so I could undo the fucking spell Ellaine had forced from me, and to get into a position of power and control, which meant pretending to be the fucking thing that everyone had come to see me as—a waste of space."

"Matthias Medea, you are *never* to say that again. You are the exact opposite of a waste of a space. No shut, up— please. Damn, I suck at this being nice thing. I just need to tell you this. You are magnificent. You did everything you needed to protect your loved ones—and that's after the hell you were put through. I bet ... I *bet*, that if I told you that when I was a teenager, my parents were killed, and their murderer then attacked me and permanently scarred me, and that I dealt with my grief by going out and drinking and fucking, all before I was even twenty-one—which by the way is the legal age you can drink here, none of that eighteen year-old stuff you have in the UK—then you'd say,

'Vella, don't be so hard on yourself'." She held his gaze. "Well, I'm right, aren't I? That's exactly what I'd say."

"You are the amazing one, Vella." And inside Matt, two things happened simultaneously. A pain deep, deep inside him eased. Like Vella had opened him up, and stared down the worst of him and yet, she still cared *about* him. And at the same time, his chest tightened to the point he could barely breathe.

Love her? Of course, he bloody well did.

Vella moistened her lips and stepped closer.

Heat and awareness flowed through his veins, and he mirrored her move. If he lunged now, he could have her in his arms in a second. His tongue in her mouth. Her body under his—

"So, if you're not angry at me," she whispered. "Why did you stop me from kissing you?"

"Because what I *wanted*," he gritted out, "was to drag you away, anywhere, and bury my cock deep, deep inside you. Fuck, Vella, every night I dream of being snug inside your hot, glorious body, only to awake up on the verge of either exploding—both cum and magic—and then you're not there, and instead, I'm imploding like a black hole is sawing through me. I can't imagine how our first time together will be anything but hard and fast, and I want more than that for you—"

Her lips crashed into his.

Matt licked into the wet heat of her mouth. She sucked his tongue, pulling him deeper till he was fucking into her mouth—exactly like he wanted to be inside her.

Vella wrapped one leg around his waist and ground against the thick ridge of his cock. Breaking their kiss, she groaned and whispered, "I need you."

"Vella, Vella, Vella." The satisfaction of saying her name,

of having her *hear* him say it, touched a deep, primal need inside him and he reached up her thigh, and into her wet panties, and everything in him refocused, laser-precise, on the glorious, slick inferno of her body. *Taste her, now.*

VELLA HAD NEVER NEEDED SOMETHING—SOME*ONE*—SO profoundly in her entire existence.

Needed his heated sandalwood scent to fill her lungs. Needed his part-British, part-Fireball Whisky voice rasping in her ear. Needed his touch ... fuck yes, right *there.*

She moaned as his clever fingers delved deep, her internal muscles clenching around them until her already-slick body turned liquid.

"Fuck." Matt's breath hissed through his teeth, and suddenly his hands weren't on her body but hitching her legs around his waist, dispensing with her heels, and he strode five steps until her back hit the blue glass wall.

He dropped to his knees, and as he looked up at her, Nocturnal's strobing lights turned his midnight hair electric blue, and his silver eyes crystalline moonlight. Her breath caught in her chest. Time stopped.

Mine.

"You smell delicious." A feral glint entered his gaze as his strong hands ran up her thighs, bunching her skirt as he went higher and higher. "And I am fucking ravenous."

He yanked her panties down; she kicked them free. One shoulder nudged her thigh; she spread both wide.

"Ah, Rapunzel. Look at you. Glistening. Beautiful. And all mine."

He gripped her hips, his head dipped, and then, oh yes! He licked along her flesh, from opening to clit, and sensation flared, and she couldn't stop herself from arcing back against the cool glass.

"Matt," she keened, even as she dug her finger into his hair, steadying herself as much as luxuriating in being able to touch him.

And his wonderful, wicked tongue laved her clit, over and over, and the pressure gathered, and tensed—

"I need ... I need ..."

"Come for me, Vella. I'm going to drink you down." And then he was tonguing her entry; hot and thick, he stabbed into her, rubbing the bundle of nerves at the apex of her pussy, and oh Goddess, the friction. The pressure. The sensation—

"Matthias!" Her orgasm crashed through her, and for long, blissful moments, that sweet pleasure filled every single atom, but when she opened her eyes, her body remained heavy, needy, simmering ... a cauldron so hot it would take the merest spark to send her boiling all over again.

"Speedy there, Rapunzel?" He breathed against her.

She swallowed hard and sagged back against the glass. She picked up his hand and licked his fingers where he'd touched her. Tasted herself on his skin. "Matthias Medea, when you do that to me, hell yes."

"Vella." His beautiful eyes deepened to gunmetal.

"Let me guess ... You'd like me to lick somewhere else?"

"Gods yes. Vella, so fucking much." His voice deepened to gravel. "But fuck, baby, I can't handle it. Not yet. I am so fucking ready for you." His nostrils flared, and a flash of red hit high on his cheekbones. "Rapunzel, you don't know what you do to me."

"I know what I'm going to do. But where ..." She followed his gaze when he turned.

"My desk." His eyes sharpened, and his nostrils flared.

"Oh, you like that?" Somehow, her heart raced even faster.

"Vella, ever since I went down on you on my desk in London, I've wanted a redo. And this time I want to spread you wide and fuck you so hard we both see stars." He surged to his feet and picked her up. "Fuck. Can't wait any longer."

He carried her there, and she got the sense he couldn't not touch her, not even for the few feet to get them to the desk, which she totally understood because she felt it too. The need to be with him, physically.

He dropped her on the edge, but who cared because he was fumbling with his zipper, and then his thick, beautiful dick sprang free.

"Matt," Vella gasped. "The stars! They're shining up your shaft. Are you okay?"

"I will be," he gritted out. "Fuck!" His eyes flared. "Condom—"

"Pill. We're good." She dropped back and opened herself to him.

His eyes narrowed again, this time on her pussy, and a fierce, predatory expression overtook his face, as if nothing in this world or any other could stop him from having her. That look alone made her blood race, and her body throb.

He growled, and his fingers bit into her hips, and then he thrust into her. Hard. Hot. Thick.

She hissed at the delicious pressure of him filling her. Stretching her. Stroking every. Single. Nerve.

A whimper escaped her. Everything felt so. Damned. *Good*.

"Vella." He rocked his hips, surging forward another inch. "Take me, Vella." Again. "All of me, Vella, Vella, Vella."

Sensations came close to overwhelming her, and all she

could do was breathe through the exquisite fullness of *him*, hot and bruising and frigging perfect.

"Fuck." His teeth gnashed, but his gaze stayed locked on where they joined, as if he couldn't believe they were here, together. That he was inside her. "Can't. Hold. On—"

"Then don't." She undulated her hips, the movement sending a shockwave through her, and she wrapped her legs around his hips and used the flats of her feet to hold him deep.

A growl rumbled through him again, and he drew his hips back—slammed hard and hot back in and, as if an inviable tether had been cut, he hammered her harder and harder, hotter and hotter. As his teeth ground and his jaw clenched, midnight stars whirled into his eyes, obliterating the silver.

"Vella!" He rammed home so deep and hard there had to be no end and no beginning between them, and every muscle in his beautiful body locked, and the tats on his skin danced and the air in the room frigging hummed.

Vella's orgasm roared through her. Unstoppable. Ferocious. Conquering.

VELLA HAD zero idea of how much time had passed, but when her body came back to earth, Matthias still filled her, but they were wrapped tight together, torso to torso, her butt still on his desk and her legs wrapped around his waist.

"It's madness," he whispered into the curve of her neck. "How good you feel. How good you make *me* feel."

"I know the sentiment. I've never wanted to be with someone as much as you. From London to New York—and damn, I really liked it in London," she murmured. "With everyone watching, but not entirely able to see what you were doing to me." The blue glass wall caught her attention. "I wish we could do that here …"

"One day." He nibbled her neck. "When it doesn't matter whose eyes are watching us, you and I can put on a show right here. I'll fuck you from behind, and everyone will know what we're doing but won't be able to see this glorious pussy."

"Or your beautiful dick."

"You think I'm beautiful?"

"Pft. How could I not?" She rocked her hips, and tiny sparks tingled where they joined.

"Keep doing that and I'll be coming again."

"An option I am perfectly fine with." She wrapped her arms back around him as genuine happiness flowed through her. "Gods, Matt, I …"

"What?" His lips pressed against her forehead in a whispering kiss, but somehow, she felt that press through every atom of her being.

"I'VE MISSED YOU SO MUCH." Vella burrowed into Matt's chest, and he tightened his arms around her. "To be clear, missing seems way too shallow for how I've felt. Nothing has felt right from the moment I left you."

"Hey, Rapunzel." Now that Matt's heartbeat had returned to normal, he smoothed the hair back from her face. "How are you?"

Her mouth opened, and for a moment something raw and uncertain entered her gaze, only to be replaced by a small smile. "After those orgasms? Fantastic. Although, I do need to clean up." Her nose wrinkled in that adorable way she had.

Matt released Vella and took the moment to clean up and put himself back into his trousers. Mind you, the sexy little shimmy Vella did to get her dress back into place had him reconsidering getting dressed.

"Vella, come here." He caught her hand and tugged over to his sofa. She fitted onto his lap like she was made for him. "I mean it, are you okay?"

"You really want to know?" She nestled deeper against him and took a breath so deep he heard and felt it.

"Yeah, I do. You are fucking amazing—and I'm not talking about sex, although that too—but after the trauma of discovering the truth about your parents' and Sara and Ellaine, I am honestly blown away that you've been able to stand just being in the same room as Ellaine."

"I don't feel strong," she whispered. "I feel …"

"What?"

"I don't know." She lifted darkening eyes to his and gods but he wanted to slay every asshole who would want to hurt her. "Devastated. Horrified. Furious. And those aren't nearly strong enough words, but everything is muddled up like a tangled ball of searing hot noodles writhing here in my chest, and I have to just bury it all under a freezing barrier of ice. Bury it so frigging deep none of it can escape, otherwise I'll never get through pretending everything is fucking fine. And that's what I've done ever since—bury every single feeling deep, deep down, just to deal with *her*."

"Gods, Vel. That must be so fucking hard."

"Except then I think of you, or you're here, and suddenly I can't stay cold no matter what." She burrowed back into his chest, and her arms held onto him like he was a lifeline and she was sinking.

"Come here, Rapunzel." He pressed his lips to her hair.

"Matt." Her whisper was barely audible, but he felt it all the way to his soul. "I don't know what to do."

"Well, right now, you don't have to do anything other than hold on to me. I'll always be here for you—you hold on as hard and long as you want. And if—when—you need someone to vent to, even to help deal with your feelings, I'll be here then, too."

"Honestly, I don't think I've even begun to process everything that happened, let alone my feelings about it all, yet."

"But you know you need to, right? I've had years to come to terms with what Ellaine did, and you were right back in Stonehenge—I've still let that trauma fuck me up. How I react to ... feeling strongly for someone is still impacted by how I see myself as a direct result of what that evil motherfucker did. You've had ten days. Ten freaking days, Vella. It is totally understandable that you're still working out how to deal with your emotions."

"I dream about it." She lifted her head, and when her eyes met his, they filled with the same pain he'd sensed earlier. His Rapunzel was not okay.

"Do you want to talk about them—the dreams?"

She scoffed. "We don't have that long. And anyway, you're here, and I'm here, and I don't want to think about it, just for a few seconds longer."

"You don't know how much I wish we could have forever like this, not just a few moments." But, they didn't have more than a few more minutes. "Fuck, Vella. We need to talk." Only, instead of talking, he'd fucked her the moment she gave him the green light.

Bloody hell, Matt. Focus.

"What now?" Vella shifted away.

Buzz.

Vella groaned. "Hold on, that's my cell. I have to check—it could be Sara."

Vella snorted. "Sara says hi, and that once we're done 'reacquainting,' we should rescue her from the clutches of Derrick and Nevena. They're all in the VIP section."

"How is she?"

"After the news about the navitas? She is so freaking happy not to have to take the poison anymore. And thank you, that is so amazing. You realize this means we can finally leave Ellaine and—"

"Join us in the war against the Divs." Fuck yes. With Vella at his side, they could get the bone runes back, and surely with a Mors Dicen witch among their ranks, the Coven Union would agree to take the fight into the open.

"Right ... I mean, of course." Vella nibbled her lip. "Is that what you wanted to discuss?"

"Right now? Actually, no." Shit. This was going to be ... complicated. "Vella, have you sensed any kind of ... magical connection between us? It might have started after we fucked in the standing stones, in Scotland. I'm *hoping* we managed to cement it just now because it didn't entirely complete before ..."

"Before what?"

Gods but he hoped this went well. He took a deep breath and explained to Vella everything he understood about their bonding and how it had gone terribly wrong.

"*That's* why my powers have gone bonkers? And if we're still only *half* bonded, I might lose my mind and my magic?" Vella pushed off Matt and started to pace.

"Yes. But we can—"

"Hold on." She reached behind her and did something with the sheath running up her spine. "Brianna, we need to talk. Did we—yes. Yes, we did, but that's not what I need to talk to you about. Matt has just explained how bonds work in the magical community and how they could be impacting our magic and powers. Yes, I know you warned me about those standing stones. Here?" Vella's eyes flared. "*Fine.*"

Vella reached back and this time pulled out her bone-handled knife. Her jaw tightened, her shoulders lowered, and her stance subtly shifted as if she was on guard.

"Brianna. Nice to see you again." If not a little unsettling. At least he could tell who was in charge by the body positioning.

"Druid," Brianna said through Vella. "You are looking as fine as always. Now, I am speaking to both you and my Vespera. If you remain only half bonded, since you two have now fucked—I do love that word—the symptoms you experienced when you were first apart will only intensify if you separate again. So you *must* stay together, literally in the same location, until you can confirm your bond is cemented."

"In the same location?" Matt's breath punched out of him. "Always?"

"You need to limit your time apart as much as possible. And I am deadly serious, Druid."

Matt's phone buzzed. "Hold on. I need to check this message."

> Ronin: Nevena Montgomery is looking for you. I'm stalling but you need to get back here asap

"Shit. I need to go. But I heard what you said, Brianna."

"Matt." Vella replaced Brianna in her sheath, and he knew instantly by her tone and the looseness that entered her limbs that Vella was back in control. "Wait. We need to discuss this bond thing—but damn, I need to tell you something as well. Just let me sit. I can't see anything yet. Brianna, hush, yes, the bond thing is important, I get it, but I also need to tell Matt what happened today."

Important? Did that mean she wanted the bond to work? Or she realized how bad things were that it was *not* working?

"Of course." He took her hand. "Here, this is my office chair." He rested on the desk, right where they'd made love, still holding her hand. "Ronin can wait. What do you need to talk about? And hell, you're cold again. I can—"

"No. No, I just need to tell you this fast. I was at a reading of the bone runes with Derrick and Ellaine today."

"Shannah mentioned needing to tell me about it—what exactly happened?"

As Vella told him the entire story about what had happened at Div Tower, dread rose to lodge in his chest.

It was bad enough that Ellaine already possessed the Mors Dicen runes, not to mention a hoard of stolen arcana, including most of every other coven's grimoires, but now, that monster had knowledge of how to strike directly at the source of dark energy? She would never rest until she found its location. What would that mean for Vella and Sara, for Ronin and Shannah, for his ability to keep Madgwick and all his people safe?

Fuck.

"Matt, are you okay?"

Looking into Vella's amber eyes, his chest unclenched enough for him to get in a breath. "I am now that you're at my side. I get the idea of a bond is ... new. But—"

Ping. Ping. Ping.

> Ronin: Get to the VIP section right
> fucking now

Ronin: Situation here

Ronin: Need you out here now

"Bloody hell. I need to go. Ronin's getting antsy, which doesn't happen. But we'll talk about this later—you and I—after the party's ended."

"Okay, I'll wait a few minutes and join you once my vision fully returns. I'll make something up about running into an old friend."

She squeezed his hand, and Matt gave in to the urge to curve his hand around her silky cheek and didn't resist when she tugged him close and pressed her lips hard against his; he returned that pressure with every ounce of emotion that roared inside him, desperate to escape and shout his feelings to the world.

"And, Vel? You look fucking magnificent."

Gods, he wished this kiss never had to end. Their bond *had* to have cemented.

14

T he moment Matt left Vella, his skin started itching, and the power surging through his veins told him that his Druid magic was awakening—and it wasn't happy.

Shit. Shit, shit, shit. Oh, this was bad. Their bond had very clearly not cemented yet. He paused for a second, took a steadying breath.

Everything was fine. Vella was just down the hall. He'd see her again in moments.

Forcing his smooth, Magicae Councilor smile into place, Matt moved swiftly to the VIP lounge, waving off everyone who approached—and there were many, damn it.

But thank fuck he had moved fast, because the moment he entered the lounge, an angry buzz was palpable.

"Thank the gods," Ronin muttered as soon as he reached him. "Nevena's raring to find you, and the last thing we need is for that woman to roam freely through Nocturnal. Someone filmed Nevena getting rid of two Crystallo witches in the queue earlier and posted it on social media—it's gone viral, and now half the club is ready to fight the other half."

Deep within, Matt's power—already simmering beneath his skin—threatened to surge. Bloody hell, now not. Not here. He clamped down on his magic, plastered an easy-going smile on his face and dropped his shoulders so his arms swung loose.

More than his life is at stake here. So much more.

Over the years, Matt had walked such a careful tightrope, cultivating Nocturnals's rep for being mysterious and sexy with a dangerous edge, but also being damned careful nothing happened to risk a SI raid and the possibility of being shut down.

The very last thing he needed right now was a massive blow to his finances when they needed to prepare for open warfare against the Divinators and Elixirs, including funding the safe relocation of his entire Magicae coven into hiding when that happened.

Every single table in the VIP lounge was full, and the divide was easy to spot; one half were loud and obnoxious Divs and Elixirs, demanding service and being rude to his staff. The others were mainly Magicaes or Crystallos with a few hedge witches or lone shifters thrown in. They were seated in clumps at their tables, not laughing or talking, but staring at their phones and muttering darkly among themselves while throwing glances at the center booth.

The center booth was the most luxurious in the lounge, and Nevena Montgomery, exuding classic British poshness, sat between Sara and Derrick. On their table, a silver bucket held a bottle of Dom '96 and four champagne flutes filled with bubbling liquid.

To almost everyone else in Nocturnal that night, the witches in the center booth represented the ruling covens that dictated how everyday witches lived their magical lives.

"Matthias Medea, there you are!" Nevena's sweet tone—

somehow able to be heard above the music—grated on his nerves. "Please join us, you naughty thing. Where have you been?"

"I don't like this," he murmured to Ronin. "Let the staff know to be careful around the Div and Elixir tables. Call up security, too. Have them ready."

Matt met Nevena's gaze and allowed his smile to widen flirtatiously as he approached the booth and passed the neighboring table where Sylvie, Tannis and Alex sat in splendid solitude—their achingly cool fashion sense, beautiful faces and slightly bored expressions making everyone in the room long to be found worthy of inclusion in their company.

Interesting ... none of the three had touched their wine glasses filled with the alcohol-imbued blood he stocked especially for them. Behind their sunglasses and attitudes of nonchalance, Tannis and Alex's attention were fixed on Sara; Sylvie's glare hammered into Matt, her hostility almost a physical thing.

But why? Before he could ponder that thought, his cell phone pinged again, and he stopped just before reaching the center booth.

> Sylvie: Where is the BW and why have you not returned with her?

Matt forced himself not to look in Sylvie's direction, instead offering an apologetic smile for Nevena and mouthing the word "work."

Her eyes narrowed, but he ignored her obvious displeasure and sent back a fast message to Sylvie.

> Matt: She's fine, just taking a moment. Will be coming through the corridor behind me soon.

Ignoring the urge to turn and make sure Vella did indeed follow him into the VIP lounge, he slid his cell into his back pocket and, while he refocused on Nevena, the weight of Sylvie's gaze didn't ease. Hells, did she think Matt was a danger to Vella too?

Damn, but the vamp was protective of Vella. Not that her protectiveness was a bad thing—the more beings who cared about Vella's safety, the better.

"It was really too bad of you to keep me waiting so long," Nevena said when he was a foot away. She held up one hand.

When he followed through on the unspoken order and leaned over, Nevena's fingers tightened around his and held him in place while her eyes lit with something that made the hairs prick on the back of his neck.

Bloody hell. What was Nevena's game here?

Finally, she let him go, and Derrick stood to make room so he could slip in between them. Sara rolled her eyes at him, then went back to tapping something out on her cell phone.

"I'm ever so pleased to meet you again, Councilor Medea." Nevena's accent reminded him of all the public-school toffs he'd served in London and wished he could punch in the face, and when she smiled—what was up with her teeth?—her eyes remained flatter than a shark's. "Goodness, you're far handsomer than I recalled—didn't you have an unfortunate incident, years ago?" She trailed a polished fingernail down his cheek, and Matt nearly jerked, keeping still by the barest margin. "My, my, my, you *are* a very talented Magicae. I can't feel a single fault."

Matt been casting a glamor over those scars his entire adult life—to the point he rarely noticed the telltale tingle on his cheek and scalp that denoted the presence of his spell— but now his skin crawled. He kept smiling though, and forced himself to lean forward, because the character of Matthias Medea, playboy nightclub owner who only cared about sex and pleasure, was the path he'd chosen to take his vengeance, and this track *would* work. All the sacrifices *must* be worth it. "My dearest, I can do *many* things with my spellcasting."

"I've heard rumors of a magic dick." Nevena pushed a crisp one-hundred-dollar bill toward him. "I'd love to see one of your legendary shows, up in the salons? Perhaps I might"—her hand pressed his knee, then slowly traveled up to his crotch, and equal parts revulsion and fury had everything inside Matt screaming to get the fuck out of there— "join in?"

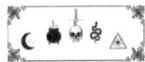

EVEN THOUGH HER vision had readjusted enough for her to make out Matthias' private room again, Vella didn't move off his couch.

She and Matthias were bonded. Or half bonded. Did you get a choice about this kind of shit, and if she did, would she want a bond with Matthias? Did he want a bond with Vella?

Yes, she ... cared for him. Her stomach seesawed. Was that what bonding meant?

"Vespera, you are thinking very hard. Do you want to discuss this?"

"No. I just need to think."

"As much as I appreciate your need to consider the half bond, you told Matthias you would join him again soon ... I suggest you do so. Matthias' unstable Druid power is too dangerous if he becomes worried about your absence."

She sighed, but Brianna had a point.

Although as soon as she reached the front of the VIP lounge, she halted hard.

What the frig? Was this for real? Matt and Nevena were all cozy in the middle booth, heads just inches apart, eyes locked on each other.

Stinging gouges ripped deep into the base of her neck and center of her palms and—

"Vespera! For fuck's sake, calm the fuck down!" Brianna roared, then added more quietly, "Fuck. Yes, I like this word."

Vella yanked out her phone, pretending to take a call and hissed, "I don't understand what's going on. This jealousy is so intense. I'm ready to fucking strangle her."

"It's the half bond you evidently didn't manage to cement. Hmm. Did you use blood?"

"What the—"

Her phone buzzed for real with an incoming message, and she paused to check the screen—whoa. Message after message, all from Sara.

> Sara: this is boring. Sharky is boring. All she does is talk about my meds and how I'm feeling 🙄

> Sara: change that. Sharky is creepy 😐

> Sara: WTF now she's creeping on your orc

> Sara: 😨🙅😐

> Sara: GTFO

> Sara: WTF are you doing? Get your ass over here now

Vella looked up to find Sara staring hard at her from across the room.

Leaning away from Nevena, Sara mouthed *let's go* and scooted out of the booth.

Vella put her finger up and replied *one minute*. Throwing back her shoulders, intending to march up to Nevena and Matt, looking as confident and sexy as possible, she strode forward—

Her feet tangled. The room spun around her. Pain exploded in equal parts hurt and embarrassment as she landed on her hands and knees.

Cruel laughter erupted from the table beside her, and five Crystallos, three women and two men, rose from their seats and surrounded her.

"Aww, is the poor little Div hurt?" said a witch with a high ponytail.

A sneery-looking bro bent down and examined Vella's wrist. "No fucking way, that's a navitas bracelet! Bet you stole it, like all—"

But even as he reached to snatch it, suddenly he was flying over Vella's head to land in a heap on the floor. Grinning, Vella sprang to her feet, kicked off her strappy heels and raised her fists. Sweet Goddess yes, she could do with a good physical vent right now. But before she could make contact, Alex appeared at her side as if he'd been there all along, fangs exposed.

"Where is your Brianna? Why are you not fighting with her?"

"I can't risk her being seen," she hissed. Not to mention

the loss of vision afterward seemed like a bad idea given the circumstances.

"Fucking vamps?" someone shouted from a table of Divs. "They let *any* fucking trash into Nocturnal."

"Yeah, they fucking *do*," a hedge witch replied, throwing a champagne bottle at the Div table, missing someone's head by inches.

It shattered against the wall.

The VIP lounge broke out into a brawl. The hedge witch launched herself at the Div table. High Ponytail threw a bottle at Vella, but Vella spun and the bottle hit someone else who cried out behind her.

Sneery-looking Bro sent another bottle flying, this time straight for Sara.

Vella shouted.

Matt whirled and sprang to his feet. His gaze landed on Vella, then tracked the bottle. He said something, and his hands moved.

Ronin intercepted the bottle—where the frig had he come from?—and Matt's gaze returned to Vella. He tensed as though he was about to launch at her.

I'm fine she mouthed and jerked a thumb over her shoulder at the unmistakable Alex, then nodded at her sister.

Matt's lips tightened, but the next moment, he whirled to use his body to shield Sara.

Alex grunted, and as she turned to check on him, three Crystallos were ganging up on him. No frigging way.

Vella ducked around and dove into the fray, landing a hit on Sneery-looking Bro, but Alex—annoyingly good—prevented her from properly getting into the middle of the fight. When she looked back at Sara, it was to find Shannah with Nocturnal security, shouting at everyone to calm down. Matt said something to Ronin, and together they leaped over the back of the booth to join his staff in the crowd control effort while Derrick sank under the table. Then, Nevena, with her ear pressed to her phone, grabbed Sara by the wrist.

Sara yelled and yanked her arm back, but instead of letting go, Nevena dragged her toward the exit.

Hell no. "Sara!"

Vella lunged through heaving bodies.

The club lights switched on. The music stopped. Panicked screams echoed up from the ground floor.

What the frig was happening now?

A voice boomed over the loudspeakers. "This is the authorities! Witches Council Special Investigators are on site. Get down! Get down now!"

The screams grew louder from downstairs moments before green orbs sailed through the air. Where they landed, frothing green bubbles rose, and the men and women caught in the vapor collapsed to the ground twitching.

Vella pivoted and changed course to avoid the nearest green bubbling vapor, but it took her away from where Nevena still tugged Sara in her wake.

But before Vella had even reached the booth where they'd been sitting, special investigators poured into the VIP lounge from the stairs, dressed in black fatigues with the Witches Council insignia front and center of their chest, dark glasses hiding their eyes, some continued launching green orbs, and others were whacking anyone they passed with batons.

WTF? Sara! She had to get to Sara! Vella redoubled her efforts, desperate to clear the crowd and vapor and SI.

Every light in the lounge exploded, plunging the entire

club into darkness. Shattered glass rained down, and the screaming ignited in a crescendo of terror and pain.

The emergency system switched on, with green glowing lights illuminating the exits, and a calm, mechanical voice said: "Alert, Darkling activity. Please shelter in the nearest lighted space. Alert, Darkling activity. Please shelter—"

The crowd stampeded. Shoved along and pushed, kneed and elbowed, as *everyone* fled the VIP lounge at once, Vella caught herself as the pack rammed her into a table, and she ducked beneath to escape the crush.

Where was Sara?

She yanked Brianna free. The charcoal veil snapped over her sight.

"A fight?" Brianna let out a whoop. "Most fucking excellent."

"Sara! Where's Sara?"

"Look!" Brianna turned Vella's head. Sara stood by herself, eyes wide and unseeing, facing a rising barrier of looming Darklings. Their faceless, pitch-black humanlike forms obscured everything behind them as they spooled out from every dark corner, growing larger and longer, and every time they touched a human, that person's skin split open in long bloody slices.

Terror gripped Vella harder than any vice could possibly manage, and she scrambled out from the table—

"Vespera, hold! I think they're protecting her!"

—her knife drawn and plunged into the mass of darkness that was the Darklings and—

15

As Nocturnal's lights shattered, plunging the club into pitch black, and the Darkling alarm system sounded, Matt whirled around. Fear hit him hard —for his family. His customers. His business—fucking hell, but he couldn't afford to lose this conduit. But one fear punched harder than all the others.

Bloody hell. Where was she?

Thank fuck his night vision allowed him to make out faces in the eerie green glow of the emergency lighting, but there were so many beings, all running everywhere.

Ronin and Shannah, their night vision as keen as his, spread out on either side, using their shifter strength as bulwarks against the stampeding crowd.

"Help me evacuate the building!" Matt shouted over the noise as he lunged for a poor sod in the fetal position, covered in green goo, with people literally walking on him.

He shifted the air barrier to shield himself, Ronin and Shannon from the SI stun gas and yanked the still-twitching guy to his feet. While injured and in shock, he seemed able to stand.

"Use the staff stairs." Matt shoved him toward the narrow stairwell. "Go!"

The VIP lounge emptied fast now that customers, staff, even the SI agents were all crowding down the faintly glowing stairwell, till only the Darklings remained, concentrated in one area—oh fuck.

They surrounded Sara, providing an obstacle between her and the stampede and—

Vella. His breath whooshed out. She was safe, thank fuck. But oh shit, she held Brianna. Everyone except his people, the vamps, and Sara and Vella had left; still, they couldn't risk a single hint escaping that Vella was a Mors Dicen witch.

"Vella! Put—"

Vella disappeared.

Matt recoiled. Stared again. Across the floor, Alex, Sylvie and Tannis were pivoting too, scanning the empty club.

Fuck, Fuck, fuck, fuck. Where was she?

Vella's gone, gone, gone. Matt's magic expanded without warning, exploding like a supernova.

His ears popped, and every single window splintered outwards, followed by a rush of icy wind and freezing sleet. The club shook and rattled and heaved. Lounge tables went spinning, champagne glasses and plates jumped and shattered on the floor, chandeliers swung in a wild clinking dance, raining shards of crystal.

"Everyone out!" he shouted, voice hoarse as he tried to rein in the power.

As strong and fast as his power had surged, it caved inwards on itself as though he'd opened up that black hole again, only this time it sapped all his energy, and he collapsed onto the floor.

Shannah and Ronin ran to him, dragging him toward

the swaying stairs. They were just behind the three vamps and Sara, and they all scrambled down as quickly as possible, slamming out through the staff doors right behind the last stragglers and into a howling blizzard.

Sirens wailed in the distance as the earth continued to rumble. Traffic had stopped, all vehicles trapped on the road, blanketed by the sudden onslaught of snow, including what looked like about a row of fifteen SI riot control carriers. But bloody hell, so many people were wounded and collapsed onto the snow.

"Freaking hell," Shannah hissed.

Horror filled Matt. His Druid power surge had done this.

"Matt, stop struggling." Ronin tightened his grip on one arm. "What are you doing?"

"Helping our ... cust ..."

"Yeah, no way, mate. You can barely talk, and you can't walk for fuck. Shannah? Let's get around the corner, down the lane behind our cars and out of sight. Sylvie, can you bring Sara?"

"Get them ... help."

"We will, I promise." Ronin and Shannah dragged Matt around the corner, sheltering between two vehicles. "Do you have anything to cover him up?" Ronin asked, looking past Matt. "Nobody can see him like this."

"Yes, I can see why those need to be hidden," Sylvie drawled. She clicked her fingers and, somehow, someone produced a hoodie and jammed it over his head, drawing the hood up tight.

"Did anyone see ..." Matt shook his head as the fog of fatigue grew thicker.

"Those?" Ronin nodded at Matt's hand, where stars visibly shimmered under his skin. "I think everyone was gone, but I'll scrub the surveillance recordings once we're all safe, to be sure."

"No. Meant Vella," Matt whispered. "She had ... Brianna ... right before she disappeared."

Sylvie said something, but her words couldn't penetrate the fog that overtook him.

THE DRONE of television commentary greeted Matt as he regained consciousness, along with a throbbing headache in his temples.

"... the worst blizzard to have ever hit Manhattan in recorded history. This extreme weather event is suspected to have been caused by a miscast spell calling by the Magicae coven, the owners of the very popular Nocturnal New York, known to host witches, and allegedly, magical creatures like vampires and shifters."

Matt's eyes flew open. He was lying on a couch in a jewel-toned living room. Sara sat on the sofa chair across from him, scrolling through her cell phone and watching the news, brows furrowed. Outside, snow fell against a pale gray sky.

Day time. How long had he been out?

The news anchor continued. "At 11:15 p.m. on New Year's Eve, there was a sudden freeze with winds of over thirty-five miles per hour, concentrated over Nocturnal's airspace in conjunction with a 4.8 magnitude earthquake that shook all of New York, including New Jersey.

"The epicenter is confirmed to be Nocturnal in Manhattan. New York mayor, Leroy Jefferson, is demanding answers from the Witches Council and a hearing with Councilor Priestley as soon as the snowfall ends and snowplows can clear the roads. In other news, reports continue to come in, of city park rats afflicted with an unusual rotting skin condition. Anyone who sights these rodents is urged to report the sightings to local officials."

Matt tried to speak and only managed a croak. Sara turned down the volume as the talking heads started discussing who would pay for the salting and snow removal, and offered him water.

He drank down the liquid gratefully, but almost choked, gaping at his hands and arms where glowing obsidian stars followed the lines of his veins. His glass trembled, water splashing everywhere as he almost dropped his drink onto the coffee table.

"I hope to fuck Nevena Montgomery didn't see"—Sara waved at his whole body—"all this." She shook her head. "Your eyes, bro, are something else."

Damn it. Another person knew his secret. "You can't tell anyone."

"That you're a dark and spooky Druid? Yeah, I get that. Mors Dicen, remember?"

Like he could forget. He rubbed his temples as the pain grew stronger. "Where's Vella?"

Sara's eyes went misty, but no tears fell. "She vanished. Again. Sylvie, Tannis and Alex are out searching for her, but Syl says they can't smell her anywhere. They think she's journeying."

Matt groaned when he learned what journeying *meant*. No wonder the headache was back, and his magic was draining out like he was losing his life's blood—he needed to be near Vella for their bond to stabilize, and right now, Vella could be any-fucking-where.

"We've got things under control, though." Sara sat up straighter. "Sylvie managed to collect Vel's purse. It was lying on the floor, right next to where ... I'd been ..." She licked her lips. "Anyway. I have her cell phone, and I've been impersonating Vella, replying to any text messages from Ellaine or Derrick. They seem satisfied that we managed to escape and get home. Nobody can do anything right now anyway. The whole city is snowed in."

"The whole city?"

"Yep." Sara gnawed at her lip. "I hacked the security system in Arcane Antiquities and jammed all the cameras—don't worry, that's totally blamable on the blizzard." She smiled, but it lacked any confidence. "Plus, I've got some recorded content on a loop from my computer using our voices to make it sound like we're in there. That way, when Vella gets back, Ellaine won't have a clue she went missing. That'll work, right?"

"I'm sure it will," he lied, because right now, Sara looked like she needed reassurance more than anything else. But fuck, where was Vella?

"You journeyed without the dark energy again?" Brianna shrieked in Vella's head.

"Stop shouting." Vella winced as, along with Brianna's voice, a headache dug its claws into her head. She struggled to shove Brianna back in her sheath by feel alone, given she couldn't see a frigging thing, but made sure to leave the bone window open so they could still communicate. And please, Goddess, wherever they were, let no one have witnessed her holding a Mors Dicen bone.

Although, given that she was freezing and the icy air smelled of snow, hopefully, wherever she'd landed, no one else was around.

"Are you hurt? You are making a chattering sound."

"Because it's *snowing* and I'm wearing a skimpy dress and no shoes." She wrapped her arms tightly around herself. "And no, I'm not hurt, although my neck and palms burn—like my toes right now."

"You feel an ice burn in your neck and hands?" Brianna inhaled hard.

"What now? It's not too different from when I access my magic; at least, it's in the same place."

"No, the ice burn is dangerous, Vella. That sensation indicates a Mors Dicen has overused their magic, past exhaustion, past everything."

"And I have to sleep, or eat, or both. I've been here before."

"No, Vespera. No, you have not. This sensation you describe is the last point a Mors Dicen reaches before they annihilate all their power—forever. I had no idea you had used so much. Good Goddess, I should not have left you alone so long."

"Great. You're saying if I get this burning sensation for much longer, I'll ... never have Mors Dicen magic again?"

"Yes, because you will be *dead*. That is the level of annihilation I am referring to. And then your Matthias shall die because your bond has not been completed, and his magic shall drive him insane and—"

"Okay, okay. I get it." Drained, weak and nauseated, Vella sank to her knees and landed in a pile of snow.

"I told you, you must not. Journeying is too dangerous."

"Not like I did it on purpose," Vella hissed. She scowled as she stared at the darkness ... except, it wasn't so dark anymore. "Finally, it's coming back."

"You can see again?"

"A little. And whoa." She was in a frigging winter

wonderland, snow drifting from the sky like in a holiday
film, heaping in pillowy piles all around her. So pretty ...
except the drifts looked like they'd be up to her thighs, and
she was in the least-snow sensible gear ever.

"What?"

"No need to snap. It's snowing, okay? But luckily, we
landed—or should that be arrived?—beneath a large pine
with a bit of a clearing around it." She peered through the
haze of falling snow in the gray light of dawn. "Yes! I know
where we are. We're back at the West Park Village a-fucking-
gain."

Cr ... cr ... cr ...

Oh no. Oh no fucking way, this could *not* be happening.
Except ... yes, indeed, inches away from the frozen blocks
Vella used to call her feet, an extremely large, extremely
dead crow, lay on its back, wings spread wide and mangled
black feathers stark against the white beneath. Its beak
gaped, and most of its rib cage showed, along with hanging
globs of flesh and ... gross stuff.

Those zombie rats hadn't been a dream.

The crow turned its head, staring at Vella with one
caved-in eye socket, and let out a loud squawk. Vella jumped
and scrambled to her feet. Damn, she was still unsteady.

"Um, Brianna, why are dead creatures coming to life
around me?"

"*And* you're a Bone Caller? This is unheard of."

The crow rolled to its feet with way too much energy for
a creature so dead. It flapped its wings in seeming irritation,
squawked three more times, and shook itself so fiercely that
one wing of matted black feathers and half-frozen gobbets
exploded outward, spattering everything, including Vella.

"Ew, gross!" Her stomach turned as she swiped at the
goop.

"What now? Fuck, Vella, if you were not so close to being dead right now, I would order you to pick me up so I might see what all this ruckus is about."

"Ruckus? I swear, Brianna, there's an undead crow—actually, maybe a raven, it's really frigging big—right now walking toward me."

The bird stopped watching Vella and instead preened its nonexistent feathers along one wing of snowy-white bones, looking way too pleased with itself.

"Vespera, you need to find shelter immediately."

"You think?" Vella snapped. "Let's see, I'm covered in bird crud, still freezing, carrying an illegal Mors Dicen relic while wearing a totally inappropriate dress in a snowscape and somehow I've lost my cell and purse."

"Well then? Get moving!"

"The Crystal Brew is close," Vella muttered. "At least I can get out of the snow there." A hot shower would be Goddess-send, but that would have to wait till she got home.

The undead raven squawked and flew—*flew?!*—up and landed on Vella's shoulder. She flinched, and it fluttered, croaking indignantly, to the ground. "Stay away from me!"

"Vella? Please close my bone window." Brianna made a tsking sound. "I must rest and ponder what this all means."

Well, frigging fantastic.

At least Crystal Brew was only one block away.

Vella stumbled out of West Village Park, feet aching with the cold, and without a doubt looking undead herself. At least the freaky raven had flown off and vanished, so that was one less issue she had to deal with.

Vella's chest warmed at the sight of the café with its friendly lights spilling from the window, and the moment she entered the shop, she could've cried with relief. But while the barista station was mostly set up, she dinged the bell on the counter because there was no sign of—

"Coming!" Jacqui's voice floated out from behind the counter. Moments later, her head popped up. Her eyes widened. "Good Goddess!"

Between the blanketing warmth of the shop and the intoxicating aroma of coffee filling the air, Vella gave in to the urge and sank against the counter, and a groan escaped her.

Jacqui stood, her gaze traveling over Vella. "Should I call 911? An ambulance? The SI?"

"No! No. Please, can I just borrow your phone? I lost mine."

"But you look like you've been kidnapped, girl—and you're covered in ... feathers? And you smell awful. What the hell happened?"

Tears sprang in Vella's eyes. No way could she handle this inquisition right now.

"Okay, okay, I can see you're overwhelmed. Here. Take the shop phone. I'll make you a hot coffee."

With her heart hammering, Vella dialed the old-fashioned handset. Please, please, let Sara be safe. The phone rang once—

"Hello?"

Thank fuck. "Sar, it's me. I'm at Crystal Brew."

"Vella!" Sara dissolved into sobs. "How the fuck did you get there? Never mind. Hold tight. Matt is already on his way."

Vella hung up and passed back the handset. "Thanks, Jacqui ... what's wrong? You're staring at my wrist like you've seen a ghost."

"Here you go." Jacqui's expression switched to a bright smile, and she plonked down a steaming coffee.

Vella inhaled the rich scent, letting the beautiful bitterness sink all the way to her soul, before taking a large swallow that she swore heated her all the way to her poor, frozen toes. "Thank you. I cannot tell you how much I needed ..." The hairs on the back of Vella's already icy neck froze even harder. "Jacqui? You're staring again."

"That bracelet." Jacqui slowly shook her head. "It's a navitas lepidolite. Definitely vintage, possibly an antique."

Vella glanced down at the cute light-purple bracelet. Sylvie had mentioned something about what kinds of stones they were, but she had zero idea about jewelry, and right now, she doesn't give a gnat's ass.

"Yeah, my friend loaned it to me for ... for a New Year's Eve party."

Wait. When she'd been at Nocturnal, it hadn't even hit midnight yet. She glanced at the clock on the wall. 8:00 a.m. What the frig?

"—that many left in the world. They're rather rare in fact."

"Sorry? What?"

"I don't suppose you heard rumors of a thief going around just taking precious arcana from other covens?"

Vella's cheeks flushed, and she took a long, slow swallow of coffee. *Shit, head in the game, Vel.* "That's terrible."

Jacqui's overly friendly smile returned. "Would you mind letting me see the navitas? I'll be careful. It's just so gorgeous."

"Um, okay, sure." Vella stuck out her wrist.

The moment Jacqui removed the bracelet, everything went black.

16

Tap. *Tap, tap, tap. Tap, tap.*

Indistinct murmuring from familiar voices roused Vella from her sleep. Sara. That was Sara's voice—even coming from a different room, she recognized the tone and immediately Vella let herself sink back into the mattress.

She snuggled deeper into the bed, warm, comfortable, with zero headache, and her magic purring contentedly in her chest. No, wait, that was the adorable fluffy white cat from Sylvie's house—huh. She was back in the four-poster timber bed. And Matthias was cuddled right up next to her too, his breath slow and even, a leg thrown over hers.

His beautiful lips were parted, and she resisted the urge to trace their shape, not wanting to wake him.

But how did she get here?

And seriously, this was getting ridiculous. All this passing out, waking up in this room. What was she, some kind of swooning Georgian lady in a tight corset? What happened to make her faint *this* time? More magic fatigue?

Tap. Tap, tap.

Wait … was that coming from the window?

Pft. Who cared. Whatever that sound was, she refused to move. She was staying right here. Matt looked so peaceful, and how amazing would it be if this were their life? Just the two of them in the early morning. Nothing more demanding than getting coffee, some breakfast, and then maybe opening up the shop.

Huh. Did she still even want Arcane Antiquities? The place next door no longer symbolized freedom or independence. Without those associations, does she even want to be a shop owner anymore?

As Vella stroked Snowflake, the gorgeous cat purred even more loudly, and her mind wandered over the last events she could remember and *oh shit*. She'd passed out covered in dead crow—raven—whatever. Vella carefully shifted around, trying not to disturb Snowflake, and peeked under the quilt.

"For fuck's sake, Sar." She was clean *and* wearing Sara's pink-and-purple fuzzy pajama set covered in soppy, glittery bunnies. Ugh. But Sara had looked after her while she was unconscious, and that made her insides melt.

Tap, tap, tap. Tap. Squawk.

Motherfucker. Something *was* at the window.

Damn it, she didn't want to look outside—had been forcing herself to *not* look out the huge sash window, currently obscured by firmly closed, plum and lilac velvet curtains—with sunlight glowing through the lighter-hued fabric.

Squawk.

Vella located Brianna in her sheath on the bedside table and flipped open the bone window. "Brianna? Wake up."

"Why are you whispering? Are we in danger?"

"No, we're safe at Sylvie's, but … just wait one sec."

Taking a deep breath, Vella slid out from beneath the kitten and Matt who snuggled into each other—Vella paused a moment to take a mental photograph. Talk about cuteness—and tiptoed to the window.

Easing the curtain open, she froze.

The animated skeleton of the chicken-dinosaur thing, with a giant black beak and long black-tipped claws, tapped at the glass, behaving for all the world like a living, overly friendly raven.

Tap, tap, tap.

Oh crap. This room faced the street, the usually very busy New York City street where if anyone looked up—

She wrenched the window open and hissed, "Get in!"

The raven strolled into her room, fluffing its nonexistent feathers and peering around like a curious cat.

"Bloody hell!" Matt jerked upright, the blankets pooling around his waist, showing off his delicious chest and torso. Her mouth went dry.

The kitten opened one sleepy green eye. Shut it again.

Damn it to the Goddess and back, she should be over there enjoying that amazing body, not just ogling it, which she would be doing if not for the undead raven currently making itself at home.

"Brianna!" Vella whirled around. "The raven is back—still half dead, but now it's here, in this bedroom!"

"Fuck me, Vespera," Brianna whispered. "Your powers are astonishing. A Bone Caller!"

"But how? I didn't try to make this happen."

"Your magic is still misbehaving. Never fear. Once your bond cements with Matthias, your magic will stop acting in ways unpredictable to us."

"And if we haven't ... bonded?"

"Daughter, what are you doing? He is your mate! You

commenced the ritual within the henge. You care for him. You find him physically appealing. You are fate-matched; otherwise, the magic would not have blessed your bonding. Why are you holding back?"

"It's complicated," she gritted out.

"Unless you are withholding information from me, which I sincerely hope is not the case, then the only complication here is coming from you."

Shit. Shit, shit, shit.

"We must make time to really begin your Mors Dicen training as soon as you are fully replenished." Brianna let out what could only be described as a war cry. "You will be a wonderful leader for the Mors Dicen!"

Leader? Damn it, but Vella was so sick of people wanting things from her.

"Vella!" Sara burst into the bedroom, scowling at her iPad. "You won't believe what that bitch wants me to do now. She expects me to fill out this form with detailed notes after I take my new potions, and I know—"

Squawk!

Sara froze. Her mouth dropped wide, and she gaped at the raven who eyed her with its empty socket before letting out a friendly warble.

Matt snatched the blankets up to his chest. "Come on in, Sara, take a seat. No, no, don't bother knocking."

Sara, still staring at the raven, sank onto the foot of the bed and started petting the kitten, who seemed more than happy with the attention as it yawned and stretched.

Seriously? Vella shut the door firmly. No more frigging interruptions.

"Brianna," she gritted out. "A little info, please. What is a Bone Caller?"

"Bone Calling is another *rare* Mors Dicen ability,"

Brianna replied. "I told you about the legend of Morrigan, remember? She was rumored to reanimate bones. But how it all works, I know not. Except that it requires either great sacrifice or great power. How I wish Tara were here with us now. Knowledge is her expertise. A Bone Caller ... I am stunned. Oh, and Queen Morrigan had a familiar. The animated skeleton of a cat. So perhaps, Vespera, meet your new familiar?"

"Vel?" Sara tucked her feet up on the bed. "Is everything okay?"

"Vella, what is Brianna telling you?" Matt's voice was low and soothing, but she could sense his tension. Was he pretending to be calm for Vella's sake, or maybe Sara's?

"She said I have a ... familiar." This was for real? Vella repeated the rest of Brianna's words, all the while staring and staring and staring at the raven.

"Wait, you've been unknowingly bringing dead animals back to life?" Matt scanned the room. "What, not like spiders or anything ... creepy, right?"

"Spiders aren't creepy," Vella murmured. A raven familiar? "This is so ... cool!"

"Ah, yes they are." Matt shifted the pillows.

"But you like snakes."

"Because snakes are beautiful and intelligent."

"So are spiders, not that I *think* I've made any undead, here at least. It's all been outdoors."

"You could've said that first," Matt muttered.

The raven hopped onto Vella's shoulder, and this time, she had zero urge to flinch. It touched its beak to her nose before gently preening a few strands of her hair. Her heart filled, and she couldn't stop herself from grinning and nudging the raven's beak back. "Hi."

"I want a familiar, too," Sara muttered, her eyes huge.

"That is your familiar?" Matt held up one hand. "Grand as this all is, one small issue. Having this ... creature out in public isn't wise."

Damn. He was right.

"But I have the perfect solution." Matt considered the raven, his silver eyes almost glowing, then he rubbed his hands together and took two deep breaths.

He whispered a series of words—and whether it was the magic or just Matthias Medea's devastatingly delicious ass mixed with all that sexy competence, but her body heated, and as whatever magic he made built up, power collected in her palms too ... like some kind of echo—and suddenly her raven was covered in black feathers.

"Oh, you handsome thing," she blurted out.

The raven warbled and fluttered back to the ground right in front of the floor-length mirror.

"Vella?" Matt sat back on the bed, eyes narrowed. "It—it's taken the spell, like, I'm not fueling it anymore. I've never seen anything like this before."

An image flashed in Vella's mind ... a raven sitting on a nest full of eggs, and the raven squawked rather definitively. "Um, the raven, I think, is telling me she is female. Also, I'm naming her Morrigan."

"Ooh, nice choice," Brianna murmured.

Morrigan let out a triumphant *caw* and flew back to Vella's shoulder.

"Well, that seems settled," Vella murmured. "Hey, Brianna? I was entirely wiped out when I first ... ah, met Morrigan. Any clue what happened? Or even why I journeyed from Nocturnal?"

"I have been pondering this, and I think that perhaps it's a combination of your half bond making your magic erratic and all the Darkling energy you absorbed. That all had to go somewhere, and maybe that's why you journeyed and accidentally created a familiar."

Vella did another recap for Matt and Sara before pausing. "Sar? What's wrong? Why are you looking ... guilty?"

"Um, Vella, actually, I think I need to tell you something." Sara fiddled with the pendant crystal around her neck and cleared her throat. "I think that my Mors Dicen powers might be coming back, since I stopped taking the poison. Last night? I feel like maybe I called those Darklings."

"Mors Dicen can call Darklings?" Matt's jaw went slack.

"Brianna, can a Mors Dicen call—as in summon—a Darkling?"

"I have never heard the like," Brianna breathed. "But then Darklings were never injuring people in my experience, either. I need further insight as to what occurred."

"Sar? Tell us everything." And damn it, why hadn't Sara told her sooner? Didn't she trust Vella?

Although, given how much Vella had hidden from Sara in the past, what right did Vella have to expect Sara's unreserved truths all the time?

Sara nibbled on her lip and then leaned forward. "At Nocturnal, after you left with Matthias to ... chat, I got stuck with Nevena, and she just went on and on about my meds and about the new potions she wants to try out on me. She kept asking me for details about the worst I've ever been, the pain, the symptoms." Sara shuddered. "No lie, she looked excited when she was asking me about how badly I hurt. There's something seriously wrong with that woman."

"Why is she asking you that?" Vella's protective instincts reared up.

"Good question! Then the brawl happened, and Nevena was on her phone, and seconds later, the SI raiders were bursting through the doors. I'm like ninety percent sure *she's* the one who called them in. *Then* that bitch grabbed my wrist to haul me out of there, like I was some kind of possession, like she owned me. I was so mad, and I swear, it was like I could *feel* the Darklings just hanging around, and I reached out and called them, and they answered. They got between Nevena and me, and that's how I got away from her and out of the club." Sara's grin turned bloodthirsty. "And here." Sara pulled out Vella's cell from her back pocket and handed it over. "I should have given this back to you sooner. I've been covering for you. You've had a few messages from Derrick and *Caorthannach*."

"Anything important?" Seriously, how good would it be to never take that motherfucker's call again?

"Derrick sent an update about Nevena. They got separated at Nocturnal, but she's going to send new potions to experiment on me with and demand my input on how she's torturing me, by the fucking hour. Ooh, I wish the Darklings had killed her."

Matt sat up straighter in bed. "Sara, if you're right and you can call Darklings, this could be a game changer. Instead of a heist, maybe we raid Div Tower: liberate Tara, the bone runes, the grimoires, even some stolen arcana."

Sara's grin turned feral. "Fuck, yes. We have to try."

"No way." Vella shoved her hand on her hips and glared at both Matt and Sara. "It's too dangerous. We don't know how any of our Mors Dicen powers work. What kind of *sacrifice* does calling Darklings require? You can't do it."

Sara scowled back. "No, Vel, you don't get to tell me what to do anymore. Not how to use my own Mors Dicen powers or whether I'm fighting back. In fact, Matthias, I want to officially join the Magicae coven, if you'll have me. I can learn how to cast spells, and I can use it as a disguise for my Mors Dicen powers, like you hide your Druid."

Vella's breath whooshed from her as though she'd been gut-punched. Sara wanted to join the Magicae coven? And Matt thought Sara could help him in a raid?

"Vella!" Brianna let out an excited cry. "I can hear Sara talking right now. Daughter, hello, and welcome!"

"Hell yes! I can make Mors Dicen magic." Sara pumped her fist. "I knew it. And I can fight too—hey, Vel? Where are you going?"

"I need—I need—" Vella walked as fast as she could without running into the bathroom and slammed the door behind her and braced both hands on the vanity.

At least in here, she didn't have to watch Sara and Matthias sitting together, plotting to put Sara into harm's way.

Morrigan warbled and nestled into Vella's neck, a comforting bundle of soft feathers and warm weight.

What she needed was to scream, over and over, until this ... awfulness inside her head was depleted. But what good would that do? She had to stay strong and not let herself crack, not let the ice barrier crack—at least until she'd accomplished what she'd set out to do—save Sara.

Except, Sara didn't need saving anymore. At least, not now Sara had the navitas pendant.

Vella sank onto the cool tiles and wrapped her arms around her head.

Sara, *her* Sara, wanted to fight, which meant putting herself at risk, endangering her life. The very life Vella has fought *her* entire life to keep safe. The pressure, the weight, the fucking burden of worrying for her sister, of being controlled by Ellaine, always desperate to find a cure.

And now, Sara was well and wanted to basically throw

herself off a cliff. And she expected Vella to be totally fucking cool with it. Never mind that Vella had dedicated her entire life since they were kids to look after her. Couldn't Sara see that? Did she really have zero appreciation or fucking empathy for how Vella felt?

If it weren't for Sara and finding her cure, Vella never would have given up Tara or the first set of aetts, and betrayed the Mors Dicen.

She'd probably be fully bonded with Matthias right now too. They could be ...

She'd be ...

Vella slid down till she lay flat on the cold marble tiles of the huge bathroom, Morrigan settling on her chest solid and warm, and stared up at the high ceiling.

Actually, Vella had zero clue about what she'd be.

What *would* she want to do if she were a different version of Vella who hadn't had to look after Sara? If she hadn't been so focused on locating a cure?

Did Vella even like history and ancient ceramics? Or had she been pushed into it by her fake aunt as part of her role as an arcana thief? Arcane Antiquities had kinda been for Sara, too—they'd needed an excuse to get out from Ellaine's evil tower, and a shop had seemed like the perfect solution. Maybe not particularly from passion but necessity and something Ellaine wouldn't disapprove of out of hand.

And why hadn't she fully bonded with Matthias? Yes, she'd longed for him, pined for him even these past few weeks, like a missing limb. Her magic was always seeking him out, even now, with their separation, she could feel him *not* here.

But why hadn't they fully bonded at the standing stones? She and Matthias had been through a lot together, and the Goddess knew he was so damned gorgeous he set her panties on fire, and more than that, he was loyal and determined and even kind—sometimes, anyway. And when he wasn't kind, he was capable and ruthless and, yeah, she liked those things too.

And ... he'd become a friend. A friend she cared for. Maybe even, in some alternative reality, a friend she could've fallen in love with.

But here and now? Was that kind of emotion even possible? Was Vella the kind of person who could fall in love? Because facts were, she wasn't even the same person she'd been two weeks ago. The Vella who had left New York to find the runes on a hunt through the UK had been ... naïve. Untested. Unproven.

But who was the Vella she'd become?

She used to think she knew who she was; only now that the truth had been revealed, she never really had. Because Ellaine Priestley had done more than steal Vella's parents and life, she'd stolen her identity.

And how could Matt possibly love her, or she love him, if she didn't even know who Vella ... Vespera was?

What even was her real last name?

Shit. This was so frigging messed up.

"Vella?" Matt's voice echoed through the door. "Your cell's ringing—I think you need to take this."

17

"I t's Ellaine." Vella's stomach clenched, and Morrigan gave a warning warble before gliding across the room to the windowsill.

Why was Ellaine calling? What next level of hell was this phone call about?

"Even Morrigan knows this is bad." Sara scrambled off the bed. "What does the evil queen want now?"

"Let's find out." Vella hit the receive-call button. "Hello?"

"I have an urgent job for you."

"But—"

"The woman Derrick saw in his vision is Katherine Stanley-Turner, a human socialite here in New York. I've procured a meeting with her for you to provide an appraisal of her ceramic collection and have personally divined the meeting to confirm you have a thirty-second window where you can see the bowl while there. You need to be at her complex at one thirty today."

"Wait. This is today? In a half-minute window?"

"Yes. Do not interrupt. Upon entry, you will meet Stanley-Turner's assistant, Martha, who will offer to provide afternoon tea. You will ask to see the collection first, and at approximately one thirty-nine, Martha will enter the room with a tea service, and you shall have the time that they are both discussing tea to complete your task. The bowl will be in the bottom shelf of an open timber cabinet."

"How—"

"I have personally divined the scene twice, and on both occasions, you held the bowl. Given the proximity of time and location, I am confident of the outcome. Once you have secured the item in question, you will return to Divinator Tower, and we will discuss what the bowl represents in regard to Derrick's vision."

Shit. Shit, shit, shit.

At this short notice, there was no way Vella could get a replica to swap out to avoid actually stealing again, but also ... Vella had asked multiple questions of the bone runes: where were the other two aetts, and where—and what—was a cure for Sara. Which of those queries did this vision relate to?

"I'll be there."

"Excellent. Do you need a car?"

"Just to pick me up afterward."

"In that case, Derrick will meet you there. He will also actively divine the situation during your meeting—we do not need any more instances of you disappearing from view mid-job."

Vella's blood went cold. Shit. Of course, Derrick had told Ellaine about what had happened when she'd taken the navitas. Was Ellaine suspicious?

"Ah, no. No, we don't." Vella swallowed the hard knot that lodged in her throat. "I'll see you this—"

The call ended.

"What just happened?" Matthias took her hand. "You look ... haunted."

"I just got a job for today. What's the time? Crap, two hours' notice. Ellaine doesn't do shit like this."

"Wait—what are you doing?"

"Getting dressed. I'll fill you in as I go. And shit—I need to change into something beige." She gritted her teeth. "I hate beige."

"THANK you for meeting me during the day," Katherine Stanley-Turner murmured as she led Vella into a sitting room decorated with contemporary furnishings in pale golds and whites with deep brown accents.

Was Matt okay with Vella being across the other side of the city? How was his Druid power reacting? Was Sara looking after Morrigan? The raven had been sitting on the windowsill when Vella left, giving off a decidedly pissed-off vibe. Was Vella going to accidentally journey again? Was the freaking bond going to cause more problems? What even *was* this frigging bond?

So many questions.

"It's all these awful Darkling attacks." Katherine stared out the window onto a decent-sized terrace. "I have insisted on doing business while it's still light."

Shit. *Focus, Vel.*

"It's my pleasure to be here, any time of day." And any other day, it would've been.

A huge glass and timber cabinet, filled with the ceramics Vella was here to see, filled most of one wall. "Well, Ms. Stanley-Turner—"

"Katherine, please."

Vella nodded. "Katherine, I'm thrilled to view your collection."

"It's a pleasure to share it. Martha will tell you, I don't let just anyone see my beauties. Martha is going to serve us something to eat; however, would you like to eat first or start with the collection?"

"As I've just spotted that pair of ewers—Wedgewood, black basalt, correct? They're the 'Sacred to Neptune and Bacchus' John Flaxman design—I'd love to start there."

"Oh, you do have a good eye."

"Hard to miss these beauties." She glanced at the display cabinet. No sign of a small dish with a painted figure on the inside. "Is this your entire collection?"

"Oh my, no. There's more throughout the house. And you do sound like you love your ceramics—you spotted my second-best pieces right away."

"Love is an understatement. I mean, I can appreciate how pretty they are as much as the next person, but the real value is understanding who made it and when and why—oops. I get carried away sometimes."

"Oh, I think that's wonderful. Well, let me show you the rest."

Formal lounge ... living room ... study. No sign of a small butter-yellow dish.

"There is one more room," Katherine said as she led Vella out of the study. "And I wasn't going to show it to you; however, seeing your love of all things ceramics, I think I shall after all." She gestured to turn left into the main corridor instead of back toward the living areas.

"If that suits you, I'd love to see everything you're happy to show me." Vella forced a casual smile, but the moment they entered what had to be Katherine's bedroom, her pulse picked up pace.

Open-shelved timber display cabinet, running an entire wall. The window opposite looked over the New York skyline. This had to be it.

Knock, knock.

They both looked up as Martha entered the room. "May I serve afternoon tea, Katherine?"

"That would be lovely."

Anticipation buzzed through Vella, and she glanced at her cell screen for the time. Two thirty-eight.

Tap. Tap, tap, tap. Tap, tap.

"What is that?" Martha looked over her shoulder toward the balcony.

"I can't see anything." Katherine turned and stared too. "Oh. What ... is that a bird?"

This *had* to be the moment.

Keeping both women—now peering at the balcony—in her sight, Vella dropped to her knees and felt for the back of the bottom shelf. Something cool with scalloped edging met her fingertips.

Fast. Smooth. Careful.

Slide it out of the shelf. Into her purse. Stand without making a noise.

"Surely not," Katherine was saying. "It looks dead."

"I'll call the super," Martha replied. "They need to take care of it either way."

"But why is it still tapping? Oh, it's stopped. How odd."

Vella steadied her breath and joined them.

Oh shit. Morrigan was at the door. Morrigan was the distraction? And back to looking like she had when they'd first met, half bones, half flesh.

Cr ... cr ... Morrigan approached the door again. *Tap, tap* went its beak on the glass. It turned its head and peered at Vella, and—did she wink?

"I'll call the super now." Martha bustled back down the corridor. "I'm sure they'll handle this."

"Or put it out of its misery," Katherine added. "Really, how it's alive is beyond me with all that damage, the poor thing—oh my, it's flying."

"I guess it looked ... worse than it was?" Fuck. Fuck, fuck, fuck. Did either of the women suspect Vella was a thief? When would they notice the dish was gone? Was her smile too forced? Could they see the pulse pounding in the vein at her throat while she tried to pretend everything was fine?

"Well, let's have afternoon tea." Katherine turned a beaming smile on Vella.

Vella shifted her purse onto her other shoulder. The weight of her stolen cargo rested against her side. "Lovely," she lied through her teeth.

As SOON AS the afternoon tea wrapped up, and with a headache already forming, Vella headed straight to the sidewalk. She'd left Matthias over two hours ago ... how long before his Druid power, or her Mors Dicen magic, went haywire again? The sooner she got back to him, the better. But before she could check her cell phone for an ETA update, a sleek black town car stopped in front of the condo complex. The rear door opened, and Derrick gestured for her to hop in.

"How did it go?" he said as soon as the door shut behind her.

Considering she'd just committed theft *yet* again, this time from someone who on any other day Vella would have been thrilled to discuss ceramics with, she'd say: shit.

"Exactly like you said," she replied instead. "Bottom shelf, cabinet and the view and all." Which meant the bone runes were good ... very, very good. Just what else was Ellaine going to be able to do with them?

"Vella? Did you hear me? Can I see the dish?"

"Sorry. Of course. I was just thinking."

"Are you okay? You really do look tired, and after what happened last night and now this—"

"No, no. I'm fine. But yeah, tired is an understatement. So this is it." She carefully turned the dish out, reverse side first.

Her breath whooshed out. Oh shit. She'd stolen a Sèvres. Somewhere, the ceramic gods were furious at her right now.

"You seem ... stunned." Derrick traced a finger over the exquisite, scalloped edge.

"I am. I've actually never held a piece of Sèvres before."

"Did you say sev-ruh?"

"That's the maker. See this symbol in blue here? Those two crossed L's are the sign of Sèvres. French porcelain, and the letter c in the middle of the L's makes this manufactured in the year ... let me think ... 1780." With her heart pounding, she turned it over. "Wow. Look at the gilt edges and the repeating pattern the entire way around. This is glorious. But the painting on the inside—I've never heard of it depicted on a Sèvres dish before."

"What is she meant to be, a mermaid?"

"No. She has a serpent tail—see the end? The upper body is classical in style, though."

"What does it mean?"

"I don't know. But the pattern of the dish—and the maker—I am familiar with. And there are few enough sales that I think I can track this one down easily enough." Vella punched an internet search into her cell phone for the pattern with the additional art.

The screen filled with results.

"Bingo. This piece last sold at auction two years ago ... now all we need is to find the previous owner. I need Sara for this."

"Vella?" Sara answered within one ring. "We—"

"I'm in the car with Derrick, everything went to plan, but I need your help right away."

"Uh, sure. Hold on." Muffled voices echoed in the background for a second—was that Ronin? "What do you need?"

"Can you hack into an international auction house for me? I'll send you the details. I need to know who they have as the previous owner or owners on file."

A voice rumbled something in the background that Vella couldn't hear.

"Leave it with me," Sara muttered. "Where are you going now?"

"Div Tower. Reporting in as ordered. But message me with whatever you find, ASAP?"

"Sure, sure. Hey, um, just ... be careful."

"Okay." What did *be careful* mean? The call ended, and Vella stared at the screen.

"Vella, everything okay?" Derrick asked.

"Absolutely. Sara's just got a lot going on, and I don't want to push her too hard."

"I get it. And hey, we will find her a cure." Derrick picked up her hand. "I wasn't a fan of using these new runes, but I have to say I've never had a vision so accurate with the detail. So we follow wherever this vision leads—"

"Wait, what do you mean, you've never had a vision so clear?"

"You know our visions range in accuracy with geographical proximity and time to event, but another factor is initial intel. Your question, and Grandmother's, were so nebulous I didn't know if I'd get a vision at all. But then to have the clarity of the color and the indents in the pattern, and the view through the window—that's damned rare. It felt like I was watching a movie with super-high resolution. If I can find a way to withstand the storm and force of the vision, I'm tempted to use them again."

"I thought you said they're dangerous?"

"They are, to anyone incapable of holding that strength of vision. But ... they're also powerful. I can understand why Grandmother believes they'll lead us to a cure for Sara and to a way to rid the world of Mors Dicen magic once and for all. Vella? Hey, Vel? Are you sure you're okay?"

"Yep. Absolutely." No. No she was *not* okay.

Ellaine wanted the bone runes to show her how to erase the power of all Mors Dicen, and would anyone else really care if Ellaine were successful? More likely, most of society would cheer her on.

Look at Derrick: the Kool-Aid Ellaine had shoved down his throat his entire life had worked, because he believed the Mors Dicen's witchcraft to be so bad, they deserved to have their power taken from them forever. So how did Vella change his—and the rest of witchkind's—perception of the Mors Dicen?

18

Matthias entered the Council chamber lobby, located on the thirteenth floor of Div Tower, with his Magicae Councilor façade perfectly in place. The Div's servers were ready with coffee as always, and the rich, bitter scent filled the room; however, he was the first to arrive for the meeting he'd been ordered to attend.

Vella had left two and a half hours ago, and while his Druid power wasn't surging, his veins felt achy and heavy, and the headache was back again.

Breathe, calm, focus. He could do this.

By the time he reached the coffee bar, Nevena joined him. Either she'd already been in the building or had taken an elevator immediately after him.

"Councilor-elect." He dipped his head and smiled as she joined him. "Fancy seeing you here. One could almost think this was a Council meeting."

"Perhaps it is? I do wonder what Councilor Ellaine has in store for us." Her lips turned up in a mischievous smile. "Such intrigue!"

"Alas, while you enjoy the intrigue, I bemoan losing my sleep. Last night was rather long."

"And yet you handled it so well. I didn't know you had such a … competent side to you."

"Competence born out of disaster. What a thing." He gave a mock shudder. "I am just grateful you weren't injured."

"As am I." She linked her arm through his, and he allowed her to steer them into the Council's meeting room; the servers following with their coffees. "Shall we sit at this end? The view over the park is so pretty. Ellaine—apologies, Councilor Ellaine—is lucky indeed to have her headquarters in such a stunning location."

Lucky was one word for it. Perfectly situated to feed off the energy of over eight million people. But he just smiled and held out a seat for Nevena, then took one at her side.

He nodded at the pennants hanging on the walls of the chamber. "Technically, if this were a Council meeting, you would be sitting beneath your coven's insignia, and I mine." He nodded at the snake within the circle hanging at the other end of the table. "Fortunately for us, this is not an official meeting."

"How do you know that?"

"Official meeting invites are sent via the Council website. This came from Councilor Ellaine personally, and as you know, Councilor Ellaine would never operate outside of protocol." Outside of all moral, ethical and fucking plain decency boundaries, but never protocol.

"Oh, of course. You know I really do appreciate you helping me understand the flow of Council politics and policy. You have been … very kind, Councilor Matthias."

"Kind is not a word normally associated with me."

"And yet." Nevena smiled and sipped at her coffee.

"Well, I wonder when—Councilor Ellaine." Nevena got to her feet so fast her seat would've flown back into the window if Matt hadn't grabbed it.

Interesting. Was Nevena's innocence and enthusiasm an act, or real?

"Councilor-elect Nevena, Councilor Matthias. Thank you both for seeing me on such short notice."

Matt let Nevena do all the gushing but nodded in perfect time to her placards and assurances they were more than thrilled to be there at Ellaine's beck and fucking call.

"Well, I am sure you are wondering why I have called you here." Ellaine sat at the head of the table, beneath the Div insignia of the all-seeing eye within the triangle. "While today is not technically a Council meeting, I wish to inform you I've decided to move the date of our next official meeting. We were due to meet on the fifteenth of January, but given we have pressing matters to see to, we will now meet on the sixth instead."

"Is there anything you wish us to be prepared with, Councilor Ellaine?" Matt made himself idly swivel in his chair. "I can have one of my people take on any menial tasks to assist in a smooth meeting."

"For the meeting, no. However, given the events that occurred at your place of business last night, I suggest you get your house in order."

"Ah, I did wonder why the SI decided to pay us a visit?"

"My understanding is that word reached the investigative team that some … unsavory types were indulging there. To protect all witches and nons, they decided to move them on. I really think you need to better manage your clientele, Councilor. And how fortunate, that is one of the reasons for our meeting. The SI will be undergoing several changes."

"Oh, and what are they?"

"To start with, should the SI need to visit an establishment more than once, that establishment will be closed. Permanently."

Matt's gut clenched. Motherfucker.

Was it the vamps? Was Ellaine trying to get them out of the city altogether? She must hate that she couldn't divinate anything about the vampires—not where they were or who they were with. Or was she looking for an excuse to close *Matt* down?

"Is everything well with you, Councilor Matthias?" Nevena pointed at the server hovering by the door. "You, get the Councilor some water."

"Of course, I am well. No water needed. And Derrick is still responsible for the special investigative team?"

"He is," Ellaine replied. "Under the Council's guidance, of course."

Under Ellaine's guidance, more like it. So, Derrick could've seen the vamps at Nocturnal and called in the SI.

A lackey approached the door and murmured something to Ellaine. "Perfect timing," she murmured. "The rest of our party has arrived."

Moments later, Vella and Derrick entered the chamber.

It took everything in him not to stare at her, and even though he'd seen her less than three hours ago, he still had the urge to grab her and run away. Instead, he gave her the briefest of glances and nodded once as if the sight of her meant nothing.

For her part, Vella didn't even look at him as she stared at Ellaine.

Gods, did she feel the same revulsion as he did?

Matt forced himself not to sit straighter and instead focused on so-fucking-gently stirring his coffee.

Focus, Matt. Breathe, control, focus.

"This sounds most fascinating," he finally drawled. "You made an acquisition on behalf of the Divinator coven?"

Ellaine shot him a look, but he just smiled back. Easy. Relaxed. Amused.

"I did." Vella finally looked at him, but she'd retreated to icy-Vella. Which he understood. Standing before Ellaine at any time was fucking awful—and he'd had years to get used to the feeling. If this was what it took for Vella to get through dealing with these motherfuckers, so be it.

VELLA HAD NEVER BEEN inside the actual boardroom of the Council chambers before. A wall of glass on one side looked out to Central Park, and the internal walls were filled with enough screens to allow chapters from covens all over the world to call in.

Of course, her gaze wanted to lock on Matthias sitting at the far end. Why was he here? Had he arranged this, or had Ellaine called him?

Is that what Sara had been talking about?

No, Vel, do not look at the spellcaster. Focus on anyone —everyone—else but him.

"So what brought this urgent meeting together, Councilor?" Matthias lazed back in his chair like he didn't have a care in the world.

"We have a lead that may assist in locating the remaining aetts of bone runes." Ellaine took the seat at the head of the table. "Vella, inform us of what you found today."

Right. She was up. Sweet Goddess, please let this be the right thing to do.

"Our inquiry led us to a French porcelain dish decorated

with a small painting of a dark-haired woman who has the lower body of a serpent."

"And that is a lead, how?" Matthias languidly stirred a cup of coffee one of the servers had brought in, as if he had zero interest in the subject of the bone runes. Did anyone else find him ridiculously sexy?

"We have good reason to believe that this dish is in some —yet unknown—way associated with them."

"Don't tell me, another treasure hunt?" Matthias' lips turned up in a sardonic grin.

"Actually—"

"Councilor Matthias. Please do not interrupt." Ellaine's lips pursed. "Velvet, continue."

"The artwork on the inside of the dish is unique and not part of the normal collection, which meant we were able to track it to an auction house where it was sold two years ago. But importantly, the figure in the dish, I think, is meant to be a reference to Melusine, sometimes referred to as Melusina, a mythological character known as the Builder Fairy."

"Who is this Melusine?" Nevena leaned closer to Matthias. "This is fascinating."

"Mmm." Matthais' tone was boredom perfection.

"There are several versions of the myth, but a common example is that Melusine was a wealthy, beautiful woman, and these attributes caught the eye of a poor king."

"Naturally," Matthias drawled. "Because how pedestrian … a poor king. Apologies, please continue." He waved a hand through the air, every inch the sophisticated, wealthy king of all he owned.

She shot him a look but tempered it straight away. He was playing a part, damn it. So she had to as well.

"As I was saying, Melusine agreed to marry the poor

king on the provision that he would not come to her rooms once a month. They were happily married for many years, during which time she built the kingdom many castles and towers and even whole towns and produced the king several sons as well. But after a time, the king's curiosity won out, and one month, he followed her and saw the truth—that she had the lower body of a serpent. Personally, I think this is an allegory for—"

"Velvet. Is your opinion at this stage necessary?"

"Apologies, Aunt Ellaine. Suffice it to say that upon witnessing her husband break his vow, she left him."

"Leaving one's husband after a betrayal," Matt murmured. "Seems fair."

"That is the myth. Where it becomes interesting is that there is a town particularly linked to Melusine called Lusignan in France. Legend has it that many of the buildings there were built by her. Now, from the auction house we have ... determined ... that the bowl with the Melusine-esque painting was sold by the Durand family, who live in Château de Durand, just outside the town of Lusignan. The château is currently a bed-and-breakfast, and according to their website, has been in the one family for hundreds of years."

"Velvet, are you saying there is something at this Château de Durand that will lead us to the bone runes?"

"I think that the dish from Derrick's vision came from that château, and so yes, it's a logical step to see what other information the château *might* be hiding."

"Very well." Ellaine steepled her fingers and regarded them all. "Vella, you will go to this château."

"While I applaud your niece's reasoning"—Matthias spun in his chair—"I find myself curious as to what this has to do with the Magicae coven?"

"Given the value of the runes we are seeking, and that you are already aware of what we are after, I feel it best to ensure Velvet has all the support she needs to ensure her safety without bringing anyone new into this situation. You also have the already established cover story of Velvet assisting you with decorating your clubs. Should anyone ask why you are traveling together, you shall say that your contract has recommenced and that is why you are in France."

"And what do the Magicae get out of this union? Apart from wonderfully decorated clubs, of course. After all, you will keep the runes."

"You get to work with the Divinators and Elixirs, and help bring your coven into the future, rather than remain a relic of the past. That is what you want, after all?"

"You know me so well," he murmured. "And Councilor-elect Montgomery?"

"Nevena wishes to atone for their previous Councilor's poor choices and so will assist with the search."

What? Vella sat up straight. "I don't need anyone else—"

"Yes, you do. Matthias' magic spells are useful; however, even they have their limitations, and you, Velvet, have no magic at all, whereas Nevena is one of the most skilled at her craft. She will provide you with another layer of protection, and an offense if you need it, when she is able."

"Able?" Matthias glanced between Nevena and Ellaine.

"There are several Elixir coven responsibilities that I must attend to right away. But once those are tidied up and out of the way, I'll join you quick as a flash." Nevena rubbed Matthias' arm. "And as Councilor Ellaine says, the Elixir's wish to help in any way possible after Charles' lack of judgment." She smiled at Ellaine.

Ellaine stood. Of course, everyone in the room went

quiet too. "I have a meeting to attend; however, Derrick, please work with everyone to ensure travel plans are put in place immediately. Vella, a car and driver are waiting downstairs to return you to Arcane Antiquities so that you may pack. And remember two things: this search must be kept quiet—the less people who know we seek these runes, the better—and your priority is to return the bones here to the Divinators so they may be safely protected."

Pft. More like hoarded and used to control witchkind.

Fear twisted the knots in Vella's stomach all over again. But one thing she knew—no way could she let Ellaine get those bone runes. And if Vella was the only one who could find them, then she was going to France.

"Well, Derrick, happy to leave the plan making in your hands." Matthias' customary casual tone screamed status quo, but Vella caught something in his tone. She glanced at him, but he never met her gaze. Instead, he turned to Nevena. "Councilor-elect Nevena, thank you again for last night. It was a pleasure to have you at Nocturnal, even if under such ... unfortunate circumstances."

"Councilor Matthias, the pleasure was all mine. And Vella, I'm thrilled to be working with you. In fact, after hearing about—and now seeing—your passion for ceramics, you'll have to come to London and give me your professional appraisal of my collection."

"Oh, I—"

"Perfect, can't wait. Well then, everything is sorted." Nevena turned her grin on Matthias.

Oh shit ... That wasn't her usual shark smile. That was see-something-you-find-delectable-and-want-to-eat-it-and-now-you-can. Now Vella knew for sure that at least one other person recognized how sexy Matthias Medea was.

"Councilor Matthias," Nevena practically purred. "Would you like to walk me out?"

"Sounds delightful." Matt held the door open for Nevena and gestured for her to precede him. "Derrick, I'll wait to hear from you."

As soon as they were alone, Derrick rolled his eyes at Vella. "Because gods forbid a Magicae actually do any work themselves. Such a useless lot. Well, Vella, what do you think? How long till you can be ready?"

Useless? Matthias?

"Not long," she managed to say past the sudden urge to laugh hysterically. "I just need to make sure the shop's covered, and a couple of other little things." Like what to do with Brianna.

"Then I'll get my PA to arrange the accommodation at the château."

"What if they're booked—"

"They'll change their plans when they know who is coming." He gathered up his laptop and stood.

Of course, they would—because who would ever say no to the fucking Divinator coven?

"In that case, I'll just wrap this up and see myself out." She faked a smile, and then, finally she was alone, and she let her smile fall away before dropping into the nearest chair.

Frigging hell. She was going to France. With Matthias. And Nevena at some point.

But right now, she was in Div Tower, and everyone was busy …

Brianna had said Vella shouldn't journey until her magic had settled, but she was so close to the vault, and to Tara and the bone runes, if she could just find somewhere to hide, she could get them back right now.

She darted for the door at the far end of the boardroom and entered a smaller room filled with electronic and technical equipment, with yet another door leading off to somewhere else. She tried that handle, and it opened to a small office filled with desks, several occupied. Many unfamiliar heads popped up and looked at her.

"Oops, wrong way." She closed the door, backtracked through the technical room and into the boardroom.

Damn. She could always stay here and lock the doors?

She reached under her shirt and opened the window on Brianna's sheath. "Brianna," she whispered as she made her way to the entry. "Listen, I'm at Div Tower, alone, and this is too good an opportunity to lose. I'm going to get Tara."

"Really? Are you certain?"

"I thought you were all 'get-Tara-now.' I'm just going to lock the entry door."

"I am, but you must be careful. How are—wait. You cannot journey, not until your magic bond with Matthias is cemented!"

"But—"

Two voices echoed from the other side of the doors.

Shit. Someone was there.

"But what, Vespera? Vespera? What are you—"

"Shh." Vella lowered her voice to the barest whisper. "Someone's here. Need to listen." She eased one door open.

"—watch them very, very carefully." Aunt Ellaine's cool, precise voice echoed through the gap.

A voice Vella couldn't quite make out responded.

"If there is any sign of a romantic relationship between Vella and Matthias, I want him killed," Ellaine continued, as casually as if she were talking about the weather.

Vella froze.

Kill Matthias? No frigging way. And who was Ellaine

talking to? Did they know Vella was still in the boardroom? Surely not; otherwise, Ellaine would never have said that. And what if they came in and found Vella?

But what was more important? Finding out who had orders to kill Matthias, or being caught in the boardroom?

Vella put her cell to her ear, pretended to be on a call, and opened the door.

Damn it. Ellaine was alone in the boardroom foyer, but the far door clicked shut, like someone had just left.

Ellaine spun. Concern raced over her expression, but in a flash her composure returned. "Velvet. You should be preparing for your trip—what are you waiting for?"

Ellaine had just ordered the possible killing of one of the best people Vella had ever met, yet stares at Vella as if *she* were the insect here.

But two witches could play at gaslighting. Vella called up that ice barrier until it was such a tight shell around her that not one frigging ounce of emotion could get through.

"Yes, Aunt Ellaine. I did want to talk with you. I've arranged with one of Sara's author friends for her to stay there while I'm away," she lied without pause. "You know Sara likes to have people around, and with you and Derrick so busy, I thought it best."

"Hmm." Ellaine's frozen gaze bored into her for a long, silent moment. "Well, if something happens to Sara while she is away from our tower, it will be on your head, Velvet Knight."

I am not—I will never be—Velvet fucking Knight. And the only thing happening to Sara is that she'll be able to breathe again.

19

Vella packed fast, and within an hour of arriving home had given Sara a hug, nuzzled Morrigan—who then flew off with her feathers ruffled in what appeared to be an avian huff—and returned to the town car.

"Look after yourself," she'd whispered into Sara's ear. "And Morrigan. And tell Sylvie where I'm going."

Damn it, so much to say in such a short time.

And where was Matthias? And how the frig did she manage this new threat to his life? He needed to be near Vella or risk his Druid secret being discovered—meaning he and his entire coven would be killed. But if he and Vella slipped up in any way and let their feelings for each other show, that would also get him killed.

Her stomach filled with rocks.

He would be furious at the threat, zero question. Although, she didn't *have* to tell him ... but no. She'd gone down that road with Sara, and look at how keeping information from her had turned out. So fine, she'd tell him. But she'd also make it clear they couldn't be together—romantically—until they could do so without risking Matt's life. The risk to Matt was not worth taking.

Something burned in her chest, but she scrubbed a fist over that sensation.

This was for the best—they could stay physically near each other to appease the bonding issue, just not have the relationship grow ... more.

Not yet, anyway.

This time of the day, the private airfield was still at least an hour's drive, so she took out her eReader and opened up the latest book on managing trauma she'd found.

Ellaine might've banned all the witchcraft books outside those she had written or approved, but she hadn't managed to ban *all* books.

As Matthias waited at the same airfield he and Vella had flown out of on their first rune hunt, he leashed the anticipation prowling through him behind his usual façade. Although so much had changed since then. *He* had changed so much.

And now, Ellaine was changing the playing field with the damned SI raids. Now *that* was a problem. If he lost Nocturnal, he lost one of the main funnels of funds and other assets into the war against the Divs and Elixirs.

Ping.

Ronin: Hack successful. Found comm trail from E to human government to ban any non-human group, as specified by the Witches Council, from gathering in public places and from owning property. All infractions to be reported to the Council for 'disciplinary management'

Matt: Fuck. Now E's getting the humans to do her dirty work too. Which groups?

Ronin: Not specified but chatter is the vamps are going to be monitored soon, if not already

Bloody hell. Was that also why Ellaine had moved the Council meeting forward? And if she was after the vamps now, how long before she came for the shifters? They were all beings born of dark energy, after all. And once she'd cleared those hurdles, how long till she turned her focus on tightening the screws on hedge witches and the Magicae and the Crystallos?

Matt: Good work. Can you keep watching their comms? Need to know everything you can find out about any new plans E is making

Ronin: On it. That motherfucker is not closing us down

Ronin: One more thing. Sara keeps asking Shannah and me to let her join the fight

Matt: She has a right to fight back. And she has the navitas

Ronin: 💯 but she's still being fucking poisoned. And she's reckless.

Matt: Fine. Hacking only for now. I don't
want Vella distracted and she gets
protective where Sara is involved

Ronin: Good call

Of course, Ronin would think that was a good call. Ronin's awareness of Sara was on another level, outweighed only by how hard Ronin fought whatever he was feeling for her.

But before Matt could say anything else, Vella's town car pulled into the airfield, and then she was there in front of him.

Black coat, black wide-legged pants, black gloves ... hair streaming down her back, and her lioness eyes ... well, they weren't glowing. In fact, the bruises beneath them looked even more pronounced. But given she barely slept last night, that was hardly a surprise.

And for all the exhaustion on her face, she still made his mouth water.

Dangerous. Capable. Strong. And so damned beautiful his body went hard and tight for her. The competing sensations of being soothed by just being near her, along with hot, clawing desire, made his head spin.

Gods, what had she done to him?

"Rapunzel," he murmured when she reached hearing distance. "Change of plans." He gestured at the car he had waiting.

"Hello to you, too. Thought we were taking Ellaine's plane—"

"Alas, it suffered a mechanical issue and didn't pass the preflight checks. We're taking mine instead. You've flown with me before, so I take it no issues?"

"Of course not. And how lucky your plane was ready."

"Fortunate indeed." He grinned. "Now, I take it you have everything you need for the flight?" He stared at her purse. He couldn't ask outright if she had Brianna—not until he could call the spell to hide their conversation—but knowing Vella, there was no way she'd left her behind.

"Yes." Vella rubbed her lower back. "My back has been a little stiff lately, but I brought something to help with that."

"Good call." At least they didn't have to worry about Brianna being found if someone searched her townhouse while they were in France.

"You warmed the seats," she murmured as she slid into the front passenger seat.

"You can drive if you want? I know you like to drive stick." A memory of their escape from poison-wielding assassins in Scotland roared through him.

"Thanks, but since we're not on the run, I'm happy to be driven today."

"As you wish, Rapunzel." He closed the door and within moments was sitting beside her. "My plane is in a different hangar."

"Wow, so we're driving for all of ..."

"Five minutes. But three hundred seconds in your company is never a waste." He waited, but she didn't make any snarky, smart-ass comeback. "You really are tired, huh?"

"Sure." But she didn't meet his eyes.

Now, for damn sure, something wasn't right. Vella back down from a fight—play, verbal or otherwise? Never. But why? Was it just the fatigue?

"Well, here we are," he said as he stopped inside the hangar beside his new Dassault Falcon 10X. The stairs were extended, and his staff were ready. All he needed was one remarkable, stubborn, captivating witch and her bone-handled knife.

But her eyes were closed. He sighed and gave in to the urge to smooth back several errant strands of deep red hair at her temple. Just that contact had his power surge through his veins.

Damn but she was special.

"Rapunzel," he whispered. "I hate to wake you, but I'm positive you don't want me to carry you on board."

"Not asleep," she muttered. "Just resting my eyes. And I'm pretty sure you'd break your back if you tried to carry me up any steps. I'm no lightweight."

"I have carried you before, if you recall? And there they are, lioness."

"What?" She sat up, and he eased back.

"Your lioness eyes. They're something else, you know that?"

"Pft. Like you can talk, Mr. My-silvery-scarf-makes-my-eyes-glimmer?"

"Oh, you like my eyes, do you?"

"Your head is way too big already for me to answer that."

"Never. Not from you." And wasn't that the truth? It didn't matter what anyone else had ever said to him—now, only Vella's words carried the weight of what he wanted to hear.

"Okay. I'm good." She hopped out and pulled her coat tight. "Man, your car was warm."

"You're welcome." He held out a hand, and as he helped her out, butterscotch and something else, something purely Vella filled his senses. His mouth watered, and he leaned closer for another lungful of her—

"Stop, Matt." She shot a hand between them. "Get back."

He did as she said immediately, but the fear that flashed over her face had him pause.

"Okay, now I know something is going on. This isn't just about you being tired. What is up?"

"I'll tell you on the plane. Just—keep your distance till we're really alone, from human and Div foresight, okay?"

He nodded, but inside he was seething. What had the coven of fuckery done now?

His pilot and the two-person cabin crew greeted them, gave them the standard safety talk and a tour of the jet. Cockpit. Galley at the front, with a door to close off the forward section. Main cabin with seating for ten, dining table, couch, and a bar. Full bathroom. Rear storage.

"That'll do," he cut the cabin crew off. "We have business to attend to. Hold refreshments for half an hour."

As soon as they were alone, he pointed to the nearest seat. "Strap in for takeoff, and then please tell me what the fuck is going on?"

20

"And that is why you and I need to make sure absolutely no one thinks we're together." Vella held Matthias' gaze. Frigging hell, please let him see the sense in her plan.

Matt sat facing her, but he unclipped his seatbelt and tunneled a hand through his hair, messing up his bun.

"You're taking this remarkably calmly."

"This isn't the first time, nor is it likely to be the last, that someone's wanted me dead." He unbuttoned his cuffs and rolled the sleeves of his white work shirt up, revealing the intricately patterned snake tattoos running down each sinewy forearm. "And you definitely didn't see who Ellaine was talking with?"

She wrenched her gaze to his. "No, not at all. Did Nevena leave with you?"

"She decided to go back and talk to Derrick about the trip. What about Derrick? Did you see him at all?"

"He left the boardroom before me, although he knew I was still around, so would he have let Ellaine tell him that right there?"

"Good question. But it could've also been any other Div witch—any of their mid-level or higher foreseers could use their foresight to watch us this far away, though their accuracy will drop. Okay, so … someone … has orders to kill me if they think you and I are romantically involved. Why? Why the fuck does you and me being together matter to Ellaine's plans?"

"I wish I knew. But I'm worried, Matthias. Everything has gotten so messed up. I was so sure," she whispered. "So frigging certain that taking the runes back to New York was the right thing to do. But I fucked up big time, and Goddess, I—I wish I could go back in time."

His face filled with compassion, but did she deserve that? Goddess, she wanted to. Just like she wanted to launch at him and wrap herself around him. Be wrapped up by him. Let someone else protect her and tell her everything was going to be okay. Let her cry on their chest.

But instead, she blew out a shaking breath and closed her eyes. Better to not see how he looked at her in case she gave in, and then there went the icy shell she needed to keep her shit together.

"I'll leave you to sleep—"

"No." She sat up higher in her chair. "I can't."

"Yes, you can. You know, for the past two days I've been pretending that the pallor in your cheeks doesn't make my chest tight with worry. But no more. You need sleep, damn it."

"You don't understand."

"Your dream … it's a nightmare, right?"

She nodded, her throat suddenly too tight to speak. "I'm working on it," she finally squeezed out. "I'm reading books on trauma therapy. Napping when I can."

"But it's not enough." His jaw tightened. "Every time I

think the hatred I feel for E has reached its limit, something else happens and that seething emotion deepens again. But I can help spell you into a deep sleep, and hopefully avoid the state where your dreams come in."

"You can avoid them entirely?"

"I can try. What about your books? Have you found any ways to help there?"

"Not yet." But if Matt could help her sleep without the nightmare? "I'd like to give that a go, later though. Because right now, you and I need to be clear about how to handle this new threat. You have to look after yourself, as well as everyone else."

"You know I need to be around you. As in physically close to you. Just breathing in your scent or standing in the same fucking room ... it soothes me, Vella. I can't for the life of me explain it in any other way but you're a calming breeze when I'm on fire. You're a blanket when I'm cold. You're oxygen when I don't think I can breathe. It's that simple. And yes, I know what Ellaine said is an issue— Gods, Vel, please don't cry." His face twisted.

"I'm not," she gritted out. "And this isn't 'an issue.' This is your life."

Vella blew out a hard breath and gathered herself. Matthias' words were like a decadent velvet blanket—warm and beguiling and tempting her to lose herself in how they could make her feel. But that was the problem. His words *could* make her feel, look at him shattering her control right frigging now. And that was a danger, for both of them. *Focus, Vel.* Tears burned in her eyes, but she willed them back.

No. Crying.

"I promise you, it's going to be okay. My life has been at risk for the past twenty years. Another person out to kill me is nothing new."

"Well, it's new to me!"

"Okay, that's fair. I get it."

"And stop looking at me like that—like you're measuring me, trying to work out how to handle me."

"Not handling." His lips tightened. "But I am trying to figure out exactly what you're saying—what you want to do. Didn't we already agree to keep our relationship a secret?"

"But that was before. Look at how we are when it's just the two of us. What if this were E's plane? We couldn't even have this conversation. And all it takes is one slip, and it doesn't even have to be in front of Ellaine or one of her lackeys. Someone who knows nothing about this situation could see us, then make a random remark that gets back to Ellaine and wham—goodbye Matthias."

His gaze followed her mouth as she spoke, and she leaned back, closed her eyes to stop from doing something foolish like licking his tattoos or biting the lobe of his ear beneath those flashing rubies.

Heat pooled low in her belly.

Damn it, down girl. Why did just being near him send her hormones into overdrive? It wasn't like she hadn't had two exquisite orgasms less than twenty-four hours ago.

"Okay." His harsh exhale echoed in her ears. "What are you proposing, Vella?"

She sat up and shifted back as far as she could go. From this distance, it would take her at least five seconds to yank her seatbelt free, launch at him and ride them both into another one of those orgasms he was so damned good at. Plenty of time to come to her senses in the case of any more foolish urges.

Focus, Vel. You can do this.

"Right." Shore up the walls. Batten down. Every. Last.

Feeling. Don't look into his eyes. "We won't be together—romantically."

"You want to turn your back on the bond?"

"I'm not saying that." And no, not for anything in the world did she want to stop what she and Matt had started. But right now, want and need were two different things. Which meant putting Matthias first, because if she didn't protect him, who else would? "Brianna said we need to be physically near each other, but she didn't say anything about needing to be romantically together. So if we can just … pause the progression of our emotional connection, then we can focus on making sure no one has yet another reason to kill you today."

What the frig? Didn't he even want to save his smoking-hot ass?

"Vella," he said her name carefully. Precisely. This time, she couldn't not look at him. "I don't think turning your back on your feelings is even a possibility—after all, that's what the bond is, an extension of how we fucking feel about each other." Something lit in his expression. "You're trying to keep *all* your feelings contained. I'm right, aren't I?"

"Yes. Yes, I am. Is that such a bad thing? Just while I'm pretending to be a fucking traitor to my true coven—who remember, the rest of the world hates?"

"Not everyone hates the Mors Dicen. Ellaine did a damned good job of seeding fear and anger through some countries, yes, but look at France? They have a rich history with Mors Dicen witches too, and I know other parts of the world do as well."

"Fine. Just the place where we live hates us. But I still need to prove my loyalty to Ellaine, while also *really* plotting how to liberate Tara and the first aett, and stop her from getting the rest of the bone runes."

"And then?" A hooded look entered his eyes, and frig, she was suddenly on high alert. Matt was pissed. Like really, truly, angry.

"And then once this is all over, we explore our feelings—"

"Bullshit." He leaned forward, midnight stars suddenly glittering in his eyes. "I know what you're doing. And it won't work."

"FUCKING GODS, Vella, you think you can protect me by hiding your feelings. And you expect me to do the same because you're scared for *me*?"

"Um, Matt? Your eyes are ... doing that thing. And we're on a plane. Is this good?"

Fuck, no, it was not good.

Control, breathe, focus. Control, breathe, focus. But fuck, the power still roiled and bubbled and frothed in his veins. Matt clenched his jaw against the rising tide.

"It's spreading." Vella's eyes widened, and she pointed at his hand. Pinpricks of black stars grew brighter and brighter, following the lines of his veins.

"Hold my hand," he bit out. "I need to ground."

"Here?" Vella's eyes were wild, but she fumbled with her seatbelt and dropped to her knees in front of him. Grabbed his hand. "How?"

"I need an element to connect to."

"Matt, there's only air. If you release here, what will that do to the plane?"

"Fuck. Fuck, fuck, fuck." He held onto her hand for all he was worth. "Don't let go," he gritted out.

"What about … another type of release?" She glanced down at his lap. "There's a bedroom back there—"

"Hell. Maybe?" Would a hand job do the job? He could manage a few pumps—fuck knew, that was all it would take, he was so on edge. The bathroom was only feet away. His power surged. His veins throbbed, containment close to impossible.

"Oh shit," Vella whispered. "Matt, your snake tats are moving! They're coiling over your skin."

"That's my Magicae power." He clenched his jaw. "Everything's getting tangled up inside me."

Her gaze darted to the galley door. Clinks and voices indicated the crew were getting something ready.

"I hope your crew stay in the galley for a few more minutes." With her free hand, she reached for his belt.

"Vella?" He sucked in a breath. "What are—"

"You know exactly what I'm doing." Her gaze locked on the fucking tent he was making in his trunks. "How long do you need?"

"Vel, I can do this—"

She drew his cock free and gripped him, and a bolt of pleasure shot up his spine, and it was all he could do not to shout out.

"Matthias Medea, let me give you a head job and stop arguing. Shame we don't have any blackberry jam." She stared up at him through her lashes, licking her lips, and, fucking hell, if his heart didn't stop and his world tilt—

Glorious, wet heat enveloped him.

Gods but this woman slayed him. He curled a hand around her head. Around her jaw. Rubbed her lips where she surrounded him. Lost himself in her eyes as she took him deep. As she tongued the vein running up his length.

As she sucked his head and then took him deeper still. As she cupped his balls and hummed around him and then shifted so he hit the back of her throat and—

"Fuck!" Pressure spiked. Stars filled his vision, and he erupted down her throat.

Vella's gasp filled his ears, followed by a long hum, and finally, "sweet frigging Goddess."

And when his breathing returned, and he could open his eyes, her beautiful face filled his vision.

"Vella. Vella, Vella, thank you." He pressed a kiss to her palm. "I know that wasn't on the expected flight log."

"It's not like I didn't get as much out of that as you did." The flush hitting high on her cheeks and the sated glow in her eyes backed up her words. "And I do care for you. You know that, right? I just …"

"What?"

She drew in a deep breath, and her mouth opened, but nothing came out.

"I'm not talking about the magical bond, Vella. Forget the bond for a moment. I just want to know what you're thinking. Feeling. Needing."

"You know I care about you, Matt. Of course I do. But I'd be lying if I said I could commit to anything more, at the moment. I just need, for now, to not worry about this thing between us. But I'm here, right? And I'm not going anywhere."

Damn it, she was willing to get physical with him—but without the emotional connection?

"Vella, clearly, I like being physical with you." Understatement of the eon. "But I won't lie and say I like the less-emotional part; however, I want to respect your wishes, so yeah, I'll try your plan."

"And hey, like I said, head jobs on tap … that's a good thing, right?"

"Guaranteed head jobs. Dream come true." He smiled like he could tell she wanted, but fuck, he'd trade all the guaranteed head jobs in the world for the knowledge that Vella loved him. And wanted his love, in return.

He just had to trust her when she meant this was a temporary arrangement. And hope like hell their quasi-bond didn't fuck things up anymore.

"So, if you and I are on the same page, we just need to make sure the bond isn't an issue." Vella's gaze flicked to the galley where the crew were still audibly busy.

"Don't worry, anything my team overhears or sees won't go any further."

"Still, you know how most of the world feels about this. I'll just—" She reached under her shirt and whispered, "Brianna? Yeah, I'm here. On the plane. Yep, he's here too. Because I'm trying to keep this conversation private—I don't want to risk anyone finding out about you. We've been … busy—fine." She rolled her eyes at Matt. "Brianna says hi."

"Hello back."

"He said hi, too. Brianna, this bond thing, does it require a deeper … emotional connection? I mean, can Matt and I just agree that we like and respect each other, and yes, are physically attracted to each other, and that will stop our magic and powers from going loco? Yes, we do. Yep. Is that possible? Uh-huh." She wrinkled her nose in that adorable way of hers. "Okay—maybe. Yes, I'll tell him. I said I'll tell him." Vella scowled and took a breath.

The door to the galley opened. "Sir, would you like refreshments now?"

"Just a few more moments, Eric." Matt inwardly sighed as Vella froze. "I'll let you know when."

"Of course, sir." The door clicked shut.

"Well, Vella? What did Brianna say? I get the sense she wants you to be specific."

"She said that magical bonds have been cemented for various reasons throughout history ... like two clans coming together for the betterment of all. So it is possible the bond might be satisfied if we agree to work together toward a common goal."

A common objective would be enough to stop his Druid power giving away his secret? He should be happy, damn it. So why was he disappointed?

"Yes, Brianna, I'm going to." Vella shook her head. "Swear it's like dealing with a child sometimes. Yes, I know you heard that. Matt? One more thing. Brianna wants me to be explicit that she can't say with full certainty that a lack of ... emotional commitment ... won't continue to impact the bond."

Matt eased back into the chair. By the scowl on Vella's face, he was damned sure Brianna hadn't used the term emotional commitment. But fine, he got that Vella wasn't ready to say the love word yet.

"It seems we have a shred of hope, at least?" He forced himself to smile.

"Why are you smiling like that?" Vella's frown was half cute, half accusatory.

"Like what?"

"It's your fake grin—the Magicae Councilor one where you pretend to be all lazy and uncaring, but behind it, I know you actually do care."

"Seeing through me already, Vella?" He dropped the forced expression and stared at her exactly like he wanted to. "Is this better?"

She swallowed and nodded.

"But, Vella, no promises—if your magic, or mine, becomes an issue, we do this my way."

"Which is?"

"Screw every other fucking person who wants to keep us apart. I get to own every inch of your skin, every moment of the day, for the rest of our fucking lives. And you get to own mine right back. I will be yours in every single way possible. And we fucking let our emotions out. Wild, raw, every fucking thing we feel we share it with each other."

And while she didn't say yes or no, the scent of her arousal bloomed in the air, butterscotch sweet, to mingle with the residue of their shared orgasms, and he knew she liked that idea.

And apparently, that knowledge was enough because after a lick of heat, his Druid power subsided. For now.

"Right. Well, since we need to work on a common target ... let's talk about next steps." She lowered her voice. "Like how to get Tara and the bone runes back, as well as finding the second and third aetts so Ellaine *doesn't* get them. And I've got a suggestion."

"I think I have an idea there, too. But you go first."

"Like you said back at Sylvie's place, we raid Div Tower. But I'll find a reason to get inside, and then journey using the dark energy to—" Vella winced. "No, Brianna, clearly not until my power is fully restored and I'm not in danger of *that*."

"You want to go in alone?"

"Don't look at me like that. It's safest for everyone, surely you realize that. Now, what's your idea?"

"It's a couple of ideas. And to start with, I know you're beating yourself up about bringing the runes back."

"With good reason. Look what's happened! What I allowed to happen."

"Actually, something good might've come by bringing the runes back to New York after all."

"Good—how can you say that?"

"Look how much we've learned. For starters, in the New York Div Tower, only Derrick and Ellaine are powerful enough to use the bone runes. And one of them needs to be an anchor, so if we can nullify that threat—"

"Nullify?"

"We remove Derrick from the equation."

"Like, kidnap him?" Vella leaned forward. "Oh shit. You mean permanently. You want to *kill* him? Brianna! Not you, too."

Hmm. Brianna agreed with Matt? "I always liked your Bone Guide, Vella."

"Don't encourage her." Vella shot him a glare. "Derrick is ..."

"Complicit by misinformation at the least? Or more likely, a willing participant?"

"I don't know! But you can't just go around contemplating killing someone."

"They do, Vella. All the fucking time. However, there's more to discuss from your reading. Maybe the biggest thing of all is that we finally know what Ellaine is after."

"What do you mean?"

"The day you did the reading at Div Tower and you heard Ellaine's conversation in her office, you told me she said 'finally, I've found it.' That means she already knew about the power source."

"And that's important, because ..."

"Because the Coven Union doesn't want to move forward with any plan to openly retake the Council without knowing what Ellaine is after. But now we have that intel. I'd like you to share your knowledge with the Coven Union."

"What?"

"And I'll review ... options ... for Derrick."

"Matthias Medea. No one is killing Derrick." There was nothing adorable in Vella's scowl this time.

21

They arrived in the picturesque village of Lusignan at half past two in the afternoon. Following the hire car's satnav directions to the château, Vella drove them past a crumbling gatehouse, around two giant spruces, with more crumbling ruins off in the distance, and then—

"Wow," she breathed. "I knew the château would be beautiful ... but I wasn't expecting something so spectacular."

"This run-down place?" Matt's glance was curious rather than awed.

"Absolutely. Run down is perfectly fine with me. Look at everything—the age, the history, the lives this place has seen."

"So that's why you liked Madgewick," Matt murmured.

"There were other reasons," Vella muttered under her breath, and while Matt didn't say anything, his lips curved briefly—the first smile she'd seen since they'd argued on the plane about killing Derrick—before she parked in the valet space.

"Tell me, darling, are you still pissed?"

"Darling? Pft. And am I still angry that you want to preemptively kill someone without knowing if they're a baddie? Yeah."

"I didn't say kill—"

"Yet. You said *not yet*. Which means it's still on the table for you. If you can get your grimoire."

"Vella, I've seen how far you would go to save Sara. How can you think I would go to any less lengths to save everyone I care for, too?" His gaze held hers, but she looked away.

The awfulness of those words wasn't something she wanted to even think about.

But fuck, was she wrong? She'd been so incorrect about everything else; what if she was making another mistake by not green-lighting Matt's plans?

"Are we going in?" Matt nodded at the château.

"Yeah. We'll continue this argument later." Vella smoothed her hair back in its ponytail. "Let's find the next aett now."

Anticipation had her stomach tightening, but she didn't look back at Matt as she got out of the car, only tugged her jacket closer, the reassuring weight of Brianna along her spine more comfort than anything else, and strode up the steps just as the large double timber doors opened and a man possibly in his forties—trimmed beard, sweet eyes behind rounded glasses, stepped out.

"Hello, welcome to Château de Durand," the man said with a definite British accent. "I'm Jamie Allard, your host."

"Hi, we have a reservation under Knight and Medea."

"Of course, of course, Councilor Medea, Ms. Knight, we're thrilled that you're staying with us." Jamie gestured for them to enter, but Vella couldn't move her feet. "And I can see you staring—you were expecting a French accent, I'm guessing?"

"Just a tad." Shit. They needed to talk to actual family members who might have knowledge of the château, not someone who had no connection to the history of the place. "The website listed you as a family-run establishment for centuries."

"It has been—and it is—I'm the last of the line. I took it over a couple of years ago after the place had been left to fall into disrepair. I know it doesn't look like much yet, but you should've seen the place when we first moved here! Now, can I take your bags?"

"No need," Matt said easily. If he was thrown at all by the news of their non-French host, he didn't show it.

"Then let's get you inside where it's warm. Councilor Medea, all the arrangements have been taken care of, so I can either show you to your rooms—you're both on the second floor—or take you on a tour if you prefer?"

Exposed timber beams, sandstone walls and flagstone floors, beautiful thick rugs and a stunning collection of true antique furniture stopped Vella mid-stride, and everything else flew out of her mind.

"This is gorgeous," she breathed.

"Yes, she is." Pride beamed on Jamie's face. "This section of the château was built in 1592, and then, of course, the family added onto it over the years. Your booking mentioned you're here as part of your work with arcane history? I'd be thrilled to show you around whenever you want."

"Thank you, I'll take you up on that offer. I'm always looking for items to add to Arcane Antiquities' shelves, but specifically, I'm assisting the Nocturnal Clubs with adding authentic elements of arcane history to their décor. Some period pieces for the right placements within the interiors, that kind of thing, and when we heard you are open to selling pieces, well, you had to be our first stop."

Jamie let out a long sigh, and his gaze traveled around the room. "Sadly, the renovations—let alone the maintenance—are such an expensive task that occasionally I need to part with pieces from the house, not that I want to, but that's the way of life, hey? I'm hoping the bed-and-breakfast element of the château will eventually earn enough that I don't need to sell any more of our history."

"Would you be open to a loan instead?" Matthias' gaze caught on a gleaming reddish timber chaise.

"Now that sounds even more interesting." Jamie's eyes lit up. "Councilor Medea, your room has the loveliest view of the orchard and the ruins of the original chapel built on the grounds at least a century earlier. Beneath there is where my ancestors stored their most precious possessions."

"What was that?" Vella forced herself to maintain a calm expression, but her heart picked up. Was their host going to talk about the second aett so easily?

"Their sparkling rosé." Jamie laughed, thankfully unaware of the disappointment fizzing louder than any bubbly wine in her belly. "Personally, I'd have been storing my jewels, but hey, two hundred years ago, clearly people's priorities were different."

"Never underestimate the value of a good drop," a polished voice called out from behind them.

Vella froze, then slowly turned as Nevena Montgomery walked down the stairs.

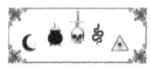

Fuck. So much for Nevena not joining them right away. Damn it, Matt had been looking forward to some real one-on-one time with Vella.

But also, he needed to work out if Nevena working with Ellaine, or just an eccentric Elixir witch trying to look after her coven?

The first option was more than a possibility, given her grandfather's direct involvement in the coup and so many deaths. But if she wasn't, the second option also made sense. No one knew better than Matt how vital keeping Ellaine as an ally—even a false one—was for the survival of those you loved. And so far, Nevena had treated Matthias exactly as he pretended to want: the magic-dicked spellcaster who cared more about money and sex than anything else.

But until he knew for certain where Nevena stood, he had to treat her as the first.

"Councilor Nevena." He stepped forward out of instinct —keeping Nevena's focus on him, and away from Vella. "What a delightful surprise. I didn't realize you were able to join us so quickly."

And fucking hell. Any hope of getting time alone with Vella to search the château evaporated faster than magic from a failed spell.

"So good, isn't it? I was able to wrap my work up faster than expected. And I think we can drop all the Councilor-this and Councilor-that now, can't we? After all, we're not in the chambers, and what Ellaine doesn't know can't upset her!" Nevena's gaze flicked to Vella. "Oh, I'm just so excited to see you both."

Matthias' radar went on high alert. What was Nevena—

"As we are you," Vella said so smoothly Matthias had to check himself from staring at her. When had she become so good at lying? "Ever since you mentioned your ceramic collection back at Div Tower, I've been wanting to ask you about it."

"And I would love that too." Nevena's laugh seemed genuine. "Your obsession with antique ceramics is all I ever hear about. I can't wait to see it in action."

"Well, you've come to the right place—I'm salivating over most of what I see here at Château de Durand already."

"So, what do you think of those?" Nevena pointed at the figures carved into the timber of the writing desk in the ground floor parlor. "Are they a clue?"

"I don't think so." Vella set her teeth for the millionth time that afternoon. When she'd pretended an interest in talking to Nevena about ceramics, she hadn't realized that would entail the Elixir witch following Vella *all* afternoon. "These look more Gothic Revival—but as I said, furniture of this period isn't my specialty. So, that's all the ground floor rooms. Are you sure you need to stay with me? I can look around on the next floor—"

"Oh no. I am here to make sure you can do your job for the Council without any harm, and especially as Matthias is busy on all those calls, I'm more than happy to be your shadow."

"Yay." Vella had to turn away to hide her true feelings. "How lucky for me."

"So, tell me about Matthias, one girl to another." Nevena leaned in close like they were besties or something. "I understand you and he became rather friendly while you were working together to find the bone runes back home. My home, I mean—in the UK."

Shit. Why ask that? Had Nevena been given the if-in-relationship-then-kill order, or was she just curious about Matt ... or, more than curious: interested? Huh. Nevena had appeared to find him attractive, and everyone knew the rumors about Magicae's magic dicks.

Except they weren't rumors.

Was Nevena sounding Vella out to determine if Matt was available?

"I—"

"You know"—Nevena linked her arm through Vella's—"you can tell me everything."

"We're not in a relationship." Vella did her best not to stiffen up. "And the rumors about us being together ... I was just doing my job, that was all."

"Of course, of course." Did this woman ever stop smiling? "But it never hurts when the job is enjoyable, right?"

Ew. Was that how Nevena saw Matt? A job, and one she could have fun *doing*? "You know, I might look outside before it gets too late." Maybe that would dislodge Nevena? "Jamie said there's an old orchard and graveyard, as well as the ruins of the original structures where his ancestors stored their wines centuries ago. Unless it's too cold?" Shit. She couldn't be too eager. "I would totally understand if you'd prefer to have dinner—"

"Did someone say dinner?" Matthias sauntered into the room as if he'd cast a spell and magically appeared, looking effortlessly graceful and delicious in black pants and shirt, and pale-lavender wool coat that somehow made his silver eyes shine more than ever.

And damn it, she might be angry about his idea for Derrick, but he still made her heart pound.

Vella snuck a look at Nevena. The Elixir witch needed a mop to clean up the drool.

"Matthias, you snuck off." Nevena's pout was the perfect mix of playful and hurt. "You naughty thing."

"Sadly, work called—but here I am, back with you and only one room missed. And in a stroke of good fortune, I ran into Jamie who suggested a small bistro in the village for an early dinner." Matthias' charming smile was directed fully at Nevena. And even though Vella knew that look was all for show, an uncomfortable sensation burned in her belly. "How does that sound?"

Dinner with Matt and Nevena? No thanks. But with Nevena out of the way, she could start searching the next floor far more thoroughly.

"I was actually thinking about staying in tonight, so you and Matthias can go and have dinner—"

"Great idea. We can get to know each other so much better." Nevena took Matt's arm and turned him around.

"Vespera," Brianna hissed. "Recall that you cannot be away from your Druid for long until you have cemented the bond."

Shit.

"Actually"—Vella ran after them—"turns out I'm hungrier than I realized. I'll come with, after all."

22

T hree hours later, Vella barely held in a yawn as she trailed Nevena and Matthias into the château.

Jamie met them inside the front door with a cheerful grin. "Fires are set in each of your rooms, and evening drinks are being served in the ground floor parlor. We have another guest already enjoying the room, and you're welcome as well."

"Vella, since you're so tired, why don't you head up and get a good night's sleep?" Nevena patted Vella's arm. "I'll keep our spellcaster entertained for the evening."

Vella set her teeth and restrained the urge to yank Matthias out of Nevena's grip. "You know, a drink sounds great." She stepped ahead and entered the parlor.

Alex sat beside the fireplace, the flames burnishing his blond hair a rich gold, and tilted a glass of something dark red in her direction before taking a sip. "Vella! How lovely to see you again."

"Alex. What—" She caught herself and walked to him. "Hello."

"And who is this?" Nevena stopped beside Vella.

"Alexander Kravchenko, but you may call me Alex." He winked at Vella. "I've been pursuing Ms. Knight here with a business proposal, but as she is always so terribly busy, I have followed her here to convince her to work with me."

"Alex, it is absolutely lovely to meet you. I'm Nevena Montgomery, Councilor-elect for the Elixir coven. And this is Matthias Medea, Councilor for the Magicae coven."

"Charmed." Matt's teeth bared in what ... might've been a smile? Vella stared at him, and finally, his face morphed into his Magicae Councilor expression. "Any friend of Velvet is a friend of ours."

"The pleasure is all mine." Alex gave a small bow, then focused on Nevena. "Your accent ... London?"

"You have a good ear. So please, you have to tell us how you and Velvet met?" Nevena sat on the other side of the fireplace and leaned forward as if Alex held her total interest. "She must have made quite an impression for you to pursue her so ... ardently ... around the world."

"What a lovely turn of phrase," he said with his thick accent. "Initially, I brought a family heirloom to Ms. Knight—"

"Oh, I'm sure she would be fine for you to call her Velvet, isn't that right?" Nevena gave Vella a bright smile. Seriously, how was the woman even awake, let alone this fucking happy?

"Just Vella is fine," she gritted out through the best fake smile she could manage.

"Thank you, Vella." Alex grinned at her. "Well, after the appraisal, I learned Vella also styles businesses with arcane décor. And, as among my businesses I own a small hotel, nothing on a scale like your friend"—he nodded at Matthias—"I knew Vella would be the ideal person to work with."

"How delightful! Your timing is perfect as this château is

owned by a Crystallo family, who are open to selling off their collection."

"Actually. Great point." Vella grabbed his free arm. "Why don't we take a look at some pieces now?"

"Why, Velvet, I thought you were tired. Perhaps the arrival of your friend"—Nevena smiled at Alex—"has boosted your energy."

"Must be." If she forced this smile much longer her cheeks would start twitching. "And how could I not give Alex a fast tour after he's come all this way?" She tugged Alex to his feet. "Matthias, Nevena, I'll probably go to sleep after this, so I'll see you in the morning."

She yanked Alex's arm, and he followed her with zero resistance out of the parlor.

As soon as the door closed behind them, she yanked him up the stairs to her bedroom and pulled him inside.

"Vespera, have you pulled me into your room to make the most of your Primus? I am pleased to confirm I conducted a signal sweep while you were out, and your room is free of any tracking devices. As I am fluent in French, among other languages, I can also be of assistance if you require any translations while we are here as well."

"Huh? No, we're in here because we can talk. And don't call me Vespera—it's Vella only. Even when you think we're alone. And how did you know this is my room?"

"I know your scent."

"Oh." She restrained the urge to sniff under her arms. Her *scent*? "But what's this Primus business?"

"Sylvie has concerns that the Druid is not applying himself to the task of your protection well enough. However, as Primus, I can also provide for your security. For instance, tonight I will sleep here—"

"Pft. No way, dude. Where is your room anyway?"

"This level, on the corner opposite the Elixir witch." He wrinkled his nose. "She smells ... wrong. However, that may be the outcome of administering too many potions on her own person."

"She uses potions on herself? How do you know?"

"Her blood stinks. The stench on the Elixir is so strong I can smell it without a taste." He shrugged like stinking blood was common knowledge. "The outcome of large and systematic change at a molecular level—"

"Hold on. What do you know about molecular levels?"

"Vampires know a lot of things."

Huh. How had she not noticed his smile was really a thing of beauty?

"Right, anyway. I don't need you to guard my room. In fact, as lovely as this is, I don't need you at all. Sorry if that sounds harsh, but it's true."

"No, it is a falsehood. You were attacked at the Druid's club, and you are journeying in your dreams. And I recall during the fight at Nocturnal, you said you could not use your"—his eyes darted to her lower back as if he could see Brianna strapped there—"full capabilities, which I suspect is due to the resulting impact on your vision. Therefore, I am here to teach you how to fight without the aid of weapons."

"Huh?" Vella paused. Was this something else she didn't know about Mors Dicen traditions? "I can handle myself, trust me."

"Without your Bone Guide, you have some skill, yes. However, within our family, I teach our younglings, and others, how to fight with their bodies. One form I find useful for those of lesser physical strength is jujitsu, so now I am here to teach you this."

"You don't mean right now, do you?"

"No. You must be rested, and it is clear you are not. However, tomorrow morning, after breaking your fast, I shall meet you by the pond."

"But it will be freezing. I don't think training outside is a good idea."

"Your Brianna will. You should discuss my plan with her, and you will see it makes sense. Now, do you wish for anything else of your Primus?"

"Actually, yes. What is a Primus?"

"Not what. Who. I fought Tannis for the right."

"Dude, did your chest just puff out?" An uneasy feeling snaked through her gut. "Alex, what does a Primus do?"

"It means I am the first vampire elected to see to your protection, to your succor, to your pleasure."

"My—" Vella choked on a lungful of air. "Stop, stop hitting my back, I'm okay." She hauled in a breath through watering eyes. Frigging hell, should she be alarmed, slightly turned on, or in hysterics? Maybe all three?

"Right. Well, you know what?" She got past the muddle of reactions fighting for supremacy. "I'm just gonna ... think ... on this for a while, so you go back to your room, or downstairs or wherever you want, really, as long as it's not in here with me, and I will talk to you tomorrow." She held the door open.

"At training," he replied as she closed the door in his face.

A definite hysterical laugh escaped her. Sweet Goddess was the universe playing games with her or something?

And shit, Brianna!

"About time," Brianna said the moment Vella took her out of the sheath. "I have been closed all afternoon."

"I was with the Elixir Councilor-elect, so I couldn't risk getting caught out. But I think we're okay now."

"Well, since you have not practiced today, shall we get to work?"

"Brianna," Vella groaned loud and clear. "I've been awake for ... frig, too many hours to count. And you know I'm not sleeping well."

"All the more reason to train."

"You sound like Alex."

"The vampire? What did he say?"

"He wants to train me in jujitsu—it's something like what the MMC fighters you watch do—"

"Yes."

"And if I said he wants to train when it's practically freezing, you'd say—"

"That practically is different from actually. And I believe this training will complement your Bone Wielder training. Look at the fight in your Druid's club—"

"Damn. Alex said you'd agree with him. Why do you always have to make sense, Brianna?"

"Because I am me. Now, take me in your hands so I can see this room you are in. And then we shall practice your bone wielding. While you should not journey until the bond is settled, you can still physically fight, and you will need to be prepared for our retrieval of Tara."

"You are merciless." But Vella got to her feet and rolled her shoulders.

"And you are a Bone Wielder."

"Yes, yes I am." Vella swallowed a sigh as the charcoal veil dropped over her vision, turning everything black and white again. "All right, what are we training in tonight?"

"How to control me. Becoming proficient in directing your Bone Guide is the most vital step toward becoming the ultimate weapon for the Mors Dicen."

Knock, knock.

"Shit. Someone's here. Putting you under my pillow."

"I doubt it is 'someone' but rather 'your one.' Have you completed the bond yet?"

Vella hid a groan, but at least she hadn't been holding Brianna long, and by the time she opened the door, her vision had returned.

"Quickly, let me in." Matt pushed past her and closed the door just as fast. "I had to fake a phone call to get away from her."

"What do—"

"Am I right?" Brianna cackled. "I am, I know it. But there is to be no fucking around. You are to train, tell him that now."

"Brianna." Vella glared at where the knife lay hidden. If only her Bone Guide could see her expression. "Hush."

"What? I am right and you know it. Now, I am waiting."

"Matt? What's going on?"

"You-know-who was determined to have some one-on-one time of the naked variety. I only just got out of there." He dropped into the armchair by the fire, and a shudder rippled through him. "Gods, at least I can breathe now."

"Well, the other you-know-who is ordering me to tell you we can't fuck around as I have to train."

"No fucking around. Got it." Matt's lips curved. "Mind you, given how angry you were at me earlier ... I doubt fucking around was on the cards. I'm right, aren't I?"

"Pft, you and Brianna are always so smug."

"If we are smug, it is because we are correct. I do like your Matthias more and more."

"Oh, hush," Vella muttered to them both. "Let's get this training over with."

23

Matt couldn't help but eye Vella over the breakfast table. He'd been up since before six a.m., having snuck out of the bedroom while she'd been sleeping, and over the past two hours, everyone else gradually joined him in the parlor, with Vella last.

She wore her floor-length, wide-legged pants, but with a fitted black shirt hugging her curves that had him consciously keeping his gaze on her face, which also meant he kept coming back to the dark smudges, even more pronounced, beneath her eyes. Shit. How could he help her get some sleep? Maybe there was a way as well as magic. He opened his cell phone and made an internet purchase.

"Matthias, always on your cell phone." From the seat next to his, Nevena clucked her tongue at him.

"Just buying a book."

"Ooh, what do you normally read?"

"I don't, really," he lied through his teeth. "But you know how it is with being the boss—you need to be seen to do the things." He shifted his attention to Jamie. "Did I hear you're meeting Vella this morning to look at several prospects for my clubs?"

"Yes indeed. After morning tea in the Marigold Parlor."

"I'd love to join you, but in the meantime, would you have a business room I can set up in? I have some meetings to attend this morning."

"Absolutely. This floor, left wing, you'll find the guest study."

"Thanks. Well, Nevena, that's my morning. What about you?"

"I'd like to see the orchard. I never know what fruit variants I'll find, and I try to get a sample from everywhere I go in the world for future potions. Oh, and Jamie? Did I read there used to be a vineyard here?" She took one delicate nip of toast after another until she'd finished the whole slice without stopping.

Jamie stared at her, then visibly caught himself. "Yes! Where the orchard is now. I had an orchardist visit when we first moved in, and they said it looks to be around a couple of hundred years old. So the vines haven't been here for a long time, I'm afraid."

"What a shame; I'd have loved to see that. But old fruit trees will do just as well. And Vella, what are you up to this morning before meeting with Jamie?"

"Alex has arranged a session out by the pond. To train."

"Train in what?" Matt blurted. Fuck. So much for not showing any interest in Vella around Nevena.

"He's qualified in jujitsu, and I'd like to know how to handle myself in a fight. You never know, especially after what happened at Nocturnal."

"If you're concerned about personal safety, I could make you a potion to knock out an assailant." Nevena leaned forward. "It won't take me long at all."

"Good to know." Vella's smile was the perfect polite, cool Div turning up of lips. "I'll keep it in mind."

"Well, now that we have all our plans for the morning, I'll head to the orchard. Jamie, would you mind if I asked a little more about the history? I can walk with you to your meeting and then head out. Have a lovely morning, everyone." She left them with an easy smile.

"Something is not right there," Vella muttered under her breath as the parlor door closed behind Nevena and Jamie.

"Are you really training with him?" Matt played with the handle of his coffee cup.

"Alex? Yeah, Brianna thinks it's a good idea after what happened—"

"I still can't believe the SI invaded Nocturnal." Matt's jaw tightened as he held on to his anger. "That should never have happened."

"Do you know why?"

"That's what I'm about to talk to Ronin and Shannah about."

"Matt, your eyes." Vella hissed. "The stars are back."

"Shit." He took a deep breath and stared at his hands. *Focus, breathe, control. Focus, breathe, control.*

"You're good." She glanced over her shoulder at the closed door. "That was close."

"I could teach you," he whispered. "To fight."

"Pft. Somehow, I don't think we'll keep our hands off each other if you're teaching me how to fight. Which is why I'll train with Alex."

"You and he must be getting close."

"Turns out we have a lot in common." Vella shrugged. "And I'm going to accept his commission to help with the hotels."

"You can't."

"Yes, I can."

"Not when you're working on my commission."

"Your 'commission' is a sham, so we can do what needs to be done. And after this is all over, I'll need an income, so getting a client like Alex is important."

"Except it's not a sham because you are doing the job," he gritted out. "And if you do another job, others will question why you'd take a smaller role over what I can offer."

"Wait up. Are we talking about the commission here, or something else? You know, it doesn't matter—I said I'd meet Alex and that's what I'm doing. You can keep Nevena out of my way—she's been following me around asking questions, and right now I've zero patience left to deal with her."

"Patience, you? Not something I've seen in you so far, Rapunzel."

"It's *Vella*. And you're right, I'm not a patient person—and I'm not planning on changing. So deal with it."

AN HOUR after wrapping up her time with Alex, Vella pulled her hair into a ponytail and squared her shoulders. Time to meet Jamie in the parlor on the first floor, and figure out where the second aett was hidden.

No question where the yellow parlor had gotten its name. Marigold and buttercup fleur-de-lis bombarded the eyes as they covered every square inch of an even paler yellow wallpaper that wrapped around all four walls, with the pattern and colors even repeated in the upholstery on four utterly charming armchairs and two matching chaises, and the rest of the room fitted out in similar hues. All in all, a warm room with a mix of sunny yellow and gleaming timber—but those weren't what really heated her body.

That reaction was owned by Matt where he sat at the Chippendale-style table with his laptop open, although its screen was off, a dainty teacup raised to his mouth. The picture of masculine grace and ease.

"Where did you disappear to?" he murmured over the teacup.

His hooded gaze tracked each step Vella took into the parlor room, and something ... predatory ... in his movements sent a shiver of awareness through her.

"I had a nap." She stopped short of him. "Why?"

"In the daytime?"

"I know; you're as surprised as I am."

"Actually, it shouldn't be a surprise. I can see how exhausted you are." His voice dropped. "Nightmares?"

"Just the one. But I slept for a good twenty minutes beforehand. I think working with Alex made the difference. Hey, why are you angry at me now?"

"Nothing." He set down the teacup with enough deliberation that Vella knew he was lying, but whatever—he didn't want to tell her, she wasn't probing further.

"So where is Nevena?" Vella ran a finger over the edge of the buttercup coffee cup in front of her. Sarreguemines, 1940s. Stunning, really. And perfectly matched for the room.

"Still in the orchard as far as I'm aware. You know, you should wipe the drool up before you make a mess. So, where's Alex?"

"No idea. I guess doing what vam—he does during the day." She picked up the matching sugar bowl. "And this beauty is droolworthy any day. The entire coffee service is. Sarreguemines, made right here in France. Pretty special that Jamie has a set."

"You really do love ceramics, don't you?"

"I love history, period."

"Have you ever wondered why?"

"I was always drawn to it, I guess. Now, I think it's because I never had a history of my own, and I somehow, subconsciously, recognized that fact. But by the time I was a teenager, it was clear I wasn't going to be of use to the Divs, and I thought the next best thing would be to find a purpose in an area that I enjoyed, and that might also help the coven, like helping them recover powerful arcana." She shook her head as bitterness filled her mouth. "Now? I hate what I did."

"Hey, Vella? Don't be so hard on yourself. You didn't know—"

"But I also never questioned. No, worse than that. I didn't look. I didn't look hard enough."

"You are now."

"But is that enough?" Vella couldn't contain a shiver.

"Enough for what?" Matthias leaned closer.

"You know, after Lucretia told us about the witch trials in the 1600s, I've been reading up on them. Humans used to believe that witches were actually on trial for their sins, and if they were declared a witch, their penance was to die. What will my penance be?" she whispered. "To make amends to everyone I've hurt?"

"Vel? Vella." Matthias jostled her arm. "We all have things we regret—and at no time were your actions done out of malice or intent to harm. Give yourself some credit. But if you want to make penance, then go for it—but find a way that doesn't take you away from your purpose. And those human witch trials? They weren't about sin and penance, they were about power and the ability to hurt the weak. How many of those tortured and killed were innocent? You and I know most of them were never witches, and so what if they were? They were healers and midwives."

"I know that. Rationally, I know all that, but sometimes my head just gets in the way. And I want to do something about it. No, I need to do something about everything I took—"

"*Vella.*" He leaned right into her personal space. So close his body heat rubbed against her icy shell. Tempted her to throw her plan into the fire and fuck Matt's brains out amid the marigold—

"Oh, you're early." Jamie's voice had them spring apart.

"I was just telling Matthias about this coffee set. Sarreguemines, right?"

"Oh, you have a wonderful eye, Vella. I wish I did!" Jamie beamed like she'd just given him an award. "So what do you think of the yellow parlor?" He ran a hand along the timber joinery around the window. "Apparently, they even painted these at one point, and as much as I want to restore the grand old lady to her former glory, that is one move I don't think I'll make."

"At least the multiple hues keep the room from being ... too over the top?"

"I can see you're trying to find something nice to say."

"No, the room is honestly spectacular. And even if I don't want the full décor in my home, I can still appreciate it for what it is—a vignette of a moment in time, probably one hundred and eighty years ago. What you have here really is special."

"You mean that, don't you?" Matt cocked his head to one side as if trying to figure her out.

"Of course. Don't you see the craftsmanship that's gone into making the furniture alone? And it's not just that work, it's a peek into a world we can't imagine, how they lived, what was important to them—like the wallpaper, to still have this hue after all these years ... I'm amazed, actually."

"And it hasn't changed at all. Do you see the sampler?" Jamie pointed at an embroidery piece hanging behind glass on the nearest wall. Other framed works surrounded it, but they were all paintings.

"What exactly is a sampler?" Matt asked, pausing mid-sip with his coffee.

"A very old tradition where young girls would embroider or cross-stitch a design to demonstrate their capability with stitching." Vella joined Jamie by the frame. "And this is a good example. I'm glad it's behind glass to protect it."

"Legend has it that this sampler is never to be moved or a terrible fate will befall the family. So dramatic." Jamie chucked. "Have a look behind the frame—just don't take it down."

Vella did as Jamie said, and sure enough, the vibrance of the wallpaper behind the sampler was exactly like the rest of the room.

She eased the frame back into place and stepped back. "Wow, just saw the date stitched into the edge; the sampler was made in 1697. Do you know what the message reads?"

"Luc translated it for me when we first moved in and started cataloging everything—see the book on the timber wall cabinet? That's where we listed the original inventory of the room when we arrived. I can check to be sure if you want, but I think it says something like 'by the witch's eye, in the sacred vines, two make one, the truth revealed.' Not a particularly great poem, but it came with the house and the legend, so I've left it be."

"I love old pieces like this. Even if the prose and stitching aren't the most amazing things, this right here is a peek into the past."

"Can I tell you a secret?" Jamie leaned in. "One thing I do know is that my ancestors mixed ground crystal fragments into a lot of the art and even the wallpaper—I'm sure that's why it still has such a hue."

"Oh, wow—I didn't know that was something Crystallo witches did." Vella traded glances with Matt and saw the same interest mirrored in his eyes. "Is it a practice still employed?"

"I don't know." Jamie shrugged. "But Luc, my hubby, is coming home tomorrow, and he knows way more than me."

"He's a Crystallo too?"

"Mm-hmm, and actually practices, unlike me. I can't wait for him to meet you—he will be thrilled to meet so many Councilors and representatives."

Really? Somehow, Vella didn't think so, but maybe the French Crystallos weren't as angry as the US and UK covens?

"Well, that sounds lovely. So, there's something here you're thinking of parting with?"

"Before you started talking, yes. I was thinking the tiny table and chairs weren't very useful, but seeing them through your eyes has me rethinking them now."

"I totally understand, and lovely as they are, I don't think they're the type of items that I'd look to furnish Matt's or Alex's establishments with anyway. Although I see some interesting ceramics over in that cabinet, can we check them out? Pieces like that layer in the ambiance."

"Of course. And oh my gosh, please feel free to look at all the small things—they're more dust collectors than anything else. But if there's crystals in them, I'll have to check with Luc—I sold a piece when we first moved in and he went through the roof afterward."

"Oh no. What was it? I'll make sure to keep away from anything similar—no way am I starting a tiff between you and your husband."

"It was a little porcelain dish, with a lovely painted character. The factory was a good name"—Vella almost choked at Sèvres being called a 'good name'—"so I got a great price for it, but Luc was not happy afterward!"

"Ceramics are a passion of mine." Vella stopped at the walnut wood cabinet. A collection of urns and ewers in all sizes stared back at her from behind glass panes.

"I've also got drawers of jewelry if you want to see that. They're in the room up the hallway."

"Thanks, Jamie, but these are perfect for now." Nine pieces in total across the three shelves.

"Are you sure? Some of the gems are truly gorgeous."

"Don't worry," Matthias drawled. "I'm sure she'll look at those as well, but right now she's in her happy place with ceramics. Why don't you show me around a little while we're here? Vella might be happy with the porcelain or china or whatever it is, but I'm more interested in the art."

"Of course." Jamie beamed.

And then, thankfully, they left her alone, and it was just Vella and the cabinet. She eased the door open.

"Can I touch?" she called over her shoulder. "I'd love to look for some maker's marks. I'll handle them professionally."

"Go for it." Jamie's voice floated back as if he'd called over his shoulder too.

"Ooh, *bonjour*," a strange voice murmured from the cabinet. "*Merci de votre visite.*"

Vella's heart leaped. Was that—surely not. She closed the glass door—the voice stopped. Opened it again.

"*Et qui pourriez-vous être?*" the voice continued.

Oh wow. Wow, wow, *wow*. Another Mors Dicen. And of course, lead glass had been used for the doors. And there must be a lead lining around the interior of the cabinet's timber, too.

She leaned closer. Middle shelf, back center, a small ceramic urn had a silver plaque with small pieces of—yes, those were bone fragments!—in a fleur-de-lis mosaic.

She snuck a look at Matt and Jamie. Both stared at a gilt picture frame holding an eighteenth-century depiction of a famous battle. Probably not from the eighteenth century— in fact, the paint looked a little too bright—unless there was more crystal in the pigments?

But no matter, there was no one else around.

She eased the door open again. "Hello," she whispered. "I don't speak French. Any chance you speak English? Who am I talking to?"

"*J'mappelle* Gerard."

"Gerard? Right, I understood that. But the rest? I have no idea what you're saying—"

"Vella? Who are you talking to?" Nevena's voice breezed through the yellow parlor, right behind Vella.

Shit. Vella's heart shoved so hard in her chest that she almost lost her balance.

"Talking to yourself again, Vella?" Matt interjected. He rolled his eyes as he joined them at the cabinet, smoothly drawing Nevena's arm into his. "Remind me never to share a long plane ride alone with an art historian. Can't tell you the number of times I'd think she was talking to me, only to see her looking at a picture in one of her books and realize she had no interest in my attention at all."

"Not want *your* attention?" Nevena laughed. "Now that I find impossible."

Vella forced a laugh, but inside, her heart raced. What were the chances Nevena would realize that Vella had been talking to a dead Mors Dicen witch?

"So this is where I find you all. And what are we doing today?" Alex sauntered into the room, a grin in place. "And wow, so much ... yellow." He gave an obvious shudder.

"Just the usual," Nevena answered. "Vella is talking to herself, and Matthias and I are enjoying ourselves. But don't worry, your Vella is perfectly sane—she often talks to her artifacts, apparently."

Vella's teeth went on edge. Why was Nevena treating her like a child? Was this some ploy to keep Vella off guard? Did she see through Matt's lie and suspect the real truth?

"Well, I may not have the history to compete with all these pretty things." Alex's drawl elongated, teasing out every syllable. "But I'd be happy to listen to you tell me about them just to hear your voice—so talk away, don't let me stop you."

"You two really make the cutest couple. Why don't Matt and I leave you to talk? Matt, darling, I want to discuss an item of Council business anyway, and it's best away from these two young ears. Plus, the room has gotten quite chilly suddenly, and I'd prefer to chat somewhere ... warmer. What do you say?"

"Of course, Nevena." Matt bowed his head. The motion made the snake tattoos up his neck curve, and their eyes flashed. Their tongues flicked.

Vella blinked. What the—she looked again, but the snakes' eyes were back to normal. Their tongues nothing more than delicate, stunning art.

And oh shit, Nevena was right there! Though if she had seen the tattoos move, she gave zero sign of it as she chatted away, hands waving, about her first Council meeting.

Was Matt's magic going haywire again? But Vella was right there, so it shouldn't be the bond causing the issue. Was something else making his magic react oddly?

"As you say," Matthias continued. "Let us find somewhere to discuss business ... alone. And Jamie, perhaps you could bring us something to eat and drink? I'm sure our Councilor-elect would appreciate something"—his voice dropped—"delicious as a refreshment." He didn't even blink in Vella's direction before gesturing for Nevena to precede him out of the room.

Nevena and Matt *alone*? And he was okay with that? Even if Nevena wasn't some asshole Elixir killer—which was still Vella's most plausible suspicion—the woman clearly had a thing for Matthias.

"Vella? What is going on?"

Vella swung back to Alex. "Sorry, I think I should go check ..." Huh. Alex spoke French. "Alex, close the door. Quickly. I need you to translate for me."

24

V ella wrapped up her appraisals of the first-floor rooms just before six o'clock and ran to her bedroom. She *needed* to talk to Brianna. She unlocked the door with the metal key and—

"Hello." Matt sat by the fireplace, coffee cup in hand, the shadows in the room hiding his face.

"Frig." Vella jumped. But then closed the door behind her quickly. "How did you get in?"

"You're not the only one who can break and enter, darling." He eased forward, and the stars in his veins and eyes were dazzling. "I swept for bugs, so we're clear to talk."

"Ew. Darling again? Rapunzel is way better. So?"

"You know, when you scrunch your nose like that, you really are adorable. And so, where to next?"

"How did your 'alone' time go with Nevena?"

"Tediously." He drained his coffee. "You have no idea how much I wish this were a good scotch. Now, how did you go? Alex speaks French, and while I couldn't hear the bones talking to you, I recognize the expression on your face easily enough."

"You knew the bone would speak French?"

"I didn't *know*. But we are in France, and that cabinet looked old—you said so yourself, so the likelihood was high. That's why I got Nevena out of the room. I take it your time alone worked?"

"Matt, good Goddess, yes, it worked! Gerard Duvauchelle, late eighteenth-century Mors Dicen witch. Last spoke with another Mors Dicen around one hundred and fifty years ago—and he knows about the runes!"

"Tell me."

"He was originally from the Thur Valley here in France, near the eastern border, and his family were guardians of one of the aetts! He came to the château as a Bone Guide in 1692 with his great-great-granddaughter, Isobel—the last of their line—when she married into the Crystallo coven family who lived here, a love match apparently. But Isobel died young, along with their sons, sounded like a virus hit the whole household, and Gerard's line died with her. The husband remarried, had more children, but none from the Mors Dicen line."

"So that's why the runes disappeared—the knowledge of them went to the grave with Isobel."

"But Isobel was a guardian of them, whatever that means, so maybe she hid them here somewhere?"

"Did he say anything else?"

"One more thing—and this is important. Apparently, there's a book involved somehow. 'The most terrible book in existence' were Gerard's exact words. They used the book to keep the runes safe. And remember, in his vision, Derrick said the book would be the key. This has to be it!"

"Where is Gerard now?"

"Still in the cabinet. I'm going to ask Jamie if I can buy his urn as a personal piece. I don't think Jamie will be surprised, given my preoccupation with the ceramics he has, although technically, that urn has the least monetary value among his collection."

"And if Jamie doesn't want to sell?"

"Then I'm going to commit theft again." Damn it to the Goddess and back. "This is a life and death matter, not to mention poor Gerard stuck in that cabinet all these years. He needs rescuing, too. But right now, I have to talk to Brianna."

"In that case, I'll stay here. I can watch your back in case you have any unwelcome visitors."

"You already did your bug search. What else do you mean?"

"As in if Nevena pops by. She's been turning up wherever you are."

"I noticed. But I think that's because she's actually turning up wherever you are, and I just happen to be there."

"Vella, why do you think I'm wherever you are?"

"Because we're working together."

"You know better." The shadows might've hidden his gaze, but suddenly the tension in the room exploded, and she couldn't stop herself from walking to him. Stopping at his legs.

The tension in the room seemed to seep into her body. Settle low in her belly. Match the rhythmic beat of her heart. *Pound ... pound ... pound.*

"Rapunzel." He growled her name more than spoke it. The tension in her belly pooled lower. Hotter.

"Matthias," she whispered back.

Knock, knock.

Vella froze

"Vella?" Alex's voice echoed through the door. "Would you have a moment?"

"What is he doing here?" Matt's eyes narrowed.

"No clue. But be quiet when I open the door and stay out of sight in case *she's* hanging around."

His jaw clenched, but he didn't argue, so she eased the bedroom door ajar.

"Alex, how can I help?"

"I am here to see if you need anything before this evening's plans? As your Primus I am good for—"

"No. Nope. I'm good. Just going to do some work here in my room before dinner."

"Shall we train again in the morning?"

"Yeah, sure. Absolutely. Early though. Let's do pre-breakfast." She tried to close the door.

"Good idea." He rested a hand on the door and held it open, a small smile on his lips. "You did well today, and I can see you becoming proficient if you pursue your training."

"Good to know." She took his hand off the door. "Right, I'll see you in the lobby for dinner—we're meeting at seven, right?" This time, she closed the door fully and turned back to Matthias.

"You know if you clench your jaw any tighter, you're gonna break a tooth, right?" She blew out a long breath. "I need to talk to Brianna, so you either stay and don't make a sound, or you can go and join Alex."

VELLA LET the familiar itch of her Mors Dicen magic scratch over her neck. "I've got news," she blurted, pitching her voice low as soon as she opened the window on Brianna's sheath.

"What?" Brianna said in the same volume.

She gave Brianna a fast recap of the information from Gerard.

"Well, this is excellent news indeed. And your next step is so easy."

"It is?" Vella looked at Matthias. He might have had zero clue as to Brianna's words, but he must have picked up on Vella's confusion because his gaze locked on her.

"Everything okay?" he mouthed.

She nodded before responding to Brianna. "So what is this easy next step?"

"Vespera. You are Mors Dicen! You will go to the grave-yard—you told me there is one on the grounds, correct?—and if the deceased Mors Dicen daughter has not reincarnated, ask her where the bone runes are."

"What if something ... odd happens? Like more undead creatures pop up?"

"Why would it? You have bonded ... Oh, Vespera. Seriously?" Brianna's sigh sent a whirlwind through Vella's mind. "You will go to the graveyard and speak with this Isobel if possible. If she has reincarnated, we will find another way. And then ... then you and I will talk. Alone. He is there, is he not?"

Matthias' eyes were narrowed, and who knew what he was making of this conversation right now, but she muttered under her breath, "Yes." Then said louder, "Fine. Graveyard it is."

"What time is it?"

"Just before six, so actually, we won't be able to go for a few hours yet. We're going to dinner in an hour, then we need to make sure everyone's sound asleep. Why do you ask? Crap. We're gonna practice, aren't we?"

"You're learning, Vella. But I will say, congratulations, my Bone Wielder. So much has happened in the past two weeks, but I feel, truly feel, that you are walking the path to success."

"Thanks, Brianna. Have to say, I feel that way too." Vella rolled her shoulders. "All right, let's train."

MATT PROCURED a second knife that Vella could practice with, and after helping move the furniture in her bedroom, sat and watched in silence as she trained with Brianna. Vella gripped the second knife, her legs set in an attack stance, her body tense.

"Matthias, how long do we have?" Vella spoke, but the tone was clearly Brianna's.

"You've been training for twenty minutes, so if we're going to make dinner, you need to wrap up in the next ten minutes for Vella to have time to regain her sight."

"Very good. I shall speak my next comment out loud so you may hear as well. Vespera, I am going to throw this knife at Matthias. You will stop me. Yes, you *can* do this. If you wish to fight as a true Mors Dicen witch—especially for when we rescue my beloved Tara—*you* must be the weapon. You just require the proper motivation, and now, being the excellent trainer I am, you have it. Save your spellcaster from being stabbed in the chest."

"Brianna?" Matt slowly stood. "Do you know what you're doing?"

"I do. Let us see if Vella does."

Vella's mouth tightened, her arm drew back.

Bloody hell.

Adrenaline spiked and Matt tensed, ready to move—her arm stopped. Thank fuck. Getting stabbed wasn't on his plans.

Vella's arm released and she threw the knife. End over end, it whistled through the air. He leaped to his feet, darted left—

Pain sliced across his chest. "Fuck." He shoved a hand to where the blade had glanced across his skin. "You cut me."

"I aimed for your arm," the dry-toned Brianna replied. "If you had not moved, it would have been a mere nick."

"And if you'd told me that first, I wouldn't have moved." He eased his fingers back. Blood ran down his chest. "Shit. This is really bleeding."

"If I had told you, Vella would not have had the proper motivation. No, Vella, it's not bad. And no, I shall not apologize. I am your Bone Guide, and I am more interested in ensuring you have the proper capability than whether your lover loses a little blood. Fine. But we shall train again tomorrow after your session with the vampire."

Moments later, Vella tossed the bone-handled knife onto the bed. "Matthias?" Vella turned slowly, her gaze unfocused.

"Yeah, I'm here. Good to have you back."

"Shit. How bad is it?"

"Well, it's not fun, but it's nothing terrible."

"Do you have a healing spell?"

"Yes, I just need a flame for the spell." Keeping one hand on the wound, with blood running down to his pants, he used his Druid power to strike the flint on the fire and waited till a small flame took hold in the kindling. "With flame the flesh is made anew, bind this wound as if thread to sew, with my words, make this be."

But instead of healing, the pain cut deeper, and more blood ran.

He hissed and pressed more pressure to the slice—now a gash. Damn, he was close to needing stitches.

"What's going on?" Vella was feeling around with her hands, coming toward him.

"My healing spell didn't work. Looks like I'm healing naturally. And watch out—you're about to walk into the fire."

"Shit, thank you. But it didn't work? Why not?"

Good fucking question. "Come to my voice. Yep, I'm here." He grabbed her hand and pulled her to him.

Tiny pinpricks danced over his chest. They gouged deeper, hotter, until a searing pain sliced through exactly where the knife had hit. Oh shit.

"Why did you just whistle?" Vella settled onto his lap. "Are you still bleeding?"

"Not now you're here." The cut had healed over, faster, neater, than any healing spell he'd done before. "So, dinner, then a little graveyard trip?"

"Yep, and we need to tell Alex."

"Why? What does Alex have to do with anything?"

"Because neither you nor I speaks French."

"Right." Bloody hell, did the vamp have to be everywhere?

"Matt? Sure you're okay? You don't sound it."

"Just peachy." Or he would be when one blond-haired vamp no longer needed to be so hands on with Vella, because bloody hell, he was jealous of Alex. Jealous of how much fun they seemed to have. Of how easy they were around each other. Of how Alex could show his affection for Vella openly and honestly.

And while Vella cared for Matt, he had no doubt of that, in her own words, she'd told him she couldn't feel 'more than caring' at the moment ... but what if the reason she *couldn't* feel a deeper level of emotion was because she just didn't love him?

25

M idnight had long since passed when Vella finally led Matthias and Alex past the pond to the little graveyard.

After the knife wound—and Brianna was still on her shit list for that stunt—Matt had snuck to his room, showered and changed clothes, thanks to all the bloodstains. By the time they'd gotten into the village, reports of Darkling sightings had meant no one else was around and the bistro was shut, so they'd gone back to the château where Jamie had offered to cook, and then his husband, Luc, had arrived. Where Jamie was kind and gentle, Luc was distrustful and uneasy—definitely no fan of the Witches Council—and for some reason, Nevena had seemed to take that as a sign to start a frigging PR campaign about the good that the Council did for witchkind.

And now here they were, graveyard-visiting in the middle of the night, with a thick carpet of freezing fog curling around every step, amping up the creepy factor.

Fitting, really. As long as there were no more undead animals—or other things.

Moonlight picked out the lichen on the larger headstones inside the graveyard, and as they approached the low stacked-stone fence, one by one, the hairs on the back of her neck prickled.

Silent. Eerie. And Vella had zero clue if the next shiver that shook through her was from the cold or the fear. Probably both.

"Now what?" Matthias' voice cut through the silence.

"Shit." Vella jumped.

"What?" Alex whirled.

"Nothing. I just—wasn't expecting Matthias to talk."

His silver eyes gleamed in the dark. "You're freaking out, aren't you?"

"How you two aren't, is beyond me. Can we just get this over and done with?" She reached under her shirt and swiveled the window on the sheath open. "Okay, Brianna, we're here. Any advice on how to avoid talking to dead people I don't want to talk to?"

"This is why you practice. But yes, only a Mors Dicen witch can hear you talking unless you are in direct contact with the bone. Should you happen across the bones of someone else, simply don't touch them, and they will not hear you."

"Not a problem. I don't intend on touching any bones here tonight."

"It really is odd, isn't it?" Alex murmured.

"What?" Vella glanced over at him.

"Alex is learning what it's like to hear a one-sided conversation between you and Brianna." Matthias' eyes darkened. "You get used to it. So ... there appears to be a few Isobel De Durand's here."

"Must be a family name."

"Okay, split up and look for the year—there can't be much more than fifty graves. It was the late 1600s, right?"

But Vella didn't need to look. The itching in her neck grew stronger as she crossed to the right side of the grave-yard until she carefully stepped along the narrow pathways to a headstone marked with two coven insignia. "Found it," she whispered.

Matthias and Alex were with her in a second, both far nimbler and faster than she'd been.

"So now what?" Vella whispered again. "How do we know if she'll even hear me beneath all the earth?"

"It depends," Brianna whispered back. Huh. Maybe Brianna was as uncertain as Vella now? "If the witch is buried within a lead coffin—an occasional practice with wealthy Mors Dicen witches to give them their slumber—you will need to raise her bones. And if she has indeed rein-carnated and her soul no longer resides with her bones, then nothing you do matters."

"Right. So we need to dig her up." Vella turned to Matthias. "I think this is where you come in. You moved the earth back at Stonehenge—could you do it here, as well?"

"Of course."

He dropped to his knees and put his hands on the dead ground, but nothing happened.

"Matt? You okay?"

"Just a second." He scowled and shook his hands, then placed them on the ground again. Still nothing. "Fuck."

"Um, Matt? You need a hand at all?"

"Just give me a moment, okay?"

"Sure." She exchanged a glance with Alex, who may have looked confused, although in the dark it was hard to tell.

"Fucking hell," Matthias muttered. "Come on ... yes."

The grave soil caved away from the center out, mounds building high on each side, higher, higher—

"Done," Matthias whispered. Was that sweat on his forehead?

Before she knew it, Vella found herself at his side. "Hey, you okay, Medea?" She put her hand on his arm, and the shudder that went through him made her shake too.

"I am now." He smiled, and the moonlight seemed to reflect in the silver of his eyes. Caught on the rubies in his ear. She leaned closer.

"So, is that what you were after?" Alex's drawl had her freeze. When she faced him, he had an odd look on his face, and his gaze shifted between Vella and Matthias with clear calculation.

Shit. She backed away. Regret shimmied in her belly, and damn if she didn't see it in Matthias' gaze too.

Focus, Vel. Head in the game.

She shone her cell phone torch at the grave. "There's no wood." She peered closer.

"Most timber caskets decompose after several decades." Alex tucked his hands into his pockets.

Vella shot a look at Matthias. He looked as nonplussed as she felt. "Right," she said. "Not sure I want to know that you knew that. Anyhow, Brianna said the coffin might be lead lined."

"Told you," Brianna whispered so softly that Vella could hardly hear her.

"Matthias, you brought the ... wheel-thing, right?"

"Tire lever. Between Alex and me, we should be able to move the lid. He's got super vamp strength, and I've got a spell."

"Great. Uh, Brianna? Will Isobel be decomposed?"

"I do not know. Disturbing hundreds of years old witches is not in my repertoire."

"Mostly," Alex called out. "There'll be bone and hair, maybe teeth. Some fabric, perhaps. No fluids or gases after this length of time, though."

"Again, don't want to know how you know that. Although good news about the bodily fluids and other ... stuff." And he'd called Vella odd?

Matthias leaped down to the coffin, his steps so light he barely made a sound, and Alex followed, without making any noise either.

Man, they were both ... impressive.

Vella's cell phone torch shone on Matthias as he edged the tip of the tire lever under the lid of the coffin. Alex took hold of the level from the other side and pushed as well.

The lid groaned. Creaked. At least she hoped that was the lid.

"Did it move?" she whispered.

"*Il a bougé*," a feminine voice whispered back.

The hairs on the back of Vella's neck prickled all over again.

"Vella?" Matthias called out. "Can you hear anything?"

"Um, yeah. Someone is there—and they're talking. Hold on, she's saying something—"

"*Qui es-tu pour t'immiscer dans mon repos après toutes ces années?*"

"Alex? Help me translate this." She repeated the words the female had said, as best as she could, anyway.

"I think you are being asked 'Who are you to disturb my slumber'—maybe rest?—'after all these years?'"

"Right. Can you tell me how to say 'Hi, sorry to wake you up. I'm Vell—Vespera, fellow Mors Dicen witch.'"

"Tell her you are a daughter of my line," Brianna whispered.

Vella repeated Brianna's instructions and added, "And then say, I need to ask about a set of ancient bone runes that your family were the guardians of, to save them from falling into the hands of an evil motherfucker."

"That's a lot of words," Alex called up out of the grave.

"Let's just try. But chunk it down into easy-to-say parts because I've never spoken French before."

It took time, but finally, they found their rhythm with Alex translating between Isobel and Vella.

"The bone runes were hidden by my grandmother—not even I know where—and she encoded the secret of their location in the most hideous book in her library, a book no witch would ever think to touch, let alone read. But to ensure future generations of our family could locate the bone runes should the need arise, she had a cipher wheel made, with each half given to the eldest son and eldest daughter to safeguard after her passing. My mother then passed her half to me, and when I moved here, I brought my part of the cipher wheel with me."

Oh shit. Another puzzle? Vella's heart sank, but still, a clue was better than nothing. "Do you recall where you hid your half?"

"Beneath the chapel, in the caves where I always felt so at home. Mors Dicen love the earth, after all."

"Thank you." Vella's breath whooshed out. At least they were close by. "Do you know anything at all about the other half?"

"I do not, I am sad to say."

Damn. They were so close to figuring out the location.

"However, when our household became deathly ill, I could not risk the secret of our aett being lost forever, so I wrote my cousin a note requesting from him a single line that would enable our future descendants to locate the cipher wheels. I never saw his response, but before my passing, I asked my husband that if a response ever arrived, that he would have an embroidered sampler made incorporating a poem I had written along with my cousins' words, and to ensure it hung forevermore in our home."

"A sampler? I remember seeing one when we took the tour. Jamie—your husband's many-times-removed grandson—showed it to me and told me a legend about it never being allowed to leave the wall."

"Then he did it! Vespera, you have lifted such a weight from this day. I thank you."

"What about the book?" Matt called out. "Vella, ask her if she knows where that is."

"Here in my home, in our library. But be warned, it is the most awful book known to witchkind. We used it as our code-keeper for this very reason, as no witch would want even to touch its hideous pages."

A hideous book? "Um, do you remember the book's title?"

"*The Malleus Maleficarum.* Known as the—"

"*Hammer of Witches.* Yeah, I've heard of it. And I know why you call it awful." Vella didn't need to hide her shudder. That book has been used to persecute witches for centuries.

"That evil man pretended to prescribe such ways to prove our brethren witches, but in truth sought coin and power and cared nothing for those he inflicted such pain upon."

"It is vile, but I can see why your grandmother used it as a hiding place. Isobel, thank you so much. You have possibly saved all witchkind with your information tonight. But may I ask, why all the secrecy in your time?"

"For our safety. For everyone's safety. Our coven was persecuted, Vespera, daughter of Brianna. There were some among the Divinators who pretended not to be witches, while pointing witch hunters at others of our kind, starting with our coven. Those Divinators played at court, standing in the shadows of the human rulers while whispering in their ear of futures that would bring the Divinators money and power themselves. They lied and called us practitioners of unnatural magic who used blood to deepen our bonds and tie souls to our bones in evil rituals. They sowed distrust and fear even among witchkind, making us hated, when all we wanted was to live our lives as the universe intended, making magic born from the earth and connecting to our ancestors through the bone."

"Isobel. It sounds so much like how it is now. And what about the Mors Dicen, were there many in your days?"

"We were few, but our hearts beat strong in many lands. I do recall traveling to Ireland, to visit the scarce Mors Dicen relatives I had, shortly after my marriage. While there, I saw the breathtaking armory of our forebearers, and when one of my relatives grew ill, they took them to the wellspring of our power to save her. I journeyed with them."

Oh wow. Wow, wow, wow. Vella grabbed Matt's hand. "Isobel, do you ... do you recall where the wellspring was?"

"From the village of Galway, we traveled for three days and nights to the northeast to reach the place. But more than that, I know not. Vespera?"

"Yes?"

"Are you really here to take charge of the bone runes?"

"Yes, I mean, I'm here to make sure they don't fall into the hands of anyone bad."

"Then I thank you. I was never a Bone Wielder, but all these years I kept myself from reincarnating, awaiting the day a witch of our coven would find me and seek the bone runes. Vespera, daughter of Brianna, do not let them fall into the hands of anyone wishing to do harm. In my family, we know of an ancient prophecy that says one day, a witch will hold all the runes and stand at the wellspring of our magic, and on that day, the fate of *every* witch, every magical being, will be sealed."

Oh shit. "Was that fate good, or bad? Isobel? Can you hear me?" Vella held her breath. Waited.

"Bone Weidler," Alex called. "Do you need another translation?"

"No," Vella whispered. "Isobel has gone. For good."

———

26

After closing Isobel's coffin and refilling her grave, Matt walked beside a very quiet Vella, Alex silent behind them, through the rising mist to the edge of the crumbling chapel ruins.

"Jamie did say that his family kept their prized possessions here," Matt murmured. "But how do we get under this pile of rocks?"

"No clue," Vella whispered, her breath fogging the icy air.

"Here, I'll warm you up." Matt connected with his Druid power and warmed the air around her.

"It's even colder." Vella's teeth chattered. "Thought you ... were warming it?"

Fuck. Twice in an hour his Druid power had come out wrong. Why? He was with Vella—shit, they were shoulder to shoulder, so his power should be working.

Focus, breathe, control. Focus, breathe, control. Heat the air, heat the air, heat the—

"That's better. Thank you." But she still didn't smile.

"Vella? Is everything okay?"

"No. Not really. I can't stop thinking about Isobel's words. How the Divs used our coven's—yes, Brianna, I know, I said 'our'—rituals to demonize us. And how Ellaine did the same thing twenty years ago, and if we let her, will keep doing it. But how do I fight not just years, but centuries of disinformation?"

"Is that what you want?"

"I guess ... yes. Yes, I do. And yes, Brianna. I agree, we deserve to live our lives how we want as well." She shuffled her feet and—

Vella fell backward.

Matt darted to catch her arm, but before he reached her, Alex was there, supporting her back, and together they eased her back onto her feet. Matt kicked at the mist, the movement swirling the air enough to see a stone at Vella's feet before the mist resettled, obscuring it from sight again. Shit, this was dangerous.

Alex muttered. "Vella cannot see where to step with the mist at knee height."

"We are in agreement there." Matt frowned at the nearest pile of collapsed stones.

"Hey, you two? I can see it's dangerous but don't talk about me like I'm not here. I'll be careful. Yes, Brianna, I'm okay. No, I'm not holding you—I can't see when I let you go, remember?" Vella looked around. "If there really is a clue to the second aett beneath our feet, I'm not leaving it one second longer than necessary." Fierce determination filled her expression. "So, let's do this."

Gods but she was amazing. "Vella, as anyone ever told you how incredible you are?"

"No."

Matt froze, floored by the simplicity of her response. "You're telling the truth, aren't you?"

"I can taste her blood if you wish to verify—"

"No!" Matt and Vella said at the same time.

But Alex's gaze stayed on Vella's neck, and there was no mistaking the intent in the vamp's eyes.

Protect. Mine.

Instinct shoved everything else aside, and Matt stepped in front of Vella, a growl escaping.

"Ah, there he is." Approval entered Alexander's gaze, and he backed up, raising his hands. "You *do* wish to be her Primus. You know this means you must be able to protect her and make decisions that are in her best interest; otherwise, that is a role I am prepared to take."

Fucking gods. A Primus did more than just defend their mates.

Instinct roared through Matt again, and this time he tracked to his left, keeping himself between Vella and the vamp. Just a little closer and he'd be ready to strike.

"Vella is more than capable of looking after herself," Matt murmured. Voice low, soft, unthreatening. Stepped closer still. Repositioned his body angle when the vamp countered his move. Was he onto him? "But if you think I won't fight to defend her with every part of my being, when she does request my help, you are dead wrong."

He lunged. Grabbed Alex by the throat and used the wind to lift him high. Bared his teeth and let every ounce of the danger he represented show on his face. "Threaten to bite her again, motherfucker, and you'll see exactly how *I* fight."

"This I like to see." Alex grinned. "And while I believe the Bone Wielder has selected you over me, I shall remain ready to step up—in *every* way—should she need."

"Fucking hell you will." Wind roared, and the vamp slammed back to the ground.

"Shit! Matt, what the hell?" Vella ran to the vamp and helped him to his feet. "And Alex, what the frig are you doing?" She whirled and stared at them both. "You two dial back the ... testosterone, or whatever is going on here right frigging now. Didn't you hear what Isobel said? The three aetts need to be kept safe for the fate of us all—witchkind, vamps and shifters. That means we focus on getting *them*, not fighting each other over nothing. Got it?"

Matt glared at Alex, but then Vella's hand slipped into his and everything within him ... soothed. Bloody hell but she really did calm him. He took a breath, and her scent filled his lungs.

The urge to murder the vamp receded.

"At least it's warm again," Vella muttered.

"I shall stay here," Alex muttered. "Stand guard in case anyone approaches."

"My apologies, Alex," Matt murmured. "I shouldn't have—"

"You did exactly as I hoped you would. I wished to see a demonstration of your ability, given you are who she has chosen. And it is the truth I can be better used as a lookout up here."

"And I appreciate Vella has another who is willing to get hurt to see to her safety."

"Seriously?" Vella yanked her hand from his. "You two are unreal. I'm tempted to find the second aett on my own at this stage."

"No need." He caught her arm and brought her back to his side. "Let's find this cipher wheel. And, Vella? For what it's worth, I think you are the most amazing person I've ever met. And it's not the bond talking. I've been in awe of you from the moment we met, and you just keep proving why, over and over." He squeezed her hand.

"Thank you." Vella's frown gradually eased to a small smile, and when she squeezed his hand back, relief sang through him.

"I can try one more thing, though." Using his Druid power again, he sent a breeze through the mist to clear a path around their feet. Thank fuck it worked this time. "And look at the stones rising in the east corner—they look thicker than the rest of the wall."

"The original staircase?"

"Possibly. If it were a staircase, maybe it went above *and* below."

They picked their way through the ruins, stepping only where the mist parted until they reached the corner.

"Can you make anything out?" Vella let his hand go and touched the nearest rock.

"Only that the stones have totally collapsed. But I can try to move them ... if they're stable enough. Stand back—if this falls in, I don't want you caught near them."

Once Vella was safely out of range, he knelt and, with both hands, touched the rocks. He had to let the wind go that was keeping the mist at bay and instead felt for the earth ... Steady. Impermeable. Solid. Ageless. And connected.

One by one, he willed the stones to move like a giant Jenga puzzle, until enough were shifted to reveal a staircase descending into pure darkness.

"Here, I think we'll need this." Matt stood up and called his witchlight spell, holding his hand out to illuminate the steps. "It's a spiral staircase. Want to lead the way?"

"What? You don't like caves?" But she didn't hesitate before starting down them.

"It's more I know you *do*."

They made a complete spiral before the steps opened to a tunnel leading off on a slight decline.

"Are you still comfortable in the lead?"

"Absolutely. I'm loving this." She grinned at him over her shoulder before continuing. "Although, if this is a phobia, you know it's perfectly fine."

"Believe me, darling Rapunzel, I have one phobia, and this isn't it."

"Ooh, the mighty Magicae has a phobia? Do tell." The tunnel opened up into a cavern, easily thirty feet wide, with what looked like smaller caverns leading off in the distance. "Frigging hell," Vella breathed. She ran a hand over the wall. "This is all hewn from the rock. And wow, those are tree roots. Do you think we're under the orchard?"

"Based on the direction we've been walking, I think we are. And look above the next cavern." He raised his hand so the witchlight illuminated a crescent moon with the crystal stem carved into rock. But he didn't need to enter far to know what was inside.

"Wine bottles?"

"Jamie did say that was their treasure. Let's see the next cavern."

"Matt! It's a skull and sword." Vella darted in front of him and ran her hand over the carving. "The Mors Dicen insignia." Her face lit up. "That has to be the place."

"Okay, okay. Don't get too excited. Let me use the witch-light first." He held his hand out—

"Matt? Matthias? What's wrong?"

"Uh, Vella?"

Something in Matt's tone had Vella go on high alert, and she spun back to him. "You don't look so good. What is it?"

"There are spiders here," he gritted out.

"The ones up there? Those cobwebs?"

"You know how I said I had one real phobia?"

"No way! I mean, I got you weren't a fan of them back in New York, but an actual phobia?"

"It's the way they crawl. Their legs ... just ... shit." He shook as if a shiver had crept over him. "I have to go in there, don't I?"

"No." Yes. "I mean, I've got my cell light for a torch, so you don't have to go in—you're teasing me, right? This is a joke—oh shit, your face. This isn't a joke. You really don't like spiders."

"Let's just get this over with."

"Do you need to hold my hand or something? What kind of reaction do you have?"

"My knees feel like they're made of jelly, and sometimes I ..." Matt turned away.

"What? I missed what you said."

"I said I freeze up, okay?"

"You know that most spiders don't want to actually hurt you, right? They're more afraid of you than you are of them —well, most times, anyway. And look—these appear to be some kind of orb weavers. They aren't even poisonous, although yes, they can bite, but it won't do more than hurt for a while—okay, just hold your light up, don't touch anything and I'll do any searching near spiders or cobwebs."

Oh shit. Spiders filled the cave. Cobwebs blanketed almost every rock from the floor to the ceiling.

"Do you know how special cobwebs are?" Vella kept her tone conversational.

"I have no idea what you're talking about."

"Arachnoidal structures have a value that goes far beyond what most people know. I read this paper on them while I was at university." She launched into a recital of everything she could recall.

"Okay, you can stop talking now. I'm not going to freeze or faint."

"You were going to pass out?"

"I told you my knees went to jelly—"

"I thought you meant you'd have to sit down or something, not that you'd frigging drop to the floor. Shit, Matt. You need to work on that."

"No. *We* need to find the cipher wheel and get out again before some crazed pack of spiders attacks, sinks their fangs into us, creeps over us with their spindly legs and then turns our insides into soup before drinking us dry."

"Wow, that was ... detailed. Although technically, a group of spiders is called a cluster when they're tightly packed. When they're more spaced out, they're called a clutter. Cute, right? Hey, you don't have to scowl at me. I'm just helping you understand arachnoids—right, well, if you can just make the light a bit brighter?"

"Good call."

"Wow, that's bright, all right. I think a medium glow would've been enough; it's like a star burst into existence right here." Vella shielded her eyes.

"Less complaining, please, Rapunzel, and more looking."

"I don't think we can see anything through all the cobwebs. We might need to feel ... *I* might need to feel around."

"And get bitten? How about I do a flame-thrower spell and we wipe them out?"

"No! These spiders haven't hurt you or me, and there is

no way under the good Goddess's sun or moon I'm letting *you* hurt *them*. Just stand there with your light and let me work on this. Arachnoidal structures all have something in common ... and if I'm right, the cobwebs on the back right wall protrude further into the cave than the others."

"Shit, you're right. But it's also big enough for you to walk in. What spider would make that?"

"Not one. Lots and lots ... Hey, lean on me. No, don't sit —there's a nest of webs."

"Fuck." The light wobbled.

"Shit, you're losing control, right? Stay here. Be right back." Vella darted for the web at the back of the cave, scooped up the mass in large circular motions around her arm, a giant swirl of spider-filled super-sticky cotton candy, and within moments, the secret of the cave was revealed.

"Yes! Matt, I see something." Vella eased through the gap she'd made in the web and, on a natural ledge in the rock, found a small, blackened box all on its own, as if the spiders had been hiding it. What clever spiders! "Coming out—"

The echoes of Matt's retches filled the cave, louder than her shout of success.

Back in the main cavern, Vella held up the box. "I've got it!"

"You still have ..." Matt gestured at her arms.

"Hey, sweeties. You can't hitch a ride with me." She picked off two spiders crawling up her arms and walked them back to the spider cave.

Matt stared at her arm before visibly shaking himself. "Do you want to open it here or back at the château?"

"Pft. No way are we waiting a second longer." Holding her breath, she unhooked the small latch and lifted the lid.

A metal disc, roughly the size of her palm, sat in the box. Vella's breath whooshed out. How incredible.

"Those are letters etched around the edge, right?" Matt leaned closer.

"Yeah. I'm going to get it out. Can you hold the box in your other hand?" With great care, she eased the disc out, and tingles shivered up her arm. "Wow," she breathed. "The center is hollowed out, and look at the patina on the metal. It's beautiful. How amazing to think this is hundreds of years old, made by hand, and based on the weight, I'd say brass." Excitement bubbled up, made her chest go tight. She rubbed her thumb over the indent. "There's something else here."

Matt let out a low whistle. "It's the skull of the Mors Dicen insignia without the sword."

"We found it! We really are on the right path. Now we just need to find the book and work out where the second half of the cipher wheel is."

"At least we know the book is here. I might lead the way out, if that's okay with you?"

Vella couldn't help but laugh. "Matthias Medea, you can go first. I'll guard your back from the itty-bitty spiders."

"There were millions of those itty-bitty spiders. They

could have swarmed and overrun you, and you'd have been spider stew in a minute."

They reached the spiral staircase way faster than it had taken to come down the tunnel.

"Swarmed." Vella shook her head as they reached the main castle ruins. "I don't think you know how spiders work. And also, ew—spider stew? You really have spent way too long—

"Vella! Matthias!" Alex's urgent whisper preceded him by moments. "Nevena is in the orchard, talking to someone. I didn't stop to see faces, but they appeared to be male, six-foot, with yellow hair. I came to get you right away."

"Oh shit. Why? And who would meet her here?"

"Fuck." The glow of Matt's witchlight flickered. "What the hell is she up to? Okay, Alex, can you go back and find out who she's talking to? Vella and I will take the long way to the chateau, around the other side of the lake, to make sure she doesn't see us."

Vella's stomach dropped. Frigging hell, what was Nevena up to? And who was the yellow-haired man she was meeting? What if her meeting was to do with Matt's death threat?

27

Bloody hell. What had Matt missed? Who was Nevena talking to, and why in the middle of the night, in the orchard?

Calling a spell to hide the sound of their footsteps, he clasped Vella's hand tightly and together they jogged in silence all the way back to the château and into Vella's room.

"What is she doing?" Vella went straight to her window and peered out. "And who would she be meeting?"

"Two questions that must be answered." What if Nevena was in France for more than one reason ... "Fuck."

"What?"

"Vella, Ellaine insisted on Nevena coming to France, but what if Nevena was never here for the bone runes ... or not only the bone runes?"

"As in she's who Ellaine ordered to kill you?"

"Not just that either. Historically, the Divs sent Elixirs out into the world for one reason only—to kill. But Ellaine has another goal in France right now besides finding the runes and killing me off. She's trying to build a Div Tower in Paris, but she's facing a lot of local resistance. I need to call

Ronin; he's been hacking Ellaine's communications to identify her plans. I'll see if he's found anything relating to Nevena and Paris."

He put his cell phone on speaker, but set the volume low, and Ronin answered within one ring.

"Thank fuck," Ronin said before Matt could say a word. "Hold on, I'll get Shannah. Vella's bird is going loco in her bedroom, and Shannah was trying to calm her." The line went quiet.

"They're at Arcane Antiquities? And with Morrigan?" Vella's eyes went wide. "What's going on?"

"No clue."

"We're back." Ronin's voice came through the speaker again. "Matt, are you with Vella?"

"I'm here." Vella crossed the room and grabbed Matt's arm. "Why? Is something wrong?"

"Vella, have you heard anything from Sara?" Shannah's voice echoed into the room, threaded with a level of concern Matt rarely heard from his strong, capable cousin.

"What? Why?" Vella grabbed the rear pocket of her jeans and took out her cell. "Nothing. What's going on?"

"Sara's gone," Shannah replied.

"Hold on, I'm calling her now. Shit, voicemail. Sar? It's Vel. Call me back right away. As in as soon as you get this." Shit. Shit, shit, *shit*. Vella punched the end-call button. "Shannah, what happened? What do you mean by 'gone?' As in she's left town?"

"Sara went back to the shop this morning, said she had something there to do with a client, and we agreed I'd meet up with her this afternoon when she was finished at Sylvie's. Well, Sara called me fifteen minutes ago and said that as soon as she got there, Ellaine arrived and demanded she go with them to Div Tower."

"What? Why—"

"Vella, let Shannah talk. Shannah?"

"Apparently, Ellaine told Sara that she'd a vision of your imminent death, and if Sara wanted to know what it was, she had to sit in on a reading with her and Derrick, and she had the bone runes."

"She blackmailed Sara into doing the reading?" Vella dropped onto the bed. "*The* bone runes?"

"Sara thinks so. Vella, Sara said she heard a voice from the bones, but then Ellaine did the reading and divined the location of a family of witches. As soon as the reading was over, Ellaine told Sara the vision about you had changed and you were fine, then she and Derrick left, and basically locked Sara in the reading room until someone came and let her out hours later."

"What?" Vella went still. "They fucking locked her in—"

"Shannah. What family? Did Sara say what Ellaine was after?"

"A Crystallo witching family named Allard."

"Fuck. You said this happened this morning? How long ago now?"

"From what we know, maybe six hours. Why?"

"What about Sara?" Vella grabbed Matt's arm. "I don't know who these Allards are, but if Ellaine took Sara once—"

"Shannah, what about the tracker we've got on Sara?"

"She took her purse, good news there. Ronin's tracing her now."

"Okay, as soon as Ronin confirms her location, you go after her. Ronin, I need you to stay focused on Nevena. She's up to something here, and we need to know what."

"Of course."

"Wait." Vella leaped up and grabbed his cell phone. "Shannah, did Sara say anything else?"

"Just that she needed to fix something."

"Thank you!" Vella hit redial on her cell. "Come on, Sar. Pick up ... pick up ..." Sara's voicemail message echoed into the room. "Shit. Shannah, did Sara say *what* she needs to fix?"

"Nothing. But, Vella. I'll find her, promise. And Sylvie is helping too; she and Tannis are out looking for her now."

"Shannah, I'm hanging up now to call Ruby. Get me an update on Sara's location as soon as you have it. And, Shannah? Thank you."

"I fucked up, Matt. I shouldn't have let her stay there alone."

"No one saw this coming, Shannah. Believe me. But I should've—and that's on me, not you. Just be safe, please. Whatever the hell is going on, I don't like this one fucking bit."

Matt gently took his cell phone from Vella and ended the call.

"Matt?" Vella's heart pounded so fast she imagined it racing out of her chest, but she somehow kept her voice steady. "Who are these Allards? What does this have to do with Sara? What does she need to fix?"

Vella: Sar, please tell me you're okay.

Vella: You don't have to answer my call if you don't want. Just let me know you are getting this. Please.

> Vella: Also, what happened with the reading? Shannah said something about someone named Allard and there's a witch here with that surname

VELLA STARED AT HER CELL. What was Sara doing? Was she okay? Three little dots appeared beside Sara's name on Vella's cell.

"She's replying!" Vella held her breath.

> Sara: There's Allards there? If they're Crystallos, you have to get them somewhere safe. Maybe Madgewick—you said it was protected there?

> Sara: And stop calling. I won't answer. It's my fault, Vel. I led Ellaine to them at the reading, and I have to do something to help now

> Vella: What do you mean led Ellaine to them?

> Sara: In the reading, E asked where witches with a last name of Allard from the Crystallo coven would be in the future. Why would she do that unless it's for some fucked up reason? I looked up all the local Crystallo Allards as soon as I got my laptop and found the nearest. I'm on the way there now.

> Vella: WTF? No. If E is after them then she could be there too. You have to go back to Sylvie's. Now.

> Sara: Morrigan is in your room. Tell Sylvie so she can let her out
>
> Sara: Muting chat now BBL

"BE BACK LATER? Fucking hell. Fuck, fuck, *fuck*." Vella stared at her cell. "Ellaine is after Crystallos now? Why?"

"I'm calling Ruby." Matt punched something into his cell.

"Matt?" Councilor Ruby's thin voice wavered into the room. "I don't have time—"

"I'm sorry, Ruby, but you need to hear this. There's a credible threat against one of your families—"

"It's too late," she whispered. "Our crystals resonated with their departures from this world already. I have to go."

"Wait—why?"

"Because they openly resisted building her tower." The line went dead.

"Sweet Goddess," Vella breathed. "They were killed because they dissented to the Tower going up?"

"Ellaine will have come up with some BS reason." Matt's hand clenched around his cell phone to the point his knuckles went white. "For the good of witchkind. Gods but I fucking hate this. We need to stop them."

Vella's mind whirled. Sara. The aetts. The murderous motherfucker who had to be stopped.

"We have to get the runes," Vella whispered.

"And we will, I promise. We'll work out what the clue means—"

"No, not the second aett. The bone runes that Ellaine has right now." Determination filled her up—to stop Ellaine fucking with her and Sara, from going after any other witches. From using Mors Dicen bones to ever hurt anyone ever again. "Those are the runes we need to get. She's too dangerous with them."

"I'll get the jet on standby. But let's get to the library now and get the book so it's safe."

"Good point—"

"Shh." He grabbed her hand. "I hear ..." His face drew tight. "Fuck, someone's screaming. Downstairs." Matt took off, and Vella followed him out of her bedroom.

By the time they reached the stairs, the screams were loud enough for Vella to hear.

"They're coming from outside," Matt called as he leaped down the last steps and ran across the lobby to the entry. He flung the doors open—

Nevena and Jamie staggered toward them, and her gaze latched onto Matt like a lifeline.

"Darklings. Run," Nevena cried out before crumpling to the ground.

Jamie fell to his knees, bloody slashes were visible through his jacket sleeves, and more slices crossed one cheek, but his eyes stayed open, and he didn't topple any further.

But the blood ... so much blood.

"You help Jamie, I'll take Nevena." Matt reached them first.

"Here." Vella got one arm under Jamie's. But with so much blood, she couldn't see where he was injured. "Where can I touch you?"

"Underarm ... okay." But even so, Jamie hissed when she put an arm around him, and the sticky wetness seeping through his shirt could only be one thing.

"Here we go. Heading to that chair there." Vella eased back, using her shoulder to do all the lifting, and together they staggered to their feet and shuffled toward the nearest seat. "I'm going to ease you down; there you are. I need to take your jacket off to see your cuts."

"How is ... Councilor Nevena?" Jamie let out a cry as she freed his arms.

Oh shit. They didn't look deep, but there were so many, and blood dribbled from them all.

"Unconscious." Matt stood; his lips compressed and the fury in his eyes said everything.

Nevena had to be involved in the death of the Allards; now her life hung in Matt and Vella's hands. And based on Matt's expression, he wasn't going to do a single thing.

"Please help her," Jamie gritted out. "She saved me. I'd be so much worse if not for her. And I need to call Luc. He's coming home soon, but it's not safe."

Vella took Jamie's cell and ran over to Matt. "I need to stop the Darklings—"

"Go. I'll call Luc and use my magic to help Jamie. You stop *them*."

Vella raced outside and ran for the Darklings.

28

B undled beneath the blankets in her bedroom, Vella's chest had been rising with even, steady breaths for a good hour before Matt could breathe easily again himself. What a fucking nightmare.

Knock, knock.

Alex entered the room, his worried gaze going to Vella before finding Matt where he sat in the chair by the window.

"No sign," Alex whispered.

"Damn. Wonder where they are? And thank you for doing that. I didn't want to take my eyes off Vella in case she frigging disappeared again or went and called more—well, you know. Any word from Sylvie?"

"Good news. She and Shannah caught up with Sara in Camden, up in Maine. Apparently, she was on her way to a Crystallo family there."

"The tracker worked. Thank fuck."

"Actually, no. Sara dumped her purse—they found it at a truck stop north of the city."

"She what?" Shit. Ronin must've been loco. "Then how—"

"Shannah said Morrigan had gotten out of Vella's bedroom and basically led Shannah and Sylvie to Sara."

"Thank fuck for Morrigan, then." And Sara's safety would mean one less worry for Vella when she woke.

"Agreed. Now, I need to clean up all the blood downstairs. It's rather tempting, and I don't wish to be hungry here."

After Alex left, Matt placed more wood on the fire and continued a steady stream of Druid power to spread the warm air through the room.

But he was still so attuned to Vella that he registered the change in her breathing pattern moments later, and when he turned around, her face contorted, and she started to writhe under the blanket.

Shit. The nightmare.

He eased onto the bed and soothed her hair back from her forehead. "Vella, you're dreaming. Vella? Can you hear me?"

"Matt!" She bolted upright.

"Hey, Rapunzel. You're safe. I'm—"

She launched herself into his arms.

"Let me guess, the nightmare?" he eventually murmured into her hair.

She nodded and burrowed into him, her breathing still shaky. "It's awful."

His own exhale whooshed out, but he just sat there until her breathing had evened and the shaking stopped.

"Want to talk about it yet?" he murmured. "I've been reading about trauma and nightmares ... Turns out sometimes talking about the actual events in the dream can help."

"Thanks, but I'm okay now." She tightened the embrace briefly, then let him go. "The hug helped, though."

In an effort to banish the empty feeling in his arms and chest, he stood and pretended to restoke the fire before turning back to her. "So, how are you feeling?"

"My stomach feels like I drank an entire bottle of whiskey all by myself." She winced and looked around the room. "What time is it?"

"Six-thirty. You've been asleep here for over an hour."

"Six—oh shit, Sara! Is there any news? Where's my cell? I'll call her again."

"Sit back, it's okay. Sara is fine. Sylvie and Shannah found her and are taking her to the lake house." He explained everything that Ronin had told him, including Morrigan's involvement.

"Morrigan did that?" Vella's eyes welled, but she scrubbed them dry. "Okay, that's good. Sara's good. What about everyone else? How is Jamie? What did you do with Nevena? And damn, I am so sick of blacking out and waking up in a bed."

"Jamie's doing well. Got an update from Luc not long ago. Jamie is being discharged shortly, but Nevena has been transferred to a larger hospital in Paris."

"So she's alive?"

"Jamie is adamant she saved his life, and when I tried to use my magic on him, he got so upset I had to stop and do the minimum to keep her alive. Fuck, but I hope that was the right call."

"She really did save him? But he's a Crystallo *named* Allard. Can we trust her or not? And the Darklings ..." Vella froze.

"Do you remember what happened?"

"I kept inhaling them, but they were spread everywhere

over the estate, and I've got zero clue where I ended up when they were all gone, except I was walking for ages trying to find my bearings, and Brianna suggested letting her help, so I opened the window for her to see through my eyes, and then everything went blank."

"Alex had followed whoever Nevena was talking to, but lost them up at the road, and by the time he got back to the château, Luc had arrived, and the ambulances, and once they were all gone, Alex and I went out looking for you."

"Where was I?"

"We found you just beyond the graveyard." The memory of *how* they'd found her sent a fresh wave of unease through him.

"Um, why did you just ... shudder? What happened, Matt?"

"You were unconscious, to start with. That was freaky enough. But you were also surrounded."

"Oh no. More undead rats?"

"Some. And foxes—small dogs—maybe? And ... there were humans there too. Not sure how long they'd been dead, but definitely human."

Vella's eyes went round. "Humans? What. The. Fuck?"

"That's more or less what we said. We finally got past them, and that was hard, but every time we moved you, they followed."

"Wha—where are they now?"

"We had to go a really long way to get back here, but eventually"—a long fucking time later—"we lost them. I cleaned you up, and you've been out ever since."

"Matt! They're still there—"

"Not exactly. Alex went back out to watch in case they came here, but there's no sign at all."

"But that means they could still be out there, doing ... whatever undead things do."

"Yeah. But they haven't followed you here yet, so that's a good thing. And Derrick also messaged. Word of the attack landed in New York just after we got you back here, but I reassured him you were resting and not cut into ribbons. You know, I detected a genuine sense of ... concern from him? You will need to call and reassure him yourself, as of course, he didn't trust me at all."

"And Ellaine? Any inquisition there yet?"

"Not directly, but Derrick mentioned she's unhappy due to having no updates for the past forty-eight hours."

"Yikes. Not even any concern for Nevena? And hold on, Nevena ..."

"What are you thinking, Rapunzel?"

"I have an idea for Alex."

Matt could feel his hackles rising but managed to grit his teeth instead of growling. "And that is?"

"You had him watching me for days, right?" Matt nodded slowly. "Well, he's obviously good at staying hidden because I never saw him until I journeyed to the park. So maybe ... maybe he could watch Nevena and see what's going on there? She might not be the evil bitch we thought, and instead just be polished and articulate and sleek and—" Everything Vella wasn't. "Or she's in this up to her eyeballs. Either way, I don't trust her at all. And I think we need to be certain."

"Good idea. Let's go tell him he has a new mission."

"You agreed pretty fast there, Medea. Want to tell me what your problem is with him?"

His problem? Matt tunneled a hand through his hair. Frustration and embarrassment bit at him equally, but at least he could be honest about his feelings here.

"I'm jealous, okay. Jealous that he's training you, jealous that you smile around him. That you sleep after working out with him. That he can get his hands on you, and I can't."

"What—why didn't you say anything?"

"Because it doesn't change anything, okay? I need to pretend to the world that I don't care for you when you know that's not true. And it cuts me. Gods, but it cuts me."

"Matt. I am so sorry." Vella dragged in a shaky breath. "I hate this," she whispered.

"Just … just tell me one thing. Do you feel something for me, Vella? I know we have a fucking world to save, and that we don't always agree on the *how*, but regardless of all that, I have to know if you actually feel something, not only as a friend, or only as the witch helping save your sister, but a man you want to pursue a relationship with once this is all over."

"Matt." Her breath hitched. "Of course I do! Yeah, I wish the timing was different and that we didn't need to convince every-fucking-one else that we don't feel anything for each other—but I will do that, Matthias Medea, because your life is too important for me not to. And yes, I'm also struggling with my emotions, and that makes it hard to even talk about this. But—" She took his hand and pressed her lips to his palm. "I care."

"Bloody hell." He hauled in a shuddering breath. "I needed to hear that. Okay, so before the Darkling episode, we were going back to New York. And while yes, I agree we need to get the bone runes away from Ellaine, without you or Sara, she can't use them. So right now, Nevena is in the hospital, you and Sara are out of Ellaine's grasp, and you and I have a strong lead on the second aett."

"You think we should go for it?"

"I do. And the jet is still ready—we just need to figure

out where the next half of the cipher wheel is, and then get the book."

"The book—and the sampler! Have you looked for them?"

"Vella, I wasn't leaving your side for anything. The whole world could've been burning, and I was staying right here, watching over you."

"Oh." Her lioness eyes turned a molten gold, and the bloom of her arousal hit the air.

Matt's body responded, everything in him tightening.

The fire gilded her creamy skin and her kissable freckles and her fiery red hair. Gods but he wanted her.

But what he wanted meant nothing right now because they couldn't waste the opportunity to search the château with no one else present.

So he forced himself to stand. "I need to change, but I'll meet you in the marigold parlor."

"Vespera, tell me what happened, right now. One moment we were heading back to the château, and the next, you went silent."

"I will, I will." She filled Brianna in on everything Matt had told her.

"You called bone again?"

"Yeah, and now we have zero idea if some undead animals ... and humans ... are roaming the French country-side. Brianna, I need to know, is this bad? What do the undead do? Like, are they zombies?"

"What is a zombie?"

"Um, undead people who eat brains?"

"The undead eat brains?"

"No, well, some do, in books and movies—but, I don't know! I never thought I'd be *making* them."

"In truth, I have no idea, Vespera. We need to find more Mors Dicen Bone Guides to ask what happens to bones after they have been called."

"Isobel said she went to Ireland and saw a whole armament of Mors Dicen weapons; maybe they have Bone Guides there?"

"That is a very good idea. We must go there immediately."

"Now, as in *right* now? Because the next thing we're doing is finding the second aett so we can make sure Ellaine doesn't get her murderous mitts on it, then we're going back to New York to get Tara and the first aett."

"In this I approve, although ... as much as it grieves me to delay you finding my Tara a second longer, finding the armament may assist you in all your quests."

"Good to know, but a side trip to Ireland looking for a place we have no idea if it still exists isn't on the to-do list right now."

"Then, what are we doing right now?"

"Meeting Matt and figuring out the clue in the sampler." Jitters still shook Vella's stomach, but everything in her settled when she opened the door, and Matt, standing in front of the sampler with his cell phone in hand, turned to her and smiled.

"Vespera ... are you okay? I swear I heard your heart make a ca-chunk sound."

"I think it did," she whispered. Dear Goddess, how had she gotten so lucky to have such a magnificent being in her world?

"Talking to Brianna, I take it?" Matt's brow rose.

"You guessed it. And your scars are showing, so I'm guessing you've called your privacy spell?"

"Look at us, correctly reading each other's behaviors so well."

"Nothing like a good brush with the undead to bring you closer together." Vella stopped in front of the sampler. "And look at all that work around the edges. Those are grape vines, right? And maybe crescent moons and crystals. I'd never have thought a Mors Dicen had made this."

"Well, they didn't. The words might be Isobel's and her cousin's, but whoever Isobel's husband had embroidered the piece, we know they weren't a Mors Dicen."

"Good point. So, found anything?" Vella nodded at Matt's cell.

"Take a look." Matt turned his screen so she could read it. "I ran the text through an online translator, and this is how it came out."

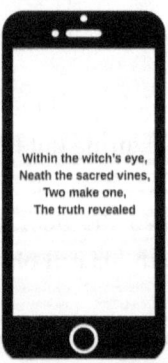

Within the witch's eye,
Neath the sacred vines,
Two make one,
The truth revealed

"Another code," Vella murmured. "Well, if it's hidden the secret of the second aett until now, I wholly applaud their efforts. And I think we can safely say that 'Neath the sacred vines' refers to Isobel's half. The chapel is the sacred part, and the vines were what would have been above ground when the poem was written."

"Which leaves us to decipher what 'Within the witch's eye' means. It sounds almost as bad as digging up Isobel. Gods, I hope we don't have to dig up any more dead witches."

"Me too. Okay, another internet search?"

"Witch's eye ..." He punched something else into his cell. "Here we go. Plenty of references. Symbolization, television shows, books. Shite. There are pages and pages of references."

"Try adding 'place' into the search—we know we're looking for part of the cipher wheel, so it's got to be located some*where*."

"Clever girl, Rapunzel. Okay, top two options. A lake in Japan, and L'oeil de la Sorcière—the remains of a castle, known to locals as the Witch's Eye, and located in the village of Thann, in the Thur Valley."

"Wait. Gerard came from the Thur Valley." Adrenaline and excitement rushed through her, and Vella grabbed Matt's arm. "That has to be the place! At this rate, we'll have completed the cipher wheel and found the second aett in no time."

"Then that's where we need to go." Matt did something else with his cell phone. "And ... it's a six-hour drive, or a ninety-minute flight. So the only thing we still need from here is to find the book."

"Vespera, did I hear that right? You have found the location?"

"Yep, you heard right, Brianna; we've figured out where to find the second half of the cipher wheel. All we need is the book, and we're heading to the library now."

Excitement chased them to the ground floor, along the hallway and through the last door.

At her back, Matt let out a long whistle. "We've got work to do, Rapunzel. How do we quickly find one book among several thousand?"

"We don't have to search that way—remember when we first met Jamie in the marigold parlor and he said he and Luc had cataloged everything in the house? He pointed out the book of the room's contents, right? Jamie is way too organized not to have done something similar here, so look for a book or a register or something."

"Like those?" Matt pointed at a table by the window holding several massive bound books. "They look as though they could be guest books or something similar."

As soon as they reached the table, Vella eased the first book out. "Bingo. You got it straight away, Medea."

"Not just a pretty face." He winked at her, and no way could she contain the urge to grin back. Goddess, they were actually doing this!

"But also definitely a pretty face," she teased back. "And bless Jamie's organized socks. They're alphabetical and all."

"Okay, so we need *The Hammer of*—"

"No, look for the M book; its Latin name is *Malleus Maleficarum.*"

"M ... M ... Here it is. Oh shit." He held the open book out to where the title was handwritten in the ledger. "It's not here."

"What—" Oh no. The record book had a column for the status of the items, with titles listed as one of three options: in library, out of library, or sold. "Out of library. Shit, shit, shit, shit."

"What does that mean?"

"Well, at least the book isn't sold. But I guess Jamie could be getting it restored, hardly a surprise given the age, or he loaned it to someone? Either way, we need to talk to Jamie."

"He'll be coming back from the hospital soon. We'll ask him when he gets back. And the trip to Thann is only ninety minutes, so we can afford to wait, plus we need to find Alex and ask him to watch Nevena."

"Good point."

"I know you were ready to go, but this won't take long."

"I was just ... ready to get this over with, you know?"

"I get it." Matt rubbed her arms, and she gave in to the urge to lean on him, just for a moment. "Fortunately for us, we have a jet on standby as soon as we're ready to go."

"So many books!" Alex practically bounded over to them. "Alas, I am not a reader, but still, they look rather pretty."

"Did you sleep or something? You've got a lot of energy after the night we all had."

"No sleep needed after a little snack thanks to all the blood left downstairs—that is thanks to our host, Jamie, though. I advise against touching the Elixir witch's blood at all costs." Alex wrinkled his nose. "Now, what is the plan?"

Vella froze, and she sensed Matt do the same. But then she eased again, because who cared? It wasn't like Jamie was going to mop up his own blood and intravenously take it back.

"We have a plan, Alex, and we need your help."

And please, please let this work.

29

Matt followed Vella aboard his jet, shaking his head.

"Stop looking at me like that," she muttered.

Like she was amazing and capable and fucking breath-taking, but also that her cheeks were so pale they made her freckles bright enough to draw a map, and the smudges under her eyes were darker than Morrigan's bespelled feathers?

"I merely suggested you could've slept during the drive here, and since you didn't, perhaps you could try on the flight to Thann." He nodded at the cabin crew and took a seat opposite Vella.

"Yes, please, I'll have a coffee," Vella said when the cabin crew offered refreshments. "I know you're trying to help, but I've already had a nightmare once this morning and really don't want to go there again. I'm a grown-ass woman, Medea, who can decide when to sleep or not. Plus, I want to call Sara, only ...." She scowled at her cell phone as she looked at something on the screen. "I have zero idea what time it is back home."

A stubborn-ass woman, more like it. But all he said was, "It's half past nine here, so half past three back home. Morning, to be clear."

"How do you do that?" Vella blinked. "Okay, not calling Sara right now. At least we have other work to do. After your nap, you research the Witch's Eye, and I'm going to look up Jamie's copy of *Malleus Maleficarum*. He said the exhibition he loaned it to is called 'Illuminating the Ages: Medieval Manuscripts.' I'm Googling it now ... here we go. The exhibit is currently on display at the British Library, in their London building."

"London?" At least that wasn't far as the crow flies. "Okay, we'll go after we get the other half of the cipher wheel. I'll tell the pilot to refuel and lodge the flight plan."

"And I'll see if I can find a contact to arrange a private viewing of Jamie's book."

Ping.

"It's Ronin," he murmured when Vella flashed him an uneasy look.

"Pretty late for him, isn't it?" Vella gnawed at her bottom lip.

Yes, it was.

Ronin: News on Ellaine and the tower. Just got confirmation she sent Derrick to Paris yesterday morning your time to complete negotiations on the tower.

Ronin: Guessing you want me to track Derrick's movements and hack all his files too now?

Matt: Fuck. Yes, if you can. If you need resource support let me know and I'll put out a call to anyone we trust

Ronin: Will let you know if I need it

Matt: Also Vella thinks there might be a secret entry into the basement of Div Tower

Ronin: Adding it to the list

Ronin: And still reviewing Nevena. Hard terrain to cover, digitally speaking

Matt: Any other news on the Council meeting?

Ronin: Not a single fucking thing which has me worried. It's like E is intentionally keeping any records about the meeting off her digital footprint

Matt: Damn. Okay, good to know. And thanks. Great work on the tower and Derrick. But get some sleep if you can. Got a feeling things are heating up

MATT SANK BACK into his seat as he shut the cell phone screen off. Just what else was Ellaine planning for their meeting? And Derrick! What the fuck was he doing here in France? *Golden-haired* Derrick.

Like an impeccably balanced spell, the pieces of the puzzle locked into place.

"Bloody hell," he breathed.

"Matt? You're worrying me."

"Nothing is wrong with Sara." He tunneled a hand

through his hair ... Vella wasn't going to like what he had to share.

"But something *is* wrong. What's going on? Matt?"

He read her a fast recap of Ronin's messages and watched the moment realization crossed her expression.

"Hold on. You think Derrick is the golden-haired male who Alex saw talking to Nevena?"

"It must be. Who else would Ellaine entrust?"

"Yes, I agree she would send Derrick to advance her Div Tower plans, but—"

"The evidence is right here, Vella."

"The evidence? Just because Derrick is in France and has blond hair doesn't make him complicit in those murders!"

"I know you don't want him to be, but we can't ignore the facts. I need to tell Ruby and put her people on alert."

"And the whole 'remove the threat' plan? Are you going to talk to Ruby about that too?"

"The time for talk is over." The look on Vella's face made his chest hurt, but what the hell was he meant to do? Innocent witches were being killed, and those responsible were right here in France, no doubt planning even more deaths. By all the gods, yes, Ruby needed to know.

Matt took out his cell again and brought up Ruby's contact.

Buzz, buzz, buzz.

Vella scowled at her purse and fumbled through it before taking out her cell phone. Her eyes narrowed as she read the screen. "Frigging hell."

"Who is it?"

She turned the screen so he could see for himself before she answered, and the knots in Matt's chest shifted to his stomach. Why was *she* calling now?

"Aunt Ellaine," Vella gritted out. "Yes, still in France, pursuing the clues as instructed. No, not at the château, but hopefully we'll have the second aett soon. Yes, I'm aware ... at the hospital. Matt helped her. Yes, we know our responsibility." Her eyes narrowed, and twin spots of red hit high on her cheeks. Fury overtook her expression, and while she regained her composure, her eyes didn't lie. "Sara has left our house?" Vella made a mock gasp, and he hoped like hell Ellaine brought the reaction because sitting beside Vella, there was no doubt her outrage was all directed at the evil queen. "No, no, I did not know. Of course, if I hear anything, I will tell you right away."

As though her muscles were locked up, she placed the cell phone on the table with extra care.

"You can throw it if you want," Matt murmured. "The gods know I've certainly thrown enough items after dealing with her."

Vella hauled in a deep breath, and the rage in her eyes cooled. "No, I've got it. I just needed a moment."

"I can see that, and I'm impressed with how you control your reactions. But you don't need to 'have it' with me; I'm always going to be a safe space for you to vent."

"Thanks." She smiled, but it didn't reach her eyes, and something clenched inside his chest. Was she still pissed because of their disagreement over Derrick? "But you need to know the evil queen gave us new orders."

"What now?" Matt went still. Staying ahead of the Div Councilor had been his adult life's mission ... but what if he missed something? Exactly what was Ellaine up to now?

"Nevena is expected to be cleared for a medical transfer out of the hospital tonight, and *Ellaine*"—Vella's mouth flattened—"expects us to meet Derrick there and the three of us will take Nevena to her London home."

"But she sent us here for the second aett—you even told her we were close—so why wouldn't she want us to pursue that?"

"Do you think she wants us in London?"

"Absolutely. I don't like this, Vella."

"Same. But what else can we do? And we are going to London anyway."

"That's what has me worried."

VELLA TIGHTENED her coat as she and Matthias stood at the base of the hill where L'oeil de la Sorcière towered into the clear azure sky above them, a stony corpse watching over the valley.

Corpses. Pft. She'd had enough of them, thank you very much. Except for Morrigan. Morrigan, she adored.

"If you're too cold, I can go up alone." Matt nodded at the steep ascent.

"That's not why I shivered. I was thinking about any more undead ... encounters."

"Got it. I'll keep an eye out. Is Brianna awake?"

"She's here."

"She?" Brianna said. "Is your Druid asking about me?"

"He is." The same Druid who had refused to back down from telling Ruby that Derrick was a direct threat to the Crystallo coven. So now, without question, there would be a ton of Crystallo witches gunning for her cousi—Derrick.

"Say hello to your Druid. And I am judging by the coolness in your tone that you and he have had another argument? It really is time for us to discuss how you are applying yourself to this bonding, Vespera. It really may be time for a blood rit—"

"Not now. We're about to go up the hill to the witch's eye."

"You can't put me off forever."

"Tell me about it," she muttered.

"Everything okay with Brianna?" Matt gave her a side-look that screamed he'd correctly guessed Vella and Brianna weren't in agreement.

But Vella didn't want to go into that either, even more so when she was pissed off with Medea. Instead, she shook her head in answer to his question, then gestured at the trail ahead. "While there's no one else around, we should start up."

"Vella, I get you're angry at my decision, but we still need to work together to get this cipher wheel. Will you at least listen to what I found on the plane?"

On the plane ... that would be *after* he'd called Ruby.

"Just because we disagree about how to achieve the goal we both want, doesn't mean I'm not listening. What did you find out?"

"The eye is actually a stone ring, measuring roughly ten feet in diameter, with the stones about two feet wide and two feet deep the entire way around. It's all that's left of a thirteenth-century castle that was built here to guard the valley. Rumors have abounded for years of an evil witch who ruled the village, and some people say the eye is the last of her magic here in town."

"Evil ..." Bitterness lodged in Vella's throat. "I bet that was because they were Mors Dicen. You heard what Isobel said about how we were already persecuted back then." Vella scowled and looked around. "Pft. If the villagers already feared our coven, of course the Mors Dicen would be the evil witch in the tale."

"You can change it, you know. Just because it's always been that way doesn't mean it has to stay that way."

"Oh, I will be. Once all this is over, and I can take a moment to think about something other than stopping Ellaine. Was that it for the witch's eye? Anything else we need to know?"

"Nothing more." His mouth flattened, and she knew he was pissed off because she was pissed off, but damn it, he was the witch looking to kill off another person without ironclad proof they deserved to have their light snuffed out. And proof—that was all she wanted. Because if she knew that Derrick was involved for sure ...

Her chest went tight. She would hate it, yes, but she'd understand the need to stop him from doing any more harm.

But no, Matt just wanted to end the threat now.

And damn it again because that part she got. What wouldn't she do to save Sara ... pft. Look at what she *had* done to save Sara. Vella had risked all their lives.

"Vespera? While I know not the cause of the disagreement with your Druid, remember that a sword is only as good as the hands that wield it, and even the best hands cannot fight without a blade. You and your Druid are meant to be together; otherwise, the bond would never have happened for you. And I have no question that, whatever your disagreement is, you will find a way through it. Just remember you travel this path together for a reason."

"Thanks, Brianna," she whispered.

Matt cocked an eyebrow, but didn't say anything, and once again she sensed he knew she and Brianna were talking.

And while none of them spoke again for the next twenty

minutes, Vella reached the top not as tense as when they had started the climb.

Her breath caught and she stilled. Frigging hell, this was no stone corpse guarding the valley. This was history; this was thousands of lives being touched; this was magnificence.

Matt got up closer to the stone still. "It's spectacular," Matt murmured. "Come and stand here. If you look through the center of the eye, you can see the entire township and most of the Thur Valley. You are a beauty, aren't you?" He ran a hand over the stone. "It's so much taller than I thought it would be, like a giant silvery-stone donut."

"A giant donut? This is a monument."

"Apologies." He cocked one of those brows again. "A giant stone ring monument, then. Now ..." He pulled out his cell. "The inscription read, 'Within the witch's eye.' See?"

"Within ... what does that mean? The center of the stone eye is a void so you can see through it to the town." Vella stepped back. "Maybe inscribed into the stones somewhere? But ... I don't see anything."

"Perhaps on the cliff side, or the top? I'll have to climb up and check. Stay here."

"You can climb that?"

"Think I can ... slowly ease one stone brick at a time out, enough to get a fingerhold. There we go. Good girl," he crooned. "That's it, let me in, just a little more."

Good girl for a rock? Pft. He'd never said that to her ... Oh no, no way was she jealous of the damned donut.

"I'm up top."

"Can you see anything?"

"Yes, actually. No clue how a Mors Dicen managed to get up here, but there's a skull and sword carved into the stone. Maybe your forebearers were stonemasons?"

"Seriously? Not another clue." Frustration dug its claws into her. Damn it, she'd thought they'd find the—

"I don't think so. I sense a gap in the stone. It's hidden inside the stones, like a cavity. I can move the bricks to open it up, but I have to be careful—one wrong move and the whole thing might crumble."

"Really? I'm not getting my hopes up, though. Just be careful. Don't want your maddening ass splattered all over the hill below."

"Why, thank you, Rapunzel; that's so lovely of you. I'll do my best, shall I? And yes indeed, I've ... located the opening."

"Why does that sound bad? Are you okay up there, Medea?"

"It's pitch black in there. If more spiders surround this part of the cipher wheel, you are toast, Vella. Toast. Here goes. I've got something."

"What? Matt, tell me!"

"You really are impatient, aren't you? I'm easing it out now. It's heavy, wrapped in a disintegrating piece of cloth. I have to get the stones back together and then get down. Hold on."

Moments later, he dropped to the ground beside her with less noise than if he'd taken a single quiet step, not dropped from ten feet.

"How do you do that? The whole drop silently thing?"

"I'm a Druid, Vella. I used the wind to cushion my fall."

"So you wouldn't have gone splat on the rocks if you'd fallen?"

"I've never tried it to know, but I assume I could stop my fall somewhat. Now, do you want to do the honors?" He held out his hand.

Vella couldn't have breathed even if she'd wanted to as

she unwrapped the cloth. It must have been thick once upon a time, maybe an oilskin? But it had done its job well, because nestled within its remnants, a small bronze disc peeked out.

"It's smaller, still with the letters around the edge, but without the indent in the center," Matt murmured.

Vella traced her thumb over the center. "And it has a sword, without the skull. But I think I know why. Here, hold my purse."

Vella laid the disc from the spider cave flat in her palm, then fitted the smaller disc inside, lining the sword up so that if the skull had been visible, the two would have married up to make the Mors Dicen symbol.

"Perfect fit." Her breath whooshed out. "They're complete. The cipher wheel is together again, for the first time in hundreds of years."

"Hey, breathe, Vella, are you okay?"

"Yeah, just—this is special. Really special. Anyway, you're right, I need to focus. We have this cipher wheel; now all we need is the book, which means it's time to go to London."

"And collect Nevena and Derrick on the way. Let's hope both our magics behave; there's a morgue at the hospital, and I really don't want to meet any more of your undead friends."

30

"Lots of security," Matt murmured after he and Vella were cleared to park their hire car in the controlled patient collection area by the rear entry of Nevena's Paris hospital.

They gave their names again at the entry, and Matt strode inside, Vella matching his pace in silence.

She was still pissed, no question. Bloody hell, but he hated being at odds with her about Derrick, yet how could they find common ground when they both believed so strongly in their positions?

At least the morgue was in another section of the hospital ... having their unpredictable magic *not* be a problem for once would be nice.

"I can't see Alex anywhere," Vella murmured. "He's meant to be here watching Nevena."

"He can't be too far away," Matt replied under his breath.

"Councilor Matthias." A dark-haired French woman met them at an otherwise empty reception desk. "Hello, I am Lea Laurent, Medical Director. Councilor Priestley requested our assistance with moving the patient, and while I feel the transfer is too soon under any other circumstance, I also understand the immediate concern."

Fuck. What immediate concern?

"Perhaps," he murmured, "you can tell us more."

Lea's gaze cut over Matt's shoulder. "Mr. Priestley, there you are. Councilor-elect Montgomery is in the transit lounge. We have vetted everyone else on this floor, and they are either patients or staff. Our security guards are standing by at the exit doors."

"Ours are inside," Derrick replied. "Vella, gods, it's good to see you." His gaze dipped to Matt. "Medea."

"Derrick." Vella gave Derrick a fast hug. "What's going on?"

"Yes, Derrick. What the fuck is happening?"

"Watch yourself, Medea," Derrick growled, before he nodded at Lea. "Thank you, get Councilor-elect Montgomery ready to move out now, please."

Matt ground down on his jaw to stop from grabbing Derrick and forcing him to fucking explain what fucking situation Matt had just brought Vella into.

Luckily, Derrick ignored Matt, so he didn't see the rage Matt couldn't hide for anything right then and instead caught Vella's hand.

"There's been two attacks since Nevena's arrived. I think they're Crystallos, and if I'm right, the coven has gone utterly mad. Grandmother is furious, and Councilor Ruby will have a hell of a lot of explaining to do on Tuesday. Getting out of here is the only option—we can't risk another attempt in case they're successful next time."

"Crystallo witches are trying to kill Nevena?" Vella shook her head like she couldn't believe what she'd heard. "Right now?"

"I get it's beyond fathomable, but it looks like Grandmother was correct; old hatreds are flaring up again." His lips tightened.

"How are they attacking?" Matt did a fast recon of their surroundings. Four points of access: the external to the rear of the building, three corridors leading into the hospital, straight ahead, east and west. No obvious guards but several medical staff in the distance. No windows. "Is it mass force or a single person? And, Vella, get between me and the exit, just in case."

"First time an orderly had a syringe. I caught them just before they injected it into Nevena. After that, I started divining the immediate future and saw three people in medical scrubs, one holding a crystal-handled knife about to stab Nevena and me. The guards got there just in time. But if they try again and have other weapons ..."

Fuck. Fuck, fuck, fuck.

If the Crystallos succeeded and Derrick was onto them ... or if another attack went sideways ... Bloody hell, was Matt really saving Derrick's and Nevena's asses?

"Okay. Derrick, I'll set up a perimeter air spell from the three internal corridors, but no one will be able to get past that barrier."

"*You* can do a spell that strong?" The suspicion in Derrick's voice made Matt seethe.

"It's in spell-development," he gritted out. Fucking hell, it wouldn't be a spell at all, but Derrick could never know it was Druid power, not spellcaster magic, making the wind. Matt bared his teeth. "Get your grandmother to approve the spell, and I'll use it more often, shall I? Otherwise, get Nevena so we can leave. The longer we're here, the more likely we'll face another attack, and I don't want Vella caught in any crossfire. Got it?"

Derrick's gaze cut between Matt and Vella, and his eyes

narrowed, but without a word, he turned and ran down the west corridor. Moments later, four special investigators in their black fatigues and SI badges marched up the corridor, one pushing Nevena in a wheelchair; Derrick was at her side.

"I can't believe this is fucking happening," Matt hissed.

"I know," Vella whispered behind him. "But even if you're right about Derrick and Nevena, if the Crystallo coven are openly implicated in either Derrick's or Nevena's death, Ellaine will do everything in her power to wipe out their entire coven. So many will die."

"Why do you think I'm helping?" he whispered back. He said louder as Derrick reached them, "Confirming, your people have secured the rear parking lot?"

"Correct," Derrick gritted out. Sweat beaded on his forehead. "Divining the immediate future. We're clear to the exit."

"Matthias," Nevena called out through a wobbling smile. "Thank you for coming."

"Where else would I be but right here?" Had he managed to say that with a straight face? Because bloody hell, he'd rather be *anywhere* else. "Now, I need my hands free for any spellwork," he said as they reached the car. "Vella, you drive. Derrick, back seat with Nevena."

"On it. Keys?" She grabbed them as soon as he threw them at her and took off around the front—

"They're coming!" Derrick pointed to the brick-and-concrete building beside them. "Guns! One—two. Third floor. Fuck, the vision cut off."

Bloody hell. Matt dropped the wind barrier in the hospital and instead grabbed hold of the wind with his elemental connection.

The air refused to move.

Fuck, not now! Fear shot through him, and he dropped the connection, tried again. Come on, come on, come—cool friction slid along his skin, yes! He sent a wall of air rushing toward th—

Crack. Crack. Crack.

Glass exploded. People screamed. Vella cried out.

"THEY'RE JUST SCRATCHES," Vella hissed as she shifted the gear stick and sent the car hurtling around yet another bend.

"I think this is the last of the glass." Matt dug into her arm again.

"Ouch, no need to probe that hard." She took her gaze off the road for a second and glared at Matt—

His eyes glittered with rage, black stars beginning to whirl in them. Oh no. No, no, no. That couldn't happen here. Not with Nevena and Derrick both in the back seat.

"Matt," she hissed as she focused back on the road. "It's going to be a starry night, don't you think?"

"I'm not—" Matt recoiled into the seat.

"Vella, are you okay?" Derrick leaned forward. "I can drive—"

"No! No, you focus on divining. Watch out for any more attacks. As I said, I'm fine. Just some scratches."

"Let her be, Matthias," Nevena said from the back seat. "I'll make a poultice when we get home and have them mended in no time. Matthias, you need to conserve your spellcraft in case we run into any real issues or experience any dire injuries."

"Exactly," Vella gritted out. Pft. Take medication from

Nevena? Even if she wasn't directly involved with the plan to kill the Crystallo witches, that would be a hard no.

Beside her, Matt had closed his eyes and whispered something under his breath. Frigging hell, he'd better get control of himself. It wasn't like she could stop the car and give him a head job.

Thankfully, whatever he did, it worked because he finally returned to looking at her arm. Which stung, a lot.

He'd lost his cool back at the hospital, but with bodies everywhere and more shots ringing out, no one had had the time to stop and ask questions. Matt had picked her up off the ground; his face stark white, eyes blazing, and covered her body with his as they'd ducked down behind the car.

More shots had rung out, and with guards and special investigators and who knew who else running around, Vella had screamed at him to get in through the driver's side. He'd tried to put her in first, but she'd shoved his hands away and yelled for him to use his magic to get them out of there safely, and with adrenaline flooding her system, she'd hopped into the driver's seat, barked at Matt to put the car into drive and release the handbrake—because her arm hurt *a lot* at that point—and she'd sent the car screaming out of there.

"Sorry," he mouthed. Then he cleared his throat and said out aloud, "They're not actively bleeding, but they do require dressing. If you pull over, I can at least drive—"

"Nope. No need. And honestly, if we get any more surprise attacks, I'd rather have you free to do your spell thingy and save our asses."

"See? Vella is being smart. Matthias, you really need to listen to us." Nevena sighed. "So, which airport are we going to?"

"Le Bourget," Matt answered.

"That's where I flew into … goodness me, when did I fly in? It's all a blur these last few days."

Yeah, getting attacked tended to blur out the small stuff: the inconsequential details like what day it was, or what color panties you'd worn that day, as if the brain recognized the need to focus on which direction the threat came from, and which way did you need to run the fuck toward?

Memories of the last time Vella had driven a car on the run with Matt speared through her, and she glanced at him.

His gaze locked on her, and when he smiled, with the slightest curve of his lips, she sensed they were remembering the same day.

"Grandmother just messaged," Derick called out. "Nevena's coven has prepped the medical room at her house in Canary Wharf to handle any impacts from blood loss."

"And you're all welcome to stay with me tonight, of course. I have excellent security."

Stay at Nevena's? That would be another no. And wait—Nevena had a medical room in her house?

"Let's just focus on getting you home, shall we?" Matt murmured in his perfect Magicae Councilor voice.

ZERO ADDITIONAL INCIDENTS had them taking off for the short flight to London within the hour. The setting sun cast a golden glow through the windows, and as soon as they were cleared to move around the cabin, Vella grabbed her purse and locked herself inside the bathroom.

Yikes. She looked like she'd been through hell. She'd been side-on to the glass doors when they'd shattered, her head turned toward the car, but that side of her body—from her knee to her neck—had taken the brunt of the flying glass.

At least private jet bathrooms were large enough that she could gingerly ease her pants and top off without banging her already sore body. And standing in her bra and panties, cool air sending goosebumps over her skin, the full-length mirror revealed the full extent of her impact with both flying glass and concrete.

Tap, tap.

"Vella?"

"Matt?" She froze, then whispered back, "What are you doing?"

"Coming in."

"It's locked—"

The latch clicked open. The door eased ajar.

"What the frig? How did you do that?"

"Emergency access latch, just under the locked sign." Matt slid through the gap without making a sound and secured it again behind him.

"But if they see you in here—"

"Vella. Fucking gods." He rubbed the back of his neck as his gaze traveled over her, head to toe. Fury darkened his beautiful eyes, but he took hold of her hand as gently as if she were priceless porcelain. "Baby, you are so messed up," he whispered.

"Matt! What. Are. You. Doing? They will—"

"They're both dead to the world. Sleeping, I mean. Derrick had already run out of juice from all the divination, and with so few of us up here in the sky, he doesn't have any energy sources to tap from, so he'll be out at least till we get to London. And Nevena is still recovering from all the blood loss, so she was out in no time."

"Still, *if* they wake up and find you in here—"

"I'll say I was helping with your wounds." Pain clouded his face, and Vella squeezed his hand. "Which I am."

"I really am okay, Matthias. It's only on one side."

"I did this," he said hoarsely. "I called Ruby, and some-how, she sent people to the hospital, and you got hurt."

"Hey, spellcaster. Matthias! Don't make me shout at you. You did what you thought was right—and yeah, that action had unintended consequences. I've learned about that the hard way. But all we can do—any of us—is the best with what information we have at any time, and we are sure as shit not responsible for the actions of others. Could you have reasonably foreseen that Ruby would send people to kill Derrick and Nevena? No? Then all we can do is learn our lesson and not make the same mistakes again, but no more toxic guilt! You are not responsible for what Ruby did. And if her peeps want to be sharpshooters, they need to aim better."

"Gods, Vella. When I heard the shots, and you cried out ..." He sank to his knees and wrapped his arms around her, pressing his cheek into her stomach. "My power failed me. Failed *you*."

"What do you mean?"

"In the parking lot *before* the shooting started, I called the wind, but it didn't come, and I had to start all over again. If it had worked the first time, I'd have stopped their fucking bullets, and you wouldn't have been hurt." His arms tight-ened around her uninjured side, and he dragged in a harsh breath. "You are so important," he whispered. "Important to *me*. Not because of a fucking bond, or because of your power, or even because you can help us within this war, but because you, Vella, Vespera, Mors Dicen witch, are fucking the most incredible being I have ever met."

Vella's chest went tight, and she couldn't suck in a breath if she wanted, because his voice filled her ears.

He took a breath, whispered a tangle of words, and his

breath blew over the scrapes, cool. Soothing. Welcome. That beautiful sensation spread over her body, and she sighed as quiet bliss overtook her, heated her, spread delicious tingles to her core.

"Vella?" His eyes had turned to molten silver, and his voice deepened to roll over her like Fireball Whisky: rich, hot, decadent. "Can I make you come?"

Puddle, now.

She shifted her legs, and he took the invitation.

"Ssh. Not a sound now, Rapunzel," he whispered against her panties, then he oh-so gently drew them down and off, and she leaned back against the vanity, as his strong, capable hands cradled her hips and his wicked, wonderful tongue delved and licked and his lips closed over her clit and he sucked and laved.

Her breath caught. He groaned against her.

His tongue slid further. Surged up and into her. Rasped over the sensitive nerves at her entry, stroking her into a fever again and again and again, and his fingers plucked at her clit and her blood turned molten, just like his beautiful, stunning eyes.

Her body strained. Pressure gathered.

She flew apart.

31

A s their plane descended into London, Vella eyed a still-sleeping Derrick and Nevena before leaning toward Matt and whispering, "Are you sure you like the plan?"

"I think it's our only plan right now, unless you've changed your mind and want to stay with Nevena tonight?" Matt murmured back.

"Good point. Okay, I'm ready for you to wake Derrick. But you're sure you can rouse him and not her?"

"Yes ... reasonably. Sleeping spells aren't the type I usually reverse. And Sylvie just messaged."

"Did she say what happened to Alex at the hospital?"

"He was pretending to be a doctor to stick close to Nevena, but when the SI started checking everyone's credentials, he had to get out of there."

"At least he's okay. Anything else from Sylvie?"

"She confirmed Alex will get the next flight to London and continue watching Nevena on one condition."

"What?"

"I don't let you get hurt again." Matt's lips pinched.

"Pft. Those vamps take their vow damned seriously. What about you? You need protecting too."

"Vella, they're serious, and so am I. What I said earlier about my magic failing? We need to face facts. It's happening more and more, at the château, and then today." His jaw clenched.

"It's not just you." Unease crept through her. "I'm still making undead peeps. Damn it, I thought we were getting better. I thought the bond was cementing."

"At first, it felt like we were. Can you ask Brianna if she has any ideas?"

Vella sighed. Brianna was already unhappy with Vella's bond resistance, but Matt was right; they had to figure out how to control their powers because the risk of being caught mounted every time his magic went loco.

"But that will have to be later," he said, looking out the window. "We're about to land, so I need to wake Derrick up now. Ready?"

"Ready. And tonight," Vella whispered. "I'll talk to Brianna."

Matt leaned forward and touched a fingertip to Derrick's hand, then slowly whispered his reverse sleep spell. In his seat, Derrick fidgeted—

"Done," Matt mouthed at Vella before he lazed back in his seat and picked up the scotch he hadn't touched all flight. His Magicae Councilor persona slid into place ... a cool smile playing about those sinful lips, a mocking glint in his clever eyes. Hmm. Was this all fake-Matt, or was there part truth in his smooth, confident, sexy air?

How did no one else see the ruthlessness? The fierceness? The loyalty? The *power*?

But then, by showing the world what they wanted to see, they never looked into him ... at him ... further.

"Welcome back to the land of the awake, Derrick," Matt murmured. "Nice nap?"

"Fuck you, Medea." Derrick ran a hand over his stubbled jaw. "Where are we?"

"Just landing at The Windsor by Heathrow. I'm sure you're familiar with the VIP private jet airport here? I do hope the limousine your grandmother arranged is waiting."

Derrick swung to Vella, and his expression softened. "How are you? Nevena said she'll make something for the scrat—wow. They're healed?"

"Matt did a spell while you were asleep." *Do not let on how he did that spell.*

"Good," Derrick grunted. "About time a spellcaster used their magic for more than making themselves pretty." Derision filled his gaze, and Vella restrained the urge to leap in front of Matt and defend his smoking-hot ass.

"But why?" Matt laughed. "I rather like looking at my pretty face in the mirror."

Pft. Vella coughed to hide the laugh that escaped her. *Focus, Vel. Work to do.*

"Derrick," she cut in, keeping her voice pitched low. "I've been thinking about tonight. I know you said we could stay at Nevena's, but she needs rest, and we need to follow the clues to the second aett." Truth. But now for the lie. "Matthias has arranged to meet someone he thinks can help with the clue at his hotel, The Carrington Arms, but I'm still nervous after what happened at the hospital. Would you come with us? He said we can crash there for the night, of course."

"Stay at Medea's hotel?" Derrick's gaze flicked between Vella and Matt. "I suppose Nevena will need her rest."

"Great." Huh. He'd agreed to that fast. Vella resisted the urge to look at Matt as the fine hairs on the back of her neck prickled. Why did something feel off here? "We just need to wake Nevena—"

"No need, Velvet. I'm awake." Nevena let out a cheerful yawn and glanced out her window. "The Windsor by Heathrow. Lovely, we're back already. And now that we're all off to Canary Wharf, I can't wait for you to see my home."

Vella shut her mouth. She and Matt had agreed he would be the best person to convince Nevena why they shouldn't stay with—

"Actually, Councilor-elect Nevena." Derrick held up his cell phone. "Given you're well enough, of course, you and Councilor Matthias are due back in New York for the next Council meeting in three days, so my preference is that we three continue to look for the second aett, while you rest."

Now Derrick was intervening for Matt and Vella? This time, Vella couldn't stop herself from surreptitiously meeting Matt's gaze, but whatever his thoughts about Derrick's intervention were, he hid them well.

But also, the meeting in three days' time ... Vella's stomach tightened. Just what was Ellaine up to?

"Oh, how dreary. The company would've been divine." Nevena pouted, but then her smile brightened again. "Never mind. I'm sure I'll be back to myself in no time. Matthias, once we're in the limousine, would you be a sweetheart and use your spellcaster magic to help speed along my healing process?"

"Anything to help you recuperate will be my pleasure."

Ew. Of course, Nevena wanted Matt's magic ... that cool, soothing, healing spell of his had been pure bliss.

"Jealous, darling?" Matt murmured to Vella as he leaned over the gleaming timber bar in his hotel lobby. He waited till his bartender caught his eye. "Chris? Ms. Knight's drinks are on my tab."

"Pissed off that you had to give Nevena your magic, more like it," Vella murmured back. She smiled at Chris and nodded toward the liqueur shelf. "I'll have a Fireball Whisky, neat, please." She lowered her voice again. "And I know why she wanted it—your healing is pure bliss."

Matt couldn't hold back a laugh. "No one has ever described it like that before; mostly they say it tingles or itches, or sometimes borders on outright discomfort as the magic pushes the body through the healing process faster than normal."

"What? That's not how I felt your magic. I mean, the tingles ... somewhat."

"Darling Rapunzel, you seem to experience my magic wholly differently from anyone else."

"What? As in the spontaneous orgasms—which, by the way, I need to ask about. I had one several days ago, out of the blue. Around one a.m. I was making a hot chocolate when, wham, I literally came too hard my favorite coffee mug broke."

"And you're blaming me for that?"

"It must be you. The only other spontaneous orgasms I've had are from when I've gone down on you—like on the plane and at Madgewick—and that one other time when we were at the B and B in Scotland, the night before we went to Edinburgh Castle. You were having a shower; I was in the bedroom—"

"Bloody hell." Heat prickled on his cheeks. "You felt that?"

"Felt what?"

Matt masturbating to daydreams of Vella.

"I was ... relieving the tension." Fuck it, he was being honest with her, wasn't he? He dipped his head beside her ear. "Giving myself a hand job and fantasizing about it being you in the stall with me, your hands ... your mouth ..."

He leaned back and sipped his soda water to cool down.

"You were imagining me in there?" Vella squirmed in her seat, and a delicious, familiar scent bloomed in the air. One Matt was so addicted to, his cock stiffened in a second. Hard-on ... let's see, how many was he up to now? Had to be in the million range.

"Hold on." Vella shot up a hand. "Does this mean all your previous sexual partners go around popping off O's when you have an orgasm?"

Well, well, well. What a good question. And the fact that Vella could feel his sexual pleasure even when they were an ocean apart? His blood began to pound. Gods just that thought had him hard enough to come right there—except, shit, they had a job to do.

He cleared his throat. "To my knowledge, never. And although I can check if you like, my guess is that it is the—"

"Bond," she groaned.

"Everything okay?" Derrick said from right behind them.

Matt froze. Fuck. Had Derrick heard any of that conversation? He flashed a warning look at Vella before turning around, fixing his Magicae Councilor expression in place.

But whatever Derrick had or hadn't heard, his gaze was on the crowd in the bar as he scanned everyone carefully, before settling back on Matt. "Any sign of your contact?"

"Actually, no. Looks like they're not showing tonight." Not that they ever were. "So, what do you think of The

Carrington Arms? Voted third-best, small, luxury all-suite hotel in the world last year."

"Small?" Vella laughed. "It's five stories, set in what must be an old castle."

"Small for a hotel, and this entire Victorian beauty—not a castle—was home to a single family before falling into disrepair. I picked it up for a song a few years ago and had a wonderful time restoring all her original glories."

"Do you know who this home belonged to?" Derrick's jaw ticked. "It was a Divinator family. They only left because they decided to start fresh lives in the US."

"Wait, not your family?" Vella paused with her whiskey mid-sip.

"Our family, you mean?" Derrick's gaze locked on Vella.

"I—yes, of course, that's what I mean."

Fuck. Matt stepped in front of Vella and steered Derrick to the table set aside for them. "Now that is fascinating. I had no idea. You'll have to tell me so I can have my decorators do some research. I do so like to be thorough when other people are doing the work, of course."

"Sure." Derrick sneered and held out Vella's chair for her. "So, since the contact's a no-show, what now? What was this clue of yours?"

"Vella has concluded we are looking for a book called *Malleus Maleficarum,* apparently on display here in London. Alas, my no-show was also my only"—nonexistent—"contact with the British Library. What about you, Derrick? Know any bookish types who can arrange a private look at an item in a public exhibition?"

"Actually, I have an idea." Vella sat beside Derrick and gave him her full focus. "Could Aunt Ellaine get us an appointment? I hate to ask her, but maybe if you did? The sooner we get the book, the sooner we can track down the second aett."

"You really think this book you're looking for is part of the clue?"

"Absolutely."

Derrick looked from Matt to Vella as though trying to work out the answer to a question only he knew, but Vella kept her gaze straight on Derrick, and eventually, he nodded.

"I need to check in with Grandmother anyway, but I'll go somewhere ... quieter."

"Thank you, and an early appointment would be best. As you said, Matt needs to be back in New York on Tuesday."

Matt didn't say anything, but his gut clenched at the mention of the meeting. What new restrictions or punishments—or both—was Ellaine going to force upon them now? Whatever it was, he needed to be there so he could prepare his people, bloody hell, all their people, for whatever the hell was coming was for them next.

What more harm and havoc did she need to—

"Matt? Matthias?" Vella grabbed his arm. "Did you hear me? Your stars are showing," she ground out.

As if Vella's words had triggered a dam opening, power surged through his veins.

Breathe, calm, focus.

"Shit. I need to ground, now. Make something up for Derrick—he'll believe anything salacious. And our two rooms interconnect, so once I see you on the surveillance system heading upstairs, I'll wait ten minutes and come in."

32

"Where did Medea go?" Derrick's top lip curled as he joined Vella at the table again. "Let me guess, he had a *friend* he had to meet? Someone else after his magic dick?"

"Something like that," Vella managed to reply without losing her shit. Goddess, bring on the day she could tell everyone to shove their holier-than-thou opinions about her spellcaster up their asses. "You were gone a while; how did it go with Aunt Ellaine?"

"She had a ... concern she wanted to discuss. But before I get into that, let's get champagne. I know you prefer that to whatever it is Medea ordered you."

"Actually, I'm good with this." She took a deep breath. "But you go ahead and order for yourself."

Derrick's eyes flared for a second, but he went to the bar and got his own drink, and satisfaction warmed in Vella's chest. Such a small thing, and hell, all she'd done was say no to a drink. But she'd made the choice *she* wanted, and that was a first around Derrick.

"So what's the concern?" Vella asked as soon as Derrick returned.

"Grandmother believes Medea sees you as a meal ticket."

"To what?" Vella froze. What the frig was Ellaine on about now?

"More power on the Council. Listen, I don't want to see you get used, Vel, and you haven't exactly had a lot of relationship experience, but Magicae are excellent at fucking their way to their objectives. It's literally what they do. And ... and I'm sure you know the rumors about Magicae sex."

"So, they're good in bed." Pft, understatement! "What makes you think I'd be interested in exploring that?"

"After solstice, there was talk about you and Medea at his London club."

"That was for a reason, you know that. Aunt Ellaine understood it."

"But Grandmother doesn't know you like I do, Vel." His voice lowered. "After everything we've been through, you think I can't see when you're trying to hide something?"

Damn it, Derrick was right. They had been through some shit together. He might've been older, but Vella had witnessed plenty of times where Ellaine had punished him for some minor infraction, just like she had Vella. Different reasons, sure, yet the same outcomes. Pity snuck into her chest, but she shut that feeling down. Derrick still drank the Kool-Aid, and she could never forget that.

But shit. Shit, shit, shit. If Derrick did see through her lies ... she couldn't risk him thinking she had a thing for Matthias. What if he were the one Ellaine had given the kill order to?

"Please," she scoffed. "I did what I had to. I'm also a twenty-three—almost twenty-four—year-old witch who's happy to get her rocks off every now and again. Doesn't mean I'm ever going to forget what happened to my parents." She let every ounce of her truth fill her voice. "Derrick, believe me when I tell you this, the scars of what happened to my mom and dad are something that will forever taint those responsible. There is no other way I can be. And even if I was interested in the Magicae for sex, he and Nevena got all ... chummy in France. She had some serious hands-on vibes, and after what Charles did, I'm putting Elixirs high in my don't-fuck-with column."

"Gods, I'm relieved to hear that."

Vella made sure her exhale was slow and quiet. Derrick sounded like he'd believed her ... please let that be the case.

"So, how did you go with Aunt Ellaine and the book viewing?"

"Success. She got us an interview with the curator of the exhibition at one p.m. Apparently it couldn't be any earlier as the curating team is busy. Grandmother also wants me to actively divine the situation, so you and Medea will have to go in alone."

Vella restrained a wince. Not having to worry about Derrick being in the room when she viewed the book was a bonus. But if she did need to use Mors Dicen magic, Derrick would get a giant black hole in this vision, and he'd have to wonder why.

But she also had Derrick right here, and he seemed to be willing to talk. This was too good an opportunity to pass up.

"Hey, do you know why the Council meeting got changed to Tuesday? Is there big news coming?"

"Grandmother has hinted that changes *are* coming, but even I don't know what." Derrick's lips tightened, and he did a fast scan of the room. "And I wouldn't mention the Council too loudly, Vella. You saw what happened in Paris."

Yes, yes, she did. Bile sloshed in her stomach, and she put her drink down, unable to take another sip.

"I heard it had something to do with a new Div Tower," she said carefully.

"That's to protect our people over there—once they have a formal base of operations, any Div in the region Europe can use the Tower."

"And Divs using the Tower can strengthen their magic by feeding off the energy of the millions of Paris residents."

"Feed isn't the right term, you know that." Derrick's lips pursed. "Yes, our magic is enhanced by the energy humans produce, but we don't hurt anyone in that process. And trust me, we give far more back helping to guide and direct humankind with our predictions."

Kool-Aid. So, so, so much drinking of the Kool-Aid.

"And what about anyone who disagrees?"

"Luckily, humans have their democracies, and for the most part, when their leaders see what good we can do, they welcome us with open arms. We just have to convince the majority, and that isn't hard."

"You said mostly, though. What happens when you don't convince someone?" *Frig, stop, Vella.* Why was she pushing so hard here? But something in her needed to know: was Derrick responsible for directly killing someone simply because they disagreed with his point of view?

"Like I said, it's rare. But I guess we keep working on them until they do come around."

"And what if there are witches who disagree?"

"It's different, of course. Witches are governed by the Council, and every coven has agreed to take the Council's orders as law. After all, every coven has a representative at that table to speak on their behalf before any law is changed or made."

Not every coven—not anymore. But also ... "What about the hedge witches and vampires and shifters? They don't have a representative on the Council table."

"Hedge witches need to get on board. They know they can join a coven any time they want, but for years, they've flouted the conventions the rest of witchkind have lived by for centuries. Our forebearers, in fact—" Derrick glanced around the bar. "Our family, who lived in this very building, were among the pioneering witches who brought the Council to life, what, three hundred years ago, now? And look how much better life has been since then."

Better? *Better!*

"But everyone is entitled to their opinion, Derrick."

"Witches can think what they like, but they have to act as their coven wishes. That's the model we live under."

"But what if they don't want to?"

"I guess it depends on how far they go to dissent. But why all the questions? I know it was hard with Sara before solstice, but she seems genuinely well now. We even did a reading the other day, and she was amazing."

Vella almost puked right here and then. Except, she couldn't give up here. "I heard about that too. She said she got stuck in the reading room afterward?"

"What? No, we all left. Grandmother sent me to France immediately after, but I heard her tell Sara she was ordering a car to take Sara home. There must have been a mix-up in the room. Was Sara okay?"

"A bit worried. First time being in the reading rooms and all that. So ... how did the reading go?"

"We used the first aett of bone runes, and the reading went far smoother than last time. It feels like I'm getting better with each session with them. You should've seen the clarity of detail, and the range of location—I literally did a reading from New York for a vision occurring in France, and with crystal clear clarity, which has never happened before."

"Oh? What were you divining for?" Damn, how much longer could she hold back the bile?

"I can't discuss specifics, but let's just say it was for context around how to succeed with the meetings I had in Paris. But it paid off, and I can't wait to use them again. Hey, Vel? You look like you're going to be sick—hold on." He darted over to the bar and came back moments later with a glass of icy water. "Here you go. Maybe you should stick to champagne after all."

"Yeah, that's it." She took a sip of the water.

"I'm worried about you, Vel." Derrick rubbed her back, and it took everything she had not to cringe. "I'm here, anytime you need. Just like old times."

A hot lump lodged in her throat at the memory of the boy who'd snuck food into her bedroom when she'd been grounded and peeked in on Sara to see if she still lived after Ellaine had withheld her medicine. If she could only trust that boy hadn't become a man intent on murdering inno-cent witches. But it was looking more and more like she couldn't.

DERRICK DIDN'T NEED MUCH CONVINCING that Vella needed to go to her suite, and she got back just in time to heave the water and whiskey into the very fancy loo.

Sinking onto the heated tiles afterward, she dropped her head to her knees.

Derrick could actually be guilty of murdering those Crystallos, and even if he wasn't, just by being able to use the Aetts of Cogadh meant he was a risk to all witchkind.

When Vella got Matt's grimoire out of Div Tower, Matt would undo the protection spell and kill Derrick.

Unless Derrick had already killed Matt because he was secretly sent to.

Shit. Shit, shit, shit.

She needed to talk to someone ... She reached under her shirt and opened the window on Brianna's sheath.

"Hey, Brianna. You there?"

"I am here. How goes it with your Druid? Have you settled your bond?"

Vella sighed. "It's complicated."

"You have said that before. Would you like to explain why?"

"Honestly? Not really." Vella sighed and got to her feet. "But I need to. I need help. We thought the bond was cementing, but now we're both losing control of our magic, and it's getting dangerous. Do you have any other ideas?"

Brianna's sigh was an echo of Vella's. "Why don't we practice as we talk? In my living years, I always found action made thought come easier."

"Sure. Why not? Just let me put a few things somewhere safe. I don't want to risk damaging anything in here, and the Goddess knows Matt's hotel is luxe on steroids."

"Your Druid is certainly a complex character. Do you have the second knife?"

"It's in my luggage. Hold on, okay. I'm ready."

"Excellent. Then let us begin. I take it the Druid is not nearby? He did make excellent motivation for you to control me."

"No, and we are not doing that again."

"I suppose leaving blood in your Druid's hotel is rude, so I shall provide no argument today. Is there something else we can aim at?"

"I'll stack some pillows on the bed ... there. Hopefully, the cost of replacing them will be enough motivation for me to stop you from throwing the knife and cutting them to pieces."

"Oh-ho. You think you can stop me this time?"

"Gonna try, that's for sure."

Vella turned the window on the knife sheath around until her skin met Brianna's bone, and the charcoal veil fell over her eyes.

"I will pick up the knife first. Now, I shall throw it. You stop me—"

Vella's arm moved in a blur ... *puff* ... feathers billowed into the air from the pillow.

"No matter. We shall collect the knife and reset ... Now, again."

Vella's arm muscle twitched. She strained everything to hold it from lifting.

Puff ... more feathers.

"I CAN'T DO IT!" Vella hauled in a shaking breath after half an hour of fighting with every muscle to stop Brianna from making her throw the knife. "Why the frig isn't it working?"

"Because you are not opening yourself up to me fully. Vella, after all that we have been through, after giving me your trust at Madgewick, why do you not trust me still?"

"What do you mean? Of course I trust you."

"Really? Vespera, in this, you must be honest."

"Well, I mean, you did abandon me because you disagreed with my plan for almost two weeks. And then you forgot to tell me I could die by using too much of my magic. But ... I trust that you mean to do the right thing by our coven."

"Then between you and me, there is still work to be done. And for that, I am genuinely sorry, Vella. I meant my words when I apologized; I should never have left you alone. That was not ... good of me. And I vow here and now, I shall never abandon you again."

"Thank you." Vella's throat clogged up, and something in her eased. "I guess I needed to hear that, too. And I vow to you, Brianna. I am going to fight for our coven."

"And you have my thanks for that, Vespera. I see you beginning to feel part of our coven. However." Brianna cleared her throat. "I fear there may be something else ..."

"Yes? Brianna, you don't normally hesitate. What is it??"

"Perhaps ... perhaps it is not only me you don't trust, but yourself, Vella. You must open yourself fully to the bones you wield. That means every emotion, every sensation—good and bad or otherwise."

"I can't."

"Can't or won't?"

"The same thing," Vella whispered. "You don't understand. I'm battening everything down inside me—I don't, no, I *can't*—let that out. It's the only way I can handle this shit right now. If I compartmentalize enough, if I can keep myself from getting emotional, I can get through pretending I am okay talking to the fucking murderous bitch." Thick bile rushed up again, and she bent over.

Don't vomit. Breathe in. Don't vomit. Breathe out.

"Then you will never fully wield bone, Vella."

She got back to the bathroom just in time for her stomach to erupt.

"Vella?" Brianna's voice was as gentle as she had ever heard it. "You may need more help than I can give you."

"But you're my Bone Guide, you're meant to be the one to help me."

"I can help you learn your craft, but you have other issues that I am not sure I can aid you with. Your bond with the Druid, what's happening with the Darklings ... accidentally Bone Calling creatures back to life ... why you cannot control me ... I think—I think your magic is leaking, and I do not know why. You should meet with the rest of your coven, as perhaps they have answers that I do not. The faster the better."

"That's not an option right now, Brianna."

"Vespera." Brianna's sigh made the hairs on the back of Vella's neck prick. "There may be one element that links all the issues you are facing."

"What? I'm ready to fix it—"

"Not it. *You.* You are the common link."

Vella's breath punched out of her. Her? Vella was the issue?

"Of course, I may be incorrect," Brianna continued. "It could be an external factor; however, either way, you need help to work through this problem and as I have not been able to get you to see reason, perhaps you will find someone within your coven who has the answers you need. And Vespera?" Brianna's voice dropped to a whisper. "What good will any of the aetts be if your magic becomes so unstable as to destroy you?"

Brianna claimed she needed to rest, so Vella slid the bone-handled knife back into the sheath and shut the window, and with the depth of the silence in her head matching the depth of darkness in her vision, felt for the bed and dropped onto it.

Brianna said Vella didn't trust herself, but of course she didn't. How could she? Vella had trusted Ellaine all these years and look at what had happened. How could anyone trust Vella's judgment, even her?

But if her magic was leaking, what was she meant to do?

"Vel?" Matt's voice echoed from the doorway. "Practicing with Brianna, huh?" His scent filled the air moments before the bed dipped, and one of her hands was picked up. "Guess it didn't go well."

"What gave it away?"

"Well, unless you cut the pillow into ribbons to tie me up, then covered the room in feathers in some kind of tickle-kink, that's my theory. Hey, that was a joke. Kind of." Her hand was squeezed, and she squeezed back, pretending everything was okay.

"Did Derrick get the evil queen's help?"

"Yeah. Later than we wanted though." Vella filled him in about what Derrick had said regarding their meeting with the curator, then took a deep breath. "Derrick also said he thinks I've developed feelings for you."

"Well, the prince of evilness has some smarts after all."

"Don't pretend you don't get the issue. What if he's been ordered to murder you?"

"I honestly don't believe Derrick could kill me outright."

"But he could track you and work with the Elixirs to poison you in an instant. He's good, Matthias, and frig, he wants to use the bone runes again."

"Maybe he'll get lost in a vision. One less Div to worry about."

"Matt, we don't know he's part of this for sure."

"Actually, we do. At every Council meeting, Derrick sits right behind Ellaine, so he's heard all those orders she gave to detain and control witches over the years, and never once did he offer another option or try to stop her."

Vella pinched her bottom lip as worry for Matt—and for Derrick—warred inside her.

Because Matt was right ... Derrick *had* been behind

Ellaine in every meeting since becoming her Second on the Council. And between what Derrick could do with the first aett, and the possibility of his threat to Matthias, maybe removing Derrick was the right option?

"You're freezing." Matt rubbed her arms. "Come on, let's get a few hours' sleep—"

"It is cold." But the shiver that shook through her was so much more than just temperature. "Did you turn the temp down?"

"Shit." The warmth picked up again.

"What happened?"

"I was using my Druid power to warm the air and keep us hidden from any Div foresight, then it turned icy ... This is getting bad, Vella. Did you talk to Brianna about the bond? What did she say?"

Vella swallowed hard. "That the problem is probably ... me."

He was going to be so mad at her, but she took a deep breath and recounted Brianna's words.

As she talked, Matt's movements, even his breathing, grew so quiet that no other sound echoed in the suite, and once she'd finished, only the pounding of her own heart filled her ears.

"Matt?" She moistened her lips. Damn it, she'd never wanted to read someone's expression more than she did just now. Was he furious at her? "Matthias? Are you—"

"Vella, let me get this right." His breath inhaled like a hissing snake. "Brianna thinks the reason both our magic is leaking is that the bond isn't cementing, and that is because you don't trust her, or yourself."

"That's a fair summary."

"Then I have to ask ... what about me?"

"I—I..."

"Do you trust me?"

"You don't get it! It's not that I don't want to trust you—or myself, even—it's that I don't know how. I get the bond has started between us—"

"Fuck the bond. I don't give a dead god's ass about the bond right now."

Lightning crashed outside. The windows rattled.

"Matt!" Vella squealed.

"Fuck. I have to go. My power's bursting out. Just—we will finish this conversation, Vella. Later."

33

Banners advertising the Illuminating the Ages exhibition decorated the ground floor lobby of the British Library, but as Vella and Matt joined the queue for the main reception desk, Vella couldn't stop thinking about the night before.

Vella was the problem. And Matt remained furious.

But what if ... what if Vella was just too broken, and there was no way to fix her? To fix them?

Her stomach clenched and she crossed her arms.

Matt had barely spoken to her all day, and when he had looked her way, his jaw had been tight and his eyes flat, and she couldn't shake a creeping sense of loneliness.

Damn it, they needed to talk. Except, what else could she say?

She would've at least tried, except he hadn't returned before she'd finally fallen into an exhausted doze. Guilt and frustration and fear had sent her straight into nightmare town and well before dawn, she'd woken up shivering and in a cold sweat, and had laid there huddled under her blankets, calming her mind until Derrick had insisted on an early breakfast.

Derrick had also stuck by her side all day, to the point that when Matt had joined them, she couldn't have said anything anyway.

And why *was* Derrick glued to her side all of a sudden? Was it Ellaine's orders? Was it his plan to catch Matt mid-relationship? Or was Derrick beginning to get suspicious that Vella had been making Mors Dicen magic?

So many frigging questions, and zero answers.

And even now, Derrick sat across the lobby on one of the public couches, pretending to read a book while he divinated their immediate future.

Zero chance of talking to Matt.

She uncrossed her arms yet again. Rechecked the time on her cell phone ... 12:59 p.m. Why were so many people in the queue today, of all days? What if they were late and the curator refused to meet with them? She crossed her arms again.

"Personally, I don't understand why anyone would want to visit an exhibition about moldy old books," Matthias murmured. "I mean, look at that manuscript in the display cube. You can't read it. You can't touch it. What good is it, even?"

What was Matt even talking about? These books were priceless snippets into the history of their world and the people who lived then.

She spun around to see the example he'd referred to.

A clear Perspex cube sat on a plinth in the middle of the lobby, showcasing one of the manuscripts from the exhibition, teasing at the treasures inside. Vella peered closer ...

"That's a Book of Hours," she breathed, shaking her head in

genuine horror at Matt's dismissal. "That copy was owned by a fifteenth-century duchess. I read about it while researching the exhibition. It's renowned because one of the letter illuminations contains a decoration believed to be the duchess, only it shows her as a skeleton looking at her reflection in a handheld mirror. There's only one like it in the world, and you are mad—"

Oh. She shut her mouth. He hadn't meant that at all, had he?

She was antsy, tired, and anxious about *everything*, and he'd found a way to distract her.

Even pissed off, he was still finding ways to help her. She gave him a small nod and mouthed, "Thanks."

But instead of returning the gesture, his eyes remained disinterested, and he gave a mock shudder. "All these books."

Yep, still steamed.

The couple ahead of them in the queue turned and glared. Matt gave a lazy shrug. "What can I say? I prefer the movie version."

Thankfully, before anyone got into an argument, it was their turn at the counter, and the receptionist directed them up to level two, to yet another reception desk, where they were taken through a door marked Staff, past several work desks, and into a small, windowless staff room.

Matt remained coolly unresponsible at her side, but right now she had a job to do.

Focus, Vel. Deal with the book now; figure things out with Matt after.

A woman with curly hair tied back in a ponytail and direct eyes followed them in, a box cradled in her arms. She wore a long necklace filled with keys that might've been pendants or might've been actual keys. Hard to tell.

"Hello, I'm the curator of the Illuminating the Ages exhibition." She eased the box onto the table.

"Thanks for meeting us on such short notice," Vella said with all the professionalism she could muster. "And for taking the manuscript out of the exhibition for a few minutes." She hoped. Who knew how long this was going to take?

"As the request came from the minister, of course we will assist; however, I hope you can appreciate that this is a highly unusual request. And while we don't have private rooms here; again, thanks to the minister, we have made an exception and cleared out this office for your use." The curator pierced Vella and Matthias with those dark eyes, then unlocked the box with a key from the chain around her neck.

Wow, how many strings had Ellaine pulled?

"And we thank you," Vella murmured. "Sincerely. I promise we'll be careful."

"Careful? Oh no, you will be meticulous in your handling of this precious manuscript. To start, it will not leave the table. You will wear gloves even though you are never to touch the manuscript, period." She held up a tapered piece of clear Perspex and wiped it over with a cloth from the box. "This is a finger. You will only use this to turn the pages. Is everything I've just said clear?"

"Absolutely," Vella replied.

"Of course," Matt drawled.

The curator stared at Matt for one extra moment. "And you will be on camera the entire time," she continued.

"I can guarantee we will treat this manuscript with all the respect it deserves," Vella said. Subject-matter-wise, the book deserved zero care, but it remained a historical record, and for that alone—so that in the future the horrors perpetrated against the vulnerable in the name of witch-hunting would be visible for all to see—she'd try to leave it intact.

The curator pursed her lips, and her expression turned even more flinty—crap, had Vella not sold the lie well enough? But finally, with extreme care, the curator lifted a red leather-bound manuscript from the box and placed it on the wedge in the middle of the table.

What a manuscript. No wonder the exhibition had wanted to loan it from Jamie.

"Look at the gold leaf pattern bordering the edge—that style is pure Gothic—and the flourish in the center." Vella leaned closer. "It's so intricate."

"Step back, please." The curator used the finger to ease the manuscript's cover open, and from the side of the wedge, she swiveled out a wide sheet of clear plastic on a retractable arm and stopped it in place over the manuscript. "The viewing pane will stay between you and the manuscript at all times, and you have thirty minutes. After then, I am returning for the manuscript no matter what the minister says. And I will be watching you from the desk outside, the entire time."

As Matt leaned over Vella's shoulder to peer through the viewing pane, her familiar scent made him want to nuzzle into her soft skin, but even if they had been alone, would he? Because even after everything they'd been through together, after everything they'd done together, how could Vella not trust him?

For most of his adult life, he'd fucked when and where he'd wanted, and it had never mattered if his partner, or partners, attached any feelings to the act.

Actually, it had been the opposite. Vella had been right about what she'd said at Stonehenge—he hadn't wanted any emotional entanglements back then because he hadn't been open to anyone mattering to him.

But the truth? He was the one losing out by not having a real romantic love in his life. And he'd be fucked if he'd let Ellaine cause him to lose out on anything more.

Only he'd gone and fallen for someone who wasn't letting herself feel *anything*. And bloody hell, he even understood why—Vella's method of dealing with Ellaine was to tightly control all her emotions.

But what if ... A chill trickled through him. What if, when Vella did let herself feel again, she *didn't* love Matt?

What if the bond had gotten it wrong and they were just two people caught in a situation who happened to have great sex?

Although fuck, that wasn't even right. Making love to Vell was unlike any experience he'd had before. But what if to Vella, their sex had been just that—a good time? The gods knew he'd filled the role of guaranteed orgasm for plenty of people throughout his life; maybe that was enough for Vella too?

"Matthias? Did you hear me?"

Bloody hell. Head in the game, Matt.

"Look at the annotations scribbled in the margins. And multiple passages underlined. Those could be a ciphertext, right?"

"Perhaps, but there's a lot to work through."

"So many," she whispered. "Too many."

"We'll need photos of every page."

"Oh no, we're not leaving the manuscript here. No way am I allowing someone else to get the clue."

"Well, Madam Thief, you're the expert. How do we steal the book?"

"Not a title I ever thought would come in handy," she muttered. "Firstly, if we take it right now, there's no question who did it."

"Do we care? This is important, you said so yourself."

"True. Okay ... so how to get around the cameras and one highly vigilant curator? We could make a distraction—something that will take the curator's attention."

"I can handle that, but something tells me our curator won't go anywhere without this book."

"That's it! She has to think she's got the manuscript. Matt, you're good at glamours."

"And?" He resisted the urge to feel for the scars running back from his jaw across his skull.

"The best—probably only—solution is that we make a fake manuscript that the curator believes *is* the right one when we leave."

Make a fake, out of a glamour spell ... "That's doable. But it will need to be two spells: one for the book we're stealing, and one for whatever we leave in its place. I'll need something similar in size for the glamour to work. And the spells won't last long, half an hour max."

"We don't need long, right? Just enough time to get out of here. And we'll bring it back once we have the aett and this ... monstrosity of a manuscript isn't a clue anymore. But what can you glamour? There's nothing else in this room."

"You stay here and keep looking at the text. I'll find something."

Outside, the curator stood at the nearest desk, staring at a monitor, and the moment he closed the door behind him, she lifted her head and met his gaze.

"My associate is still viewing the manuscript," he said

unnecessarily. He hadn't expected the curator to stay so close, but maybe this could work ... "Actually, you might be able to assist me. My friend loves the fancy books"—he pretended not to notice the curator's cringe at his choice of words—"and I want to get her a memento of the exhibition. Is there a gift shop here?"

Ten minutes later, he was back and, after being admitted back through the staff door, purposely strolled up to the desk where the curator stood, her gaze glued to the monitor.

He held up his purchase. "Got her a replica of another book from the gift shop. The cover might be plain black, but the pictures inside are pretty."

"Pretty. Sure." She spared one glance at the cover before rolling her eyes and returning to stare at the monitor.

He kept the forced grin in place as he rejoined Vella and shut the door behind him. "Got it."

"Frig, that was well done. Okay, place the gift shop book on your lap so it's out of sight of the camera and do your glamour on it first."

"Can do. But I'll need to look at the *Malleus Malificarum* cover to make sure I render my spell closely enough to pass a visual inspection."

"Wait, Matt. You've already got one glamour spell running." Vella glanced at his face. "And between the books that will be two more."

"No, I've never run three glamours concurrently, if that's what you're asking. My best guess is we'll have forty-five minutes max, thirty to be safe, before the magic fails and I'll need to restore my energy somehow. I suggest we do this fast and then hope like hell I don't need to make magic for a while."

VELLA'S PALMS itched as Matt murmured his spell, but she clenched them and willed that sensation away.

"Done," Matt whispered. He leaned back, making room for her to see the book on his lap.

"Whoa," Vella whispered. "You are good. It's the same—even down to the texture of the leather. How did you do that?"

"Plenty of practice." His lips twisted.

Of course, he was talking about his scars. Pride welled in her chest. Sweet Goddess, he was something else ... after all he'd been through, he continued to take everything that had been done to him and make a positive difference. He was perhaps the best example of a person she knew.

If she *could* love someone, it would be him. Zero question.

"Vella? Did you hear me? I need to do the real book."

"Of course. That spell took you about thirty seconds, right?"

"The texture of the leather and the variation of the gold foil took longer to fit into the spell. The next spell will be faster as it's a plain black cover."

"Okay. I'll stand up and pretend to look at the book from the back. Am I between the book and the camera?"

Matt glanced over her shoulder. "You've blocked the view of the book, but the curator is at the reception desk right outside, so I'd better act fast. Here goes."

He raced through the next incantation and, between blinks, the manuscript on the wedge had a different cover.

Vella couldn't stop herself from gasping. "Dude, you are fucking amazing. It looks so real—and it changed so fast.

Okay, now quickly but smoothly, slide the fake *Malleus Maleficarum* into the box. I'll slide the real manuscript straight off the wedge and onto your lap." *Focus, Vel. Careful, smooth and fast.* "And ... done!"

The door flew open, and the curator stormed into the room. "Did you touch the manuscript?"

Vella feigned a remorseful expression. "Oh shoot. I just replaced it in the box—sorry."

"That isn't the point. You were instructed not to touch the manuscript, even with your gloves." The curator scowled and peered closer at the manuscript cover.

Oh shit, it looked right, didn't it? Vella met Matthias' eyes above the curator. His expression had morphed into a bland, easy expression, but she wasn't fooled. He tilted his head at the door.

Did he want her to run? She tensed—

"You're lucky it doesn't have fingerprints." The curator lowered the lid of the box and took the key from her necklace. Locked the latch. "And now this important historical artifact can go back on display where it should be. And may I please ask, if you ever *must* obtain a private viewing, we would appreciate an early session—I could've had this set up for you to view any time before eleven a.m. and no other paying customers would miss viewing this manuscript, simply because you know the minister."

Vella froze. "You could've seen us earlier, as in earlier *today*?"

"Yes, as I said when your PA called last night."

Oh shit. Why had Ellaine set the meeting for now?

Aware that Matthias was still at her side, Vella cleared her throat. "Well, I—we—appreciate your help."

34

Cradling the book to his chest, Matt stuck to Vella's back like scales on a snake, all the way out the staff door and down to the ground floor, because a deep fucking unease had joined the emotions already curdling in his gut.

Why had Ellaine not set up an early meeting as they'd asked for?

He scanned the faces of everyone they passed carefully.

"Matt," Vella hissed. "Matt! Where's Derrick?"

"Over there—" Fuck. The golden-haired Div had been sitting in the lobby thirty minutes ago, and now ... was nowhere to be seen.

Tap, tap, tap.

He paused. What sound was—

Vella froze, and her gaze traveled behind him. Her eyes went wide, and she mouthed, "Oh shit."

He whirled around.

The manuscript in the clear cube that Vella had commented on earlier was no longer on its stand but instead sat right up against the glass. Vella shifted to his side, her arm brushing his.

The manuscript bashed into the plastic.

Vella jumped. Two people walking past squealed. More people nearby stopped. Looked over.

Horror dawned on Vella's face. "I think ... there might be actual bone somewhere in the book."

"Are you talking to it?" he hissed.

"No!" She swallowed hard and started backing away. "We should go. Like now."

The residual tingling of spellcraft in his palms dwindled. "Fuck."

"What now?"

"One of my glamour spells has dropped."

The stolen book he cradled still had its false cover. He felt for the telltale feel of magic over his scars.

"Stop them!" The curator's voice rang out through the space.

"Guess we know which one," Vella hissed. "But why? You said it would last half an hour."

"I'll give you one guess why," he gritted out. At the rate his spells were fucking up, this bloody half bond was going to get him—and Vella—killed long before it had a chance to drive them mad. "Go!"

He grabbed Vella's hand and ran down the last set of steps. Guards rushed after them, but the entry was only fifty feet away. Forty. Thirty—

Five more guards ran in through the front doors.

He skidded to a stop. Bloody hell. He could call the wind to knock everyone off their feet, but with so many children around, if they were caught too ... Change of plans. Matthias put on his Magicae Councilor smile. "Well, this is a rather lovely greeting."

He glanced at Vella, but her smile was too tense to be anything other than a grimace, and her hand dipped inside her jacket. Shit. What was she doing?

"Vel, no. We can do this another way."

"We can't get caught, Matt. We must get the manuscript out of here." Her chin set with that maddening determination he admired the hell out of, and she slid her purse around till the strap crossed her body. "I am here, Druid." Brianna's tone replaced Vella's.

"These aren't our enemies, Brianna. They're humans just doing their job—"

"And impeding ours. Never fear, I shall find us an escape without causing death unless it is required. Keep the manuscript safe, Druid. You run for the exit, and we shall keep them busy."

Bloody hell. Who was worse—Brianna or Vella?

Vella pivoted, her arms loose, her stance screaming she was ready to attack.

Any other time, he'd love to fight beside her, but Vella clearly couldn't control Brianna, and Brianna's concept about the rules of engagement with people who posed a low threat was questionable.

Matt did his own fast calculation. The guards at the door advanced, while behind Matt and Vella, other guards had ushered everyone else back to clear a space—thank fuck.

He swished his hand through the air and connected his Druid energy to the minuscule breeze. Energy pulsed through him, living with every beat of his heart and pulse of blood in his veins, and he gathered it, more ... more ... turned that tiny wind current into a gust—hurtled it at the guards by the front door.

Swoosh. Swoosh. Swoosh. The gust took the legs out from under the first three guards, and they fell on their asses.

The fourth ran for Vella.

She leaped high, somersaulted over the guard's head and kicked him hard in the back so he went sprawling to the ground, before landing square on her feet and grinning at Matt.

"Told you we could do this, Druid."

"No time to gloat. The rest are coming. Run!" He raced to the door, yanked it—

The gale he'd sent for the guards coalesced into a roaring storm opposing his wrenching of the doors, and nothing he could do would open them against that pressure.

Blood rushed in his ears. His heart raced so fast, he swore it would burst out of his chest any second. Fuck!

He searched for his connection to the wind to sever it—

"Stop the wind!" Brianna yelled.

"I'm trying!" But energy kept pouring from him, stronger and stronger, surging against the doors. Unyielding. "I have to get control," he gritted out. "If it turns toward the library, a heap of people—kids—are getting hurt. You go, get Vella past the guards behind us and head for a rear exit. Get her to Midland Road. I'll meet you there."

VELLA MIGHT AS WELL HAVE BEEN a passenger in a locked car as Brianna took control of her body the moment Matthias said to run.

"We don't have to go just because he says so," Vella yelled.

"Your Druid makes sense—and before you say he is not yours, I would rethink that statement." Brianna cackled and darted around another guard running at them.

"But he might need our help!"

"He is handling himself superbly. I have to say, I am rather glad for your sake to have found someone so compatible—ooh, look, this one has a truncheon. Is he going to attempt to hit us?"

"Maybe—" Brianna had Vella leap and do another kick midair, and then they were past that guard, but instead of running on, she skidded to a halt.

"Vella. There is a book trapped inside a glass cube, and it is bashing against the walls to escape. Should I let it out?"

"No! That's another example of my batshit magic. I think the book must have bone in it, and for some loco reason, they're trying to get to me."

The book bashed into the box again. It toppled off the plinth.

Smash.

"Well, as the book has escaped, and is now coming for you, would you like to see what the bones want?"

"No! We need to get out of here—" *Smash.* "Shit, that was loud. What was that?"

"Impossible not to hear that." Brianna spun Vella around. "It seems your Druid has broken the glass entry doors and the windows beside them. Excellent, his wind has run away outside, and now these younglings are not in danger. We shall continue with his plan and make our exit through a rear doorway, although humans are running everywhere, and the way out is no longer clear. We shall go up!"

"There won't be an exit—"

"We will make our own."

Brianna had Vella run back past the reception desk and up the stairs.

Footsteps pounded behind them, and Brianna sent Vella into a spin, darting down corridor after corridor, between shelves and tables, until they reached a windowed wall.

"It appears we are boxed in here."

"Brianna, you said that way too casually." Vella's stomach dropped. "Wait—we're going out another window?"

"Well, if you had considered my advice and gone to your coven, this situation might've been avoided. Although, I have been thinking about how to help your Druid. His power is out of control, too, correct? There is one place he may be able to go for help."

"Do you mean Madgewick?"

"No, not for his witchcraft. For his Druid power. Avebury is the ancient site where Druids met from dawns long before my memories. It was rumored one of their gods still has a source of power there. Maybe that could help."

"There's a Druid god?"

"Once upon a time, younglings were warned not to run three times around the Devil's Chair—the first of the stan stones at Avebury—as they would summon the devil. Now, this window needs to be smashed." Brianna took Vella to a wall where three polished brass-looking bollards were lined up, each connected with a velvet rope. She hefted one up.

"You want to smash a window with this?" Vella eyed the glass. "It's too thick."

"The base looks solid and sharp enough. We shall throw it hard."

"Really? Brianna! Shit, shit, shit—" Vella found herself running back to the window, flinging the bollard—

Another smash. More broken glass. A fast look outside revealed they were facing yet another brick building with a footpath and street between them. And a two-story drop.

"Brianna? There's nothing below but concrete. Please be careful."

"Of course. No—now is not the time to fight me, Vespera. You trusted me once before; you should do so again now."

Fucking hell. Was she for real? But yes, she was. And right now, going out the window—if Brianna could get them to the ground safely—was better than being caught by the guards, and possibly the police.

"And, Vespera? Given we do not know who or what else is down there, I am going to have you take me from the sheath and hold me in your hand so that if we need to fight, we can slay."

"I don't think that's necessary, we're at a library." Her hand reached beneath her shirt, and she slid the bone-handled knife free. "Fine. So now we're getting out of here one-handed?"

"Correct." Brianna had her climb through the smashed window, jump out and somehow scale the bricks till they landed on the ground.

"Sweet frigging Goddess, Brianna. You did it!"

"Vespera! There is—" A roaring sound filled Vella's ears, muffling Brianna's voice, and a ferocious gust of wind threw her off her feet and sent her banging into the concrete.

Pain burst in her knees. Her shoulders. Her knees again.

Over and over, she tumbled until finally, the wind let her go, and with a groan, she rolled onto her back. Head on the ground. Staring up at the darkness.

Oh shit. She'd dropped— "Brianna? Brianna!"

She groaned as she caught her breath and steadied herself on stinging palms.

No sight. Body hurting. No sound of Brianna. Which way was she even facing? *Focus, Vel. Figure this out.*

She gingerly sat up, felt for her knees. The fabric of her

pants was torn, and a hiss escaped when she touched ragged flesh. Ouch.

She rolled over to her knees, gritting her teeth against the pain, and reached out as far as she could ... come on ... come on ... "Brianna! Can you hear me?"

Surely Brianna was close by. But why couldn't she hear Vella? Oh, frig. What if Brianna had been broken? Could that even happen?

And what about Matthias? Was he okay? He'd said to meet at the rear of the building, but was that where she'd jumped, or had she gone out a side window?

Crick ... Cr, cr, cr ... crick ...

Vella froze. "Hello? Is someone there?"

Crick ... cr, cr, cr ...

Vella yanked her hand back. "Brianna? Brianna!"

"Vella?" Matthias' voice reached her from a distance, right before pounding footsteps came to an abrupt halt nearby.

"Matt! Thank fuck. Do you have the manuscript? And I can't find Brianna. Can you see her?"

"Yes, I have the book. However no, I can't see Brianna." His voice didn't change position, and his steps didn't come closer.

"Are you injured? You sound strained."

"Don't worry about me." There was another pause. Footsteps moved to her right but still didn't come closer. "You, though—your knees are bleeding. How badly are you hurt?"

"I'm banged up, but don't think anything's broken, although, there are these weird sounds. And I can't find Brianna. I lost her when the wind hit."

"She's not with you? Hold on, I'll find her." Running footsteps echoed off into the distance.

"Did you find her?" Vella called out. "Matt?"

Cr, cr, cr.

Vella jumped. The hairs on the back of her neck prickled.

"Hey, Matt? The sounds are getting closer."

The footsteps returned. "I can understand why," he muttered. "Vel? You're surrounded."

"By what?"

"Rats."

"They're all dead, aren't they?" she whispered.

"And in various stages of decay. They've got you circled, and any time I try to step through an opening, they close it, so I'm going to jump over and land right in front of you. Don't move, here goes ..." His arms surrounded her, and the connection and relief that flowed through her took her breath away. "Got you," he whispered.

He did. He *always* did. Her chest clogged up.

"Vella? Remember when you teased me about not being able to carry you? We're about to prove that statement wrong. Here we go, up in my arms now. Hold on, I'm about to take a big jump."

"Can anyone see?"

"There's no one around."

"Huh?"

"Most ran off when my wind tore through here, and the rest after seeing your ... entourage. They're following us, by the way."

"Fucking hell," she whispered into his neck. "This is batshit."

"Agreed. How much longer will your vision be out?"

"Another fifteen minutes—twenty, maybe. And I need to find Brianna. You still can't see her?"

"No sign at all. Do you think you've moved much since you last had her?"

"I've got zero clue. All I know is we jumped to the ground just fine, then your wind sucked me off my feet and tumbled me around, but that only felt like a few minutes, and I didn't walk anywhere. She has to be here. Brianna? Brianna!"

"Fuck, Vella. I'm looking everywhere but can't see her. Can you hear her?"

"No." Ice shot up her spine, and she couldn't restrain a shiver. "How can she just be gone? She doesn't have feet to get up and walk away."

"We need to face facts—Ellaine set the meeting up for this afternoon specifically. Derrick's disappeared. And now Brianna is gone."

"Motherfuckers." Panic and fury gripped Vella with dual claws. "If they hurt her," she gritted out. "I will gut them all myself."

"There's more ... I'm almost burned out."

"Matt!" Vella gripped his arm. "You used all your magic?"

"Correct. I'm going to crash soon."

"Shit." This was bad. So frigging bad. When Matthias crashed, he passed out and became totally vulnerable. "Shit, shit, shit."

"I do love your bloody way with words, Vella."

"Yeah, I'd prefer to have something better to say. It kills me to leave without Brianna, but we need to get you somewhere safe. Your hotel?"

"Unfortunately, no. If anyone is looking for us, that will be their first place to look."

"What about if we get a car? Once my sight returns, I can drive us out of here."

"Good plan. We're right beside King's Cross. Hold on, I'm looking now ... Okay, found a hire car company on

Euston Road—that's the next corner. We can be there in a few minutes."

"Can you make it that far?"

"I will. Bloody hell," he muttered under his breath.

"What?"

"People are starting to come back—nope, they're running away as soon as they see your rodent entourage. They might be little, but they are nimble and do not stop for anything. When we get to the hire car place, you stay outside." He let out a long whistle. "Did Brianna know how to put your zombie squad back to sleep ... let them be dead again ... whatever the hell you call it?"

"She had zero clue."

35

"Matt?" Vella called his name for what felt like the hundredth time after she'd pulled into the empty parking lot of a small café on the outskirts of the village of Avebury.

He needed sleep to recover from the magic fatigue, but how much was enough? He'd been out the entire three-hour drive to get here, and another fifteen since then, but night was closing in and if there was something here that could help Matt control his power, they needed to find it fast.

She added a chest shake for good measure. "Matt, you need to wake up."

"We there yet?"

Thank frig. His silence had been unnerving, and given how batshit their magics were, a small part of her had been terrified his deep sleep might be something more sinister. But all she said was, "Good to hear from you. Can you open those pretty eyes?"

"You think my eyes are pretty?" His teasing tone made her eyes sting with relief.

"When I can see them, yeah. There you go." She swallowed the lump that had lodged in her throat. "I hate seeing you defenseless."

He levered the car seat up, and for one moment his silver eyes radiated warmth, then as if a veil had slid over them, they filled with a somber coolness that made her chest go tight.

"Ronin called your cell while you were out. He said to tell you he'd wipe any surveillance recordings from the library, but there were so many people there, he's already seeing social media lighting up with different recordings."

"Bloody hell. If Ellaine hasn't heard already, she will soon."

"She'll think you're using unsanctioned magic again."

"Better that than any inkling it wasn't a spell at all. At least I'd already seeded the wind spell idea with Derrick back at the hospital in Paris." He shifted in the seat to look out the window and sat up straight. "Vella, where are we?"

"Avebury, in a county called Wiltshire. It's another henge of standing stones. Brianna said ancient Druids used to worship here, and there might be a power source that can help control your power. Through that hedge." Vella pointed at the windscreen. "There's another bigger parking lot on the other side of the village, but this café has a small gateway that leads there too—it's buried in the hedge—and staying away from people right now seemed like a good idea. And although I don't know where we're meant to go, Brianna mentioned a story about a stone at the southern end of the largest circle."

Crap. Brianna. Where was she? Was she okay?

Focus, Vel. One problem at a time.

She cleared her throat. "Have you been here before? Do

you know why Brianna would suggest we come here to help your Druid magic?"

"Never, and no clue. I recall my mother talking about a site a few hours from home that she'd wanted me to visit with her when I was older, only ..."

That day had never come because she'd died before Matthias' Druid powers had manifested.

Vella gave in to the urge to touch him, to offer some comfort, but Matt pulled back from her hand before she could make contact and left the car.

Cold air filled the interior; its icy hit less of a slap in the face than the fact Matt didn't want her touch.

Looked like he was still steamed ... and so he should be. He'd been there for her time and time again, but Vella just kept struggling to support him in the same way. Damn it, if only this could be easy—if only fixing herself could be easy —maybe then she could be there for Matthias like he wanted. Like he deserved.

Swallowing the lump that lodged hot and thick in her throat, she followed him through the hedge.

Her breath caught.

Massive stones emerged from the tufted grass. Ancient and primal. Resolute.

"There's magic here," Matt whispered. He turned his hands over, as if searching for something in them, then he nodded to the right. "This way."

"How do you know?"

"I can feel it."

She caught up fast because she sensed it too. And it was ... uncomfortable.

"Imagine living there," Vella whispered. She rubbed the back of her neck and nodded at the houses and cottages, a mix of slate and thatched roofs, off in the distance. "They're inside the stone circle. I wonder if they're witches—if they can feel it too?"

"What else did Brianna say about this place?"

"Just that children were warned against running around the biggest of the stones and that it was called the Devil's Seat."

"Look there." Matt pointed at a giant stone in the distance. "It has a hollowed-out section that looks like you could sit on it." He strode over, and Vella had to jog to keep up as he reached a stone that had to be twice as tall and twice as wide as him.

Her gut seesawed.

"Uh, Matt? Maybe we should think this through."

GODS, what was this place? Energy hummed in Matt's hands, more potent than anything he'd known, and it was coming from the stones ... these giant craggy outcroppings called to his blood.

Something told him that if he made magic here, it would contain a potency unlike anything he'd accessed before.

He sat in the hollow of the giant stone.

Energy crackled through him.

"Matt," Vella hissed. "Your stars are showing."

"I can't stop it. Brianna was right. There is a power source here because it's like I'm being lit up with Druid energy. My connection to the elements is so strong I can taste them—the metallic earth, sweet moisture on the wind. The char of a flame from a fire burning in one of those houses. It's all part of me." Kneeling, he pushed a hand through the thick green grass to the soil.

Déjà vu filled him. Only weeks earlier they had been at

yet another sacred standing stones site, descending into the ground.

The soil split open.

"Just like at Stonehenge," Vella breathed. "Those are steps. Oh wow. We're going underground again."

"Yes, we are."

Matthias pulled his coat tight and tried to ward off the chill icing his veins—and not because of the frigid afternoon.

"I wish I had Brianna," Vella murmured.

"Me too. Hold on, let me light a witchlight." His spell ignited immediately, so at least his spellcraft was restored. "Here we go. Follow me down."

Warm, moist, metallic air made his nose tingle as they descended the earthen steps into a deep, dark tunnel.

"It smells ... different ... this time," she whispered. "Stonehenge felt stale and dank—I remember it so clearly. But this place seems almost alive."

"Yeah, and not in a good way." Matt's senses went on high alert, and he caught Vella's hand and used his witch-light to reveal her face. "Stay close, although if we get separated, the opening has left a pool of light, so you should be able to find it again as long as we don't go too far."

"You don't have to tell me that twice. But there's something else here; I can feel it." She eased closer to him, her arms trembling against his. "Darklings?"

"I sense something, too. But it doesn't feel like the Dar—"

Matt's witchlight shut off, dropping them into such darkness that the tiny patch of light from their entry point barely penetrated.

Oh fuck. He hadn't dropped the spell, and he wasn't exhausted, so something else had cut his magic.

"Matt? Why—"

"Smart humans," a voice rumbled from beyond them.

Matt froze. Vella did too.

"I think we found it," he murmured. He grabbed Vella and yanked her backward, placing himself between that voice and her.

"It? You found *it*?" The voice sounded closer.

"Vell?" Matt backed up slowly, using his body to crowd Vella in that direction too. "For now, walk, but get ready to run."

"What about you?"

"I think I need to stay." He fought the instinct to yell for Vella to run, and to take off after her, because his instinct also screamed the ... thing ... talking was by far the deadliest threat he'd ever dealt with. And no way was he giving it his back.

But he could pull the earth down in this section of the tunnel and use the cave-in to give Vella time to get out of there.

"Why do you fight the inclination to run, mortal one? Do you not wish to live another day? See out your existence with your skin attached to your flesh? With your eyes and tongue and ears not the last witnesses to experience your annihilation at my hands? If I had hands."

"What are you?" Vella's whisper echoed into the tunnel.

"I am the antithesis of magic. None may occur in my presence unless I wish it so."

Fuck, that was why Matt's witchlight spell had failed. But thankfully, whatever creature this was, it didn't know Matt was a Druid and that his night vision was strong enough to make out a figure approaching, maybe twenty feet off. Whatever it was, it moved with absolutely no sound and on four feet, but the body shape was more human than animal, except for antlers brushing the top of the tunnel.

Fuck. Fuck, fuck, fuck.

He stepped back again, pushing Vella another step closer to the opening. Another step. Another.

"Foolish witches," the thing whispered. "To venture into my tomb, thus not knowing who you face. And ooh ... I have scented you before. Yes, I know now. The two who came to visit the ancient site where Bone Witches hid their treasures. You escaped a brush with me then, yet this time you have not been so cautious—in fact, your hero here convinces himself to strain against the basic need for life ... to leave my presence while still possible. Tsk, as if that would ever happen."

Matt's breath punched from his chest. This was the thing beneath Stonehenge? And oh shit, the two sites were connected? And these tunnels were its tomb?

"We are ... here for another reason." Matt risked a glance over his shoulder. Perhaps twenty feet to the opening.

"To present yourself as an offering? Oh, I do approve of that reason. After all, I have not had tributes in many a thousand years. Your flesh would be most welcome."

"Matt, any ideas?" Vella hissed in his ear. "I'm not planning on being anyone's dinner today."

It wasn't in Matt's plan either, at least in Vella's case. But he needed to buy time to get her nearer to the entry.

"We're here on a quest," he called out. With his hand, he drew circles in her palm, just like they'd done with Charles at Stonehenge. *Stall for time.* They just had to reach the opening.

Come on, Rapunzel. Did she remember? He did it again.

"My Bone Guide said you might be able to help us," Vella blurted as they took another step backward. "My name

is Vespera, and I am here on behalf of the Bone Witches—
the Mors Dicen people—to seek your guidance."

"Ooh, the pretty Witchling wishes to speak on behalf of
a great coven? I grant you this one boon, Witchling. Tell me
a story that does not bore me, and I will answer you with
one question."

"Three."

"Two. But take heed, if you enter this bargain and a
single drop of disinterest befalls me, then you and your
companion shall be my feast. What do you say?"

"I say that you could make us your feast whether we
agree to your bargain or not. So, I think you want us to keep
you entertained. You said yourself ... you have been here
alone for a long time."

"Smart Witchling." A creepy laugh echoed into the darkness. "Well, you have not bored me yet. Begin."

"There once was a child of witches, whose branch of
magic had become feared by others because their power
could not be controlled. One day, a bunch of evil witches
killed the child's parents and stole the child, and then raised
that child, pretending she was theirs."

"How ... delightful. Witch against witch. This story is
entertaining me so far. You may continue."

Matt sensed Vella clench her teeth and squeezed her
hand again. Took another step back.

Surely not many to go now.

"The witch grew up into a lioness of a woman," he
picked up her story. "And while she didn't know her truth
for a long time, eventually, she found it, and when she did,
she decided that none would ever cause harm to her loved
ones again ... and so she decided on a way to bring about
the demise of those who had hurt her. She met a Druid who
—" The thing was five feet away now. "Vella. Run!" He

turned and shoved Vella toward the entry, then spun back to the thing.

"Oh no," the thing purred.

"Matt!" Vella shouted. "The opening's closing. Shit. It's gone. I can't see anything."

Focus, Matt. Head in the game. The thing could control the earth.

"Leaving after visiting for such a short time?" The thing laughed, and the stench of its breath made Matt's stomach churn.

"It seems we have intruded." Matt felt for Vella's hand. Squeezed it even as her breathing rasped in his ears. "I think it's best if we come back another time." Or never, but Matt didn't say another word as he touched the earthen wall with his other hand and connected again to the soil, reopened the earth to the standing stone.

"Druid? You are a Druid? Why did you not say?"

Suddenly, light filled the tunnel as Matt's witchlight spell roared back to life. Matt shielded his eyes, sensed Vella doing the same.

"I thought you had all left me," the monster said.

"You know of the Druids?" Matt's heart picked up.

"Know them? They *are* of me. Of us. The Druids were our children, but when my siblings left your world, and I alone stayed, they grew weary of their differences and cast off their power, choosing to become human ... all except you. Druid, you are the prize I have waited for. Blood of mine, I call by right—"

Fuck. Oh fuck. Dread filled Matt. They weren't dealing with a monster; this was far worse—

"Matt, what's going on?"

"Sun by day, moon by night, fire to burn, earth to build. Air to breathe, rain to flood. Blood—"

"He's calling an ancient spell. I don't know how, but I can feel it in my—"

"Calls blood," the thing finished.

The ground rushed up to meet Matt, and then for the second time that day, everything went black.

36

"Matt!" In the dark, Vella lunged for him, managed to get a hand on his arm and stopped him from hitting the earth hard, although no way could she stop his fall entirely. She dropped beside him, felt for his chest. Her heart only started again when his beat beneath her hand.

Shit. How did she get him out of here? Over her shoulder, the tiny sliver of light from the entry Matt had reopened seemed so far away.

"What did you do to him?" Vella snarled at the monster.

"Ignited my blood tie to this Druid." The monster smiled, and its fanged teeth gleamed. "Long have been the days since I tasted mortality. Since I roamed freely from the ground beneath these standing stones."

"What—what will happen to Matthias?"

"His soul shall join with mine, and we will roam the world."

"What does that mean? You can't just claim him. Matthias is mine—"

"Ah, you do not understand. Your Matthias is already

part of me, and I part him. Who do you think Druids are, Witchling? They carry my bloodline, and you cannot stop this from happening."

No. No, no, no. But how did she stop this?

"Wait, you said ... you said that if I told you a story that didn't bore you, you would answer two questions for me, honestly. Is that still so?"

"Yes. But your story did not—"

"No. You already said my tale entertained you. So these are my questions." Shit. She had to do this carefully. So, very, very carefully. "What are all the ways that two witches who are partially bonded—and whose powers are out of control—can get control of their powers again?"

"This is easy. And you think to ask a question in such a manner to ensure you have all the answers, but you have erred, Bone Witch, for there are only two answers. You either complete the bond, or a god can choose to sunder it."

Frigging hell. This was something witches really needed to know before they went and got laid in a dramatic henge.

"And your next question?" The monster stalked closer. Its fetid breath hit her cheek, made her eyes sting and belly revolt, but she inhaled through her mouth, focused on Matt. *Come on, Vel, you can do this. For both your lives, you can do this.*

"What are all the ways that I, with my current skills and possessions, and in this current place, can stop you from doing the plan you just outlined with Matthias and me?"

"You would try to trick me?" The monster roared. Spittle hit her face. The ground shook.

"I will do whatever it takes!" she shouted back. "The one you want—the Druid—he loves me. If you kill ... eat ... me now, he'll know and will fight you for the rest of your existence. He will spend his life moving every mountain in every world to stop that from happening, and I believe he is more than capable of doing so."

"So ... the bond your first question referred to, it is between you and this Druid?"

"Why?" She'd thought that had been obvious, but maybe not?

"That is a third question, and one you have not earned an answer to. However, I shall answer your question, but to do so requires more information as your addendum presumed I have knowledge of your skills. So, Bone Witch, have you reached the Knowing yet?"

"The what?"

"Ah, you have not. In that case, I have all the information required to respond. Should you wish to see the Druid and yourself spared the fate I first selected, you will have to find a different fate to barter with, for you have not the magic nor the physical prowess to battle an Old God—"

"Hold on." Vella shot a hand into the air. "Whoa, whoa, whoa. I thought you were a monster. You called yourself a monster. You have giant horns."

"I have many things. But I am also one of the Old Gods who first came here, only to be entrapped beneath these standing stones, their power restricting my ability to move outside their perimeter. Now, do you want your answer or not?"

"Fine. I just feel it's a little unfair to put me, a virtually new Bone Witch, up against an actual fucking god."

"Fairness? Where was the fairness when witches entrapped me all those eons ago here beneath the ground?"

"But you're a god—the antithesis of magic. Those were your words."

"They tricked me, the clever, cruel witches, into lowering my guard and took advantage of the time when I was not suspecting them to make a curse upon me. Be certain I will never allow that to happen again."

Witches tricked an Old God? Respect trickled through her for those witches, followed by determination. "So ... if you're an Old God, and Matthias is descended from you, does that make him a god too? And yes, I know, no more questions. That was more rhetorical than anything, since I think I know the answer there." Vella hauled in a deep breath. *Come on, Vel. Almost there.* "Okay, you were saying the only thing I can do to avoid getting eaten is to provide you with a different option."

"There is one idea I have ... but you must be give it willingly."

Sweet fucking Goddess, the slyness in the Old God's voice was so clear. But with Matt still unconscious, and Vella without Brianna, what choice did she have right now? "Can I just check though ... any chance your name is Bel? I studied arcane history, and with your horns, the name seems right."

"Oh, I do like you indeed, Bone Witch. I hope you make the right choice, for that is a name I have not heard in a very, very long time. But prevaricating will not aid you in your escape."

"Fine. Spit it out."

Vella gritted her teeth and heard him out.

"And now," Bel purred after he'd finished explaining Vella's alternative. "I suspect you wish for the Druid's power to be returned to his control?"

MATT'S SENSES were on fire before he opened his eyes. Where before he'd felt connected to every element, now they were him, and he was them. The dirt beneath his hands was both solid, and yet as light as air, as if he could sink into it, become it.

"Matt? Matt, can you hear me? Hey, motherfucker, you said he'd wake up!"

Matt opened his eyes, and Vella's beautiful face filled his view, her ferocious lioness gaze locked behind Matt.

"If you go back on your word," she snarled. "It won't matter if you're an Old God or just a plain motherfucking monster, I'll chase you down, grab you by those damned horns and drag your ass back here, no matter how many witches I have to find."

Chase down an Old God? Of course she would. No wonder he loved her.

"Rapunzel."

"Matt!" Vella's breath whooshed out, and tears glimmered in her eyes.

Fuck. Vella never cried.

He leaped to his feet and charged the Old God. "Did you hurt her? I will annihilate you—"

Sly satisfaction poured off the motherfucker, and rage shot through Matt, so hard and fast he'd shaped the earth into a cage of giant spears, shot them into the Old God before—

"Bravo, young one," the Old God purred. As fast as Matt's earthen spears had risen from the ground, they melted back into the earth, like they'd never been there. "Not only a Druid, but powerful too ... you must be one of my line whose ancestors did not cast off all our gifts." A dark chuckle made the hairs on Matt's arms prick.

Hell. What was the fucker talking about? What did the fucker know about Druid powers? No matter, he had to get Vella out of there.

"Vella, are you hurt?" He grabbed her hand but kept his gaze on the Old God.

"No. No, I'm fine." She tugged on his hand. "But I have to tell you about the bargain."

"What? What bargain?"

"Bel—by the way, this is Bel, in case you didn't know—can stop the bond from making your magic go haywire, but in return, I had to agree to a small ritual that will free Bel to roam above the earth instead of below it—still within the confines of the stones. That was the deal. Take it or leave it. So, I took it."

"A ritual?"

"You need to rub your blood over my forehead, and then you're going to cut me and taste my blood. Apparently, the witches who cast the curse to keep him here were representatives from every coven, so you and I can't free him entirely, but we can get him above ground, for the night of the new moon only, every month."

"And what about when he's above ground?" Matt kept Bel firmly in his sights. "You can't go and start eating everyone. Ordinary, harmless humans live inside the stone circle."

Bel's smile was all teeth—sharper than a vampire's. "I shall agree not to enter any abodes, as long as the humans stay inside their homes on the new moon, then they shall be fine. Of course ... should anyone *want* to venture into the circles and experience the night with me, then I shall be more than happy to entertain them. I can derive pleasure from more than just flesh and blood."

Vella hissed. "That had better be willingly offered, asshole—"

"Yes, yes, I said *if* they want." Bel rolled his eyes. "Well? Do you agree?"

"Vella wears my blood, then I have to taste Vella's—and that will release you?"

"There is also a small ritual ... I will, of course, explain the steps required."

Fuck. He didn't trust this asshole—to borrow Vella's term—one fucking bit. But what could Matt do? Was he powerful enough to out-element an Old God?

"I do have another offer ..." Bel's sly grin shot between Matt and Vella. "The Bone Witch may join me here underground every new moon instead. I sense the taste and heat of this one's cunt would be more than enough payment for—"

"Oh ew. Pervy Old Gods aren't really my style." Vella's gagging sound made Matt smile, but he'd already sent another round of spears to cage Bel against the tunnel wall, only this time he held them in place, drawing one earthen spike close enough to pierce the Old God's eye. And when the dirt tugged at his domination—Bel's attempt at wresting control of the earth from Matt—he leaned into his connection with the elemental nature of the earth and fought Bel with everything he had. Gritting his teeth, he managed—just.

"If you ever talk about Vella again," he ground out, "I will use every ounce of my power to carve you into pieces, and you will never set foot above ground again. Do you hear me?"

Bel's mouth flattened, but the Old God couldn't nod unless he wanted to impale his eye. "It seems I may have underestimated your power. But you should not misunderstand your god—"

"You are not my god." Matt let the earth subside. "But fine. We accept your deal."

Bel's eyes narrowed, but Matt didn't give a fuck what Bel

thought, so he held the fucker's stare until finally, Bel let out a laugh.

"Oh, I am pleased to see what our progeny have become."

What Druids had become ... Matt froze. Bel might be an asshole, but he had insight into Matt's heritage—information he'd thought lost forever. But for now, he filed that thought away and focused on the immediate issue. "So what is this ritual?"

Bel scratched a triangle in the dirt at his feet, then ran a hand over the tip of one horn. Blood welled.

"Come, Druid. You will wear my blood." Bel dragged his hand across Matt's forehead, and Matt held back a shiver as his skin tingled where the Old God's blood coated him. "Now, the Bone Witch must wear yours. Use my horn."

Gods but they had better be doing the right thing here.

A sting flashed across the pad of his thumb, then he turned to Vella and ran it over her forehead.

Her lioness eyes flashed, and something heavy began to churn in his gut.

"Next, you must cut the Bone Witch and *taste* hers."

"Why? Why can't I just wear it?"

"Because that is not how this ritual works. Well?"

"How much blood does Vella need to give?" Matt eyed Bel.

"A single drop shall do the job. But it must be given willingly ... to you."

"It's okay, Matt. I'm fine with it if you are." Vella held out a hand. "How can you cut me?"

"You may use my horns."

Bel pierce Vella's skin? Matt's hackles rose all over again, and he yanked one of the ruby studs from his ear. "I can use the post of the earring. Which finger?"

Vella slid her hand into his, and the weight of the trust in her gaze as she held his stare made his stomach go tight. Fuck, this better not hurt her—and he didn't mean the prick because she didn't even flinch at that, nor say anything when he pressed lightly on the wound and a bead of blood welled.

A metallic tinge bloomed in the air. The heaviness in his stomach ignited into outright heat.

Bloody hell, blood magic was by far the most potent. So much so that his coven didn't even have any in the small list of spells Ellaine had allowed the Magicae coven to train in since the coup.

"Perfect," Bel all but purred. "Now, you each stand at one point of the triangle; I take the third. You must consume the witch's blood, and then together, you and the Bone Witch call this ritual: 'with blood of witches I call this rite, remove Bel's curse on a moonless night, within the henge's boundary sight.' Simple, is it not?"

"Boundary?" Vella scrunched her nose.

"The boundary is the circle that the stones make." Matt went over the words in his mind ... the spell seemed locked into Bel's movement for when and where he could travel. "Okay, let's do this."

He lifted Vella's finger to his lips.

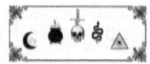

MATT'S BEAUTIFUL LIPS PARTED, his silver eyes filled with those bright glittering diamonds, and as he sucked her thumb into his mouth, all the air seemed to suck out of her lungs.

He sucked deeply. Wow, how much blood did he need?

Heat bloomed in her pussy, and damn if she didn't

drench right there and then. She squirmed, forcing herself to stay still and not leave the triangle point.

Matt's nostrils flared, and for a second, his expression seemed to mirror her urge to forget everything else and get naked, hard and fast.

His gaze shuttered, and he yanked her thumb from his mouth, squeezing her hand even as he opened his mouth.

Oh shit. The ritual. She repeated the words as Bel had given them, somehow keeping pace with Matt, and then power tingled in her palms, echoed at the base of her neck, dipped lower to throb in her pussy—

"Well done!" Bel tipped his head back—his horns gleaming in Matt's witchlight—

and let out a shout of triumph.

And she should have been alarmed as all hell at that sound, but instead, the throb between her legs was growing, and Matt's eyes were glittering and who cared where they were? She needed him. Had. To. Have. Him.

"Well, Bone Witch, my Druid does seem to find you intoxicating. These tunnels would make a fine bed to fuck, and given I am here, I could join you." Bel hissed, long and low. "Darklings."

What? Vella spun around as the tunnel filled with Darklings.

"Damn them, ruining all my fun." Bel howled and spun, his horns scraping on the tunnel walls.

"Hey, our powers," Vella yelled. "Your end of the bargain! Motherfucker, you said you'd help!" Vella spun to Matt. "Can you throw an earth spear through him to stop him from running away?"

"I already have!" Bel's echoing cackle set Vella's teeth on

edge. "Trust, young ones, trust! Now, I must be off—I can't stay in their presence."

An Old God running away from Darklings? But sure enough ... Bel's figure retreated into the tunnel, although the Darklings stayed packed closely around Vella and Matthias.

"Trust?" Vella whirled to Matt. "What is he talking about? Trust him? Trust the bond? Trust what?"

"I have no fucking clue. Do you feel different?"

Different? "Well, I've never gotten so turned on by someone sucking my thumb before."

Matt's eyes narrowed, but he just shook his head. "Not like that. I mean the bond—do you feel altered? Because I don't."

"No, not at all. What an asshole. Was this all for nothing?"

"Not entirely ... I learned that someone else exists who knows about Druid history—my history. That's more than I ever expected to get." His gaze dipped to her hand. "How's the thumb?"

"The prick barely stings. Um, what was it like, the whole drinking blood thing?"

For a moment, he didn't seem to hear her, then he shook himself and his jaw clenched. "Metallic. Hot. Not ... unpleasant. Come on, we need to get out of here."

"So, you didn't get a massive hard-on?" she said as he brushed past. "I swear I felt as turned on as if you'd just gone down on me."

Matt made an odd sound but didn't stop, until he'd reached the opening back to the henge.

"Matt, wait." Vella grabbed his hand. "We need to talk. About what I said in your hotel. Please, I know you're angry—"

A scream from above ground echoed down the earthen steps.

Another. And another.

"Bloody hell. What now?"

"Oh shit. It's not a new moon, is it?" Vella scrambled up the stairs, aware of Matt hot on her heels, and froze. Darklings were everywhere. "They've filled the field," she hissed.

Another scream echoed from the direction of the village.

Another. And another.

"They're not just here in the field. Can you do your thing with this many Darklings?"

"Only one way to know." She sprinted for the houses, found an opening between a thatched-roof cottage and raced to a street.

Darklings filled the road. Lined the sidewalks and driveways.

Adults ran indoors. A family piled into a white SUV and slammed the doors. Two children on bikes pedaled for their lives.

"Vella! I'll go for the car, do my witchfire. But those kids on their bikes—"

"I'll take care of them."

"They'll see." And she knew he wasn't talking about the Darklings. If she consumed the Darklings and saved the children, anyone looking in her direction would see Vella's actions. Her secret would be out.

"Whatever it takes." She set her teeth and ran for the children. Maybe they could out-pedal the Dark—

More Darklings poured into the street from the other end.

The children skidded to a stop, but both bikes toppled, and they slid across the street.

In the distance, adults cried out.

Focus, Vel. She ignored the urge to turn in the direction of those screams and instead ran harder for the children. Her trajectory took her to them at an angle, and she leaped over the bikes, ran past the children and into the Darklings.

Energy buzzed through her as she collided with the first of the Darklings. She danced on her toes and whirled, ran to the next. Another energy buzz.

Another rush of Darklings. More energy fizzed in her veins.

Huh. She could do this all night! She spun and ran to Matt—his witchlight had created a pool of clear space around the car, but the humans inside still couldn't get into their house, so she took care of those Darklings too. Matt called out something, but his actual words were lost beneath the energy crackling through her.

She sucked in a breath and whirled around. More Darklings streamed past the houses and filled the street, almost as if they were looking for *her*.

Maybe they were? And damn, she was happy to oblige them, if it meant more of this amazing, whirling, wonderful energy.

She ran through their ranks as fast as she could, over and over, until she couldn't stand still if she wanted because fiery energy filled every single part of her, and she had to chase after more ... more ... more ...

Something grabbed her arms, swung her around—

"Matt! It's amazing." She wriggled to get out of his hold and go after the next Darkling.

"Vella, stop!" His eyes were wild, and something like panic filled his expression. "They're gone. You've got them all."

"All?" But then how would she get more of this energy? And now she had it all, what did she do with it?

Bone. She needed to connect with bones, all the bones, every bone that existed.

"Vella? What are you talking about? There are no bones here, but there's a cemetery over—"

Yes. Bones. She needed—

Nausea swelled. She fell to her knees. Vomit surged.

Somewhere close by, lightning cracked and split the air. New screams followed. But Vella couldn't move as her body heaved and heaved.

New lightning cracked. Thunder roared and rain pummeled.

"Fuck!" Matt spun and started shouting something, but Vella couldn't understand what because the ground rushed up to meet her and everything went dark.

37

Vella opened her eyes to an unfamiliar bedroom ... again! Seriously, universe, enough with the blacking out and waking up in strange places.

Although at least this bedroom was giving off lovely cottagecore vibes with exposed timber beams, whitewashed walls and sash windows showing the night sky. Were they still in Avebury, in one of the cottages there?

She was alone, and— Vella lifted the thick blankets. "Wearing someone else's leggings and sweatshirt," she murmured.

Where was Matthias? Was he still angry? The last time she'd seen him, he'd been at her side while she ...

Oh crap. She'd vomited at his feet.

Good going, Vella. At least her purse was by the bed, and she snagged her cell to check for messages from Sara, and maybe even Derrick—though what reason could she believe for why he disappeared at the same time as Brianna went missing?

No service.

Huh. Maybe they weren't in Avebury?

Shivering as her feet hit cold floorboards, she padded down a set of creaky stairs and stepped into a beautifully rustic, homey cottage.

Alex and Lucretia sat at a small table with a rectangular tin, a bottle of red wine and two half-drunk glasses between them.

What the frig? Why were *they* here?

"Vella!" Alex leaped up and hugged her. "I knew you would wake soon!"

"Uh, hi. But how—Lucretia, hello, it's great to see you, too. Do either of you know where Matthias is? And are we still in Avebury? Alex, I thought you were in London, watching Nevena—"

"My queen?" Alex whirled to Lucretia. "Would you like me to tell her?"

Wait. Lucretia was the vampire *queen*?

"No, Alexander," Lucretia murmured. "Please let Sinead know our Bone Wielder is awake, though."

Alex bowed and gave Vella another fast hug before bounding out the door.

"So much energy." Lucretia's smile was fond. "My dear Bone Wielder, I am so pleased to see you again. And your Druid is not far away, in case you are concerned."

Relief shot through her. If Matthais was close by, accidental power surges shouldn't be too big a risk.

"Um, thanks. Am I meant to say your highness or something like that?"

"Lucretia is perfect. Only a few stubborn vampires use my title. Now, I have a gift for you; however, I shall wait till Sinead gets here."

The cottage door banged open, and a woman about

Vella's height, with curly hair more silver than red, and warm caramel eyes, dashed in.

Following so fast they ran into her back, were Ciara and Ryan, the two Mors Dicen witches she'd met on her search for the first aett of bone runes.

Okay ... The hairs on the back of Vella's neck tingled. Something told her she wasn't in Avebury anymore.

"Oh my good Goddess, you're awake!" the woman who must be Sinead said with a faint Irish accent. She shot a hand to her chest and wobbled.

"Careful, *máthair mhór*." Ryan steadied the woman. "Vespera, it is so good to see you again. This is Sinead, our last Mors Dicen elder. Sinead is also—"

"Let me tell it, Ryan." Sinead took a breath, and tears filled her pretty eyes. "Vespera, I am your great-aunt. Your mother, Honoria, is ... was ... my niece, bless her soul."

Vella froze.

Sinead was *family*?

But ... Ellaine had called herself Vella's great-aunt, and now this stranger was also claiming the title. What if this were another lie? Another betrayal to add to those she'd already been fed?

"It is true," Lucretia murmured. "Doubt not, Bone Wielder."

Vella's heart took off running because Lucretia wouldn't lie about this, would she?

The vampire—queen!—nodded as if in approval of that thought.

And if this woman was Vella's great-aunt ... The prickling at the base of Vella's neck erupted into an outright shiver.

"May I—may I come over?" Sinead took a hesitant step

forward. "I know you do not recognize me, but ever since Ryan and Ciara came home with news of your discovery, I have yearned for this moment."

Inside Vella's chest, something unfurled, something warm and alive and ... hopeful.

Had she found her coven?

Vella's eyes stung, but before she could blink, Sinead wrapped her in a fierce embrace. And then another pair of arms, and then another wrapped around them, and someone cried, but it wasn't Vella because she couldn't get a breath past the burning lump in her chest.

"All right, all right. Let the girl breathe." Sinead pushed back, and her weathered hands cradled Vella's cheeks. "Vespera O'Connor, welcome home."

She had a name? A *real* name.

"O'Connor?" Vella whispered. "Antony and Honoria O'Connor?"

"Almost. Antony was from Italy—he and your mother met while they were studying. But Antony understood the need for Honoria's children to carry the O'Connor name as so many of our leaders have had before you. And oh, Vespera, we have longed for the return of one who can take up their torch and lead us."

"A leader?" Vella stepped back. "You and Brianna sound so similar."

"And we are so proud that you found her."

"Actually, I ... lost her." Had Vella really found a new family but lost the one she'd already had? Vella's stomach roiled with bile.

"The Druid told us," Sinead said, her smile slipping. "But you found Brianna once. One of our oldest, greatest Bone Guides who has been missing for centuries—*you* found her, Bone Wielder. And I know you will again. And that is why we are honored to follow you."

Wait, what now?

Oh no. No, no, no. Vella was still figuring out who *she* was. No way anyone could look to her for guidance. Just look at how much she'd fucked up in the past.

But three pairs of eyes, not to mention Lucretia, all watched her with some kind of awe and expectation.

Her chest clogged up heavy and hot, and suddenly she couldn't even get a breath in. Air. She needed to get some frigging *air*.

"Listen, it has been ... well, I'm speechless at meeting you, Sinead." She swallowed hard. *Keep it together, Vel.* Just breathe. "And Ryan and Ciara, I am so happy to see you again. But this has all been a lot, and I just need to go for a walk and clear my head. Find—"

Myself.

Tears stung at her eyes, and that hot lump rose higher.

"Your Druid is in the third cottage up the hill," Ryan said. "I'll take you there—"

"No! No, all good. I'll go myself. Thank you."

Sinead's eyes creased with concern. "Of course, this is so much all at once. I'll get the tea on and have something hot ready for when you get back. But you'll be needing more clothes—it's freezing outside."

"Here." Lucretia rose to her feet in that preternaturally smooth way of hers and took an expensive-looking full-length black woolen coat off a hook by the door and tossed it at Vella. "Vintage Dior."

"Right. Thank you again."

Vella escaped into the icy night air, but at least cold meant her tears froze before they could fall.

AFTER WORKING by lamplight for hours on end, painstakingly transferring all the underlined annotations and text from Jamie's copy of *Malleus Maleficarum*, Matt sat back, rubbing the base of his neck as a disturbing itch gathered there, and contemplating Alex across the table.

"No signs of Vella waking up?" Matt asked again. "I can check—"

"Not needed. I just came from there." Alex smiled. "Now, how does this decoding of the puzzle go?"

"Almost done." No surprise, given he'd had hours while Vella slept to work on it. "Listen, I should go check; she might be having a nightmare—"

"Our queen sits with her; she will ensure our Bone Wielder is safe."

"Still, I should go." Matt rubbed his neck again.

The cottage door opened, and the sweet wind blew in Vella's butterscotch scent moments before she stepped inside.

He shot a scowl at Alex. "You were meant to tell me when she woke up."

"Sinead asked me to give her some time alone first, and my word goes to the Mors Dicen first, you know that."

Bloody stubborn vamps, almost as bad as stubborn Mors Dicen witches.

But right now, Vella was standing and not vomiting lightning. That was a plus.

She brushed her windswept hair over her shoulder and turned those lioness eyes in his direction.

"You don't look so good." His gut clenched. "Is something wrong?" He shifted chairs, freeing up the seat nearest the fire. "Come over and get warm."

"Nothing's wrong. Just a lot going on. And I needed the air." She blew out a long breath as she sat down, and damn it, he might be mad with her lack of trust, but inside him, everything eased just to be next to her.

Bloody hell.

She looked over the table, and her eyes widened. "Wait —you did it? Oh shit. How long was I out this time?"

"Nine hours, and it's not quite finished." Matt held in a grimace. Nine hours of wondering if she was okay, if she'd inhaled too many Darklings, if her lightning spews were deadly to her and others.

If she trusted him yet.

Bloody hell.

"Druid, are you okay?" Alex shoved his arm.

"Yes." No. But he called on the years of practice he'd had at pretending to be fucking okay and smiled his lying ass off. "It's just been a long night of identifying the ciphertext."

"Where are we?" Vella's eyes narrowed. "It's like a village from a very long time ago."

"On the ocean-side of Inis Misneach," Alex cut in.

"In-ish Mish-nagh?"

"It means Island of Courage. We're in the North Atlantic Ocean, off Ireland's west coast."

"We're in Ireland?" Vella dropped into the seat Matt had suggested. "I mean, it's good to know where in the world we are, but I don't even know what happened after the whole Darkling-vomiting-at-your-feet episode. Except, I think there was lightning?"

"Did you make it, Bone Wielder?" If Alex leaned any further forward, he'd fall off his seats.

"No clue." Vella's eyes widened as she looked at Matthias. "What did happen? Did you see Bel again?"

"No, the last I saw of Bel was him running down the tunnel toward Stonehenge. As for the vomiting, as you said, you were extremely ill, and there were multiple lightning strikes. That"—had freaked Matt out more than anything. Every time Vella vomited, lightning fucking erupted so close it almost struck them—"worried me. I had to use my Druid power to get control of the sudden ... storm, and after that crisis was handled, I remembered what you told me about Brianna feeling your coven could help with your magic. So I called Sylvie, who contacted Lucretia, who arranged for a helicopter to pick us up and bring us here."

"How was everyone at Avebury? Did anyone ..."

"Everyone survived."

"That is such a relief." Vella's breath visibly whooshed out. "I've never seen so many Darklings in the one place before. And you were brilliant—you got to those people with your witchlight just in time."

"You were the amazing one." And near-to-giving-him-a-heart-attack mesmerizing when she was hyped up on Darklings, but he'd save that for a private conversation. "You saved way more lives than me."

"No wonder you saved them all." Alex sat up and smiled like they'd patted him on the head. "What a team you make, a Bone Wielder and her Primus."

A team? Oh no, a team trusted each other.

Frustration ... and that damned hurt bubbled back to the surface, and he turned away. *Head in the game, Matt.* Whatever he and Vella were—half bonded, allies, lovers—right now they had an aett of bone runes to secure, and a meeting to make back in New York in two days' time.

"Matt, I need to check in with Sara, see how she and

Morrigan are going, but there's no reception. Do you know where I can make a call?"

"Not here." Alex shook his head. "The village we're in has no name, no cellular service, and is kept apart from the electricity grid that humans use, to lower the chance of anyone discovering who lives here."

"But how do they stay hidden from Div foresight?"

"There's always at least one vampire here, and we know the Divs cannot see us, or what happens around us, and the Mors Dicen who do are live here maintain bone magic at five points around the village to protect it. It takes a lot of their time, but it keeps them alive."

"Thank frig for that." Vella nibbled on her lip. "So you can't get a call in or out at all? I really need to check in with Sara."

Damn it, they had work to do. Yes, contacting Sara—and everyone else they needed to talk to—was important, but right now they had a deadline looming.

"Nope." Alex held up his cell phone. "But the village on the other side of the island has reception, so we go there when we need to get messages out. I'm going over today and can take you."

"That would be great."

"No. This code is our priority," Matt gritted out. "After we know where the second bloody aett is, we can leave the island and contact every fucking one who we need to talk to and find out what the hell other fuckery has happened while we've been hiding out here."

Vella and Alex traded glances, and Alex loudly whispered, "Your Primus is angry. Do you need to soothe him?"

Soothe him? Gods but Matt wanted to rip out the smiling fucker's throat. He did not need soothing.

"No, Matt's right. We need to get this done." Vella leaned

over the table, and as she shifted, the lamplight picked up the gleaming skin at the base of her throat.

Memories of how her blood had tasted beneath Avebury made his mouth water.

Bloody hell. *So much for head in the fucking game.*

He cleared his throat. "Thank you. We are on the clock to get back to New York."

"Shit. The meeting." Vella scrubbed her face. "What's today?"

"Monday," Alex said helpfully. "Almost sunrise."

"Hence the need to finish fast. The meeting is tomorrow afternoon." Matt nodded at the letters he'd written out. "These are the letters—both from the annotations and the actual book text—that were underlined in the manuscript. We have the ciphertext, we just need to decode the location of the second aett."

He slid the notebook he'd been working on across the table.

Yshqfd Ou Oesdio Yauvufushev
Kdiyfasev Hiiayuifhev

"And these discs will decode the message?" Alex held up both pieces of the cipher wheel.

"I'll show you." Vella held out her hand, and when Alex dropped them into her palm, she turned them over and fitted them together. "Beautiful," she breathed. "It's amazing how perfectly they join. Whoever made these was a true craftsperson."

Beautiful was one word for it.

"Matt? Did you say something?" Vella looked up at him through her lashes, and for a moment, the rest of the world disappeared. Gods but she was pure fucking perfection.

"No," he grunted.

"Right. Well, if we swivel each disc so the sword evenly lines up with the skull, the K lines up with the A. That's the key we need to decipher the text." She glanced at Matt, but whatever she saw on his face had her turn back to Alex. "And there you have it."

Alex peered down at the discs.

"So the Y becomes C, and the S becomes R ..."

"Correct," Matt bit out. "But let's hurry this along."

Vella's gaze flew to him, but she didn't ask the question clearly on her mind ... why the fuck was he being such a prick ... which was just as well, because what could he say? That he'd found the most incredible being he could ever imagine, and she didn't. Fucking Trust. Him.

"Wow," Vella breathed moments later. She leaned back in her seat. "So this is the code they hid all those years ago."

Yshgfd Ou Oesdio Yauvufushev
Kdiyfasev Hiiayuifhev

Cripta De Durand Coemeterium
Sanctorum Innocentium

"But it's in another language—maybe Latin?" She nibbled at her lip. "Not a big surprise there; it was a common language, but I have zero clue what it says. Matt?"

"No idea." He shoved his hands into his pockets.

"Then now it is my turn to make you happy." Alex grinned. "It translates to Du Durand Crypt, Holy Innocents' Cemetery."

"Oh wow. We have it—that's the location!" Vella leaped to her feet. "We're getting the second aett. Now we just have to work out where they are in the ossuaries, and then how to get them out without being seen by any Divs, and then how to keep them safe."

"Wait. What ossuary? I said it translates to cemetery."

"The Holy Innocents' Cemetery was closed down in the late eighteenth century."

"Closed?" Alex frowned. "Then how do we have the location?"

"Because the bones were placed in the ossuaries beneath Paris, and the big crypts have markers for where to find them. I read about them at college—I never imagined actually going there."

"Back to Paris we go." Alex whistled.

"And thank fuck." Matt mentally reviewed the timings. "We can get to France, then back to New York in time—"

"Matt? Maybe this is one meeting you shouldn't be at. What if Ellaine and Derrick are planning something terrible? We still don't know why Ellaine forced us to have the later meeting, or why Derrick disappeared. And if they're involved with Brianna going missing ... I don't want you risking your life here, Medea."

"Vella, Ellaine and Derrick are the reason I *must* go. If I'm not there, Ruby will have no support, and Ellaine will bulldoze over her like she's building her towers. And the main reason? Being at those meetings is the only way I can discover what Ellaine's plans are and warn everyone. And I'm it—no one else has a hope in hell of getting inside that meeting room."

"You could be walking into a trap, Matt."

"Every time I go there, that's a possibility. It hasn't stopped me yet, and it won't now. And I've got Ronin at my back."

"But your power has never been so dangerous before. What if you lose control and Ellaine sees? The half bond is still a risk to you—"

"And you." Matt couldn't control a shiver. "Look at what happened with the Darklings. Last word I had from Ronin, he was following up with the Avebury locals to get any footage of you off surveillance cameras and cell phones. You —we—are so close to being fucked here, Vella—"

Shit. He bit back the words that wanted to erupt.

Did she really not trust him?

And why the fuck couldn't he get over that question?

Because ... *holy fuck.* Because if she didn't trust him, how could she ever love him?

His chest fractured.

"Hey, Alex? Would you mind if Matt and I have that alone time now? We need to talk."

Vella's gaze stayed on Matt as she spoke, but Alex

nodded and left without a word. Of course, because he would do exactly as a Mors Dicen asked.

But what else did Vella have to say? What else did she want from him? Like a wounded animal, Matt's hackles rose, and instead of defense, his body went into offensive mode. She wanted to talk? Fine. It was time they had some total truths between them.

"Actually—" Vella opened the door. "It's almost sunrise, and I need air."

Air? Fucking perfect.

38

B y the time they'd reached the cliffs above the ocean, the sun's glow battled the clouds for dominance over the dawning sky.

With a deep breath, Vella stopped walking and faced Matthias.

His long coat billowed behind him like a cape out of a fantasy story, and his breathtaking, heart-achingly magnificent face—eyes stormy, cheeks like the granite rocks below them—captivated her more fully than any artwork she could imagine.

And while the rugged cliffs and bruised sky and roiling winds that whipped his hair into a fury might seem too fierce—too rough—too *much* for the smooth Magicae Councilor, for Matthias Medea, they were perfect.

Beautiful. Elemental. Powerful.

Her breath caught, and suddenly her heart pounded so fast she couldn't catch it. *Focus, Vel.* Because however she and Matthias were going to move forward, honesty had to be the first step.

"All right, Matthias, let's do this. I know you're angry—"

"Angry?" His lips pulled back in a sneer that made her belly clench. "You think what I'm feeling is fueled by anger? Oh no, *anger* is an outcome."

"Okay. Not angry—no, not *just* angry." She moistened her lips. Was the wind chapping them dry, or was it the sense that she was suddenly way more out of her depth than she'd realized? "Lay it on me, spellcaster. All of it."

His eyes narrowed, and his jaw clenched so tight it seemed he wasn't going to speak.

"Fine. This is my all," he gritted out. "After everything you and I have been through together, it fucking hurts that you don't trust me, and yes, when I get hurt, I guess I get angry." He turned to look out over the wild ocean, his strong profile versus the powerful seas, and hauled in a shuddering breath. "Turns out it's been a long time since anyone *could* hurt me."

Oh Goddess, this magnificent man was shuddering because of *her*. She'd hurt him—*was* hurting him.

Pressure clenched in Vella's chest, as if responding to the pressure of the clouds gathering around them.

"I do—I do trust you," she whispered.

Matt slowly turned to her. But there was no hope in his eyes.

"Physically? Yes. But emotionally?"

Emotionally ... The tightness in her breath constricted further. She wanted to say yes, but she wasn't going to lie.

"Yeah, that's what I thought." Matt laughed, a cold, brittle sound. "Gods know, I deserve some of the blame. I manipulated you and lied to you when we first met. And fuck, you're only twenty-three—"

"Almost twenty-four," she whispered. "And age has nothing to do with this. I just—I want to trust you, I do. I want things right between us. I want *you*, Matthias. But ...

but I don't even know what trust means! How can I?" The pressure in her chest expanded. "Look at what happened when I put my trust in Ellaine? I fucked up, Matt. I trusted her and all along she killed them. Mom. Dad. And then poisoned Sara. And for all those years, I trusted her." Tears burned in her eyes, but somehow, they didn't fall.

"Vella. I am sorry for what happened—for what she did to you, and what she took from you—but how much more of your life are you going to let her steal?" He shoved a hand through his hair. "Fuck, Vella, I have tried to do the right thing here. I haven't pushed to get you to see my perspective. I've let you set the pace the entire fucking way, and that's the problem."

"What do you mean?"

"I mean, you are not in control, Vella! You pretend you are—trying to control your emotions, but it doesn't work. And the sooner you see this for what it is, the fucking better, for all of us."

"Is this about you and me?"

"Gods, but I wish it was just you and me. But if you and I get this wrong, *every* witch might lose, because right now, you and I—we—might be the only ones who can bring Ellaine down and save them."

"Fuck, Matt. I don't know how much more I can handle." Those damned tears rushed back to her eyes. "Everyone wants me to be something. Ellaine wants me to help her frigging destroy my coven. Derrick wants me to be the perfect cousin I never was. Sara wants me to fight back and, oh yeah, let her go and risk her life, too. Brianna wants me to fight using every Mors Dicen weapon out there. Even Sinead expects me—me!—to somehow lead their fight back against Ellaine. And you ... you want the most." Her throat squeezed tight, so she could only whisper, "You want my trust."

A sob lodged in her throat.

Matt stilled, and the midnight stars in his eyes whirled faster and brighter, until there was no silver in his irises at all.

"But me? I want—I want—"

"What? What, Vella?"

"I don't know! I'm broken, okay? Brianna said it—I'm the problem. I'm broken, and I don't know how to fix me!"

"Because you're battening everything down! Vella, Ellaine fucked you over, but she did not break you. Yet you can't see that because you're shutting everything—everyone—out. You're not broken, Rapunzel. You're hurting. But you've buried all your emotions so deep, you can't even see that *not* feeling is the problem. And you know what? I think you do know what you want, even if you haven't realized it yourself yet."

Damn him, why did he have to look at her like that? Pity and sadness and pain and hurt.

A burning ball lodged in her throat.

"You want to trust yourself." His mouth tightened. "But only you can work out how to make that happen. And until you do, I don't think you can trust anyone else."

Trust herself. Damn it all to the Goddess and back, he was right. She did want that. So. Frigging, badly.

Only ... how?

That burning ball swelled. She opened her mouth to keep talking, but the words sat like a lump of smoldering bones in her chest. So she swallowed hard, because Matt deserved her full honesty.

"Matt, even if you're right, and maybe—maybe you are, can't you and I just be together while I work out my shit? We like each other. The bond will work. Why does trust have to matter so much?"

"Vella, this isn't about the bond or the fate of witchkind or anyone else. This is only you and me. But this is the part that terrifies *me*—because if you don't trust me, how can you love me?"

The churning in Vella's gut froze into a lead weight.

"And yes, Vella. Vespera, Bone Wielder, Mors Dicen witch." The midnight stars in his eyes glittered. Over the ocean, the clouds grew heavier and rolled across the water faster. "I fucking love you."

Vella's heart jammed in her chest. He loved her. Matthias Medea, maybe the best person she'd ever met, loved *her*.

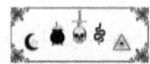

MATT'S CHEST was on fire, as though he'd swum across the ocean underwater on one breath of air, but he couldn't have taken a breath if he'd wanted to.

Because he might be out of oxygen, but his Rapunzel was the one drowning.

Her eyes screamed it. Her words had confirmed it. She was sinking beneath the weight of everyone's—his included —expectations.

"Vella." He reached out for her.

"You really think you love me?" she whispered. Her hands clenched his hands. Cold. Tight. Shaking. Her usually golden eyes, now a pale amber, were wide as she searched his. What she looked for, he didn't know.

"Yes, I do," he said quietly. "I am in love with you. But what you just said about everyone's expectations? I never realized you were feeling like that, and the last thing I want is to add more pressure."

"I should've told you sooner, and for that, I'm sorry. But, Matt, I do care for you. I care for so damned much. But more than that—as in ... love? I don't even know if I'm capable."

"Do you mean you can't fall in love? Or you don't want to fall in love?"

"I don't know." He hated the unhappiness filling her eyes. "And I don't want to hurt you, but we've been together for less than two months, and even though it feels like I've known you forever, we haven't."

"I get that."

"And the bond has forced us together. Maybe, if we'd gotten to know each other like normal witches do, had a relationship develop like it would for anyone else ..."

"Yeah, I get that, too."

"Maybe if we weren't in this clusterfuck of a situation, I could honestly say yes to that question because you are, without doubt, the man I would want to fall in love with."

"But you can't." The fracture in his chest widened into a chasm, and physical pain flooded in, taking his breath away.

He'd thought not having her trust was bad, but this—this was agony.

"Matt," Vella gasped. Her hand squeezed around his. "Oh shit. That pain—are you going to have a power surge?"

"No. No, I'm not." But why? Every other time he'd felt a strong emotional reaction in the past three weeks, his power had exploded. Until now.

Dread spread its cold fingers up his spine. "You're right."

"Wait. You are going to surge?"

"No, I mean that I'm not losing control of my Druid power."

Vella winced. "That's good, right?"

"Unless ... do you recall Bel's words in the tunnel as he

left? He said he could fasten or sever a bond. Maybe he chose the sever option."

"But he said he would help you get control of your power."

"Which he did, I haven't lost control once since then. Not seeing you high on Darklings and vomiting up lightning. Not in the past nine hours of worry. Not even now while it feels like my heart is being cut out."

Vella's mouth dropped wide, and Matt had to snap his own shut.

Their bond was gone.

Fuck. Fuck, fuck, fuck.

"Maybe ... maybe, this is for the best." Was he lying to himself, or to Vella? Or to them both?

"What? How can you say that?"

"Because you're dealing with so much pressure, and now you have one less worry on your shoulders. You don't even know *what* you're feeling. And how could you? This is all so fresh for you, whereas I've had years to deal with the knowledge of Ellaine's fucked-upness."

"Matt." Vella's eyes went flat. "Why does that sound like you're dumping me?"

"No. Gods no. I can't imagine not loving you. But you're here with your coven; you can figure out your magic, how to stop making dead things come back to life."

"And where are you going?"

"I'll get the bone runes and bring them back here; you can work out how to keep them safe, and then I'll go to New York—"

"Without me." Her chin lowered.

"If you're not at Div Tower, Ellaine can't hurt you. And I must be there, but we don't need to stay together now the bond's gone. I'll get Shannah to bring Sara to you, and you can stay here, figure out your magic, figure out"—if she wanted Matt in her life—"who you are."

Pain tore him like a saw with jagged teeth, ripping apart skin and bone and muscle all the way to his heart. He held in a hiss. Surely, with the bond gone, this shouldn't hurt so fucking much?

"Is—is that what you want?" Vella dropped his hands and stepped back. Retreating from him. "For me to stay here without you?"

"Yes." No. Fucking gods no, he never wanted to leave her. But at least here she'd be safe away from Ellaine. That was a bonus he couldn't deny.

Footsteps echoed behind him, and Vella's gaze cut over his shoulders. Tears still gleamed in her eyes, but none fell.

When was she going to see that she couldn't keep going like this? She needed to start to feel again. And even now, it wasn't so they could cement their bond; this mattered for *her*.

"What a delightfully chilly morning for taking in the ocean," Lucretia called, her voice carrying over the crash of the waves. "Apologies for the disruption of your ... chat; however, a message has arrived in the village for you, Matthias. There's a mule and cart waiting at Sinead's home to take you across the island."

"Got it, thank you," Matt called back, without turning around. Only Ronin knew where Matt and Vella were, and if Ronin needed him ... Fuck. Fuck, fuck, fuck.

"I have to go." Gods but he wanted to wrap his arms around Vella and never let go. What if she took this time to work on herself and realized she didn't love him?

That pain shot through him again, but there was fuck all he could do. So this was it. He'd say goodbye and hope to the gods that when Vella found herself, when she opened herself up to emotional connections again, she'd feel for him what he felt for her.

He took a step forward.

Vella crossed her arms tightly.

Guess that was a no to hugging her goodbye.

"I want you to know one thing, Rapunzel. You are not broken, and you don't need fixing. Just ... find yourself."

"Find myself? I don't know how!"

"Start by looking at what you do know. Like your love of antiques."

"But even that, how do I know if I truly admire them or if it's because *she* started me on this path, needing me to have this insight so I could find the Aetts of Cogadh? How do I know ... me?"

"Vella, Ellaine has taken so much from you—from thousands of witches—but please, please don't let her take this from you, too. Do you know one of the things I first loved about you?" He tried not to wince when Vella's arms tightened around her waist. "It was how you get lost in an object's past—it's like you see more than just the function, or form, or whatever most of us see, and you find the story that makes those antiques come to life. That's not something Ellaine could ever make you feel. And if there is only one thing you ever do for me, Vella? Promise me, you won't let Ellaine steal anything more from you."

Vella's eyes tightened, and around them, raindrops started to fall, whisper quiet.

"Don't stay out too long." His throat closed over like it had filled with hot lead, and with one final glance to soak in his Rapunzel, he turned around and walked away.

39

M atthias' words replayed in Vella's mind, synchronizing with every step he took away from her until, once again, she was alone.

The pressure in her chest grew too much to bear, and she spun back to the ocean, but her legs no longer supported her and she crumpled to the ground.

"Bone Wielder?" Lucretia's voice was soft as she stopped in the grass, right where Matt had been standing.

"I, uh, didn't hear you—"

"No, no. Stay there. I shall join you." Lucretia sank to the grass with her habitual preternatural grace, looking like some fancy lady from Victorian times having a picnic on the lawn ... all she needed was a croquet game nearby and a frilly parasol.

"Listen, thanks for coming over and all, but I'm not good company right now."

"Then I shall be the good company, and you the bad. What a lovely change that will be, something I am sure your Brianna would say."

"You know Brianna?"

"I knew of her. She was the Bone Guide to the wonderful witch who saved my life, that would be ... oh, over four hundred years ago now."

What ... no way. Brianna had told Vella the story of Hannah, her last Bone Wielder before Vella, and how she'd sacrificed herself to save a young vampire princess.

"That was you in the cell with Hannah?"

"That was me. Hannah was an incredible woman. And she told me so much about Brianna while we were together in that cell, which is why I know your Brianna would want me to help you, especially in her absence. So how may I do so? I can see you are troubled."

"I look that bad?"

"Hmm ... that is part of it. So, where would you like to start?"

Goddess, where *to* start?

"At the beginning, I find is best." Lucretia waved an elegant hand. "Come, Bone Wielder, what can it hurt? Unless you enjoy feeling this way?"

"No, no, that I do not," Vella choked out. With a deep breath, she told Lucretia everything. "And now I'm here, and Matt has gone," she whispered.

"Hmm ... dear me, you have had a time of it, haven't you? Lies. Betrayals. Mistakes. So much self-acceptance required, yet leaving oneself vulnerable to a repeat of all that suffering. And beneath it all, just one foundation: trust."

Vella's throat closed over and she nodded. No matter which way she went, it always ended with that one word.

"I would ask you this, Vespera: do you *want* to trust yourself, and Matthias?"

"Of course I do. But I don't know how. It's not as simple to just say those words—I need to mean them, but that's what I can't do."

"Then reframe this conversation. What choices can you make here? If you choose to trust Matthias, to give him your total belief and become vulnerable, what repercussions could happen? And be honest with yourself about it all— the good and the bad. And then ask the same of yourself. If you trust your intuition and believe in your ability to know what to do, what can happen?"

"Everything can go wrong!"

"And right?"

"Everything," Vella whispered.

"Then it appears to me, the only thing you can do is choose—choose to accept the risk and move forward or choose to reject the risk and embrace the fear, staying where you are." Lucretia dusted her hands on her coat and rose to her feet. "And now I find myself becoming hungry, and the sun far too bright for my delicate eyes. I shall adjourn and leave you to your musings on this beautiful island. The Island of Courage, I believe it's named. Or something along those lines."

Trust ...

Alone again on the cliff, Vella stared out at the feral ocean; the turbulent waters mirroring the sky above.

Trust ...

So what *if* she trusted wrongly—with herself or someone else? How many more would be hurt or worse?

Maybe ... surrendering to the fear wasn't so bad?

Except that would mean Ellaine had won. That Ellaine had broken Vella once and for all.

A keening cry escaped her, and she dug her fingers into the cool earth.

Fuck no. Letting that ... blight on this world win was not happening. Witches ... humans ... everyone deserved to live

without the Council controlling their lives. They deserved to
live.

Her mom. Her dad. Matthias' parents. Every single one
of them deserved to live their lives. Matt deserved to grow
up as a teenager without that horrific assault. Sara deserved
to live without being poisoned her entire life. Vella deserved
to not have her parents' murdered and to live free of the
threat of her sister's death.

And there were so many, many, more.

They deserved better. Vella deserved better. Tears sprang
into her eyes.

She'd be damned if she didn't fight for all of them to get
their vengeance.

Scrambling to her feet, she braced herself against
the wind as it roared over the cliffs. "I am not giving
in!" she shouted. "I am not broken!" she screamed to
the sky.

And the wind roared back.

It tore at her hair, and it scrabbled at her skin and pulled
the scream from her lungs.

It whisked the moisture from her eyes, sent it streaming
down her cheeks in an endless sea of tears.

And it ripped up the ice that had sheltered her soul and
let the pain free.

The pain was an entity all its own ... it raged and bit and
clawed and laid everything bare—and when finally, finally,
it had filled her and she could drag a breath past the hurt ...
everything made sense, and she knew exactly what she
needed to do.

The wind stopped so suddenly that her hair dropped in
a tangle, and everything went still. Everything except an odd
sensation right in the center of her chest, urging her back
toward the cottages.

"Well, that was certainly a demonstration," a man said from beside her.

Vella whirled around. "Who—"

The tin Lucretia had tried to give her earlier sat in the grass, lid ajar. Had the wind propped it off?

"I felt that scream all the way to my toes," a woman said.

"Oh shit." Vella dropped to her knees and grabbed the tin, pulling out the book she hadn't known was inside. "Hello! It's Vella. I'm here."

The small, black, pocket-sized book filled her hand, and she traced the raised skull and sword—her coven's insignia —with her thumb. This was the book Lucretia had shown her back in her London home.

"Hello, Vella. We remember you from the vampire's house. You took us out, but only for such a brief time."

"And I am sorry for that. I was still learning about myself. I didn't know then who I was, who you were."

"Well, I do not like the sound of that," a dry, unfamiliar voice said. "You should know who we are—"

"Catherine. Enough. Let the youngling speak." That was the first voice again.

"Please introduce yourselves, all of you, and tell me about you—about this book."

Cradling it to her chest, she picked up the tin and its lid and took off at a run. She needed to see Sinead and then get to Matthias before he left.

"We are the Book of Bones," the first voice replied. "I am Sebastian; this is Catherine."

"I suppose I shall say hello. I am Catherine—do not address me as Katy," a new voice said.

"And I am Elizabeth. Please call Lizzie." the first female added. "Now, tell us about you, Vella."

"I'm a Bone Wielder." Vella reached the path back to the

village. "But I'm having a problem with my magic, and I've lost my Bone Guide—"

"Lost? Oh no, that will never do," Catherine—definitely Catherine—cut in.

"It's a long story. But I can talk while I walk."

"Where are you taking us?" Lizzie asked.

"I need to speak with my elder here and find out how to make my magic work. And then I need to find an armory and get some weapons. And I have to do that fast because my flight off this island is happening soon." Just, please don't let her be too late.

"We can help you," Sebastian said. "What answers do you seek?"

"You can? My magic is leaking, and I'm accidentally bringing dead things back to life—"

"A Bone Caller!" Lizzy let out a cry.

"Yes. And I've half bonded with a Druid, only an Old God cut the bond—"

"Oh no. I do not think so," Catherine cut in. "A bond cannot be severed."

She'd reached the row of cottages, eight in total. But which was Sinead's—

The door nearest opened, and Ryan popped out. "Vespera?"

"I'm looking for Sinead!"

"She's here." He ducked his head back in through the door. "*Máthair mhór!* Vespera's here, talking to the Book of Bones and wanting you."

"Ryan?" Sebastian called out. "Good morning!"

"You too, Sebastian. What are you talking to Vespera about?"

"She said her name is Vella." Suspicion laced Catherine's tone.

"It's both," Vella gritted out. But at least Sinead was there —and Lucretia. All were standing in front of the cottage.

"Hello again, Bone Wielder," Lucretia purred. "I see you found my gift."

"What is it, Vespera?" Sinead asked.

Vella did her best to bring them all up to speed on her conversation with the Book of Bones peeps. "And I'm telling you—the Old God did a ritual and then cut our bond."

The tugging sensation pulled in her chest again, urging her to go up the hill.

"Which ritual?" Sinead grabbed Vella's arm, and she refocused on the elder.

"Matt cut himself and put his blood on my forehead, and then he drank a sip of *my* blood—" Her body heated at just the memory of how good that had actually felt.

"Drank it?" Elizabeth asked. "Not my preference, but it will do. Mind you, hygiene would be an issue underground."

"Highly unusual." Catherine. Definitely Catherine.

"I'm not worried about a little prick right now. I'm saying that Bel cut the bond—"

"Hmm, now that is interesting," Lucretia said. She tapped her blood-red lips with one immaculately enameled nail. "That does make me wonder ... However, for now, Bone Wielder, you should know that Bel is an ass. He has been trapped underground for far too long, the fool. He absolutely cannot cut a henge-blessed bond. Pft. Such arrogance. No, the bond is binding. What he did do, however, was consecrate your bond with the Druid. Your bond is now cemented."

Vella froze.

Holy shit. She and Matt were still bonded? How did she tell him that?

"Okay ... as unexpected as that is"—understatement!—
"what about the undead things I keep bringing back to life?"

"You are a Bone Caller," Sebastian said as if that
explained everything. "Your magic is calling the bones to
your side."

"But how do I stop it? Well, not all of them. I love Morrigan." She gave them the fast version of how she and her
familiar came to be together.

"And your Druid's magic combined to make her feathers? How wonderful!" Lizzy gave out a crow so reminiscent
of Brianna that Vella's chest went tingly.

Their family was really growing now. Gods, she couldn't
wait to bring Sara here.

"Okay, so how do I stop accidentally calling them—and
put the ones I've already called back to rest?"

"Once your leaking magic is no longer an issue, that will
stop." Sinead patted her hand. "A little leakage is normal
when you first bond—your magics are adjusting, sensing
where one may cede and the other grow, in both directions."

"So now the bond is done, all that leaking magic should
stop?"

"Not entirely. The adjustment period takes time and
usually starts after the bond."

"Stalled bonds are rare but not unheard of," Sebastian
called out. "Page thirteen. All you need to know about
stalled bonds. And page eight has what we know about
Bone Callers ... not much there, so perhaps you can add in
your findings?"

"Never fear," Sinead added. "You and your Druid will
eventually balance each other out. Most witches find this a
gentle process; however, you are both powerful in your own
right, so perhaps your balancing might be a little more ...
tempestuous."

"So this is all normal? I don't need help to manage my magic? Brianna thought, maybe I"—shit, this was embarrassing—"that I was the problem."

"And were you?" Sinead cocked her head to one side.

"Yes." Vella sighed and owned it. "I was. But I've figured my shit out now."

"Figuring one's shit out is always such a process." Lucretia gave an elegant shrug. "Well done, Vespera."

"Do find the creatures you have reanimated so far," Catherine added. "They must be laid back to their rest."

"Of course." Just as soon as she found them. "In the meantime, are they dangerous?"

"Why would they be? They seek you out. They are here for you, Bone Caller."

Bone Wielder, Walker ... Caller ... Good grief. How many titles did she need?

"Well, now that's sorted, I need to get our bone runes back, which means catching my Druid before he flies off without me. Did you really send him across the island with a mule?"

"Oh no. He decided to stay."

"Matthias is here?" Vella's heart spiked. "Let me guess? He's in a cottage up the hill?"

"Yes, the third one, where he spent the night."

"Thank frig." She had so much to tell him—but she also needed had to find their armory. *Focus, Vel.* "Can you show me where you keep your weapons? I'll need at least one—"

"What do you mean? You are the Bone Wielder."

"But I still need a weapon—"

"No, Vespera." Sinead shook her head, true puzzlement in her eyes. "You *are* the weapon."

40

M att stood up for the hundredth time to go back to the cliffs—and sat back down.

Alex shook his head at him. "She needs time. You heard what our queen said."

"Lucretia said 'give her space,' which I've done."

The door creaked open.

He stood so fast his chair flew back. "Vella."

"You are still here!" Her eyes lit up.

"I had to stay. Gods, Vella, I need to tell you—" He peered over Vella's shoulder. "What are you all doing here?" Matt stepped back as Sinead, Lucretia, Ryan and Ciara all crowded in behind Vella.

"Matt, I need to talk to you." Vella took off her coat, slinging it over the back of the nearest chair, then she shook out her hair, the red mass tumbling around her shoulders.

His fingers itched to dive into it, holding her still while he devoured her. "Talk ... Yes, I know. That's what I'm saying. And it looks like you all intend on hearing what I have to say? Is that it?"

"She is our Bone Wielder," Lucretia said with a smile

that belied the steel beneath her words. "We will see her Primus do the right thing by her."

"And Vella is our family." Sinead folded her arms. "We will see that her bonded mate does the right thing by her."

"Family." Vella smiled, and it was one of the sweetest smiles Matt had ever seen.

"Right. If what I have to say requires an audience, so be it." He took her hand and led her to the nearest chair. "Sit, please? And everyone else—you can hear, just give me a little breathing room. Thank you." He took a quick breath, filling his lungs with courage. "Vella ... back on the cliff, I said I loved you—but I never told you the important parts about my love. That it's unconditional. You don't have to say you love me back. You don't have to even try. You asked if it could be enough that you and I just be together, and my answer is yes. Fuck yes. If that's what you still want. If you want to stay here and learn your magic, then yes, that's what we'll do. If you want to go to New York together and we rescue Tara and Brianna and my grimoire, then that is okay too. If you want to let Derrick live and find another way to handle him—I am here for you. Or if you want to blow up every plan we made—then I am here for you.

"But on the flip side, I will burn every motherfucking inch of Div Tower down—for you. Whatever the fuck you want—I am here for you. Because that's what my love means. And I know you haven't seen much in the way of real love—but I am here to show you what it should look like. And yes, we haven't had long to learn about each other, but I'm here to go as slow as you need to be comfortable with us —if there is an us. And the reason I didn't leave when Ronin's message came through? Because you are my first priority. I have your back, Vella, and I'm not going anywhere."

Vella took in a shuddering breath, and her beautiful eyes filled with tears ... and one by one, like gleaming silver stars, they trickled over her cheeks, leaving stardust in their wake.

Fuck. Fuck, fuck, fuck. His Rapunzel was crying.

He dropped to his knees at her feet. "Please don't cry—not because of me. Cry for yourself and for your loss, but never because of me."

"These are happy tears," she whispered. She grabbed his hands and brought them to her lips. His already-racing heart did a somersault. "You're wrong about one thing, Matthias Medea. I do know you. I know you're quick to say sorry and admit when you get something wrong. That you face your fears—even ones that make your knees go weak. That you've been here for me, time after time. And you're wrong about something else, too."

Her eyes glittered like she had a secret he didn't know ...

One by one, the hairs on the back of his neck prickled, and he looked over to Sinead, whose mouth curved in a satisfied smile.

"Sinead ... when you came in, did you say 'bonded mate'?" Matt held his breath.

"She did," Vella whispered. "That's one of the things I came here to tell you. You and I—we—are still bonded. Bel didn't sever our bond; he cemented it."

"So the reason my power is stable—"

"Is because the bond is settled. Although Sinead tells me we'll both occasionally get small flare-ups as our magics balance out."

Matt rocked back on his heels. They were still bonded.

"I feel it now." Vella took his hand and rested it in the center of her chest. The rapid beat of her heart made his pound faster. "It's like this pull, tugging me in the direction of where you are. I literally can stand still and moments later find myself facing a different direction, and I ... I don't know how I know. I just know it's because that's the direction you are. And I'm sorry that I didn't realize sooner what you are to me. That I couldn't ... didn't ... tell you sooner."

"You can feel that?" he whispered. Hope crashed into his chest.

"Yes, but just wait, please? Let me tell you *my* all. It's not just the magic, Matt, and you need to know it. I *want* to bond with you. I want to see what happens when our magics truly connect, and I want to be there for you, just like you've been for me. Yes, I'm twenty-three—almost twenty-four—but my age hasn't stopped me from finally seeing what was right before me all this time. I love you, Matthias Medea. Spellcaster. Druid. Possibly the most amazing person I've ever known, and who, by some miracle after all the shit I've done, loves me. And I'm going to shout it to the wind, so your Druid power hears and knows I want every single fucking part of you. I love you."

His entire world froze. Buzzing filled his ears. And only one element remained:

Vella.

Gods but he saw *her*.

Mine.

Hers.

"Rapunzel," he whispered. "You destroy me, every fucking time."

Vella leaned forward, her gaze dropping to his mouth.

Need. Her.

Matt rose to his feet, tugging Vella up to hers with him, and picked her up in his arms.

Her lioness eyes glowed, and her lips curved with a hint of wickedness. "We're putting on a show now, Medea?"

"Next time," he growled. "Everyone? Your Bone Wielder and her Primus need to be alone now."

"About time!" Alex bounded to his feet. "That was totally lovely but really needs more spice—"

"Out, young one." Lucretia raised one eyebrow.

"Yes, my queen."

"Close the door behind you all," Vella called over her shoulder.

Matt didn't even pause. "I don't give a fuck what they do, as long as they leave us alone. We have an hour till the helicopter lands, and I plan on making the most of every one of those sixty minutes."

But one more second of not devouring her lips was unacceptable, and he crushed his mouth to hers.

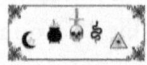

"MATTHIAS," Vella breathed into the most delicious, carnal, breathtaking kiss she'd ever had. His ferocity. His urgency.

The moment he placed her on her feet, she yanked his shirt free, fumbled with the fastening on his pants.

"Fuck, Vella." His voice was low as he crowded her back till her legs hit the bed. "I need you. Now."

He shoved her shirt up and bra cup aside, and his lips locked around her nipple. She groaned as the heat and the suction made her back arch, and together, they stripped and yanked and shoved until they were both naked and she fell back to the mattress.

Matt stood naked at the end of the bed. His sinewy snake tattoos coiled around his gleaming, delicious muscles. His dick jutted high and thick, the tip already glistening.

For Vella.

"Don't look at me like that," he gritted out. His gaze

locked on her breasts. Traveled down the curve of her waist to the roundness of her hips. The curve of her belly. The vee of her pussy.

"Why are you all the way over there?"

"Because I want you to savor our first time together with the bond cemented. You own my heart, Vella, and I want to make this special—want to worship you—but I'm already so fucking close to losing control."

Her body drenched.

His nostrils flared. Midnight stars whirled up in his eyes, but he clenched his fists and shook his head. Then he inhaled a shuddering breath and exhaled long and slow.

Cool air snaked around her ankles, slithered up her calves, goosebumps rippling in its wake. It followed the curve of her thighs, paused ... dipped ... slid its invisible tongue between her thighs, explored her fully from seam to slit.

"Matt!" She arched off the bed.

"More," he growled.

She tried to open her eyes. But the tongue of air was stroking her clit, around and around and around it swirled with such delicious friction—

"More!" Matt snarled. "Gods, Vella, you taste—"

The air tongued her entry. Ravenous.

Her body imploded. A keen escaped her, long and high as pleasure rushed through her veins.

"Fuck." His voice rasped in her ears this time right before his mouth claimed hers, so hard she might be imprinted by his lips forever, and she tasted herself in their kiss, and his body covered hers and she cradled his hips with her thighs, widened them—

The thick, silky head of his dick nudged at her entry.

"Take me, baby." He surged into her. Hot. Hard. Filling her up. "Take me, Vella. Vella, Vella. Vella!"

Pleasure sparked all over again inside her, and she did as he demanded—linked her hands behind his bowed neck, wrapped her legs around his waist, rubbed her clit against the base of his shaft—

"Fuck," he growled, even as his body ground into hers. "You feel so good, baby. So good. So good," he praised her with every thrust.

She lifted her hips and matched his pressure, used her thighs to push him out, then to wrench him back in. "Yes, like that," she gasped. Greedy for more of him, more of them together.

He thrust again. "Vella, I will do anything for you." He gritted his teeth, and, in his eyes, those beautiful stars were whirling faster. Brighter. "There is no spell that will hold me." Her body clenched. "No lie that could sway me." The tension crested. "No force in this world or any other that will stop me from loving you."

He thrust harder, deeper; his body shuddered.

"And you are mine, Matthias Medea." She shifted her hands and cradled his jaw, held his beautiful eyes. "I love you."

"Vella," he roared. And poured himself into her.

The fire in the hearth exploded to life. The windows crashed open, and Vella soared.

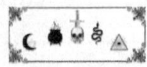

MATT, Vella and Alex reached the ossuaries beneath Paris before noon on a beautiful winter's day.

They'd been late to the helicopter to leave Inis Misneach, but Matt hadn't said a word because Vella had been hugging Lucretia and Sinead, with silver-star tears tracking down her cheeks.

"I found my courage," she'd said to Lucretia. Whatever that meant. And then she'd turned to Sinead. "I'll be back soon, promise. With Sara." She'd taken a basket from Sinead and giggled at something Sinead had said, then followed Matt and Alex to the helicopter.

"What's in the basket?" Alex asked.

"Scones with blackberry jam. A personal ... favorite." She'd given Matt a secret smile, and just like that, his body went hot and tight all over again, as though he hadn't just come with the most satisfying orgasms of his life three times in the last hour.

"You two." Alex had grinned. "I love it. But please share the scones?"

And now here they were, waiting for Alex to bring the second aett of bone runes out of the bone-filled tunnels, while Matthias used his Druid power above ground to hide their progress from the Divinators.

"No sign of anyone following us." Matt scanned the area again. "But about the *Malleus Maleficarum*. If Alex does find the second aett in the ossuaries, are you happy for me to arrange the book's return to the exhibition? Vella, you're shivering. Do you want me to heat the air more?"

"It's not that kind of shiver. This place feels ... chaotic," Vella said. She rubbed her arms, even though she wore Lucretia's coat that the vampire had insisted Vella wear. "I think I'm picking up on all the energy of the bones beneath us. Thank frig Alex was happy to go down there."

"Not sure Paris is ready for its ossuaries to meet a Bone Caller just yet. How did your call with Sara go?"

"She's still on edge after what Ellaine did with the read-

ing, but she's also determined to do something useful.
Which I totally understand—"

Ping. Ping.

Ronin's name flashed on his cell phone screen, and he
turned it around so Vella could read the message too.

> Ronin: Pulled surveillance footage from
> around the London library. Derrick was
> waiting at the back when Vella jumped from
> the building, and he picked up Brianna. The
> fucker didn't even look to see if Vella was
> okay after she got thrown around by your
> wind.

"He was *waiting* there?" Vella hissed. "The motherfucker."

> Ronin: News also just in from the hedge
> witches researching Div Tower building
> plans in Scotland. They've found a secret
> elevator linking the top floor to the
> basement.

Matt snapped his fingers. "That has to be how Ellaine
surprised you in the archives that day. And I get you're
worried for Brianna, but we will get her back, I promise."

Vella's nostrils flared, but she restrained the violence
visible in her eyes. "You're right, I know confirmation on
who took Brianna is a step toward retrieving her. And the
secret elevator ..." Her mouth dropped open. "Matt, do you
know what this means?"

"What?"

"I know how to get Brianna and your grimoire and Tara
and the first aett of bone runes—all of them! I think we
might actually be able to do this—"

"I'm back!" Alex carried a small box. "Exactly where you said."

"We have the second aett." Vella's eyes lit up. "We are absolutely doing this!"

VELLA WOKE up wrapped in Matt's arms, snuggled tight against him on the bed at the back of the private jet's main cabin.

"Why haven't we been flying with the back four chairs made into a bed all along?" she whispered into his chest.

"Not sure how that would've gone over with the other occupants on the plane."

"Good point." She grabbed her cell and flicked the screen on.

"Almost time." She tightened her arms around him. "Do you ever imagine a world where no one is evil? And, yes, sure, some people are always going to do bad shit, but I mean the true, true evil like what we've seen in our lifetimes ... just imagine that just never existed?" She took a deep inhale of his beautiful scent. "Do you think you and I would still have found each other, like this?"

"That would be the most soothing dream I can imagine. Being able to meet my parents as adults and talk to them, being able to see everyone thrive and flourish and live their lives, and being able to be who we really want to be. Yeah, I absolutely dream of that." He shifted and brushed the hair out of her eyes. His silver gaze lit up like brilliant molten metal. "And do you know ... I believe with every part of my being, you and I would still have found each other. We just would've had a hell of a lot easier time admitting we loved each other."

"Where would the fun in that be?" She pressed her lips to his jaw.

"I promise we still would've had a lot of fun." He tilted her chin up and kissed her fast. "All right, Rapunzel—or should I call you Weapon now? Either way, it's time. Let's go put on the best show of our lives."

"Right with you, Medea."

"I am also here," Alex added. "You can thank me later for not sleeping at the foot of your bed."

41

A flurry of feathers and claws hit Vella hard in the chest the moment she silently climbed from Sara's bedroom through to Sylvie's brownstone. Angry squawking chattered in her ear, and a curved black beak began a ferocious, precision-based prune of the hairs around her face.

"Morrigan! Enough! Stop!" Vella finally managed to get her purse out of the way, and both hands around her familiar, and while she'd intended on holding her back, instead she cuddled Morrigan to her chest. Morrigan gave a small indignant squawk, burrowed in under Vella's chin, and let out a small warble. "I missed you, too," Vella whispered.

"What about me?" Sara's voice echoed over her shoulder. Vella whirled around.

Sara! She threw herself at her sister. "Miss you?" She half laughed, half cried into Sara's hair. "Why the hell would I miss my pesky little Mors Dicen sister?"

"You just called me a Mors Dicen." Sara hugged Vella just as tight until they were a tangle of arms and feathers and crying and cawing.

"Of course," Vella said when they finally untangled. "That's who we are—that's our coven. And, Sara, I have so much to tell you, but right now, we're on the clock. Are you ready?"

"Hell yes, we all are. And I cannot believe we're finally doing this." Sara did a little fist pump.

"Okay, okay. Remember, we have to take this seriously; lives are on the line here. We just all do our part, and we will succeed."

"Then let's get downstairs. Everyone's waiting."

Vella's heart felt close to bursting. The last time she'd returned after hunting the bone runes, her reunion with Sara had been awful. Today ... today was frigging brilliant.

With Morrigan on her shoulder, Vella followed Sara into Sylvie's jewel-toned living room where Shannah, Sylvie, Alex and Tannis had all gathered.

Sylvie came over first, holding a small box. "Eight small animal bone fragments, as requested."

"Thank you." Heart in her mouth, Vella reached into her purse and took out the bronze box with the second aett. "Let's swap. Until we find a permanent option, a vampire keeping these is the best solution, since the Divs can't see you at all in their visions."

"We shall guard them with our lives." Sylvie gripped Vella's wrist and dipped her head. "And just so you know, our mother"—Sylvie nodded at Tannis and Alex—"has made a blood vow on behalf of our entire people to safeguard these. You will have the support of all vampires, all over the world."

Vella mentally snapped her fingers. Of course—why hadn't she seen it sooner? Lucretia was Sylvie's mother. Did that make Sylvie, Tannis and Alex royalty?

Focus, Vel. Today: rescue Brianna, Tara, and Matthias' grimoire. Tomorrow: find out more about the vampires.

Vella gripped Sylvie's wrist back, and the bracelet around Sylvie's arm caught her eye.

"Is that the navitas you loaned me? I haven't seen it since ..." Vella racked her memory. "Crystal Brew! Jacqui took it off me to look at it, and then I blacked out."

"Which happened because the navitas was your only energy source, given you had exhausted all your magical reserves. How do you feel now?"

Like she could conquer the world. "I'm good now, no navitas needed. Although I'm so sorry I lost it. But how did you get it back?"

"As well as running Crystal Brew, Jacqui works with crystals to make navitas for their coven here in the city and made this one for me. Apparently, there is a local resistance attempting to thwart the Divinators from stealing more arcana, and Jacqui is involved in some way. So she was aware there was a thief stealing arcane objects, and when she saw you wearing my navitas, she thought—"

"—I was the thief." Wow. Jacqui was in some kind of Crystallo resistance. Vella filed that away, because once Brianna and Tara and Matt's grimoire were all recovered, the more witches who could work together toward ending Ellaine's rule, the better. She refocused on the tin with the animal bones. "Well, now we have the final piece of the puzzle in place for our heist. Is everyone else ready?"

"We are indeed," Shannah said. "We've been working around the clock since you and Matt called from the jet. Tannis is our mobile command unit, aka the new SUV driver."

"I'm also providing snacks," Tannis added.

"Sara is on tech in command and control—"

"Which is the back of the SUV. But you should see it, Vel. It's totally kitted out! It's in the lane out the back."

"Someone might have gone a little overboard on Matt's credit card." Shannah rolled her eyes at Sara.

"What? I'm always playing tech backup to Vella, and believe me, you never know what systems you're going to need on a job like this."

"I am totally on board with throwing in everything you can think of," Vella said. "What about you, Shannah?"

"I'm on comms—I'll be in your ear all day as well as strategy management. Sylvie will stay here and guard the preciouses, and Alex is your on-site support."

"Ready to pretend to be my ardent lover again, Alex?"

"For you, Bone Wielder, always. Though please ensure your Primus is aware it is all for the act."

"Primus? Sounds kinky." Sara elbowed Vella.

"What do you know about kinky?" Vella teased.

"Pft. I might not have any real-world experience, but your girl's got plenty online." She waggled her eyebrows.

"Oh wow. Not sure I needed to know that. But fine, that's us all set." Vella checked her cell screen. "And Matt will be walking past the SUV—oops, mobile command center—in thirty minutes, so it's time to go." She reached under her shirt for Brianna.

Damn.

"I know you miss her," Sara murmured as she walked past. "But, don't worry, we'll get Brianna back."

"Thanks, Sar." Vella squeezed her shoulder. She just hoped Derrick had brought her back to New York.

"Hey, Vella?" Shannah tilted her head to the side.

Vella hung back after everyone else had left. "What's up?"

"Ronin said Matt was pretty upset a couple of days ago ...

something about you spewing lightning. Apparently, he was curt and yelling and close to totally out of control with his power, and frankly, Ronin was worried as shit. But now, again, according to Ronin, in the short time you two have been back in the city, Matt's chilled out and his power is under control." Shannah lifted one eyebrow. "So? It's the bond, isn't it? Uh-uh, don't try to BS me. I can already see I'm right. About time! I knew it—back at the lake house when you stayed that first night and you two couldn't take your eyes off each other—or hands now, it seems. Ronin's gonna have to pay up."

"You two bet on us?"

"And Amelia. We had a pot running about who would get confirmation first."

"You guys are hilarious."

"But seriously, welcome to the family, Vella. We're lucky to have you. And you're damn lucky to have him."

"On that we agree."

"Hey, you two!" Sara stopped in the doorway. "It's time to go. And Shannah, you should see the nano earpieces and mics I've got! They are the bomb! The earpieces go into the ear canal, so they're invisible; the mics adhere to your shirts and have this cool background noise remover so it's only our voices everyone hears, and the van is set up to take their broadcast on a secure channel. Vell—you get the extra sets for your orc and Ronin. Hand 'em over when Matt does his spell."

"Yes, boss."

"She's doing really well," Shannah murmured as they made their way to the rear access lane. "What happened with Ellaine and the bone runes, hit her hard, but she bounced back, I think, because of this heist. She is hell-bent on taking that murderous motherfucker down."

"I get the sentiment—believe me, I do—but while she's a whiz with technology, Sara is still just nineteen. And you've seen how rash she is. She rarely thinks before she acts, and I worry she'll get herself hurt."

"Well, shelve that concern. You're family, and Sara is too. I'll watch her back."

"Thank you. Now, where is—" Morrigan flew to her shoulder, and Vella stroked her downy head. "You stay here with Sylvie, love. We need to keep an eye on this place too."

"We shall keep each other good company," Sylvie murmured.

Vella stepped into the SUV, and her mouth dropped open. "Um, this looks like something out of a spy movie. How many monitors do you need?"

"Enough to watch all of you inside. Any other questions?"

"Nope! You're the tech boss." Vella took the spare seat beside Shannah, and Alex sat in the front beside his brother.

Exactly twenty-eight minutes later, they arrived at 110th Street. Alex got out and said something to the driver of a delivery van parked where they wanted to be, and within moments, the van left, and Tannis pulled in.

"How did you convince them to move?" Sara called out when Alex hopped back in.

"Just a little persuasion." He grinned and licked his lips.

The SUVs side door opened.

"Matthias Medea." Vella's heart picked up as though it had been days, not two hours, since they'd parted at the airport.

"Rapunzel." The black stars flared in his eyes for a split second. Did he feel the same way she did? Judging by his rueful smile, she'd say yes. "Got something for me?"

"Indeed, I do. Two sets of nano earpieces and mics, and one very old rusty tin with eight bone fragments—ready for your glamour."

"In that case ..." He took two breaths and whispered the spell for the glamour, and before her eyes, the bone fragments rippled as the magic swept over them.

"Perfect," she breathed. "How long?"

"Maximum, two hours, but for a safety zone ... ninety minutes."

"That's all I need. So long as they pass any scrutiny going into the vault, they'll be locked away in the case until they're called up for a reading, by which time ..."

"We will be long gone," Matt finished for her. "I also got you a present." He reached into his jacket, pulling out two small throwing knives and a holder for them. "They're not Brianna, but you are damned good with a blade, so hold on to these until we get her back."

"Thank you," she whispered. "And hey, Medea? Love you."

His beautiful eyes held hers. "Same goes, Rapunzel."

"Why does he always call you that?" Sara muttered as the van door slid shut.

MATT STROLLED into the Council chambers on the thirteenth floor of Div Tower with his Magicae Councilor façade in place and Ronin at his side at three fifty-nine p.m.

Bloody hell, let their plan work.

Ruby and her Second stood by the windows overlooking Central Park. Ruby's cheeks were paler than usual, and she gripped the crystal head of her cane tightly enough that he could see her knuckles, but her chin remained steady as she gave him a barely discernible nod.

Derrick drank a coffee in the doorway to the Council chamber; the cool, composed Div. Gods but Matt couldn't wait to wipe that look from his face. As soon as he saw Matt, his eyes widened. Good, you fucker.

The serving staff were stationed at the coffee bar, ready to go.

"Matthias, darling! I am so thrilled you're here." Nevena's plum accent cut through the lobby as she entered the room. "I have missed you terribly."

"Councilor-elect Nevena, you are a picture indeed." What kind of picture was the question? Vella would no doubt think in terms of fake or fortune ... but which was Nevena? "How do you feel before your first official Council meeting?"

"Ooh, I am excited. And nervous, of course, as I want to represent our coven as it deserves. Have you met my Second-elect yet?" She turned around, a delicate wrinkle creasing her forehead. "Henry? Oh. Perhaps he's already in the chamber. And Derrick, how good to see you again." Nevena's smile dimmed slightly.

"Councilor-elect, a pleasure as always. And Councilor Medea." Derrick's nod was as short as his tone. "We weren't sure we would be seeing you after you disappeared from the library in London."

"Actually, you disappeared. When we reached the lobby, you were nowhere to be seen. We tried to call you," Matt lied smoothly, "but we couldn't get a single message through. However, I do have good news. We found the second aett of bone runes. Vella said she will be calling Councilor Ellaine to arrange the drop-off after she sees her sister."

Derrick's eyes flared.

"Oh, well done." Nevena clicked her fingers at the servers. "Two coffees, here now. Councilor Matthias' usual, and I'll have whatever he is having."

Matt waved a languid hand at Ronin. "Anything for you?"

"I'll get something stronger later. I need to use the facilities before we start. I'll see you in there." Ronin had never mastered the lazy Magicae façade, but he did a passing job at boredom when it came to anything Council related, and he kept that look as he left the room.

"Your Second is a waste of a seat at the table." Derrick nodded at Ronin's back. "You should bring someone who can contribute."

"Why in the world would I do that? Ronin is here for protocol. You know how it is ... one must always be seen to do the right thing."

"Oh, we must indeed." Nevena nodded with more enthusiasm than he'd expected.

"So where were the bone runes?" Derrick asked.

"Paris. Do you know there are tunnels and tunnels filled with bones below the city?"

"They're legendary," Nevena breathed. "How exciting that must've been for Velvet."

Exciting wasn't quite the word for it, but Matt just shrugged. "You'll have to ask her. Personally, I found the whole experience rather tedious without your company, Nevena."

"Tedious?" Vella's voice was extra dry through his earpiece. "Interesting."

"Peeps," Shannah bit out. "No nonoperational chitchat. But also, you are so paying for that later, Matthias."

Nevena swatted his arm. "Oh, you flatterer."

Derrick just stared at him before taking out his cell. "I need to make some calls. I'll see you in the chamber."

At the coffee bar, both baristas were making his and Nevena's order, and while Nevena launched into the story of her trip back to New York, Matt kept a careful eye on the servers. Nothing seemed out of place, but surviving a previous assassination attempt by a server had him extra cautious.

"Matthias, be a darling and bring our coffees, would you? I want to be inside when Ellaine arrives, so I don't hold up the meeting."

"It would be my pleasure." He'd just deposited their coffees at their respective seats when the staff at the door stood to attention and Ellaine Priestley glided into the room like a fucking evil queen. Her composed gaze cut to Matt, then to Nevena, before she took in the rest of the chamber's occupants.

Fuck. What had that been about?

"Grandmother," Derrick said loudly.

"Councilor Ellaine." Matt bowed with the deference of a lazy Magicae who knew which side his bread was buttered on.

Around the table, everyone greeted Ellaine.

"We're a go," Shannah's voice echoed in the earpiece. "Ellaine is on level thirteen. Ronin, update?"

"Need one minute. Had to go through the rear access to the Council chamber. Almost ... there. Sara? You should have full access now; we're plugged into a printer connected to the on-site network."

"Looking ... yep, I'm in. And ... bypassing all their protocols, getting into their surveillance system. Here we go; you are now all live on my feed here in the SUV. Hi, everyone."

"Ronin, head back to the Council chamber," Shannah ordered. "Sara—you're up."

"Adding the fake entry log now," Sara said. "And next up ... booking Reading Room One on the thirtieth floor under Ellaine's name, and ordering Tara and the bone runes to be sent there, priority one. Okay, Vella and Alex, you're ready to go."

"Entering the tower now," Vella murmured.

Anticipation tightened in Matt's gut. Bloody hell, they were really doing this ... after all these years, the Magicae coven would get their stolen grimoire back.

"Vella and Alex are at the security desk," Sara whispered.

"Afternoon," Vella's voice echoed through his earpiece. "I have a deposit. Should be in the log. Excellent. Yep, filling it out now. This is my friend—oh, this entire level is restricted? Oh, well, perhaps he can wait upstairs in the lobby?"

"Vella is heading into the vault," Sara whispered. "Alex is heading back up to the ground floor main tower lobby."

At the Council table, Nevena stood, her face tight with worry. Shit. What had Matt missed?

"Apologies, Councilor Ellaine, my Second is running late, and I think he must've gotten lost. I am so sorry to mess up my first meeting—oh, there he is."

A tall, slim witch, late-twenties to early-thirties, took a hesitant step into the chamber. He had bright golden-blond hair and too much facial resemblance to Nevena to be anything other than family.

"Henry," Nevena called. "Please come in."

Oh shit. Alex's description of who Nevena had met with in France flew through his mind. What if Nevena hadn't been secretly meeting with Derrick, but with Henry instead?

Matt carefully turned around—while Derrick's expression gave nothing away, his gaze was locked on Nevena and Henry.

What was Matt missing here?

"Done in the vault," Vella whispered. "Heading to the archives now. Will grab your grimoire, Matt, and use the secret elevator to take it to the penthouse so the guard here never sees me take it."

Matt's heart picked up pace; this was it—

"Councilor Matthias, did you hear me?" Ellaine was suddenly in his face. Her eyes narrowed, lips pursed.

Fuck. "Apologies, Councilor Ellaine. The jet lag is getting to me. I'll just get another coffee to ensure I stay awake for the rest of the meeting."

"Which your Second would be able to arrange if they were here. Never mind." She glanced back at the doorway and snapped, "You, another coffee for the Magicae Councilor," before turning back to Matt. "Well, we shall have to start without the company of your cousin, which, after today's meeting, is probably for the best. Derrick, please distribute the agenda."

Matt went on high alert. What now?

Ellaine took her seat beneath the Divinator coven's pennant; Derrick slid a single sheet of paper in front of Ruby, Nevena and Matt.

"Our first order of business is to agree on the passing of four new laws. As you can see—" Ellaine continued talking, but Matt read faster and scanned the list.

Witches Council Agenda

Agenda Item 1. Propose New Laws

Remove all property ownership rights from vampires and shifters within a one-hundred-mile radius of any Divinator Tower.

Vampires and shifters barred from entering premises where witches gather.

Special investigators may immediately close any business not meeting the above rules.

Special investigators to have kill-on-site authority

Agenda Item 2. Sensitive material management

Items to be discussed

Agenda Item 3. Vacant Councilor Position

Set a formal date for the Elixir Councilor-elect to undertake the test for a permanent seat at the Witches Council

LEAD JAMMED IN MATTHIAS' stomach.

"Councilor Ellaine." Ruby used her cane to stand. "In good conscience, I cannot agree to these laws."

"Councilor Ruby, you shall have your opportunity to discuss and oppose this proposal if you wish during the vote."

"We have an issue," Vella whispered. The hairs on the back of Matt's neck prickled. "The grimoires are not here. The entire section is gone. Shit. Shit, shit, shit."

Matt froze.

"Vella, stay calm," Shannah murmured. "Double check. Have they moved things around there?"

"Looking now … No, everything else is the same. Just zero grimoires. Do we need to abort?"

"Not entirely. We still have everything in place for Tara's retrieval and for you to search for Brianna. But it's your call."

"Okay," Vella responded. "Then ... we continue. Heading to the penthouse now."

Bloody hell. The grimoires were gone? But Vella was sticking with the plan—a call he agreed with. If she'd taken the bone runes while they were in the vault, the pressure sensors would trigger the moment she removed them, and they'd all be in the shit. But up in the reading room was another matter. And at least from the penthouse she only had to travel down two floors to get to the reading room, instead of up thirty from the archives.

He forced himself to breathe evenly.

"Ronin?" Shannah said. "Since you're not back in the Council chamber yet, stay outside and see what you can uncover about any other archive locations—nothing too suspicious though."

"On it," Ronin murmured.

"Ruby, you may sit. And now I suggest we continue." Ellaine nodded at the agenda in front of her. "We will move to item two. Derrick, please share your evidence."

Derrick reached into the satchel at his feet and withdrew—

Holy fuck. Brianna. Right here.

"What is that?" Ruby asked.

"This is a sensitive item." Ellaine smoothed a hand down her hair. "I am moving an instant motion that all sensitive items—which shall be defined on a case-by-case basis by the Council—must be contained immediately, and that anyone found to be hiding or using them be subject to the full extent of the special investigative team's powers."

Bloody hell. Ellaine wanted to have the special investigators kill anyone just holding a Mors Dicen relic ... on the spot.

Matt's chest seized.

Ellaine's lips curved. "And now I move that we approve agenda items one and two now."

"We do not need any discussion," Ruby said immediately. "The Crystallo coven says no to this proposal."

And he was hard fuck no. But shit, he had to keep playing his part here. *Head in the game, Matt.* So while his heart raced and his body tensed to fight back with everything he had, instead, he murmured, "I feel it unwise to move with haste on matters of such importance, so I must say no on behalf of my coven."

Ellaine's eyes flared, but her expression remained calm as she swung to Nevena. "And Councilor-elect Montgomery? You have the final vote. Under Witches Council rules, a new law must have fifty percent or higher support to pass."

"Well, I am of course here to do the right thing for this Council, and my coven, and so we support what you think best, Councilor Priestley. The Elixir coven votes yes."

"Then the new proposals are passed."

A Div Tower staff member ran into the room and whispered something into Derrick's ear. Derrick froze.

"What now?" Ellaine pinned the staff member with a cool look.

Derrick slowly stood up. "Our lead special investigator wishes to speak with us in private. He's waiting outside."

Fuck. What was going on now?

42

"I'm in the penthouse," Vella murmured as she stepped through what she had always believed to be a solid wall in Ellaine's bedroom. A shiver scrabbled up her spine. "Sara, where are Ellaine and Derrick?"

"Still on floor thirteen. Not in the Council chamber but talking outside the main doors."

"That's good enough," Vella replied. "Can you see if Tara and the bone runes have been transferred to the reading room?"

"Yep. They're coming up now."

"Then that's where I'm going." Vella took a deep breath. "Alex, are you ready to get into place?"

"I am coming, Bone Wielder."

"Okay. Let's do this." She removed the Book of Bones from her pocket. Please, Goddess, let this work.

"Hey, Bone Book friends, thanks for staying quiet till now." Vella went into Ellaine's dressing room, keeping the lights off, and sat in the farthest corner.

"We are here to help," Sebastian said in a subdued voice. "Remember, when you journey in the dark energy, only the living can exist there, so you shall not be able to communicate with us, or Tara and her bone runes, until you are out of the dark energy."

Vella touched a hand to the pages where their bones were ground into the paper, and as the itching gathered on the back of her neck and within her palms, she stared into the darkest point of the room.

The black spiderweb of sparkling obsidian stars that was dark energy shimmered into her view.

Yes! She was connected.

Focus, Vel. She had a job to do.

She made her way as fast as possible through the mausoleum of an apartment to the emergency stairwell and down to the thirtieth floor.

"No, no. I have a booking *here*." Alex held his cell phone in the receptionist's face, keeping their attention off the monitors watching the reading rooms so that they wouldn't see Vella take the bone runes.

Alex's gaze shifted to where Vella stood, and while everyone else was oblivious to her presence, his eyes widened a fraction before he swung his focus back to the receptionist.

Had he actually seen her? Not that it mattered.

She followed the dark energy up the corridor to Reading Room One and passed through the door.

Tara and the bone runes sat on the table.

Vella's breath whooshed out, and she reached out with her dark energy hands and lifted Tara's skull. The bones runes inside clicked and clacked, but moments later, they too were covered in the same obsidian stars that coated Vella, meaning they would be invisible to anyone else.

Elation poured through her.

They'd done it.

VELLA HADN'T SPOKEN for three minutes. Was she okay? Had she found Tara and the bone runes? Had she gone searching for Brianna, not realizing her Bone Guide was here with Matt?

And fuck, how did he get Brianna out of here now?

Opposite him, Ruby and her Second had their heads bent, talking quietly to each other, occasionally looking at Henry.

Nevena still sipped her coffee, but her gaze stayed on Matt. A small smile curved her mouth every now and again. What the fuck was that look about?

Maybe he should just take Brianna now—

The doors opened, and Ellaine and Derrick returned. Ellaine remained perfectly composed; however, Derrick's cheeks had a grayish tinge.

"Well," Ellaine murmured. "It seems we need to amend the order of business for the day. Unfortunate news has arrived that I am deeply shocked to share." She nodded at Derrick. "I know this is hard to hear."

One by one, the hairs on the back of Matt's neck prickled.

What the fuck was going on?

"As you know," Ellaine continued. "I pride myself on ensuring our coven members adhere to the laws we set, and it has come to my attention that one of my own has been breaking our most sacred law."

Dread weighed down Matt's gut. What was Ellaine doing now?

"I am sad to report that my great-niece, Velvet Knight, has been confirmed as having conducted illegal Mors Dicen magic. I believe she is here in the tower, attempting to use it right now. Given the risk that Mors Dicen magic presents, we are evacuating the tower."

Matt froze.

Fucking hell.

"Velvet, break the law?" Nevena's eyes flew wide open. "Surely not?"

"Councilor Ruby." Ellaine gestured to the doors. "For your safety, I suggest you make your way to your city address. I will let you know once we have this matter contained. Derrick? Please help with the evacuations."

"Are you certain?" Ruby wobbled on her feet. "There has been no Mors Dicen magic in years—"

"Councilor Ruby, I assure you my information is accurate. Now, please, your safety is important to me. I have a car waiting downstairs for you."

Ruby's lips pinched, but she nodded and left with her Second, although she did glance back at Matthias over her shoulder.

"Problem," Ronin whispered through Matt's earpiece. "I'm outside the Council chamber and a dozen SI dudes just erupted from the elevator, all ordering everyone to show their ID badges and then, once they're cleared, leave the tower."

Oh shit. None of Matt's team knew what had just happened—not yet anyway.

"Councilor Priestley," Matt said as clearly as possible. "Did you just say that Velvet is accused of making Mors Dicen magic and is on site right now? I take it your people are looking for her?"

He got to his feet, but his balance was off, and he had to catch himself on the table.

"Fuck," Ronin snarled.

"Vella's still getting the bone runes," Sara said. "She might not be able to hear us when she's in the dark energy."

"Ronin, Alex," Shannah bit out. "Can either of you get up to Vella?"

Shit. Vella would be without her vision when she returned from the dark energy, and right now she had no idea Ellaine's goons were looking for her. She'd be vulnerable.

Not. Fucking. Happening. He pushed off the table—his head spun, and he had to force in a deep breath.

"Matthias, you need to leave as well. Now," Shannah added.

"On my way," he murmured. But he wasn't leaving without Vella.

"On your way where?" Ellaine sauntered over to Matt. "Councilor Medea, I am very disappointed. You have been such a good boy up to this point." She shook her head. "You really should not have gotten involved with Velvet. Luckily, the sister can do the job I need. Oh, Nevena, can you please have the SI team leader step in?"

Fuck this shit. Matt called the wind—

Nothing happened. His hand started to shake, and he dropped back into the chair.

On the table, his coffee cup went blurry. A fog rolled in, coating everything—his senses, the room, his thoughts— even the man in black fatigues who entered the room and walked over to them.

"I have your first KOS order," Ellaine said. "Velvet Knight, last seen on the vault level."

Terror cut through the fog, and Matt forced his legs to move. His arms. Anything.

Nothing.

"KOS," he whispered past his numbing lips. "KOS ... Vella. Ronin—tell, Vella, plan ... M."

"What's he saying?" Sara shouted.

"Kill on sight. Vella," Shannah bit out. "I don't know about the rest. But don't worry, Alex and Ronin are going to her now. Tannis, get ready to go—hey, Sara, get back here! Matt—get out of there, now."

"No way!" Sara yelled. "She's saved me her entire life, and I am not leaving her now. I know the tower better than all of you."

"Nevena, how is he progressing?" Ellaine bent closer. The fog almost covered her too now.

Vella. Vella. Vella.

"Based on the scars becoming visible on his face, and the lovely reaction I am feeling, he should be unconscious any moment." Nevena shifted over him too. Close enough he could touch her, if he could lift his hand.

"You ... sent to kill me?" Matt whispered.

"Yes, I was. It is my skill base after all." Nevena's grating laugh came from far, far away.

"Shit, was that you, Matt?" Shannah. That was Shannah's voice. "Did anyone just hear Matt say something?"

"You were so clever to poison both of your coffees, Councilor-elect Montgomery." Ellaine stared at Matt again. "He really never suspected?"

"I told you I'm good at what I do. I have been dosing myself since childhood, so I'm resistant to the effects now. I did think he and Vella were on to me in France, but as you can see, apparently not."

"Well, at least you can take care of the Allard witches at the chateau now. I'd like them removed as soon as possible."

"Absolutely Councilor Priestley, I'll send Henry back over once we're home. And thank you for trusting my opinion on the timing of their deaths—it was vital that Matthias didn't suspect my involvement if I was ever to get close enough to do this." She waved a hand at the coffee cup.

"You are remarkable, Nevena. So much like your grand-father. Now, Henry, be a dear and take the unconscious Councilor out through the back? His dog is still out in my tower somewhere, and I don't fancy having a mess here. Oh, and please take that bone-handled knife. I might have a use for it."

Vella, Vella, Ve—

The fog claimed Matt.

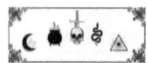

VELLA LET the Book of Bones go, and as the dark energy filling the dressing room disappeared, so did her vision.

"Vella!" Shannah shouted in her ear. "Get out, get out, get out! Vella, can you hear me? Does anyone have eyes on Vella? And shit—Sara's going into the tower."

"Fuck!" Ronin hissed. "Alex and I are one floor away from Vella. Alex, you keep going to Vella, I'll go back for Sara—"

"No, you both get to Vella. She's who they're after," Shannah cut in. "I'll get Sara. Tannis, keep the SUV running. We will be coming out to you fast and probably hot. If anyone gets separated, meet back at Sylvie's—use the rear access."

"I'm here!" Adrenaline surged, and clutching Tara's skull, Vella leaped to her feet. "But I can't see anything until my vision returns."

"Vespera?" Tara let out a cry of excitement. "You've returned! Where—"

"Long story, which I'll tell you soon." Fumbling with her purse, she made sure Tara and the Book of Bones were secure inside and zipped it shut. "But please, no sound—and that's for all of you. I need to listen."

Thankfully, none of her Mors Dicen coven members disagreed, and she stilled her breathing, let herself hear everything ...

"Bone Wielder?" Alex called softly. "Where are you?"

"In here, Alex!"

"Ronin, I have her," Alex said from right in front. "Heading back to the stairwell now. Bone Wielder, how long till your sight returns?"

"A few minutes. And thank frig you're here—what about Matt? Where is he?"

"Leaving the thirteenth floor now. And Bone Wielder, they have issued a kill-on-sight order for you. We must leave fast."

"Can you hold my hand? There are no steps between here and the elevator, and I know the way—just need you to steady me if I fall."

"Done."

By the time they reached the stairwell, the darkness covering Vella's sight had lightened off to a charcoal, and she could make out shapes.

"Vella?" Ronin stepped closer. "Can you see me?"

"Just. The darkness is receding fast."

The elevator pinged. The doors opened.

"SI!" Alex yelled. He grabbed Vella and yanked her through the emergency stairwell door.

"I'll hold them off up here," Ronin snarled. "You two go!"

"Bone Wielder, I have to carry you—"

"No arguments!" She held on as Alex fireman carried

her down two flights—and thank frig the darkness cleared from her vision.

"I can see again. Alex, put me down—we can move faster individually."

"I'll go first," he said as he set her on her feet. "In case anyone comes up from below."

"Shannah, Sara, we're in the stairwell. Coming to you," Vella gritted out as they raced down flight after flight. "Matt? Matt, can you hear me?" Why wasn't he answering, damn it? "We're not far off—"

Muted bangs echoed up from the lobby.

"That's gunshots!" Terror squeezed Vella's chest, and she pushed even faster. "Sara!"

Please let her be okay, please let her be—

A roaring howl boomed down the stairwell, followed by a giant wolf. It flew past her down the steps, banging into the landing walls, careening down each level till it reached the ground floor.

"Faster, Bone Wielder," Alex snarled. Together they ran down the stairs to the ground floor, raced through the door—

Crack, crack, crack.

People ran in all directions. Screams and gun smoke and cries filled the air.

"Vella!" Sara screamed from where she knelt beside someone.

Vella skidded on her knees across the lobby floor. Shannah lay on the ground. Blood coated her chest and her cheeks.

"She got hit," Sara sobbed. "I'm stopping the bleeding." She looked back at Vella. Her eyes flared, and she screamed, "Behind you!"

Vella whirled. An SI pointed a gun at her chest.

The giant wolf leaped and tore the SI in half in a spray of blood and gore.

Crack, crack, crack.

"Bone Wielder, you cannot stay here," Alex yelled. "They are shooting at you and may hit Sara."

Fear made her frozen heart lurch, and she staggered to her feet. "Sara, run for the van. Ronin!" she screamed at the wolf. "I know it's you. Get Sara and Shannah to the van. Tannis? We need your help. And where the fuck is Matt?"

"We have to go!" Alex grabbed her arm. "We'll run out the opposite way from the van to let Shannah and Sara escape. I'll be right behind you—their bullets won't kill me, but they will you!"

"Not without Matt," Vella snarled.

A whisper echoed in her ears, like her name being called, over and over and over. She whirled around. Where had that come from?*Crack, crack. Crack, crack.*

Alex grunted, and his body jolted. "Bone Wielder, I cannot stop these bullets forever. You. Must. Go. I heard the Druid say he would leave when Shannah told him to."

"You heard him?" Vella grabbed this arm. "Promise me, Alexander."

"I heard him. Now I do not know where he is, but he would not want you to get shot while he is escaping! Come, Bone Wielder. You know I am right."

"Fine. We clear here, then we go *back* and find him."

They ran out the rear doors, through a gap between the buildings and onto IIIth Street, just as an SI ran from a parked car and grabbed for Vella.

Alex yanked him off his feet and sank his fangs into his neck. The SI fell to the ground.

But Vella didn't even scream, because across the street,

four more SI carried a limp body toward the back of a white van. The rear doors opened. The body was tossed inside.

Everything in Vella stopped. Then, as if time had restarted, rage flew through her.

"Matthais!" She ran for him.

Two of the SI leaped into the back with Matt, and the vehicle took off, tires squealing, disappearing around the corner. The other two SI ran for Vella, drawing their guns.

Crack, Crack.

Morrigan dropped from the sky like an arrow in front of Vella. The bullets hit her. She screeched and fell to the ground.

"No," Vella screamed. Pain shot through her arm, and she stumbled, but sprang to her feet and kept running, injured arm hanging at her side, because she could not stop.

"Bone Wielder," Alex shouted behind her.

The SI re-aimed at Vella, but she didn't falter. Using her good hand, she slid out the first knife Matt had given her and threw it end over end.

One SI dropped to the ground.

She darted sideways. A bullet rushed past her.

With the good hand again, she took out Matt's second knife and launched it. The second SI fell beside the first, knives protruding from their foreheads.

Vella leaped over their bodies; forced every ounce of energy into running to the corner.

Please, please, please.

The van was gone.

They'd taken Matthias.

Despair and disbelief gutted Vella, and she didn't bother

pushing the hair out of her face as she and Alex trudged the last few steps into Sylvie's brownstone.

With her uninjured arm, Vella cradled a shivering Morrigan to her chest. The wing Morrigan had been shot twice in had lost its glamoured feathers and returned to bones, but otherwise she had no other injuries after saving Vella's life.

The pain in Vella's other arm had numbed, but although she wasn't bleeding and had no visible injury, she couldn't move it.

They'd taken Matthias.

"Do you want me to take her, Bone Wielder?" Alex held out a hand.

Morrigan burrowed under Vella's neck. "No," Vella whispered. "Morrigan wants to stay with me."

Alex nodded, but his jaw tightened as he glanced toward where hushed voices echoed from the jewel-toned lounge. They were too quiet—like no one wanted to speak loudly.

Vella couldn't stop a shiver as her stomach clenched.

What—who—would they find through that doorway?

Alex entered the lounge first; he paused, then stepped aside for Vella. Please, *please* let—

Shannah lay on the floor, her eyes open. Unseeing. Ronin crouched over her, clasping her hands. Sara sat huddled by her side, sobbing.

"No," Vella whispered. "No!" She flew to his side, fury erupting in her along with her tears. "You're a witch! Do a healing spell. I've seen Matt do it—"

"Ronin has tried," Sylvie whispered. "But Shannah's injuries were too great."

Ronin's body shuddered and tears ran down his cheeks. "I'm sorry, Shan," he whispered. "I'm so sorr—" His entire body crumpled.

Sara let out a cry and scrambled to Ronin's other side.

Goddess, why? Shannah never deserved this. Never!

"Vella?" Ronin's voice was so hoarse, she could barely hear it. "Matt—before we lost contact, he said to tell you, Plan M."

Her heart stuttered.

"Vella?" Sylvie's voice was as gentle as the arm she eased around Vella's shoulders. "We need to know, what is Plan M?"

"On the way back from Paris, Matt—" Vella's throat closed, but no, she would tell them this. "Matt and I agreed, if anything ... bad ... ever happened, that Madgewick was where we would go. Plan M for Madgewick. That's where he'll be expecting to meet us."

"He's alive?" Ronin turned, and the dullness in his eyes made her heart break all over again.

But the tiny tug in her heart that would lead her to Matthias in any world, at any time, still lived there. Which meant *Matthias* still lived.

They'd taken Matthias.

"Matthias is alive." She clenched her jaw against the disbelief, and the compassion, and the devastation in the faces all turned to her.

Blood pounded in her ears, and she stared at them all and, with every burning ounce of rage inside her, through the tears that wouldn't stop flowing, she made a promise to them all. "So, we'll go to Madgewick, like he wanted. And then we will save Matthias. We will save Brianna. And we will get our vengeance for Shannah. For everyone."

The End

Watch out for Witch Wars Book Three in 2026

DEAREST WITCHY ROMANCE READER

Thank you for reading *Weapon* and stepping back into the world of *Witch Wars*.

I hope you loved spending more time with Vella and Matthias, and I can't wait to invite you back to see what happens next in Witch Wars Book Three!

While many of the locations and places that Matthias and Vella visit during the story exist in real life, I have absolutely taken liberties with people and operations. And although research is one of my favourite parts of writing, please forgive any mistakes made in translating the Irish, French and Latin—they are entirely my own.

ACKNOWLEDGMENTS

Writing *Weapon* turned out to be way harder than I had anticipated, for reasons related to the story and challenges in my personal life. I can honestly say you are only reading this now because of a crew of wonderful writing witches (as of today, that's my coven name for you all).

To start: Sarah Calfee from Three Little Words Editing. You helped me see the possibilities of this story when I hadn't even realized I was struggling, and your approach to the structural edit was my favorite part of this entire writing experience. Thank you, thank you, thank you! I can't wait to bring you the hot mess that will no doubt be my book three first draft.

To Joanne Speirs from Nurturing Words (whose advice that thickness matters has certainly resonated with this story), thank you for being the most patient, accommodating, wonderful final editor a writing witch could ask for.

Next (and in no particular order) are the other wonderful witches who have helped me bring *Weapon* to fruition, some in small ways, others with more help than they may have realized: Jacqueline Hayley, Tanya Nellestein, Caitlin Duncan, Sarah L Richhelm, Louisa Duval, Samara Parish, Laura Wilson, Jo-Anna Apelt, Julie Morris, and Valerie Morris. And one more special shout-out goes to my little girl, Tricks. You may not be an undead raven, but your doggo cuddles are just as special.

And to my own magic man: you rock my world.

And then lastly, a shout-out to the readers who loved meeting Matthias and Vella in book one. Your passion for them and their story gave me the determination to make *Weapon* the very best motherfucking book it could be. Thank you 🤍

ABOUT THE AUTHOR

Award-winning Brisbane author, HM Hodgson writes about wicked romance (steamy scenes a must!), intrigue and magic. Magic that moves worlds and takes her to another place.

In 2021, HM Hodgson won the Romance Writers of Australia First Kiss competition with the first kiss scene from her novel, Keeper Of My Heart, as judged by producer and director, Tosca Musk. Hodgson also won the Australian Romance Readers Association award for Favourite Continuing Romance Series 2022 with The Immortal Keepers.

When not writing or reading or daydreaming about her next literary hero, you can find her sipping coffee and eating chocolate (more often than not at the same time).

Keep in touch with HM Hodgson at: www.hmhodgson.com

ALSO BY HM HODGSON

Relics and Legends

A Relic Of Magic And Gold

A Relic of Magic And Myrrh

A Relic Of Magic And Frankincense

A Wreath Of Thorns

A Spell of Longing and Death

A Sword of Stone and Magic

Cursed Nights

Book 1 Cursed Alliance

Book 2 Cursed Embrace

The Immortal Keepers

Book 1 The Last Keeper

Book 2 Keeper Of My Heart

Book 3 Keeper Of My Desire

Witch Wars

Wrath: Book One

Weapon: Book Two